the window

jeanette ingold

the window

harcourt brace & company

san diego   new york   london

Requests for permission to make copies of any part of
the work should be mailed to: Permissions Department,
Harcourt Brace & Company, 6277 Sea Harbor Drive,
Orlando, Florida 32887-6777.

Library of Congress Cataloging-in-Publication Data
Ingold, Jeanette.
The window/by Jeanette Ingold.
p.   cm.
When she comes to live with relatives on a Texas farm,
fifteen-year-old Mandy encounters the grandmother she never
knew and begins to come to terms with her blindness caused
by the automobile accident that killed her mother.
ISBN 0-15-201265-6   ISBN 0-15-201264-8 (pbk.)
[1. Mothers and daughters—Fiction.   2. Blind—Fiction.
3. Physically handicapped—Fiction.   4. Family life—Fiction.
5. Ghosts—Fiction.]   I. Title.
PZ7.I533Win   1996
[Fic]—dc20   96-1293

Text set in Fairfield Medium
Designed by Camilla Filancia
First edition   A B C D E F   A B C D E F (pbk.)

Printed in Hong Kong

For my husband, Kurt

a c k n o w l e d g m e n t s

I wish to acknowledge with gratitude the
assistance of the teachers and counselors
who answered my numerous questions and
who read and commented on the manuscript:
Fred Bischoff, Judy O'Toole-Freel, Bob Maffit,
Dennis Slonaker, and Dr. Karen Wolffe;
of willing readers Jamie and Kristy Maffit;
of students at the Montana School for the
Deaf and the Blind who reviewed the
manuscript and talked about it with me;
and of my good friends who gave varied
and valued help: Peggy Christian, Hanneke
Ippisch, Wendy Norgaard, Dorothy Hinshaw
Patent, Greg Patent, and Carol Soth.
I especially thank my editor, Diane D'Andrade.

the window

chapter 1

"S TAY SEATED, Mandy," the flight attendant says. "When the other passengers have gotten off, I'll come get you."

Right. She should try staying seated herself, when everybody else is standing up and the guy by the window wants out and stuff's tumbling from the overhead bins and you get bumped half into the aisle.

A man says, "Watch it," and some other man says, "Hey." Suddenly there's a pocket of hot silence. Everyone around has just realized I can't see.

"Those must be your folks. They've got a sign with MANDY on it."

Then a woman is hugging me, Aunt Emma I guess. Her front is soft and she's shorter than me. She laughs, flustered. "I knew you were fifteen, but somehow I hadn't pictured . . . I mean, I thought of you younger . . ."

A man hugs me, and another, hugs of wool jackets and aftershave, clumsy big hugs, and their voices rumble.

One tells me he's my uncle Gabriel. Great-uncle Gabriel. They're all greats, for that matter, Great-uncles Abe and Gabriel and Great-aunt Emma, who is Gabriel's wife.

"So, Mandy," he says, "I hope you're going to liven up our gloomy old house."

"Gabriel, hush," Aunt Emma whispers. "It's too soon."

"Don't worry about me," I say. "It's OK."

And even if it's not, I can take care of myself.

That's my gift. Other girls get blond hair and nice families and brains that tell them the right things to say. I've got knowing how to take care of myself, and how to face what I have to face.

Like that night I woke up in the hospital

and heard the nurses talking about whether they should take me to my mom. One said, "I hate for her to see," as if there was any way I could through bandages over eyes that had stopped working.

Besides, did that nurse think I couldn't imagine how my mom was? That I couldn't guess what happened to people when they got thrown from cars and smashed against utility poles?

I fussed until she put me into a wheelchair, took me to another floor, to intensive care, and I was too dumb to wonder why I was getting to go there now when they hadn't let me for days and days.

"Here's your mother," the nurse told me, and I had to take her word for it. The only sounds in the room were machine sounds.

I found my mother's arm, reached for her face, but the nurse moved my hand away. "You'll dislodge the tubing."

I listened for Mom to make some noise, even to just breathe out loud, but all the room became one steady, tiny monitor blip.

"Hey, Mom," I said, "you sure we can afford the rent here?"

I could feel the nurse get uptight, knew

she was thinking: Hard case; people like these don't have feelings like they should.

"Don't worry, Mom," I said. "I'll get along."

My mom died the next morning, without me ever knowing if she'd heard.

This is my first time to Texas. The cold air surprises me. Somehow I thought Texas, even in the north, would be warm and dusty-smelling, not damp and cold and made empty by a wind without scent. There is no sun; I would feel it through my eyelids. I would see it. I can see sunlight, bright light. There is none this day.

We drive a long while after leaving the Dallas airport, first over highway and then back roads, and then I'm inside a house and still chilly. Aunt Emma puts a bundlely sweater on my shoulders and I hear a furnace come roaring on. "Cold November," says Uncle Abe. "We'll have heat in just a few minutes."

I can't stop a shiver.

"Em," says Abe, "guess we've got another cold-blooded one," and I think he's saying that I'm mean, but he's not.

Gabriel says, "Your Uncle Abe means thin-blooded. Emma always wants the heat up."

The house smells of cooking, onion and broccoli and meats layered one meal into the next, nice smells, but smells.

And of flowers, but not sweet ones like my roommate's at the hospital. I ask Aunt Emma what kind and she says marigolds. "About the last, I guess. We could get frost any night now."

"Most people plant marigolds to keep deer away," says Gabriel, "that's how bad they smell. But Em likes them."

"An honest smell," says Aunt Emma, "and they're easy to grow." Her answer starts another question. It seems to hang in the air: This Mandy, does she grow easy?

No, I want to shout. I don't grow easy. I'm trying the best I can and messing up terribly and I don't see how the three of you are going to make anything any better.

No, I want to shout. Don't you read? It's never easy to raise a child, not even for the people whose job it's supposed to be. Mothers grow children. Not great-aunts and old uncles.

No, I want to shout. Stare at me, in this

5

bundlely sweater. I don't even know quite where to look, now that you're silent and your voices don't tell me where you are. Do I look easy to grow?

"May I see my room, please?" I ask.

Again that silence. I'd said, *May I see.* You'd think I'd know better, would have learned these last weeks what *see* and *look* do to people who can, when they hear the words said in front of someone who can't. When someone who can't says them herself.

"Certainly," answers Aunt Emma. She laughs, an embarrassed little laugh. "Actually, we have a choice for you. About what room you want, I mean. There's one here on this floor . . ."

"Aren't your bedrooms all upstairs?"

I know they are. Mom had a picture of this house, though she'd never been in it. "My mother's house," she'd say, when she'd find me looking at it. "Your grandmother's."

Again that embarrassed little laugh. "Yes," Aunt Emma says, "but there's a little room down here, a study, that we thought you could . . ."

"Whose study?"

6

"Well, your uncle Abe's, but . . ."

"I don't need it," he breaks in. "I can work perfectly well upstairs. Lots of space in my bedroom for a desk."

I ask, "What's the other choice?" I know what they're doing, trying to give me a room where I won't have to climb steps. But I'm blind, not crippled.

"The other one is on the second floor," says Emma, "but it's so tiny . . ."

It's Uncle Gabriel who interrupts this time. "Actually, there's another choice," he says. "Nobody's using the attic room, nobody has for years. It's not much bigger, but . . ."

"Let me see it, please."

I am not going to stop saying *see* just to spare their feelings. It's what I mean. And what do they want me to say, anyway? *Let me feel the attic, please? Smell the attic?* Choose it for my bedroom without learning one thing about it first?

It's Gabriel who puts my hand on his arm and walks me to the staircase. I run the tip of my long cane side to side. The bare treads are wood and very wide, worn to rounded edges.

"It's a long flight," he says.

I start up on my own, as rapidly as I can go and not hesitating once, even when I'm thinking, Please God help me find the top so I take a smooth step onto it and don't fall on my face. And I do it right.

I wait for the others. Aunt Emma comes up wheezing. I've made her climb the steps faster than she usually does. Abe doesn't come up at all.

"The attic?" I ask. "How do we get there?"

I start to unpack by myself, opening my suitcase on a high, creaking bed. It's afternoon now, and someone has cleaned and made the bed with sheets and a puffy quilt. Aunt Emma comes in long enough to hang lace curtains. "Washed and pressed," she says. "They don't give much privacy, but there's no one out there but cows."

She chatters as she works, telling me about Herefords and Angus and how the uncles are thinking of trying some exotic breed.

I hear metal snap. "There, done," Aunt Emma says. An instant later she touches my hand. "Mandy," she begins. "Mandy, I'm glad your caseworker found us. Your uncles and I had no idea we even had a niece."

I can't decide which response to pick from the several that come to me: I'm not your niece, I'm your grandniece; I didn't know about you, either; I must have been some surprise. Any one of them would lead to more talk, when all I want is to be left alone.

"If you don't mind," I say, "I'll finish unpacking now."

I find the closet and a dresser and put away my clothes, becoming angry all over again about how much is missing. Half my things got thrown away by the child services woman who closed up the apartment after Mom died, I guess because she thought my stuff looked cheap. "It wasn't your right," I told her when I learned what she'd done. She'd answered, "Your needs will be different in Texas."

At least she left me my photos. Now I stand them on a dressing table. Mom. Her dad, who died before she was born. I touch the glass in the frames.

The sun has come out now and it's

making the attic too warm. I go toward the sun, feel behind the curtains to the window latch, unlock and raise the window. Fresh, cold air rushes in, blowing the curtains against my face. I hold them aside and lean out, into the wind. There's someone calling.

I lean out farther, to hear. . . .

"Gwen. GWEN. Where are you?"

It was a child's voice. "GWEN?"

Footsteps sound on the stairs. "Mandy," Aunt Emma is saying, "I've got towels . . . Oh, child, be careful. Don't lean so far out."

"I heard something," I tell her. "Who is that boy calling? Wanting Gwen?"

There's a space before she answers. Too long a space. "There's no one out there, child. You must be hearing the curtains whisper."

))
))
))

chapter 2

I LEARN QUICKLY that this is a house of routine, with times for everything. If a time needs to be changed, nobody makes a big deal, but everyone knows. Something's changed.

Enter Mandy. They must hate how I'm making everything in their lives change.

Like Tuesday morning, my first morning in this house. Breakfast here is a sit-down, all-together affair that starts at 7:15. Tuesday I make the start but I'm late for the finish. One minute there's forks clinking against plates and talk about hay and pregnant cows and shopping lists, and the next minute I'm the only one left eating.

"Don't wait for me," I say, but they do, and I know they're all replanning their mornings because I'm making things slow, have made them change what they do.

A wave of longing for my mom, and for the easy way we lived, washes over me. Mom and I, we never had anything set enough *to* change.

"Hungry, babe?" she'd ask, whenever she thought about food. It might be five in the afternoon or nine at night. Or 3:00 A.M., when she'd been awake and I'd heard her prowling in the hall. She'd know I wasn't sleeping, either, and ask, "Hungry, babe?"

The memory is so strong I can hear her voice, and Gabriel's voice cutting through it is a jolt.

"If you're done, Mandy," he says, "let's give Emma a hand with the dishes."

"I don't think Mandy should . . . ," Emma begins.

But Gabriel's saying, "The door's just behind you, Mandy."

He doesn't leave me any choice but to start toward it, even as I'm thinking, No, I can't help and I shouldn't be in a kitchen and please, how will I keep from breaking things and what if the stove's still on?

Emma must be thinking the same things, because as soon as I step from carpet to tile, she's by my side. "Mandy, I'll walk you to the sink," she says.

I let her guide me, and, reassured I won't get hurt, I move forward until I brush against something off to the right. "The kitchen table, Mandy," Emma says. "The refrigerator is along the wall to your left."

I reach out and find its smooth, cool front.

"Next there's more counter," Emma says, and I'm going to touch that, too, but before I can her voice sharpens into a warning. "Don't, there's the stove next."

I jerk my hand back and right away hope no one has seen me do it. I will not let on that this scares me; I will not.

And tumbling after that thought is the realization I'd jerked my hand away from warmth.

As we round a corner I say what I've just learned, say it as though it's something I've known all along: "You don't have to worry about me getting burned. I'd feel heat before I'd actually touch a burner."

But I'm thankful to hear Emma say, "That's enough exploring. Why don't you stand here?"

Then someone's handing me a towel and soon I'm drying pots and lids, laying them on the counter. For a bit there's the *whish* and soft clang of Aunt Emma working at the sink and the clatter of the uncles loading things into the dishwasher. Then Emma says, "Mandy, we need to talk about what's next for you."

One of the uncles takes a frying pan from my hand.

"We're asking, Mandy," says Gabriel. "What do you want to do?"

The question is school. Where. If I want to go away to this special one where there would be other blind kids or if I want to try the high school in town.

Already my child study team has met with my aunt and uncles to go over reports from the rehab center where I was before coming here. I guess they've all pretty much decided the final decision can be left up to me. "She has potential for success in either environment" was the way it was put.

The special school, which I'd have to board at, would have more equipment and a lot of specialists to teach me all the things I suddenly need to know. And—get this bit—my "chances of social integration would be greatly enhanced."

The local high school has some stuff, too, mainly in a resource room, but I'd be expected to do most of my work in regular classes. I could count on some help from itinerant teachers, teachers who go from school to school to work with kids like me, but, for sure, I'd be a lot more on my own.

Now Uncle Gabriel breaks into my thoughts. "So, time for a command decision," he says. "Pros and cons either way."

He doesn't have to spell out the cons, and, besides, I doubt if he thinks of the same ones I do. A school of fifteen hundred normal kids—will they make room for me? Whisper and watch me? Will they laugh at me?

Don't be stupid, Mandy, I think. Of course they will, but since when haven't you been able to handle being the outsider?

Mandy the new girl, I think. Mandy the new blind girl. So what's the difference?

I don't fool myself. The difference is huge and lies, cold and sick-feeling, in the pit of my stomach. I swallow back welling saliva.

"The town school, I guess," I say.

It's not a guess, though. More a gamble, or a chance I have to take. I'm afraid *not* to try, afraid to disappear into that special school for blind kids. I'm not ready to give up, to disappear from my life. I don't ever want to be.

"The regular high school," I repeat.

There's a trick to first days, days when you're the new girl and you've got to let everyone know where you'll fit into things. Blow it, and you might as well quit trying, because nobody's going to give you another chance.

I'd had it down, always wore my good-luck T-shirt and amber skirt, my hair in a single braid pinned up like I took ballet or ran track. I'd pause at the classroom doorway, flash a confident smile, make eye contact with the kids who looked like they ran things. I wanted them to know I was there.

Of course, I'd had a lot of practice with first days. Mom and I were forever moving ahead of a rent check coming due. Or behind Mom losing her job. Or with some story Mom had read about how life's better in West Virginia, or cheaper in Arizona because you don't have heating bills, or healthier in the mountains or on the desert or by the ocean.

Over the years Mom and I moved south to get religion, north to get away from it, west to escape from some creep who stalked Mom the time we tried Philadelphia.

Yeah, I've had a lot of practice with first days.

Except I've never done one blind before. And I don't have my amber skirt. It's gone, along with all the other clothes the child services woman didn't approve of.

That evening I ask, "Aunt Emma?"

"Yes, Mandy?"

"Do I have any money?"

"Money!"

"Well, left from my mother. Insurance . . . ?"

"Don't worry about it. We've got enough."

"I mean, my own money. That I can spend how I want."

I guess the answer's no, although Emma doesn't exactly say that, but later on Uncle Gabriel gives me some folded bills. "I hear you need an allowance," he says. "Why don't you plan on fifteen dollars a week?"

"You're just giving it to me?" I ask. "What do you expect me to do with it?"

I don't mean to be rude, but I know from Gabriel's answer that's how I've sounded.

"I expect, Mandy, that you'll use it to buy what you need, that you'll save some, that you'll pay your way when you do things with friends." His voice lightens up. "Pitch in gas money, maybe, if you go somewhere."

Is this man for real? What friends does he imagine?

I want to tell Uncle Gabriel I don't need his allowance, but I keep my mouth shut. A person doesn't turn down money.

Two days later we all drive to town so I can get some clothes to start school in.

The uncles drop Aunt Emma and me off at the department store end of a mall, saying they're going to check on some motor repairs and will pick us up when we're done. "What do you want?" Gabriel asks. "Half an hour or so?"

"A couple of hours at least," Aunt Emma says. "And bring the checkbook back. Why don't you meet us about noon in the coat department?"

She's laughing as we go in. "Half an hour! Isn't that just like a man, Mandy?"

She steers me across an echoing, perfume-smelling place and into an elevator, where a woman greets her by name.

"Anne, this is my grandniece, Mandy," Emma says.

I don't have any idea if I'm being introduced to a clerk or a friend or what. I say hi and someplace inside hear the voices of a dozen teachers saying, "Speak up, Mandy."

I expect Emma to say, "Speak up, Mandy," but she doesn't. Instead, she tells how we're going to the junior department. She makes it sound like the most exciting thing she's ever done.

Then we're getting out of the elevator, which hasn't stopped quite flush with the floor. I stumble, and this woman, Anne, grabs my arm. She says, "Let me help," and she's pulling me forward before I can get my bearings again. When I try to shake off her hand, she grips me harder.

"I don't need your help," I say. "Let me go." I can hear that I'm too loud.

There's a moment of embarrassed silence, a tiny "Well . . ." from the woman, not angry exactly but uncertain. Then she's saying good-bye, and good shopping, and telling Emma she'll talk to her later. I bet.

I expect Emma to scold me for being rude, but she just says, "This way."

We seem to be the only ones shopping in juniors, I suppose because it's a school morning. Aunt Emma asks what kind of things I like, but I've hardly started to tell her when a clerk comes up and takes over.

"This is my niece," Aunt Emma says, "my grandniece," like it matters who I am. "We're here for school clothes."

"What size is she?" asks the clerk.

"I'm an eight," I say.

"Does she like pants or skirts?"

"Ask me," I say. "I'm the one who will wear them."

And then, to my horror, tears well up.

"Want to get a cola and try this later?" Aunt Emma asks.

"No," I say, "now."

"Look," says the clerk, "I'm sorry, I didn't mean . . ." and then Aunt Emma's smoothing things over and pretty soon I'm in a dressing room.

I stand there while the clerk brings in things and holds them up to me. She says, "See how this fits," or "Navy's not your color."

There's so much I want to know. . . . I mean, clothes matter. I feel the tops of collars, try to picture how a neckline is. Where a hem is hitting my legs. Everything seems long, and I say so.

"I can call in the seamstress, but of course that's an extra charge," says the clerk.

"We can take them up at home," Aunt Emma says.

I'm happiest with the jeans—jeans fit or they don't, and you don't need eyes to tell. And with one blouse, the material feels like air between my fingers and I hear Aunt Emma catch her breath when she sees it on me. Or maybe she's gasping at the price tag. Nobody talks about what anything costs, but the blouse feels expensive.

Shopping does take until noon, between the junior department and shoes. I'm picking out a jacket when my uncles arrive.

Uncle Gabriel pays for it all, and I wonder if I should offer to give back the money he gave me, but I can't find a moment when it feels right to ask. This is the first time in my life I have bought more than one thing at a time.

Emma and the uncles are ready to go out to lunch, but suddenly I'm so tired I can hardly stand up. "Please," I say, "can we go home?"

The next thing I know, Emma is shaking my shoulder and Abe is saying, "We're here, Mandy."

It takes all of us to carry everything up to my room. We pile it on my bed, and Aunt Emma says she'll help me take off tags and hang stuff up.

"No," I say, "I'll do it, if you'll tell me where to find scissors."

I can feel Emma's disappointment. A twinge of guilt shoots through me, but I can't take more help, not today.

Alone, I empty a sack, find underwear. I start with a pair of underpants, spread them flat, and run my hand all over one side, all over the other, inside the waistband. Only one tag, pinned in, and I take that off.

Emma comes back up and puts something metal in my hand. She's gone again before I identify the nail clippers she's given me instead of scissors.

The skirt and jeans and tops, they're harder to deal with than the pants were. The price tags are all attached by those stiff plastic strings, the kind that end in *T*s. The clippers work on most, but there's one tag that's caught in a seam and I finally give it a yank that makes something tear.

I'm doing the last pair of jeans when I stab my finger on a pin. I suck a bit of blood and wait and wait, lick my finger clean and wait some more. What if I get blood on my new clothes and don't know?

And then I put it all away, the underwear folded in a dresser drawer, the other things on hangers. The clothes feel right, but I wish I could see them, could be sure they're OK.

I wish I knew what sort of Mandy the kids are going to see.

I've got the window open because the attic was stuffy when we got back from shopping. Now cold wind hits me and I go over to close it.

The curtains billow up, and I duck under.

I reach for the window, again hear a child's thin voice calling.

I lean out.

"Gwen, Gwen, GWEN."

"Who's down there?" I call.

"Gwen, where are you?"

The boy sounds closer now, and I lean out farther.

Wind gusts and the next instant a curtain panel blows around me. For an instant I imagine I'm in the hospital again, waking up inside bandages. Then the house smells bring me back, bleach and dust from the windowsill.

My fingers scrabble with the curtain, searching for the edges.

And then I hear my own voice but not mine, my voice with somebody else's accent. . . .

"Abe, go away," the voice says.

chapter 3

THE WIND GUSTS again, and I'm moving with it, spiraling from November to summer, from dark to light, tumbling until I'm really seeing, watching another girl. She hangs by her knees from a tree limb, one hand holding up her skirt, the other dragging in the dirt. She looks about my age.

A little boy is with her, in the shade under the big tree, and I can hear him talking. . . .

"Gwen, you better come down out of that tree. Mama's looking for you everywhere."

"Go away, Abe."

"Mama will get you, Gwen. You know she

said you're too big to be climbing trees. I can see your underpants."

"And you're too little to matter." Gwen pulled herself up, then dropped back to hang from her knees so fast that bark scraped her legs and the little boy sucked in his breath. "Tell Mama I'll be along in a bit."

She stretched down both hands and dragged the tips of her fingers in the summer dust.

I stand back from the window, touch its frame.

What has happened?

My question is smothered in an answer that wells up, scary and impossible and, especially, exciting. Can I have seen into another time?

Mandy, I tell myself, you're losing it. Imagination plus.

But the sharp detail of leg and cotton dress is bright inside my eyelids, and the Texas accents echo in my ears. They're so real, and that moment of being able to see again so clear in my mind, that I feel disoriented.

I go to the closet and find my new clothes. Count the four pair of jeans.

Go to the door.

"Uncle Abe?" I call.

"Yes?" he calls back, his voice full and deep and ragged, a grown man's voice. "You need something, Mandy?"

"No," I call back. "No, it's nothing."

So I am where I think I am. But . . .

I go back to the window, let the chilled air blow over me. I could pull the window shut, could close out the wind. But instead, I lean out, strain to hear the voices again. Hear them, and see the people again. . . .

"I'm not going without you, Gwen," Abe said, his face puckering. "Mama'll get mad. Please come down, before she comes out and sees you."

"And tells me I'm a disgrace, at fifteen I should know better?"

"Please, Gwenny?"

A motor sounded on the road. A car, an ancient black one, turned in, making dust cloud up from the drive. Gwen grabbed the tree limb and somersaulted down.

A boy was looking out the driver's

window. "Nice," he said to Gwen, as he stopped the car close by her. His smile was just fresh enough to bring uncertainty to Gwen's face. "Your mother home?"

Then he was getting out of the car, pulling out a black case, and setting it on the running board. "I've got some good brushes, made by the blind, good prices."

"You're a salesman?" Gwen asked. "You don't look old enough."

"Old enough for what, sugar?" he asked, his smile wider and teasing.

"I'll get my mother."

Why did he think he could talk to her that way? Maybe her mother was right, maybe she did behave in a way that asked for trouble.

"Mandeeeeee."

Emma's calling wakes me up. I'm on my bed, and someone has closed the window and pulled one side of the quilt over me. I stay still, sorting out sounds and smells. A television commercial. Rolls and something sweet baking.

Lunch, I think, and then realize it feels too late for that. Aunt Emma must be fixing

dinner. I ought to be starving, but I'm not.
I'm too mixed up to want to eat.

At the window I press my face against a
cold pane and try to see through my darkness into the darkness outside. I didn't
imagine you, Gwen, did I? But who are you?
And *when* are you?

I gather one of the curtains, feel its rough
lace pattern. How can Aunt Emma say
there's no one outside this window?

Monday, the day I start school, comes
quickly and goes wrong before I've even left
home.

I'm in the kitchen, about to ask Aunt
Emma if my hair's OK, when she says, "Oh,
Mandy, let me get that tag off your jeans
for you." She snips threads from the corners of a sewn-on label, and I worry about
what else I've missed.

My nervousness makes me extra awkward
getting in the car, and my stomach hurts so
bad I wonder if I'm going to be sick.

Uncle Gabriel drives and Emma sits in
the front seat. "Aren't you coming, Abe?"
she asks through the window.

"No, Mandy doesn't need a parade," Abe

says. He's so right. I certainly don't need a bigger production than this is going to be anyway.

I've gone to the school once already, on Friday, and met the principal and the aide who runs the resource room where I'll go in the afternoons, at least for a while. There's not a regular teacher there all the time, but just specialized ones who come in for individual kids.

When we went in on Friday, though, classes were going on and we walked through silent halls. I don't think any kids saw me.

Today, this is for real.

It's late, 12:30, but Ms. Zeisloff—she's the aide—said that maybe for the first few days coming after lunch would be best. She's waiting for us in front of the school.

She tells my aunt and uncle, "We'll take good care of Mandy."

There's a pause, and I realize Emma and Gabriel had thought they'd come in and get me settled.

"Well, I . . . Mandy?" my aunt says. Then, when I don't answer, she says, "Well, call if you need anything. We'll be back for you at three."

"You have quarters?" Gabriel asks. "For the phone?"

And suddenly it's all I can do not to say, Please don't go, don't leave me here. Their footsteps click away, down the pavement.

A door opens behind me, and Ms. Zeisloff says, "Oh, Hannah, here you are."

"Locker disaster, everything crashed out. Hi."

"Mandy," says Ms. Zeisloff, "this is Hannah Welsh."

"Hi," the girl says again, "I'm taking you around for a few days. You scared?"

I can't believe she's asked me that. What right does she have to ask how I feel? That's private and I don't even know her.

"Thank you," I say, "I will appreciate your help."

And then, like I've leaned in to invite it, this Hannah girl hugs me. Where does she get off, thinking just because I'm blind I can be hugged?

The three of us go into the school

together, Ms. Zeisloff doing a running commentary about where we are.

"This is the main hall," she says. "To get to my room we turn right and go through the outside doors at the end."

Hannah's by my side. "What's the best thing for me to do?"

"I'll take your elbow," I say, grateful she asked instead of just taking hold of my arm.

We pass a room with an open door and I hear a man talking about simultaneous equations. Some kind of blower keeps coming on and off up above us, and far away a phone is ringing.

I don't know what to do with my cane and I wish I wasn't carrying it. It screams what I am.

I try tucking it under my arm, but I realize how dumb that must look.

Sooner or later, Mandy, I tell myself, you're going to have to use this thing here. May as well be now.

I stretch the cane out in front, begin the side-to-side sweeping that's still hard for me to do, that makes my wrist and whole forearm ache. Sweep it side to side and back along the hard, smooth floor. Drag it along the wall that I'm going to have to re-member.

We reach the end of the hall.

"This door pushes out, Mandy," Ms. Zeis-loff says, and I think she's going to make me try it right then, but Hannah opens and holds it for me.

The resource room is at the other side of a courtyard, in a building by itself. "It's a temporary," Hannah says, "but it's been here as long as I can remember."

Then she's saying, "This is where I leave you, but I'll come back before school lets out."

Ms. Zeisloff and I go in together, into a room of electronic clicks and whirs, of elec-tric smells, a room just a little bit too cold.

"Everybody," Ms. Zeisloff says, rapping on something tinny-sounding for attention. Most of the clicking noises stop. I wish I knew how many people were in the room.

I wait for Ms. Zeisloff to say, "This is Mandy," but instead a boy breaks in.

"Welcome to the land of the blind, deaf, lame, maimed, outraged, and outrageous," the guy says, his voice not far from my ear. "You anything besides blind?"

"Ted, sit down!" Ms. Zeisloff seems exasperated but not angry.

"All right, Ms. Z., all right," says the boy. "Just welcoming the new inmate."

"Don't mind him," a girl says. "In my opinion, Ted's got some functional psychological behavioral disorder. Besides not being able to hear, of course."

It's like being in the middle of circling madness, and I want to make it hold still so I can get a clear look. I grab on to the one thing that seems a solid lie.

"If Ted's deaf, how did he hear Ms. Zeisloff?" I ask.

"Not really deaf," the girl says, "hearing impaired. Also, he reads lips. Also, he can be a real jerk."

"But, Stace," says Ted, "now we know our new inmate talks as well as walks. And she's not stupid, folks. There's a questioning brain behind those sightless eyes."

Talk about first days.

E VERYONE'S WAITING for me when school lets out.

I try to do the introductions right. "Hannah, this is my great-aunt Emma and my great-uncle Gabriel and my great-uncle Abe." I hear how awkward it sounds, those rolling *greats,* and I wonder why I've bothered with them.

But if the others find them funny, they don't say.

Aunt Emma tells Hannah she believes she knows her mother and asks what all Hannah does. It seems to be almost everything from student government to baby-sitting.

I'd wondered why Hannah was messing with me, but hearing the list I can guess: I'm probably some sort of service club project.

Then we're driving home and I know Emma, Gabriel, and Abe all want me to tell them how things went. But I don't know myself and I'm too tired to sort it all out.

I sag back into the car seat.

At home I go to my room and flop on my bed. I am so tired.

For a long time the afternoon happens again and again in my mind, names and voices and snatches of talk and how the bumps of one, two, and three felt under my fingers.

"Some people think braille is on its way out," Ms. Zeisloff told me, "but I don't believe that."

Teaching me braille will be the job of one of the itinerant teachers, a woman who'll work with me for a couple of hours three afternoons a week beginning Wednesday or Thursday.

Meanwhile, Ms. Z. says she knows just enough to get me started.

Braille dots under my fingertips . . .

I think of Gwen, whoever she is. Gwen, whose fingertips dragged in summer dirt when she hung upside down from a tree limb.

Had I made her up?

I go to my window, open it. Run my hand down a lace curtain.

It's just a curtain, I'm thinking, when the breeze quickens, pulls it from my hand, pulls on me.

This time I lean into the dark wind, give myself over to it. In another moment I'm back all those years again, back to seeing, watching another girl in another time. . . .

Gwen snatched up her shoes and ran around to the back of the house, before her mother could come to the door and see her. She slipped into the kitchen, turned the radio on softly, and then went back outside.

Sitting against the house in the cool shade, her bare legs on the cold, rough concrete of the side walkway, she waited for her program to come on. The salesman was here with a lot of things for her mother to look at. Maybe Gwen would have a whole half hour, long enough to hear an entire program, which didn't happen often.

But news came on instead, more about Korea.

Gwen had heard it first the evening before, from Abe, who'd heard it on the radio and run to tell. "We're at war," he had shouted. "The radio says we're at war and we got eight of their planes, but they didn't shoot down any of ours."

"Nonsense," their mother had said. "Don't make things up."

But of course the story had been in this morning's paper, and then all their mother could say was, "Well, here we go again."

Gwen thought about the salesman. Would he have to go to war? How old was he, eighteen maybe? Old enough to be drafted?

A screen door slapped shut in the front. He was leaving.

Gwen ran along the side of the house.

"Bye," she called, stopping him as he got in his car. "I just . . ." She searched for something to say. Stepped closer. "My mother buy any brushes?"

"You got a name, sugar?" he asked.

She looked carefully, decided his smile was not a smirk.

"Gwen," she said. "What's yours?"

"Paul."

Paul started his car, getting the motor to catch on the third try. Wiggled the stick shift into reverse. "Be seeing you, Gwendolyn," he said. "Don't do anything I wouldn't do."

"Gwen, not Gwendolyn. And I don't see how you'll be seeing me."

"Thursday," he said. "Thursday I sell soap. I'll be back."

"Mandy," Aunt Emma says, giving my shoulder a light shake. "You've got to get up now if you're not going to be late."

I wish I didn't have to go.

It's Thursday morning, my fourth day of school, but so far I've only gone for afternoons, only dealt with the resource room. Kids are in there on varying, overlapping schedules, but I'm starting to get them figured out.

I've gotten to know Ted, who really is more funny than mean, as long as you understand his sense of humor. I've also met Marissa, who's the only other one in the resource room with what she calls a "vision impairment." Marissa can see a lot, only very fuzzy, and she doesn't want to have anything to do with me.

I'm not sure why Stace and the other boy are there. Ms. Z. doesn't give a lot of time for talking.

But anyway, today . . . Today I start my regular schedule.

First period I've got math, the same class as Hannah. We go in together, early, and she introduces me to Mr. Casie, the teacher.

I ask where my desk is, but Mr. Casie's got a table all set up for me instead. There's a computer on it, which he says he's ordered earphones and some software for.

"There's also an electrical outlet for whatever else you need, Mandy," he says. "I suppose you'll be bringing a tape recorder?"

I have a sudden vision of Mandy the camel, hunching along the hall under a load of equipment.

"I don't know," I say. "Maybe."

I wish he'd let me slip into a normal desk

like everyone else, but before I can ask there's a bell ringing and the room is filled with the racket of talking kids.

Hannah squeezes my arm. "You'll do OK," she says.

I find the chair and sit, wonder where to look. Wish maybe I had a tape recorder after all because it would be something I could be busy with. I wonder if everyone's staring at me?

I hold my hands tight together; I will not put them up to check my hair, check if my collar is flat.

It seems forever before the bell rings again and the room gets quiet.

Then Mr. Casie is telling the class who I am, and I say "Hi," hoping I'm talking in the right direction.

"Man," says some boy, "math's hard enough when you can see the stuff."

But Mr. Casie's telling everyone what page to turn to and at the same time telling me to try to follow along.

Then I realize the class is doing statistics, new material for them but stuff I've had before.

I think, Mandy, you know this.

One thing I learned years ago—the more scared I am, the better it is to jump in fast. I wait for a question that I'm sure about the answer to and put up my hand.

"Mandy?" Mr. Casie calls on me.

"You don't try to control variables in a random sampling," I say. "That's the whole point of random samples—the randomness evens out the variables."

The boy who said "Man" before says "Man" again, this time like he's impressed.

My heart's pounding and I hold my hands in my lap, hope nobody can see how they're shaking.

"Very good, Mandy," says Mr. Casie, as if I haven't done anything special.

chapter 5

HANNAH TUGS ME through the halls the way some mothers tug their children, like attachments that are a normal part of things. I hold her arm, but she does the tugging.

I've wondered how I'll find a bathroom, but we go to one between classes, without me asking. Hannah warns me, "The seat's wet, don't sit down." Then she says, "Sorry. Tell me when I overdo."

How am I supposed to figure out how to deal with Hannah when she answers what's on my mind before I say it?

The rest of the morning goes by in a growing blur of noise and smells and bits of touch too small for me to know what I'm feeling.

Changing classes is the worst, and the crowds in the halls make it impossible for me to use my cane. We get to both English and geography late; the English teacher passes over it, but I hear the geography teacher give an exaggerated sigh.

He spends the period drilling the class on a current events map, making them find places mentioned in news stories: Seattle and Cincinnati, Yellowstone Park and the Columbia River Basin. And after class, when Hannah and I are leaving, he says, "Mandy, perhaps this class is not the best placement for you. This class is based on knowing maps."

"I can do geography without seeing your maps," I tell him. "I've lived in half the places you talked about."

Jerk, I think. I'll decide for myself what I can and cannot do.

But fourth period I sit out a gym class because the teacher says she's not allowed to have me participate in any activities until the modified program she's worked out gets official approval.

After that it's lunch. Somehow Hannah guesses how much I need quiet.

"Instead of the cafeteria," she says, "maybe we could eat in Ms. Zeisloff's room. You can have part of my sandwich, if you didn't bring anything."

The resource room is locked, but the day is warm enough for us to eat outside. We sit on the grass, our backs against the building. It's blessedly silent.

Slowly the welter of stuff that is muddling my mind drains away, until for the first time in hours I feel in control. I let my thoughts drift away from school, drift to Gwen and to what I've learned about her.

The Korean War started at the end of June in 1950. Ted looked it up for me in the encyclopedia. So now I know the time that I go to when I lean past the curtains. I know when Gwen lived, this girl who pulls me through time to the year she was my age.

And I've done my math. Uncle Abe would have been about five then, which fits since he must be about fifty now, or maybe a little older.

For I'm sure that is who that boy is, Gwen's little brother. He has Uncle Abe's way of talking, words going just a bit uphill and down. The house that the two of them live in is the house that I'm living in now. And the tree where I first saw Gwen hanging by her knees still stands, only it's much, much bigger now. So big I can't put my arms halfway around it, and the ground under it is gnarled with pushed-up roots.

What I don't know is who Gwen is. I mean, I realize she must be a great-aunt of mine, a sister of my great-uncles Abe and Gabriel, and of my grandmother, whose name was Margaret. I just don't know where Gwen *fits*.

I haven't heard Emma or the uncles mention her. No one has said, "Is Gwen coming for Christmas?" or "Is Gwen's gift in the mail yet?" And you'd think they would. I've always imagined that's what real families do.

Maybe she's dead like my grandmother?

Sooner or later, I'll ask.

But not yet. For now, I like the mystery of her, like the mystery of seeing her in another time. For now, I like having one thing that is all mine, privately mine, that no one else knows about.

"Mandy." Hannah's voice breaks into my thoughts. "Are you sleeping or daydreaming? You look like you're miles away."

"Sorry," I say. I keep my voice light. "I guess I did drift pretty far off."

When I get home Thursday I go to my room, eager to leave my own world and be lost again in Gwen's. I lean out my window into the breeze, lean out and wait to hear the calling.

The breeze doesn't change, and I stay with just myself, alone.

Instead of seeing Gwen, I think of my mom and me, years ago. I remember how one morning she sent me off to one of the jillion different grade schools I went to.

"Knock 'em dead, kid," she said, even though I'd been at that particular school long enough for us both to know I wasn't going to.

She pinned a plastic Christmas tree pin on my coat. It was just the kind that kids would laugh at, but I waited until I was down the street to put it in my pocket.

I remember the hurt of that morning.

A girl named Aimee and I were picked to

stay in during recess and make paper chains to decorate the room. Aimee cut red and green strips while I pasted circle through circle, as fast as I could. Soon the smell of wet paste was all around and a chain of colored paper bunched and rustled on the floor.

We started giggling, and then Aimee draped a piece of chain across the bust of a Roman emperor. I roped more of it around my waist, and Aimee tore off enough to make a necklace for herself. We were having fun, and I was sure she liked me.

Then a couple of boys looked in the window at us. Aimee must not have wanted them thinking we were friends, because she took the chain from around her neck and went back to cutting paper strips, and she didn't say another word.

Saturday comes. Hannah telephones even before I'm out of bed. She wants to know if I want to go to a football game. "It's a play-off," she says. "The whole school will be there."

"So what do I do at a football game?" I ask.

"Walk around. Talk. See people."

"Like I could."

Hannah says, "Knock it off, Mandy. That's sick."

I'm learning Hannah does not put up with my sounding sorry for myself.

"I'll think about it."

"Mandy, the game starts at one."

"OK, OK. I'll go."

"I'll pick you up," she says. "I got my license last month."

"That's when you turned sixteen?" I ask.

"Yeah."

I hang up before I realize I probably should have thanked her.

I go back to my room and make my bed.

Go to my dressing table and touch my mom's picture. "Do you know what I'm doing, Mom? Going to a football game. Isn't that a laugh?"

But I don't hear Mom laughing back, and I realize I can't quite remember what her laugh sounded like. Tears in my eyes, I put down her picture, go to close my window.

Without warning, I find myself being pulled to Gwen, being pulled again into the wind behind the curtains, into Gwen's life that summer of 1950. . . .

"Pill bug, pill bug, curl up tight."
"It's *'Ladybug. Fly home.'* "
"But these are pill bugs, Gwen. Want to see my pill bug circus?"

Abe was stretched out on his stomach, planting toothpicks tipped with tiny bright flags in a circle in the dusty earth. A gray pill bug crawled tanklike to one of them, then felt its way around.

"How come he doesn't curl up at the toothpick, like he does when he touches my finger, Gwen?"

"Ask Dad."

Just then the screen door opened and their father stepped onto the porch, walked down the steps to the car. Abe called, "Dad, come see. I'm training pill bugs."

"Not now. Maybe later."

Abe arranged pebbles inside the circle of flags. "Seats, Gwen, for the audience. How long do you think Dad will be?"

"That depends on where he's gone."

"Do you think he's driving all the way to town?"

A few minutes later, Abe said, "I'm going to let my pill bugs go. I think they're tired."

Gwen watched him run off, then straightened two of the toothpick flagpoles. This was the most restless, boring summer. And hot. It felt like something should happen.

She wished something would happen.

Except she knew nothing would, it never did. That salesman, Paul, hadn't even come back, when he'd almost promised.

What would it be like, Gwen wondered, to be Abe? To be little again?

No, maybe that wasn't the question. Abe always had something to do. Was that because he was little and there was still stuff left that he thought was exciting? Or because he was a boy, and there really was?

"Gwen, come in here." Her mother spoke from the window above. "The beans need snapping now or I won't have them ready in time to eat. And wash off your knees. When are you going to start acting your age?"

"Never."

"What did you say?"

"I said I'm coming."

I should tell her, thought Gwen, that I don't see any point in growing up, just to spend Saturday afternoon cooking so I can serve supper exactly at 6:00 P.M. Saturday evening. I should tell her I'm never, ever going to think it's something to be proud of, just to get a meal ready on time.

"I'm coming," Gwen yelled again, louder than necessary.

She and her mother worked without talking, except once her mother said, "Gwen, did your father say where he was going?" and a little later, "I wonder what's keeping your father."

He still wasn't back at 5:30 or 5:40, nor at 5:50, when her mother called to everyone to wash their hands and come to the table.

They sat—her mother at her end, Gwen on one side, Abe and the older boy on the other—and waited.

Six o'clock came, and the chair at the far end, the only chair with arms, was still empty.

"Well," said Gwen's mother. "Well." She asked Gwen to say grace.

———

"What happened? What happened to your father?" I call.

One instant I'm with Gwen and the next I am alone in my room, and it has happened so fast I feel light-headed.

I have to know, Did Gwen lose her dad, the way I lost Mom? Did he get killed in some accident and never tell Abe why pill bugs curl up?

I wait until my head clears. Then I stretch as far out into the wind as I can.

"Gwen," I call. "Gwen? Please answer. Tell me what happened."

I think of another question. "And where was my grandmother? Why wasn't there another girl at the table?"

I'm grabbed from behind and jerked inside.

"Mandy! Mandy, don't you know how far down the ground is?"

It's Uncle Gabriel, and his voice is loud and angry and shaky, all at once. "Mandy, this room is three stories up. Don't ever lean out the window like that."

He's still holding my arm, even though I'm standing up straight now. I shake myself free. Turn deliberately until the back of my waist is pressed flat against the sill and my shoulders arch into emptiness.

"Don't worry about me," I say. "I won't fall."

"Mandy, you get away from that window. You're as stubborn as . . . Mandy, we're going to take care of you whether you like it or not."

"As stubborn as who?"

"Whether you like it or not."

"Who?"

But Gabriel pulls me in, shuts the window hard.

"Emma's made an early lunch for you, Mandy," he says. "Better fix your hair before you go down. She'll think you've been in a wind."

chapter 6

WHEN HANNAH COMES for me I try to just leave, but no way. Aunt Emma is so excited about me going to the football game that Hannah must realize this is the first time I've gone out, except shopping and to school.

And Uncle Gabriel wants us to sit down while he reads a newspaper story about the two teams. "You should know who the players are," he says.

"Hannah probably already knows," I tell him.

"That's OK," Hannah says. "Does it say our school's expected to win?"

When we're out in the car, I tell her she

didn't have to do that, pretend she was interested.

"I *was* interested. And besides, it's touching how much they care about what you're doing. You're lucky, Mandy."

Me, lucky? How can she say something so dumb? "Want to trade places?" I ask.

I expect to her to say, "Shut up. That's sick." Instead she says, "Maybe. Families, anyway."

Then she lightens up. "Want to meet mine? Mom said I could ask you over for dinner and to spend the night."

I don't know until we get to the game that we're meeting anyone else. The football field is behind the high school, on the far side of the parking lot. As we walk over from the car, Hannah's saying, "Mandy, this is Charla," and, "Mandy, Rosa," and "Blakney, Mandy."

I try to hear how their individual voices sound, but they don't say enough words for me to get down which is which. Within minutes the talk is a jumble and the only person I can pick out is Hannah.

I'm moving along OK, using my cane, one hand barely touching Hannah's arm. Then one of the other girls says, "They're lining up for kickoff. Let's hurry."

I walk faster, stumble. Someone says, "Hannah, why don't we meet you in the stands?"

I can feel my face flaming red. I want to tell Hannah she doesn't have to wait for me, but I can't. Where would I go if she left me?

Someone else has stayed back, too, and I hear Hannah call her Charla.

This girl, Charla, she wants to talk about a dance that's coming up, a girl-ask-guy holiday thing. "You're taking Ryan, Hannah?" she asks.

"I guess."

Then Charla says, "Mandy, are you going to ask someone?"

Is she joking? I replay her words, listen for the emphasis on *you* that would give her away. It's not there. What's wrong with her?

"No," I say. "No one to ask."

"How about Ted?" she asks. "Don't you two hang around some?"

Now I get it. I open my mouth to say,

"Pair up the misfits?" but before I get a word out, Hannah pinches me.

"Shut up," she whispers. "Just don't say it."

After the game, which is more loud than anything and I'm glad when it's over, Hannah and I go to my house for my stuff. Aunt Emma acts like I'm going on a world cruise, instead of just to spend the night, and I'm embarrassed that she lets Hannah know she thinks this is such a big thing.

Hannah lives in town. We have to go back almost to the school to get to her place.

"Tell me what your house is like," I ask when we drive up.

"It's brick, one floor. Looks like all the other houses around here."

I stand inside the front door for a moment and listen to how far Hannah shouts when she calls, "We're here." Listen for echoes. Notice cold coming up from the tile under my feet. Do not smell dust or mold. It's a clean-feeling, hollow-seeming house.

"Hello, Mandy."

Hannah's mother has a voice that is perfect and polite and without one bit of niceness. The voice of the kind of woman who will pry right into me.

"Now," she says, "you're Emma's niece? I don't remember ever meeting your mother." She makes it a question that has to be answered.

I wish I could wrap my arms around my insides, keep her eyes off my mom and me and my privacy.

"Emma is my great-aunt," I say. "But it sounds silly to call her Great-aunt Emma, so I say Aunt Emma . . ." I hear myself babbling, but I can't stop. "You've never met my mother. We never got down here."

Dinner is awful.

It's in a dining room, with a cloth on the table, and Hannah's parents are both there and her little brother. And nobody says a word about how nice the table looks, so I know this isn't just for company.

The food's spaghetti, which is hard for me to manage because of the sauce, and I eat very slowly and carefully, cutting small sections. Once Hannah reaches over and does something to my plate, and another time her mother whispers, "Hannah," and Hannah whispers, "Mandy, use your napkin."

Her father wants to know about the equipment I've got, and I get talking about how the school computer has an add-on that synthesizes speech, how whatever is on the screen is read out loud. It really is a neat machine, and he seems interested.

But then Hannah's little brother says, "Those computer voices are so bad," and he's right, of course.

After dinner Hannah and I go to her room, where she turns on some music, tosses a cushion at me, and says, "So, want to hear about Ted?"

"Ted?"

"Or anybody else. I thought maybe you've been around long enough you must be getting people sorted out. That maybe you'd have questions about them?"

"Or about you?" I say, I guess a little mean. But I am curious about this Hannah who lives in a perfectly clean house. Hannah, who is all the things I've never been, even nice. "That Ryan that Charla talked about, he's your boyfriend?"

"Yeah, sort of. No. I don't know."

"He's the guy who scored all those points today?"

"Yeah."

"Figures," I say, but she goes on like she doesn't hear me.

"We're friends. It just makes it easier if we say we're a couple. Takes the pressure off, from everybody else, I mean."

I think about that. Nod like I know what she means, even though I'm not sure.

"Did you have a boyfriend," she asks, "before you came here?"

"You mean when I could see?" But Hannah lets that pass, too, and I've got to think of a better answer.

"There wasn't really time," I say. "Mom and I moved around a lot."

"Maybe you'll find one here," she says.

"Ted?"

"He's good-looking." She puts a bowl in my lap. "Popcorn, made it last night."

"Would you go out with Ted?" I ask.

"No. But not why you're thinking. He's so smart he scares me. And it's hard to tell when he's joking."

Yeah.

We talk for a while, then Hannah has me

move over so she can reach under her bed. "Ever play with a Ouija board?" she asks. "We can get us both boyfriends."

I hear her click off the light. "It works better in the dark. There's enough moonlight to read the letters."

Then Hannah shows me how to rest my fingers on the plastic disk. She says in this phony fortune-teller voice, "Oh tell us, Great Ouija, who will Mandy's love be?"

Nothing happens. Hannah whispers, "Just wait."

I wait, feeling foolish at first, and then holding in giggles and trying to make myself believe.

The marker wiggles right, joggles left, suddenly moves fast three or four inches.

"It's stopped on *X*," says Hannah. "Mandy, concentrate."

Her mother opens the door. "Hannah," she begins, "why don't you find something Mandy can . . . ," but switches to, "Don't stay up late, girls."

"We won't," Hannah says. We wait for the door to close before we go back to the Ouija.

The board tells us Hannah is going to

marry someone with the initials B. T. S., and we can't think of anybody at school with those initials unless it's Boone Simon. Hannah says nobody would ever marry Boone Simon, who never takes a shower, and maybe the Ouija board is nonsense.

A while later we're lying a few feet apart in twin beds. I'm wondering if Hannah is asleep when she says, "Mandy, wouldn't it be great if you really could ask about the future and get answers?"

"Maybe," I say.

"My dad says his dad saw a ghost once, who warned him not to go fishing and he did anyway and almost drowned."

When I don't say anything, she asks, "You ever know anybody who saw a ghost?"

"No," I say. And then, I don't know why, maybe because I've never before in my life stayed overnight with a friend, talked in the dark like this, I say, "but there's this girl, Gwen . . ."

I tell about the lace curtains, about the voices, about Gwen and Abe and Paul, and Hannah doesn't think I'm crazy. She says what happens—how I lean out the window and become Gwen, become her and watch her at the same time—is one of the most exciting things she has ever heard.

"Sometimes when I'm doing something I get the feeling I'm watching me do it," she says. "Is that how Gwen is?"

"Sort of," I say, looking for a better way to tell her. "More like when you read a book, and you're seeing what the main character is doing, but you're inside and thinking her thoughts at the same time."

"Do you think Paul's going to come back? Or Gwen's dad?"

"I don't know."

Then Hannah says, "You must miss being able to read, if you used to do it a lot."

"There are substitutes," I say. "Books on tape. Braille, if I ever learn it. But, of course, it's not the same thing."

And a long time later, Hannah says, "I wish something like Gwen would happen to me, but I guess it won't. I'm too ordinary."

And the way she says it, I realize she means I must be somebody special. That she wishes, at least for this, that she could be me.

And, lying in shared darkness, I take that

thought and turn it over, and don't try to throw it away.

Sometime later, I don't know how late, we fall asleep. I wake up once, listen to Hannah's slow, quiet-whistle breathing. What a nice, nice night.

In the morning Hannah and I sit around the family room in bathrobes, drinking hot chocolate while her father reads the funnies. Every few minutes he laughs and says, "Girls, listen to this."

Hannah's brother must be sitting next to him. "Dad," he says a couple of times, "you're leaving things out."

I think we're all sorry when Hannah's mom comes to tell us we can't wait any longer to dress. "Mandy," she adds, "we'll drive you home before we go to church, so no one has to come for you."

"Thank you," I say, "if it's not any trouble."

"Certainly, it's trouble, but I wouldn't have offered if I weren't willing to take the trouble." The way she says it makes me flush and wonder how I was rude.

When they let me off, Hannah asks me, "Can I come over later?" but her mother says, "Not today. I need you at home today, Hannah."

It's not until a couple of hours have gone by that I realize I wasn't rude asking how much trouble it would be to take me home. It was Hannah's mother who was rude, with her answer.

I try to do homework in the afternoon, but I can't concentrate. I end up standing at my dressing table. I find the photo of my mother, move my hand to the smaller frame next to it, the one of my grandfather in his airman's jacket. I run my finger down until I'm touching right where his face, blurred and almost lost in shadow, would be. "That's you that didn't come home to dinner?"

Except as soon as I say it, I know I'm wrong. The photo is of my grandfather. The man whose dining room chair stayed empty, Gwen and Abe's dad, and Gabriel's, he would be my great-grandfather.

It's hard to keep straight.

And where was Margaret, my grandmother? Why hadn't she been at the dinner table with the others? Had she already left home? Gone off to have the baby she would put up for adoption? The baby who would be my mom.

"Mandy," Aunt Emma calls, "would you like some hot chocolate with us?"

"Yes, please," I call.

I think again of asking the uncles about Gwen. If I ask, will I risk losing her? Might that somehow stop me from going back to her time?

Be honest, Mandy girl, I think. Aren't you scared of what you might say if your uncles want to know why you're asking about Gwen? Scared you might blurt out, "Well, every so often I lean past the lace curtains and skip off to 1950?"

Right, go from being Mandy who's just blind to being Mandy who's got multiple problems. There'll be a million more conferences with doctors and counselors, and then the next time there's a student admitted to Ms. Z.'s room, Ted can do a new introduction:

"And this is Mandy," he'll say, "blind, PLUS she entertains the notion she can time-travel. Tell our new inmate, Mandy, is hindsight better than no sight?"

"Oh, shut up, Ted, and sit . . ."

"MANDEEE!" Aunt Emma calls.

Maybe I really am losing it. "Coming. Right now."

No, I won't ask who Gwen is.

chapter 7

WHEN I GO to Gwen again I go to
another Texas morning. This time the passage is slower, as if the wind can hardly stir.
It is a passage to a morning later in that
summer. . . .

Gwen asked, "Do you want the pillowcases sprinkled, Mama?"

"Certainly."

Her mother was ironing, going piece by
piece through a basket of rolled, damp linens. Linens they could no longer afford to
send out.

It was early, but already the day was

heating up. They were working on the screened-in side porch.

"Nobody sees pillowcases," Gwen said.

"Nobody sees your shirttails, either, but you keep them ironed."

Gwen traced a monogram with one finger. Her mother's maiden name initials. Probably embroidered before she got married, maybe even before she got engaged.

"Mama, do you miss Daddy?"

"What kind of question is that?"

"But do you?"

"Gone is gone, and there's no use crying over spilt milk."

"But, Mama . . . I was wondering . . . how are we going to live? I mean . . . do we have any . . . ?"

Gwen watched her mother's lips tighten into a straight line. "I will be starting work next week, Gwen. The bank has hired me to be a receptionist."

Gwen rolled the last two pillowcases together and tucked them into the bottom of the basket. "Do you want to do that?"

"*Want* doesn't come into it."

"But, Mama . . . how do you feel about it?" The words rushed out. "About Daddy leaving us, and you having to go out and work, and us . . . What are you going to do about us? Abe and . . ."

"*Feel?*" Her mother repeated the word as though she was trying out a strange sound. "*Feel* doesn't come into it, either. And you can help with the boys in the afternoons, you're big enough."

Gwen thought about Abe, who had hardly talked at all since he'd realized that their father wouldn't be coming back. She'd found what was left of his pill bug circus scattered behind an oleander bush, every toothpick broken and every tiny flag wadded up.

Gabriel seemed less affected, bicycling off most days to see his friends. Still, Gwen had occasionally caught him looking puzzled in a way that didn't seem right for a kid.

But now her mother was setting down the iron. "Oh, that dust!" she exclaimed as a car turned in the drive. "Gwen, is that that salesman again? Didn't Gabriel say he was here yesterday?"

Paul called, "Good morning," as he got out of the car. Then he opened the screen door without being asked and came onto the porch.

Gwen's mother picked up her iron. "What are you selling this time?"

"Nothing. I came to see if I could take Gwen for an ice cream."

Gwen's mother looked surprised, and then like she'd tasted something bad. "How do you know Gwen? Gwen is too young to go on a date."

"It's not a date, Mama," Gwen said. "It's for ice cream."

She ran down to the car, heard Paul following, even while he was calling back things that sounded polite.

Gwen whispered, "Let's go, before she says no."

They were out the driveway, out of sight of the porch, before Paul looked sideways, met her with a smile.

"You really want ice cream?"

I wake up cold on Monday morning, cold air blowing in on me from the window. Aunt Emma has stopped asking me why I leave it wide open at night.

"Fresh air never hurt anyone," Gabriel

told her the last time she asked. "When I was in the army, we always kept windows open in the billets."

Abe said I was cleaning spiderwebs. I finally figured out he meant I was clearing cobwebs from my brain.

I wiggle further into the covers, my thoughts shifting from the kids at school to Gwen and Paul, drifting from football games to a band of woods beside a summer lake. Cobwebby woods. Nice woods, I think, although . . .

"Hey, lazy bones, don't you know what time it is?"

It's Uncle Gabriel, at my door. He's gotten me this talking clock that you hit and it tells you the time.

I grab for it, hear a perfectly flat, absolutely one-tone voice say, "Seven-oh-clock— oh-seven-hundred-and-fifteen-seconds."

At school Hannah is full of plans for finding out about Gwen. "Maybe I can come over to your house and go through photo albums with you," she says. "Maybe we'll find Gwen's name written on a picture."

"I've about decided to ask Aunt Emma

who was in my uncles' family. See if she mentions Gwen."

"And if she doesn't?"

"I don't know. Go to Plan Two, I guess."

"Which is?"

"Hannah, I don't know. I don't have a Plan Two. Probably Aunt Emma will tell me Gwen's a retired librarian in San Antonio or Dallas and that will be that."

But now Hannah's the one who wants to be all mysterious and makes me promise we'll try to find out ourselves about Gwen before I ask. I get the idea that what she really wants is an excuse to go home with me instead of to her own home. And, of course, I should have her over since I spent the night at her house.

"OK," I say, "it's OK with me."

Hannah leaves me at the door to my gym class. "I'll be at your place about four," she says. "And Mandy . . . let's not tell anybody else about Gwen. She can be our secret?"

I try to remember if I've ever had a secret with another girl before. I don't think so.

Not that I'm sharing this one quite all the way. I don't think I want to tell Hannah about that last time, how Gwen and Paul were kissing in the car. It seems sort of . . . personal.

The tardy bell startles me and I turn quickly, groping for a handle on a closed door that won't push in. I find a knob instead, pull the door open, and a second later bang my stomach against something solid.

I cautiously run my hand along it until I realize it's a sink. My shoulder hits something that clatters to the floor.

This isn't the gym.

I try to think what I know about the wall by the gym door. What's along it? Hannah hasn't said there's a girls' room. What if I've barged into a boys' bathroom? I take a panicky step and knock something else over.

Then my hand finds the stiff bristles of a brush and next to that a wet cloth. I'm in a cleaning closet.

Relief runs through me and then my cheeks go flaming hot. I back out, wondering who's seen Mandy's latest mistake.

But the hall's quiet. Maybe nobody has.

I say a little thank-you as I search for another door. I find one and open it, and this time I listen for gymnasium echoes before I go any farther.

After lunch Ted's waiting for me outside Ms. Zeisloff's room. I think we must look like a couple, standing there.

"You want people to see us together?" I ask. "The deaf boy reading the lips of the blind girl listening . . ."

"I just wanted you to know I'm not coming to class today. I'm in the middle of a project that I've got to finish before it sets, and I've got a pass to work in the art room."

"So why are you telling me?"

And as fast as I say it, I feel guilty in case I've hurt Ted's feelings, which is stupid, but I about fall over myself trying to make things right. "Ms. Z.'s will be boring without you. I didn't know you did art."

"Yeah, well . . ." His voice trails off.

"Mandy and Ted," Ms. Z. says, "time to get started."

Ted must show her his pass. She says, "All right," and I hear her go inside.

The path is quiet now because the period's begun. I suddenly realize this is about as good a time as I'm going to get to ask Ted to the holiday dance. I wish my hands weren't so clammy. I hope my face isn't

getting blotchy red, the way it does sometimes when I'm nervous.

"Ted, the dance that's coming up . . .
Would you like to go?" I say, the words spill-
ing out.

I should have said it differently. What if
he doesn't understand that I'm inviting him?

I add, "With me, I mean?"

"So everyone can watch the blind girl being led around by the deaf boy who can't
hear the music?" But he's laughing as he
says it, a friendly laugh.

"Something like that," I answer.

For the briefest moment, Ted takes my
hand, and I don't know if he's holding it or
shaking it. Actually, the way he does it, so
fumbling and awkward, I doubt if he knows.

Ted says, "I accept with pleasure."

I go inside and my itinerant teacher, Ms.
Thorn, wants to work with me on a new set
of braille exercises that Ms. Z. is generating.

"Things going OK, Mandy?" Ms. Thorn
asks while we wait for the embosser to finish the page of bumps and spaces. "Did you
get the math tapes we ordered?"

She goes over what I'm doing, class by
class, before she says, "All right. Now, let's

see how you and your braillewriter are getting along."

The brailler reminds me of an old typewriter, the kind people had before electric ones and before computers. There's just one row of keys, three on the left and three on the right, that you press to form the six dots of a braille cell. In the middle is a space bar that you work with your thumbs.

I feed in a sheet of paper and get started on today's exercise, which is a page full of words like *cap, cat, can, pan.* I'm to read them off the sheet from the embosser and then duplicate them on the braillewriter.

Grade-one braille, Ms. Thorn calls what I'm doing, working letter by letter rather than with the code for common words and letter combinations; that is grade two.

It may be called grade one, but what I'm struggling with is worse than it was learning to read print when I was six years old and really in the first grade.

"I don't know why I have to learn this stuff, anyway," I say. "I can type my work on a computer like everyone else and then just listen to it."

Ms. Thorn adjusts the way my left hand

is positioned on the brailler keys. "But Mandy," she says, "how are you going to check your writing with a speech synthesizer? Or revise it? Do it letter by letter? Word by word? You won't be able to see punctuation or word spacing."

"I can't see this, either."

"You will, Mandy," Ms. Thorn says. "One day you'll be able to see braille the way I see print on a page. That's what braille does, Mandy. It lets you *see*."

Promises and hype, I think. I wonder how much is just sales pitch.

But Ms. Thorn doesn't sound like a salesperson, and I want to believe.

"OK," I tell her. "But I may be ancient before I get it learned."

Ms. Thorn coaches me for a while as I make *cat* and *can* with the braillewriter. Then she tells me she's going to check on Marissa and I should call if I need help.

Pan. My fingers hover over the keys as I try to picture the dot pattern that makes the letter *p*. *A* is easy: one dot, top left in the braille cell. Four dots for *n*. I pull the lever to ratchet my paper up one line and go back to the exercise page.

What I find seems too wide a pattern for the domino-like braille cell. I start to call, "Ms. Thorn, there's a mistake." But then I remember about the number sign, how a backward *L* of dots changes what follows from a letter to a number. I find the backward *L* and then the single dot that it turns from *a* into *1*.

I'm pleased I figured it out, but I don't think my teachers should be throwing me trick problems that I might take for mistakes.

I hunch over the brailler and think about Ted and me. About Gwen and Paul. About that ice-cream trip that was really a drive into woods by a lake.

What have I gotten myself into?

I asked Ted. Actually asked him. And he said he'd go.

My stomach knots up. How am I going to keep from making a fool of myself? I won't fit in, not at a dance.

Except . . . I like the way he took my hand.

I hear Ms. Thorn behind me, but I pretend to be so busy that I don't realize she's there. I hope it doesn't show, how mixed up I feel inside.

chapter 8

AT HOME Uncle Gabriel puts some money into my hand. Fifty dollars, he tells me, all in tens. "I figured you'd want to start Christmas shopping early the way Emma always does," he says.

I must look absolutely out of it, because he adds, "Don't forget something for your aunt. Emma's been carrying on about Christmas this year like I've never seen her before."

"She needn't carry on for me."

But Gabriel continues as if I haven't said a word. "You know, we almost had a baby once, your aunt Emma and me, a little girl that died at birth. Your being here—for your aunt it's kind of like being given the daughter she was never able to have."

I know Gabriel means well, wants to let me know I'm not just a burden. But instead he's making me miss my mother so much. Christmastime . . . of all the times, that was when we were the most separate from everyone else, and it made us close. It was like we held each other up in a lonely wind.

Gabriel's still talking about Christmas presents when Hannah shows up. He says, "Maybe you girls can go shopping together."

Hannah says, "Sure. It'll be fun."

When we're alone, though, I say, "I don't need your help, Hannah. I can pick things out without help."

"Mandy," she says, "I know you can, but how are you going to get to the stores? Walk ten miles? Are you ready to find your way around by yourself?"

That last is not a fair question because she knows I'm not.

"Besides," she says, "shopping alone is no fun. Now where are the photo albums?"

I hear her go into the living room, and her voice comes back from several feet away.

"Mandy," she says, "why don't you give yourself a Christmas present and stop being so prickly?"

"I'm not prickly."

"You are."

We find albums on the bottom shelf of the television cabinet. Hannah pages through the one she says looks the oldest, searching for photos with names under them. Mostly, she says, the pictures aren't labeled, or the labels say things like "My recital dress."

Aunt Emma comes into the room, bringing us hot chocolate. "I won't bother you girls." Then, "Oh, look at that. Mandy, Hannah's found a picture of your uncles at the beach at Galveston. Abe's so little he's in a diaper instead of a swimsuit."

A moment more and she's down on the floor with us, which I know because I hear the bones in her knees crack as she lowers herself. "My," she says, "I haven't looked at these pictures in years."

"Here's another one," says Hannah. "They're with a girl."

"That's Gwen. Their big sister Gwen."

My heart feels as if it's going to explode out of my chest. I want to ask . . . except my cheeks are suddenly so stiff, I don't think I can talk.

But Hannah says, as cool as anything, "She's pretty, like Mandy."

"She was Mandy's grandmother," Emma says. "Mandy takes after her."

"But . . ." Hannah's voice trails off.

I know I should say something, should correct Emma. Should say, "Gwen wasn't my grandmother, my grandmother's name was Margaret." But I can't, not with Hannah there. How can I let Hannah know, Hannah with her mother and father and brother and dining room tablecloth, that my family is so spaced we can't even agree on my grandmother's name?

So I don't say anything, only huddle quietly while Hannah and Emma talk on and on.

Later, in my room, Hannah says, "Mandy, do you think maybe you've just *imagined* seeing Gwen? That you've known about your grandmother all along, stories tucked in your subconscious? That being here has made them come out?"

"I haven't been lying," I say, and I feel my face get hot. "I never heard any stories about my grandmother at all because my mom didn't know any to tell."

Hannah waits, her unasked questions filling my bedroom.

"Look," I blurt out, "my mother was put up for adoption when she was a baby. She didn't know anything about her real family, not until a couple of weeks before she died."

I hear Hannah walk over to my window and open it. I imagine her leaning out while she tries to decide what to believe. Her voice comes back, muffled. "Yeah," she says, "families can sure get messed up."

And an instant later she's plopping down on my bed, starting to talk about the dance. "Do you and Ted want to double with Ryan and me? I'll drive, since it's girl-ask-guy."

We don't say another word about families, not mine, not hers. It's like we've agreed to let it rest for now.

We go through my closet, and Hannah says maybe I'd better see if I can get something new because the holiday dance is pretty dressy. "Or you can borrow something of mine," she says. "We're about the same size."

Our talk is surface talk, but even that's a struggle to keep up with. Most of my mind is turned inward, trying to understand how Gwen could be my grandmother.

After Hannah leaves I go to the kitchen, where Aunt Emma is peeling carrots. She shaves off curls for me to nibble.

"You said Gwen was my grandmother?" I ask. "Mom said my grandmother's name was Margaret."

"Margaret Gwen," says Aunt Emma. "But she was always called Gwen. That's all I've ever heard your uncles call her."

"Mom told me she was Margaret," I insist.

There's a silence. Then Aunt Emma sighs. "Yes, well. I suppose your mother just knew from the legal papers, and they wouldn't have told what your grandmother was called."

Then, before I know what she's going to do, Aunt Emma pulls me to her in a hug. "Poor kid," she says.

"I am not," I say, stepping back. "Don't call me 'poor kid.' I am not poor."

"I didn't mean you are, Mandy," says Aunt Emma.

"Then what?"

Aunt Emma steps away also. "I guess that I feel sorry for Gwen, and for your mother."

"You didn't know my mother." I'm furious that Emma thinks it's OK to pity her.

"Of course not," Emma says. "You're right."

In my room I try to bring to a standstill the turning pieces of what I've learned. Try to make them into a new picture.

I go to the dressing table, find Mom's photo, move my hand to the picture next to it. Remember how it was blurred and shadowy and that, really, the only detail was a young man's grin. "So, if you're my grandfather, and if Gwen was my grandmother, then maybe you're Paul."

I imagine Paul in an airman's jacket. Imagine him grinning. Bring that together with what I remember of the picture I am holding and know I can make the two faces merge.

But it's too uneasy a shift to make, and I try to put it out of my mind. Gwen and Paul, my *grandparents*—suddenly they're real and I don't think I want them to be. I shouldn't know what my grandparents were like when they were dating.

I make sure the window is closed tight, push the lace curtains back, and catch them behind hooks on the sides of the window frames.

And what's more, I want to be angry with Gwen, tell her I don't want to see her again. Tell her that if she didn't want to have anything to do with my mom, then I don't want to have anything to do with her. But what I really feel is bewildered. I want to ask what happened, why she did it. But not today.

I press my forehead against the cold glass. I don't want to hear more, not today.

I get out homework, but after a few minutes I put it away again. I can't do schoolwork, not through hot tears.

I pick out what I'll wear in the morning.

Then I turn on my notetaker. It's equipment that rehab got for me, sort of like a laptop computer only it's really a combination word processor and calculator with speech, and it has a typewriter keyboard. I type in *Christmas List,* and hit the key for audio feedback.

"Christmas list," a voice says.

But I can't get Gwen out of my thoughts. She's with me, a grief someplace inside that I don't know how to make go away.

I can't get away from Christmas, either, not with every place I go smelling of Christmas trees and with radio stations playing Christmas music and everybody talking about gifts. Everybody.

"Forget the presents," I want to tell people, but they'll think I mean that Christmas isn't about gifts, it's about Jesus, and that's not what I mean at all. What I mean is that gifts are a burden, and I dread gift-giving times.

Like Tuesday, at lunch. I'm sitting with Hannah's group, thinking partly about Gwen, partly about the sandwich I'm trying to eat neatly. Trying to close my ears to the cafeteria racket, which is impossible to sort into anything meaningful.

Suddenly I hear Charla's voice cutting through the noise. "I've gotten all your gifts, and they're all the same thing."

I freeze in my seat, wishing I was somewhere else. It's like hearing people talk about a party you haven't been asked to, or phone calls you haven't been part of.

"Have you all bought your presents for me?" Charla says, with a little giggle to show she knows she shouldn't ask.

Hannah says, "Not yet," and the others answer.

I pull my arms in miserably, hating gift exchanges.

I take a tough piece of chicken from my sandwich, try to look like I'm not paying attention to everybody around me talking about how they're going to shop for each other.

Then Charla says, "Mandy, what about you?"

I'm slow realizing she means I'm being included.

It's Hannah who answers. "Mandy's going shopping with me."

chapter 9

I KEEP my window closed now, the curtains bunched behind their hooks.

Before, seeing Gwen really was like reading a book. I wanted things to turn out OK, but if they didn't it wouldn't matter, not really.

Now, knowing she is my grandmother, what happens does matter. I'm afraid to see it, afraid for her and for me.

So I keep the closed window and still curtains between us. I concentrate on being Mandy, which is difficult enough.

School's getting harder, and my teachers seem to think I should be able to keep up with all the other kids. I am not going to tell them that twenty minutes of home-work for the others means at least an hour for me.

More like two hours in English, where the teacher gives notes nonstop. Sometimes I spend my whole homework time going back and forth on tapes, trying to find something she's said.

No geography, anyway.

One morning the first week in December the geography teacher meets me at the door. "Mandy," he says, "you've been re-scheduled and won't be in my class any longer."

He sounds so satisfied, it's all I can do to hold in my anger. Don't hold it in.

"You, you . . ." I'm almost sputtering with the effort it takes not to call him some aw-ful name, not to use words I don't want anyone to know I know, not to let on I care. "I was keeping up!"

A hand rests on my shoulder, just long enough to get my attention. "Mandy?" says a man's voice. "I hear you could teach this class." Somehow I know he's really saying it to the geography teacher.

The man turns out to be an orientation

and mobility instructor named Mr. Burkhart. For the next couple of months I'll be
seeing him twice a week during third period
and having study hall the rest of the time.
"O & M," he says, "that's the name of the
game."

He's nice and kind of jokey-loud, and
pretty soon I'm thinking of him as the Great
Om. I learn more in an hour from him than
I can pick up on my own in days.

Big stuff, like how to identify street in-
tersections, deal with traffic, ask people for
directions when they don't have a clue
where north and south are.

He has me practice things like trailing,
following a wall, listening for the water
fountain outside the library.

"Snap your fingers, Mandy," Mr. Burkhart says, and I hear how the sound
changes as we pass by an open doorway.

He asks questions like "Mandy, how do
you search for something you've dropped?"

The answer is very carefully, curved fingers ready to pull back at the first touch of
danger, or before I break whatever I'm looking for.

"Mandy," he says, "what are you going to

do when you're all alone in a strange place and you don't have your cane?"

He won't settle for "sit down and cry," and instead makes me learn how to feel my way forward, one arm protecting my face, a hand in front of my lower body.

The Great Om. My guide to moving through space.

He says not to try to remember it all, but after he leaves I put as much as I can think of into my tape recorder. The things he teaches, they're not like math or history lessons. I *do* have to remember them all.

So, yeah, school's getting harder.

And at home Gabriel keeps asking if I've shopped for Aunt Emma yet. Sooner or later I'm going to have to tell him I don't know what to buy. And I will feel so dumb, but it's a big thing, to get it right.

Also, I've got my dress for the dance Friday and I don't know what I look like in it, although Aunt Emma tries to tell me when I put it on so she can mark how much to take up the hem.

"The copper matches the highlights in your hair, Mandy," she says. "A nice fit— you've got a sweet figure."

Uncle Gabriel asks, "Isn't it a little old for her?"

"Nonsense," says Aunt Emma. "She's a young lady."

It's the lowest-cut thing I've ever owned, except a swimsuit, and Aunt Emma says I'm a lady in it. I hope, somewhere, Mom's laughing.

On dance night Hannah picks me up, the way we planned. We get Ryan and go last to Ted's.

"Let's all go in," Hannah says before I have to ask where the door is. Also, this way I can leave my cane in the car, and that's been worrying me. I want Ted to see me in my new dress, without it.

Ted's parents are just like Aunt Emma was after the football game, acting like this date is Ted going on a world cruise. His mother takes so many pictures she has to change film, and his dad offers us cookies. Then his mother fusses over my dress and Hannah's and fixes and refixes Ted's tie.

"I'm sorry about that," says Ted as we walk to the car. He sounds absolutely, miserably embarrassed, which is one way I've never heard him sound before.

"Parents," says Ryan, like it's no big deal. "They're all like that."

I barely hear Hannah's quiet, "No, they're not."

The dance is fantastic.

Whatever worry Ted had about not hearing the music, I realize right away it's not going to be a problem. The DJ has the volume up loud enough to feel, and certainly loud enough to blast its way past Ted's ears.

And I know I can dance. I always have been able to, even if it used to be alone, in front of a mirror.

There's a moment when Ted shouts in my ear, "Want to try?" that I'd chicken out if I could. But he's pulling me into an empty spot, and I'm moving, little movements, and then bigger and bigger.

Dancing in the dark is like nothing I've ever done before. Sometimes I brush against Ted, or get bumped by somebody else, but even that feels good. I dance, and the music goes on and on, and I can imagine what everything looks like with me in the middle of it all.

Me, Mandy, in the middle of it all.

I'm having such a good time it's a shock when the music stops.

"Mandy," says Ted, and his voice seems both unsure and proud, "you're beautiful."

No one's ever told me that before.

When the music starts back up, Ted has to ask, "Are you ready?" because I'm still standing there thinking about what he said.

I find the beat. "Ready," I answer.

We're out there for dance after dance, until suddenly it's time for the DJ to take a break and Hannah and Ryan are next to us. "Come on," Hannah says, "let's get in line for pictures."

And while we're waiting she whispers, "Where'd you learn to dance like that? Mandy, you're good."

"How was the dance?" Emma asks. She and both uncles have waited up.

"Wonderful," I say.

The room is warm from how happy they are for me.

They've got the TV on, and I sit down next to Emma on the sofa. She puts an arm around me, pulls my head to her shoulder. "A good time, huh?"

Her shoulder is bony and soft at once. I guess it won't hurt to be held, a little while.

Then, upstairs, I find someone has gotten my room ready for me. My bed is turned down, my window open, the lace curtains down from their hooks.

I don't want to be pulled out there, not now, not when, for once, things are close to perfect.

But I hear a voice calling, Gwen's mother calling her, and I can't shut it out. I'm drawn, slow and unwilling, into Gwen's world. Slow like a spoon being pulled from honey. Past limp curtains that hang summer still even though it's December, I'm pulled into a syrup night.

I feel as though I'm somersaulting slowly through the thick night into a motionless day.

Turning in slow motion to see my room. Its painted pink walls bounce sunlight so bright it hurts my eyes. A clutter of things that aren't mine—bobby pins and nail polish and movie magazines—cover the dressing table.

It is a day that feels 110 degrees, and Gwen is stretched out on the bed, looking too hot to move. I can feel the uncertainty in her, knotting her belly. . . .

"Gwen, GwwennnNNN . . . I need you!"

Gwen rolled onto her stomach. If she didn't answer, maybe her mother wouldn't come for her. Wouldn't need her enough to climb all those stairs to come get her.

Hot. It seemed like the hottest August ever.

She pulled the back of her shirt out of her shorts and waited for the fan to come around and dry her back. Rolled over and bared her front. Felt the sweat evaporate so fast her stomach chilled into goose bumps even while the rest of her poured more sweat.

She covered her ears against her mother's footsteps coming up the attic stairs.

"Gwen, didn't you hear me . . . Gwen! Pull down your clothes and get off that bed. That's no place to be in the middle of the day, anyway, and you without a shred of modesty. I don't know what . . ."

"Gwen, why didn't you . . ."

"Gwen, how many times have I told you . . ."

"I'm coming, Mama," said Gwen, sitting up as if she was. But when her mother's footsteps went away, Gwen dropped back. Remembered . . .

"Gwen, come away with me," Paul had said, his face sweaty against hers. "Gwen, I love you."

And Gwen had wondered if she would ever know him well enough to say, "You were the first person to tell me that." Probably not, he'd think she was saying he was the first boy. How do you tell someone you're from a house where nobody says "I love you"?

"Gwen," he'd said, "please come with me."

And she'd known he'd meant to Louisiana, where they'd find someone who'd not push questions about how old she was and who'd marry them. Marry them, and when Paul left to join the Air Force, his going wouldn't be an end—they'd be married.

"OK," she'd said. It had seemed so much better than staying home and snapping beans forever in the hot summer.

She'd made up a story for her mother about visiting a girlfriend and she'd gone off with Paul.

Come back with Paul three days later, in time for him to report for induction. "I'll send for you as soon as I can," he'd promised.

Come home alone and told her mother she'd had an all right visit with her girlfriend.

And now the afternoons were hotter than ever, and she had to tear up Paul's letters once she read them because they started, "Dear Wife."

Dear God, fifteen. What had she done?

Her mother was again at the foot of the stairs. "Gwen, I want you downstairs *now*, and working . . . ."

chapter 10

SATURDAY MORNING I sleep late and stay in bed even later, my thoughts going back and forth between Gwen and the dance.

Gwen, secretly married at fifteen?

Me, a success at a dance? I run my fingers along my face and wonder if it has changed from the way I remember. Am I really beautiful, like Ted said?

I hear Emma and Gabriel in the hall beneath the attic stairs. Gabriel's heavy footsteps come partway up to my door, but I hold my breath and keep perfectly still. He goes back down, says, "I think she's still asleep, Emma."

"Let her be," Emma answers. "I used to sleep in after a dance, too."

And a moment later I hear Emma laugh. "Put me down, silly. I've too much to do for dancing in the middle of the day."

But Gabriel's singing something, and his footsteps are in three-beat time. And then he switches to another song, and it's one my mother used to like.

Mom . . . I remember how she'd hum it. Her body wouldn't really move, but she'd seem like she was swaying, lost in a still waltz.

I remember her sitting in front of her makeup mirror, humming, frowning a bit because she was trying to match a magazine picture. The lipstick was dark stuff, deep red.

"It says you've got to respect your contrasts," Mom said.

Mom must have been about forty then. The deep color made her look even older, but I didn't want to tell her.

It was Christmas morning, the Christmas morning we were living in Florida, and we didn't either one of us have anything to do. I'd given her a leather key case with her name, Karen, stamped on it, and she'd gotten me a necklace with a silver flamingo, but we'd finished opening those in about five minutes and the hours had stretched out since.

Mom leaned closer to the mirror, seemed to decide she was done and she wasn't going to stay in the apartment any longer. "Come on, kid," she said, "let's join America."

So we'd gone out to join America, only America had closed down. The mall was shut, the drugstore, even the kosher deli was shut.

We'd driven to the beach and walked along it, with the old people who were walking two by two, and I thought they were having a lonely Christmas, also.

I'm still in bed, thinking about my mother and about Gwen, when the doorbell rings. I hear Uncle Abe calling, "I'll get it."

A minute more and Hannah's in my room.

"I guess I should have phoned first," she says.

"I wasn't really sleeping."

I wonder if I should tell Hannah what

Gwen has done. It would be fair—Gwen's our secret that we share. But . . . my grandmother, married at fifteen? Such a thing wouldn't happen in Hannah's family, and I don't want her to look down on me.

Besides, it's another personal thing, personal to Gwen, I mean. It wouldn't feel right to expose her like that.

Then I realize Hannah's trying to tell me something.

". . . aren't getting along," she's saying. "They whispered all night, mean whispers, and this morning Dad said he'd be gone for a few days. Mom looked like she'd been crying."

"Everybody fights," I say, the first thing that comes to mind. Actually, I don't have the faintest idea if that's true. I haven't heard Gabriel and Emma fight, and they're the only couple I've ever lived with.

But I've said what Hannah wants to hear, and soon she's rummaging through my dresser, looking for shorts.

"It's practically summer outside," she says. Her voice is too bright, and I know she's already regretting telling me about her folks. "It really is a lot warmer than usual.

Really warm for December. Maybe we can even get tans."

"In December? In the morning?"

"It's afternoon. Didn't you know?"

Hannah's like a cat, moving about my room. I can feel the energy coming off her, the way you can feel it come off the big caged cats at a zoo.

"Don't you ever feel like breaking out?" she asks. "I feel like I can't breathe in here."

Now she's dragging me downstairs, saying, "Let's sleep outside tonight. You ever sleep outside, Mandy?"

"Outside?" I echo, feeling dumb but not sure I know what she means.

"In a tent?"

We find Emma sorting wrapping paper. She says, "Certainly you can't sleep outside. It's December."

But Hannah promises we'll keep warm and the weather forecast is good, and I hear myself saying, "Please, Aunt Emma."

So while I'm getting dressed, Hannah helps Uncle Gabriel get an old tent from the barn, a pup tent from his army days, he says. They set it up by the side of the house.

Hannah and I spend the rest of the afternoon hauling stuff out to it, like we're preparing a room to move into. We run an extension cord so we can plug in my CD player. Get a cooler from the pantry and fill it with ice and sodas. Take out blankets and pillows and two big feather comforters.

I'm blowing up an air mattress, listening to hear if air's escaping out any holes, when it comes to me that I'm going to be outside at night, out where Gwen's and the others' voices have come from.

As though Hannah and my aunt have each caught some small part of my thoughts, Hannah says she wishes we had her Ouija board, and Emma asks, "Are you sure you girls won't be scared?"

Gabriel reassures her. "We'll keep our bedroom window open. The girls can call if they need anything."

We go out to stay about nine o'clock, and Hannah tells me it's a dark night, without any moon.

"Hang on to me, Mandy," she says, "I've got the flashlight." Then we start giggling because that's crazy, the dark is no different for me.

We settle in, and the temperature's dropped enough that the blankets feel good. About the time Hannah's saying we should have got hot chocolate instead of cold drinks, Aunt Emma comes out.

"I've brought you girls a couple of my flannel nightgowns," she says. "I don't want either of you getting sick this close to Christmas."

And after she leaves we pull them on over our T-shirts and underpants.

And maybe it's that, being out of the house in mainly underwear, that makes this night seem wild and wicked and not a night to just let end.

"You sleepy, Hannah?" I ask.

"No."

"I wish we could do something, go some-place."

A car drives by on the road and slows down.

"Mandy," says Hannah. "The lights picked up our tent."

She pauses, draws in her breath, whispers, "What if it's a kidnapper? Or a serial killer?" Hannah is faking fright, and I realize she feels the excitement in this night the way I do.

"Hannah, save me. I'm too young to die," I say, trying to sound terrified.

Hannah switches to her phony voice, the one she used with the Ouija board. "It might be," she says, spacing her words, "the Texas ax murderer. The one who likes young girls!"

She grabs me so fast I scream before I can help it, and she says, "Shush!"

"You two all right down there?" Emma calls.

"We're fine, thank you," Hannah calls back.

I hear her move to the foot of the tent and undo a couple of snaps.

"Mandy," she says, and this time her voice really is a bit shaky, "the car's backing up." Then, and her voice is altogether different, "Mandy, I think it's Ted's car . . . It *is*."

She's gripping my arm and undoing the rest of the snaps. "Be quiet," she says and pulls me, almost running, toward the street.

Almost running, and it feels like flying;

I'm moving fast along the lawn in Aunt Emma's nightgown. My bare feet pound on winter-dry cold grass, pound down on stinging thistles, and cool air blows up my legs. Hannah says, "Careful," just as we bump up against Ted's car.

"You OK, Mandy?" It's Ryan's voice. There's a pause and then he adds, "Pretty sexy clothes."

"You like?" asks Hannah.

Ted ignores the two of them. "You shouldn't be barefoot, Mandy. You could step on a piece of glass or something." He must realize how fussy he sounds. "You want to go into town for something to eat?"

"Now?" Hannah asks. "We can't . . ."

"Why not?" I hear myself saying, and then I'm getting in the front seat next to Ted, and Hannah's in the back with Ryan.

And for an hour we drive around town, ducking every time we meet another car because Hannah and I are in Aunt Emma's nightgowns.

Except at the hamburger place, where we get french fries and Hannah knows the girl at the drive-in window. "Sit up and say something, Mandy," she whispers. "We'll pretend we're going to a costume party."

And then, after all that hiding, we're driving along listening to the radio when suddenly Hannah says, "Ted, stop."

She reaches past me to turn the music up loud, and in another minute all four of us are out in the middle of the road, dancing. Dancing in the headlights of Ted's car, lights that shine through my eyelids when I turn toward them.

Cars go past and everyone honks, and the guys are laughing as hard as we are.

Then Ted says, "That's a police cruiser," and we scramble back inside his car.

We're sitting in the car's four corners, trying to act like we haven't been doing anything unusual, when the patrolman comes to the window. He swings his flashlight around; I see the light when it crosses my eyes.

"You kids OK?" His voice gets louder, I guess at some indication from Ted. "Everything all right here?"

"Yes, sir," says Ted.

But the patrolman says, "Girls?" and waits until both Hannah and I answer.

"Then you better get on home and get dressed," he says.

"Yes, sir," says Ted again, and then, once we're driving, we laugh and laugh like we're going to laugh forever. I say, "Ted, he meant us, Hannah and I should get dressed."

"How do you know?" Ryan asks, and the four of us about die laughing, Ryan the hardest, and Hannah tells Ted to watch the road.

chapter 11

HANNAH AND I wake up in the tent, sometime in the middle of the night. It's cold and damp, and I say, "Hannah, let's go up to my room." We go inside, climb into my big double bed, which is chilly, too, until the sheets warm.

And then we don't wake up again until Aunt Emma's at the steps, calling that if we're not downstairs within the hour we'll miss lunch.

"I can't believe we did that, go to town in nightgowns," Hannah says.

"Me either."

"My mom would kill me."

"Aunt Emma, too," I say, even though I

don't think she would. "I had fun last night."

"Me, too." Hannah pauses, and I get the idea she's choosing her next words carefully. "Mandy, don't take this wrong and get all huffy, but I want you to know I really admire you." Her voice takes on a raw edge, like she's suddenly close to tears. "I mean, whatever happens, you just kind of charge forward and deal with it, and I'm not always so good at that."

There's no way I can imagine she's joking because her voice tells me she's not, and I'm too stunned to answer quickly enough.

Hannah turns over, and when she speaks again the rawness is gone. "I guess if my folks get a divorce my brother and I will stay with Mom. Dad will probably get us on weekends."

"Is that what you want?"

"That's how it's usually done," she says. "Want doesn't come into it."

"Want doesn't come into it." Gwen's mother's words, and hearing Hannah say them makes the skin on my arms tighten into goose bumps.

Hannah asks, "Should I pull up another blanket? You shivered."

"No," and I'm thinking back, trying to remember if I'd told her those words. Maybe they're Texas words, I think, and everyone says them.

Hannah stays with me through the afternoon, even though she listens every time the phone rings, like she's hoping it's for her. We both know things must be really weird at her house if her mother's not calling her to come home.

Hannah opens my bedroom window. "Mandy, have you seen Gwen anymore?"

"No," I say, guilty because I'm lying but still not wanting to tell her about the last time.

"Come try," Hannah urges until I stand next to her. "Call," she says, insistent in a way that's not like her.

"Gwen," I yell, feeling stupid, "Gwen."

I tell Hannah, "This isn't how it works."

"You mean Gwen won't let me see her," Hannah says, jerking me inside and pulling down the window.

Pulling it down on the voice in the wind.

She hasn't heard, but I have. Little Abe is calling Gwen.

In the evening, when I'm alone again, I go back to the window. To reach out to Gwen, or to wait for her to let me go to her. I've stopped knowing which way it is.

I find her summer has turned into a chill December, and her house has become a house of careful, small moments. . . .

Gwen wandered through the rooms, touching this, looking at that, as if she was trying to memorize things.

Abe came in from outside, dropping his coat in the hall.

"Want to go play a game?" he asked.

Gwen swooped him up and hugged him so tightly he said, "Let me down, you're hurting."

Then she went up to the attic, to her room. She ran her hand along a shell pink wall and starched lace curtain. Looked across the stretching fields, already rented out now that her father was gone.

She opened a drawer and wondered what she should take.

"You're leaving, aren't you?" Her mother's voice at the doorway made her jump. "I thought so."

"How did you know?"

"Gwen, please. It can't be so bad here that you have to run away."

"There's not anything bad, Mama," Gwen said. "It's just that . . ."

"Then why?" her mother asked, but she didn't wait for an answer. She shook her head as though she had already decided arguing was useless. "Well, I can't stop you, but I won't take you back, either."

Gwen spent the next long hours by herself, waiting for evening, for Paul. He'd written that he'd found a room for her just off base, that he was using his first real leave to come get her. Gwen had planned to go off with him and then write, but somehow her mother had guessed.

Her mother came up to the attic just once more. "I hope you'll get married?"

"We already are," Gwen said.

Her mother made a strangled sound,

more like a snort than anything. "Here, then," and she thrust one of her own nightgowns into Gwen's hands. "You can't go to your husband in pajamas."

When Paul's car sounded in the drive, Gwen grabbed her suitcase and ran down all the stairs and out to meet him. And then, for all her hurrying, she looked back. Looked back at an empty porch and nobody waving good-bye.

Her mother's nightgown was on top of everything, in her suitcase.

Ted has started picking me up on his way to school. It's not far out of his way.

He honks and I go out to his car, a vehicle that he is very proud of. He got it right after he got his license, he told me, because the bus doesn't go near his house and his mother wanted to stop driving.

"His parents," Aunt Emma said, "think the sun rises and sets on that boy. If he wanted his own airplane, they'd find a way to give it to him."

This morning I'm only halfway to his car when he calls, "Mandy, come here and hold out your hands. Together and carefully."

He puts something soft and warm and incredibly light in my palms. "A baby possum," he says. "I found it by the road."

"Alone?"

"A big one was nearby, run over. I think it was this one's mother."

The baby is so small I can almost hold it in one palm, and I'm terrified I'll hurt it. "Take it, Ted," I say, "before I drop it."

"You won't. You can raise it."

"Me? You found it. Him. Her. Whatever."

But even as I talk, groping for a joke, my insides are thumping over because I want so much to care for the little thing. I'm wishing I dared trust it to one hand. I want the other free to stroke it, and find the top of its head, and how its tail feels.

At the same time, I'm panicky.

"I don't know anything about taking care of an animal," I say. "I've never had a pet. What do you feed it?"

"It's a baby, Mandy." Ted sounds exasperated, but he's laughing, too. "Milk, of course."

"And Aunt Emma probably won't let me keep it. If she wanted a pet, she'd have a cat or a dog."

"Why don't you ask?"

I pull back one hand just a little, begin to explore the hairless tip of its tail with my finger. A low growl and hiss make me wonder if I'm going to get bitten. Then I realize probably it's the baby that's frightened.

I leave the opossum with Ted and go in the house to find Aunt Emma. I was right about her not wanting a pet. "Keeping a wild animal is probably not even legal," she says. "I'll call the shelter and see what they say to do."

I won't beg. It's something I've never done and I'm not going to begin now. I turn, walk partway down the hall.

And turn again and go back.

"Please, Aunt Emma. Just until it can go out on its own?"

"Mandy . . ."

"Please?"

There's a long silent moment, a moment in which I swear to myself that if Aunt Emma says no I won't ever ask her for anything again. Won't ever ask anyone for anything. I shrug and start to say, "Never mind."

"I guess," she says, "we could try feeding

it some of the milk replacer your uncles keep on hand for calving. I should have an eyedropper somewhere."

Then she catches my arm as Ted and I are leaving. "Mandy, it probably won't live, you know. Wild things often don't."

I'd like to say it doesn't matter, but I can't. "Please don't let it die, Aunt Emma," I say. "Please, please don't."

Ted, on the drive to school, is absolutely delighted with himself, all out of proportion to saving an orphaned opossum.

At school Hannah's lining up my day, telling me we should go shopping in the afternoon.

I tell her I can't. I have to get home to the opossum.

Besides, I wish Hannah would understand that I don't want her help shopping. Finding the right presents for Aunt Emma and the uncles is something I should be able to do by myself.

The school halls are even more noisy than usual, and at lunch the cafeteria is thundering with band instruments playing a preview of a holiday concert. I can't hear what anybody is saying, can't even hear voices well enough to know who's sitting where.

"I'm leaving," I shout, to whoever's listening. I get up, only where I thought there was a space there's not and I knock a tray crashing to the floor. I reach down, touch something cold and wet, wonder how to clean up.

Someone says, "I'll get it."

I sink back into my chair. For a moment everything—the tray, all the noise—it's more than I can deal with.

"Hey," somebody yells in my ear, "you're complaining about the food?" I recognize Ryan's voice. He's trying to make me feel better.

Then Hannah's with me, and we're walking outside toward the building where the resource room is.

"I don't know what happened," I begin. I realize I owe Hannah some sort of explanation, but I'm just too tired and overwhelmed to make it. The opossum, Aunt Emma giving in to me, those blasted presents I don't know what to do about . . . This day feels like it's been thirty hours long.

"Sometimes I just want to get away from everything."

"Me too," says Hannah.

In Ms. Z.'s room I slump into a seat, and for once nobody comes and asks me if I need help. I must sit there twenty or thirty minutes, listening to the quiet click and chunk of keyboards and printers, to the hum of machinery fans, to the murmur of one of the boys reading under his breath. Slowly things calm down inside me, until I'm finally ready to get to work.

I go to my computer and begin a file for a paper I'm writing for English. The assignment is to capture an instant using sensory detail. I'm doing mine on an early summer morning, as far from Christmas as I can get.

It's pretty boring stuff, how the sunrise looked through the back window of the car the summer Mom and I drove west. How the sky went clear down to the earth. How empty the road was, empty as we were because we hadn't stopped for breakfast yet, empty like I always felt when we'd left one place and hadn't yet found the next.

I hear someone come up behind me. Ms. Z. says, "You make it seem real."

"It's just what I remember," I say.

"Being able to remember details is a gift."

And then she goes away and Ted takes her place. He must have been watching us, reading our lips, because he says, "I heard the ocean once, in a seashell. When I was little, before my hearing got so bad. But I don't have words for the sound."

I know what he's saying, that he wishes he could put sounds on paper, to keep them.

The way I wish I could know for sure I won't ever forget the sky, or the color of an empty road.

"I hope Ms. Z.'s right," I say, "about me having a gift for remembering. Because sometimes I wake up and everything is black, and for an awful time I wonder if I've forgotten how it was, what things looked like."

"Like the sun," says Ted. "Like the sun through the car window. You won't, Mandy."

I shrug. How can he know?

chapter 12

EMMA'S WAITING for me on the front lawn when I get home. She tells me right away that the opossum is alive. "Cute little thing," she says. "And hungry! He's been eating all day, eating and sleeping."

Emma's been busy, made some phone calls, bought some stuff that is supposed to be better than the cow milk replacer. "Not," she says, "that he doesn't seem just as happy eating bugs."

She leads me to where she's got him in a big carton on the front porch. The opossum's half hidden in a pile of leaves in one corner, and Emma tells me he moved them there himself.

"I'll sit out here with him awhile," I say. Then, as she goes inside, I add, "Thank you, Aunt Emma."

"You're welcome," she says, and she sounds enormously pleased.

The uncles have missed all this, the opossum, I mean, because they've been gone since before dawn to a stock show. Now their car turns in the drive. Uncle Gabriel calls to me that he's going out to the barn and will be along in a while, and Abe comes up the steps.

"What have you got there?" he asks.

"An opossum. An orphan."

"It's pretty big," he says. "Probably born in September and about ready to go out on its own."

"I'd wondered why there would be a baby now, instead of spring."

"Possums have young different times of the year," Abe says. "Carry them around in pouches like kangaroos until they grow a decent size. When they're born they're about the size of my thumbnail."

The one I'm holding suddenly seems a lot bigger, as I try to picture him just a bit bigger than my thumbnail. Without warning he wraps his tail around my finger and drops to my lap. The tail, unwrapping itself, tickles. "I think this one's going to be a circus performer."

I say that and a memory clicks in sharp, clicks in about circuses. Without taking time to think I say, "You used to have a circus, didn't you? When you were little? A pill bug circus?"

I hear Abe catch his breath, then the silence of him holding it, like he can't breathe. Then his harsh, "What makes you say that?"

And I'm frightened to tell him, frightened and feeling that I'm at the edge of something terribly sad.

"Oh," I say, "I don't know. I guess I was just thinking most kids like bugs."

This night there's no calling when I first lean out the window. I lean out farther and wait a long time, wait in air cold and heavy. And then I hear the child's thin, crying voice, little Abe's voice. . . .

"Gwen, Gwen? Please, Gwenny, come back."

"I miss Gwen," Abe said. "Will she ever come back?" He was standing close by his mother, as if standing so close would make her answer.

"Gwen's best forgotten," she said. "Go play."

But after he went outside, she stepped to the secretary, took an envelope off the top. She pulled out a letter and read over it quickly, as if she was looking again at something she'd already memorized. Pressed her lips together. Murmured, "Just what do you expect from me?"

She tore the letter three times across and three times down, and after that she tore up the envelope. "I told you I wouldn't have you back."

Then she sat in a rocker, closed her eyes, and murmured, "I did what was right, didn't I? Told you the consequences if you left?"

After a while she went to the wastebasket, pulled out the pieces of paper, and tried to fit the envelope back together. Tried, and couldn't, and gave up.

It's Saturday again. Aunt Emma is standing at the kitchen table, wiring pine boughs into a wreath. The uncles have put a Christmas tree up in the living room, and the boughs are what they cut off the bottom.

"They smell so good," I say, picking one up. Sap sticks to my fingers and I try to roll it off. The wonder is the boughs can be smelled at all among all the other smells. Aunt Emma has spiced cider heating on the stove and cookies baking. Ginger and cinnamon and apple run into the cool air that comes from a window she's cracked open, air that smells just a little of damp earth and cows and hay.

"Aunt Emma," I start, and then don't know quite what I want to say. That this is like a book, maybe, or a TV family. "Aunt Emma," I say, "you've made this house nice."

"It's you that's made it nice, Mandy. You can't imagine what pleasure you're giving your uncles and me."

Then she hugs me. Something scratchy, a piece of pine branch caught on her dress maybe, tickles my neck, and her cheek next to mine feels floury.

I start to pull away, but then I think, why? And so I give her a little hug back. I'm not sure what to do with my arms, which makes the whole thing clumsy, but I guess it's an OK hug. Emma says, "How about pouring us some cider?" and her voice tells me how pleased she is.

I take down two mugs and position them on the counter, where they'll be easy to find after I pick up the saucepan. I hear wire being clipped, so I know my aunt has returned to her wreath making. She's not even watching me, is she? She knows that I can do this. It's silly, I guess, but I feel quite proud of myself.

I'm proud of Aunt Emma, too. I know it was hard for her the day my caseworker said sooner or later I'd have to learn to cook for myself and it might as well be sooner.

"But it's so easy to get burned," Aunt Emma had protested. "And there are sharp knives, and . . ."

And we'd all gone out into the kitchen

and the caseworker had marked the stove dials with a 3-D marker. "One line at twelve o'clock for *off,* Mandy, two lines at three o'clock for *high.*"

And now, thinking about Aunt Emma and me, how we're working together in the kitchen, this leads to another thought. It's one that's tangled, but I like it—a thought that I'm fitting in here.

Me pouring us cider and it not being something to especially notice, that doesn't have anything to do with how well I can get about on my own. It's because I'm family. Doing for each other, it's how a family is.

Or should be.

"Aunt Emma?" I say.

"Yes?"

"Will you answer a question?"

"If I know the answer."

"When Uncle Abe and Uncle Gabriel were little, what was it like here?"

She takes awhile, as though she's searching through details. Finally she says, "They've never talked much about when they were little. But I can imagine."

She shuffles pine boughs before continuing. "The first year we were married, your uncle Gabriel and I, I wanted to buy the most beautiful Christmas tree we could and decorate it with him. But his mother—this was her house, and we were living with her then—said if we had so much money we ought to be able to find a better use for it. She set a scrawny little tree out on a table, put it up one day when nobody was home, like it was just one more job that needed doing."

"Do you think she loved Gabriel and Abe?" I ask.

Aunt Emma blows on the cider I hand her, then sips a bit. "I don't know. I suppose, as much as she was able. I probably shouldn't say, I was just a daughter-in-law, but . . . I always thought she didn't know how to love."

Emma's next words come in a rush. "I wish you could see the old photo albums, Mandy. Her, and her mother, and her mother's mother. Like, like . . ."

"Like coldness passed on?" I ask.

"Exactly," Aunt Emma says, sounding surprised, as if I've shown her something she's never seen before. "Like coldness passed on."

chapter 13

♪ ♪ ♪ ♪
♪ ♪

I HEAR the crying outside my bedroom window, hear it even though I stay in bed, try to smother my ears with covers.

I hear the boy's voice, crying for Gwen.

I hear Gwen's voice from a far distance, awful cries . . .

"Paul, stop falling. Please God, don't let him, don't . . . Paulllll!"

. . . Gwen? . . .

"How can he be dead? What do I do now?"

Monday is Big-Little Day at school, something done around here for enough years that no one thinks the name is funny. All the second graders in the district spend the morning in high school, parceled out one-on-one to sophomores and juniors.

"I think they're supposed to see how much they have to look forward to," Hannah tells me when I ask why.

Ted, who is standing with us, says, "Which we'll demonstrate by coloring Santa pictures, serving snacks in every class, and limiting the academics to rented videos."

"Not really," I say.

"Really," they answer in unison.

"What?" Ted adds. "You expected truth in advertising from a school district?"

Anyway, today I am to personally convince Robert Carlo, who is seven years old and wants to be called by his whole name, that high school is a great place to be.

Robert Carlo is more interested in me than in high school.

"I've never met a blind person before," he says.

"We go to math first," I tell him. "I bet we have juice and something to eat and watch a movie."

"How do you find the room?"

"With my cane."

"How does your cane tell you?"

"It's got an electronic elf inside that sends radio wave messages to my brain. In code."

There's a long pause while Robert Carlo considers the possibility. I laugh.

"My math class is around the first corner from where we are now, then six doors down. I use my cane to count the doors."

Wrong thing to tell Robert Carlo. "You ever lose count?" he asks as we walk. "Two, six, nine. Can you add forty-three, thirteen, and a hundred and fifty-five?" he jabbers. "Eight, eleven, one million . . ."

Charla goes by. "He's my next-door neighbor," she says. "You've got my sympathy."

We reach a second corner and I realize we've missed the room. "We have to go back," I say. "This time, Robert Carlo, shut up."

A small, grimy-feeling hand slips into mine, and a moment later I hear, "Mandy? I'm sorry."

Robert Carlo eats doughnuts and asks questions nonstop. Fortunately, the TV volume is so loud our whispering during the movie doesn't seem to bother anyone.

Robert Carlo wants to know if being blind hurts.

Why I bother to keep my eyes open.

If my fingers get sore when I read braille, and I have to tell him I don't read braille very well yet.

He wants to know if I can see anything at all.

"Light, sometimes, if it's very strong. And once in a great while I feel what color something is."

"No way," he says. "You can't feel color."

And of course he grabs my hand, sticks it on a book, and demands, "What color? Can you feel what color this is?"

"I said, *sometimes*."

How do I explain what I don't understand myself? How every once in a while I'll touch something and my brain will be flooded with an image of red, or blue, and when I ask I find out that's what color the thing really is?

The movie sound snaps off midsentence. For the first time I am aware that other kids have edged in close to Robert Carlo and me.

A boy who sounds like another second grader asks, "How do you take tests?"

A girl asks, "Do you have to help at home?"

Some snot says, "What could she do?"

"Plenty," I say, I guess a bit snappy. "I set the table, dust, help with feeding the cows. I wash my own clothes, make my bed every morning . . ."

The same kid says, "Your folks must be dictators."

"Right," I tell him. I start to leave it at that and then realize I can't. What if it got back to Aunt Emma and my uncles?

"My folks are not dictators," I say. "They just want me to know how much I can do."

The bell rings but nobody moves. Then Mr. Casie says, "Thank you, Mandy."

Robert Carlo takes possession of my hand again. And a little girl says, "Mandy, you have pretty eyes."

The days are going by quickly, punctuated by feeding times for my opossum. It seems every time I pick him up, he's grown a bit and become a bit more independent.

Hannah comes over on Wednesday

afternoon. The weather has turned cold and rainy, and we take cookies and soda up to my room, which is the warmest place in the house. I ask Hannah if there's ever snow in Texas for Christmas.

"I suppose, but not often, except maybe in the panhandle," she says. "Not over here, anyway. Mandy, everyone in town seems to know my folks are considering a divorce. Every place I go, people are nice." After a moment she adds, "I hate it that everyone feels sorry for me."

"Welcome to the club."

"Mandy," she says, "I'm scared."

She sighs and then, like she's forgetting the whole subject, gets up and goes to my dressing table. I hear her picking up first one thing, then another.

"Mandy," she says, "tell me again who the man is."

"My grandfather."

"He's so young in the picture. Is he still alive?"

"No," I say, "I never met him. He died years ago, before I was born, even before my mother was born."

"Then why do you have his picture out?"

I answer carefully because I've been thinking about that myself. "I guess because it was important to my mother," I say. "She always kept that picture on her dresser."

I think back, wondering how much to tell Hannah.

Think back to how my mother would look at that picture, sometimes for ten, fifteen minutes without moving. Then she'd tell me, "That's my father, Mandy, your grandfather, wearing his airman's jacket. Did you ever see anyone so proud? I think he must have just learned my mom was going to have me."

I tell Hannah, "That was all my mother had of her father. He died months before she was born."

Hannah says, "I think that's one of the saddest things I ever heard."

I agree. Still, I can't tell Hannah how sometimes I heard my mother crying in the night. How once I found her standing in front of the picture. "You're promising," she was saying, over and over. "You're grinning like you're promising to come back."

Instead I ask, "Hannah, do you mind very much about your folks splitting up?"

"It hasn't happened yet."

"If they do?"

"It's their lives," she says, and her voice has a new hardness.

"Yeah," I say, thinking I should have minded my own business. "There's no point getting upset over other people's lives."

Alone after Hannah's gone home, I go back to the pictures, hold my grandfather's in one hand, my mom's in the other.

I know exactly how my grandfather's picture looks, the image of a young man's face as it was at one moment. I memorized it years ago.

But Mom's photo has ceased being a fixed thing. I hold it and see how she looked, first at one time and then another, Mom in a set number of memories that won't ever be added to. I hunt through them, find how she'd ask me into her room and show me her father's picture.

"Look, babe," she'd say, "he's grinning. I think he knows I'm going to be born and he's saying, 'Chin up, kid. Hit the world running, kid.' He loved me, Mandy. See how he looks?"

And I'd stand there, thinking that even with just a picture, she'd had more of a father than she'd given me.

I guess it wouldn't have hurt me to say, "Yes, I think he must have loved you." But I never did.

I wonder if, like Gwen, my mom is out there, past the dark, living again in some year when she was young. I want to tell her I'm sorry.

It's the middle of the night, and I'm having trouble sleeping. I pull the covers close. Should I open the window? Hold a piece of lace curtain to my face, smell the faint bleach, the fainter dust?

I tumble, roughly... I hear Gwen's voice...

Gwen, Gwen... Stop screaming, Gwen...

"I saw a bird. I couldn't make it keep flying."

And?

"He was fast, falling fast, and his brown feathers were covered with oil and fire. He screeched with wind and terror."

You could hear him?

"His mouth cawed open and he crossed the sky, between me and the plane, he crossed the sun and came cartwheeling down."

The bird?

"Paul."

You saw him?

"Mandy, I wish I could give you my eyes."

Aunt Emma is shaking me, and I hear the uncles in the doorway.

"Mandy, wake up," Emma's saying. "Mandy, you're having a nightmare."

But I know I'm not, and I say, "No, it was Gwen. She was seeing Paul die. He was cartwheeling, down and down."

And then Aunt Emma squeezes my arm so hard it hurts and I jerk the rest of the way awake. "Is that what happened?" I ask. "Did Gwen see her husband die?"

It's Uncle Gabriel who answers. "We never heard," he says. "She never wrote home after she left."

I hear Abe's footsteps; he's going slowly down the stairs like an old man.

Aunt Emma asks, "Do you often think about Gwen?"

And, maybe because it's the middle of the night, I say, "Sometimes I can see everything going on, like I was there, when she was my age."

I wait for them to tell me I'm imagining things, but they don't.

Aunt Emma says, "There have been stranger things."

And Gabriel says, "I'd like to think Gwen knows you, Mandy. She'd be proud."

Only Uncle Abe is upset. I find him alone in the living room the next morning, not doing anything.

"You didn't like me talking about Gwen, did you?" I ask.

I think he shrugs, even though I can't see him.

"Would you please tell me about her?" I ask.

Abe's voice is gruff. He says, "I've got work to do outside. Besides, Gwen went away before I was old enough to remember."

He leaves, and I go to find Aunt Emma. "How old was Uncle Abe when Gwen left home?" I ask.

She does some figuring, subtracting ages and dates, and says she guesses about five or six.

That's what I guessed, too.

Old enough to remember at least a little. But maybe he doesn't want to. Maybe remembering her hurts him too much because he believes she abandoned him.

And then I feel so sorry for him, for them both. I want to go after him and say, "Uncle Abe, Gwen did write, but your mother tore up her letter."

But what good would that do? He probably wouldn't believe me.

Aunt Emma says, "I've often thought how sad it is that Abe can't seem to remember anything about being a child. It's like a part of his life is locked away and he can't get at it."

"Gwen loved her brothers," I say, and I know it with absolute certainty.

"Gabriel realizes that, I think," says Emma. "But I don't know if Abe ever will."

chapter 14

I MIX SOME MILK formula in a bottle and go outside to see if the opossum will come for it, before I have to leave for school. He doesn't stay in his carton anymore, although we leave it on the porch so he can get back in if he wants.

Uncle Abe thinks the sooner the opossum is completely on its own, the better chance it will have of surviving. And I know he's right. When you have to take care of yourself, about the only way to do it is to just get out and start.

Still, I'm glad when I hear the little guy come scrambling up the porch steps. He knocks at my hands and at the plastic bottle before settling down to eat. I don't know if the milk is dessert after food he's gotten on his own or if it's his whole meal.

I wonder if he thinks I'm his mother.

Don't be dumb, Mandy, I tell myself. Opossums can't think.

"Whatever," I say out loud. "I'll take care of you as long as you want." I feel so responsible and . . . so old. Like I really am sort of his mother.

Thinking that makes me think of my own mom. It's the strangest thing, how she seems to be getting younger and younger in my mind.

"It's pretty amazing, how you took care of me," I whisper. I remember back, a lot of things. My mom and me eating hot dogs together at a park, loading a car trunk so full we had to tie it shut, taking in one of her skirts to fit me, trying to make crocuses bloom on a windowsill.

She tried to be a good mother, even though she didn't have any more training at the job than I've got in taking care of opossums. Of course, if she had, maybe sometimes she would have told me she loved me.

She would have known it was something I wanted to hear.

The opossum is scratching my hand, probably hoping for more to eat.

"Sorry," I say. "Too much food could kill you."

I pick him up. "But I guess a little love won't hurt."

I've known as long as I can remember that my mom was put up for adoption when she was born, only the adoption didn't work out and she grew up in a series of foster homes.

All she knew about her real family was what she could guess from a couple of pictures that had arrived in the mail one day, when she was still a kid. They had come with a note that said, "For the little girl."

One was the picture I still have, of her father, taken just before he died. That was written on the back. The other photo was of the house where her mother grew up, this house that I'm living in now.

"Didn't anyone try to find out who sent them?" I once asked.

"Not that I know of," Mom answered. "I was only four or five."

The photo of the house got lost a few years ago, but by then I knew it by heart. Whenever we moved to a new town, I'd watch houses, hoping to find where my grandmother had come from. I had this scene that I'd imagine, how Mom and I would walk up to a door, introduce ourselves . . .

Dumb, but sometimes I'd see Mom checking out houses, too.

I hope she knows I'm living in that very house now, and that it's a nice place.

Hannah's visiting again.

"I hate my parents," she says. "All the fighting, all the time, and they try to be polite about it."

It's late afternoon, and we're walking through the back pasture, the one where there's just cows. The uncles keep the bulls in a different field. It's safe for us to be in this one.

"I'd like to live in the country," Hannah says. She stops to pet a cow that has come over, but as soon as the cow realizes we don't have food, it wanders off. "Other times," Hannah says, "I think I'd like to go away, just run off and disappear forever."

A shiver goes through me. "Don't say that."

"Well, it's what I think," says Hannah. "Sometimes I try to imagine the ways I could go away and not leave a trail that people could follow."

I think, Gwen found a way.

"The bus would be best," Hannah says. "It's hard to lie about your name on a plane ticket because you have to show ID when you check in, and cars are too easy for the police to look for."

"Hannah, I told you, don't talk that way."

But she won't stop. "I'd take a bus going in a direction where all the towns have good-sounding names. And I wouldn't get off until I was at least two states away."

There's no way I can make her understand. Disappearing is not something to joke about. A person doesn't know who she's going to hurt when she goes off and doesn't come back.

If Gwen hadn't disappeared, hadn't gone off and left her baby for strangers to raise, then all those years later my mom wouldn't have started looking for her, and . . . Well, maybe everything would have been different.

chapter 15

MOM GOT the idea one evening this past summer. I was fixing a torn swimsuit and she was quietly reading, which was not the way she usually read.

Usually she talked.

"Mandy," she would say, "it says here you can get cancer from the sun," or "California workers get some of the highest wages in the country." Stuff I'd already know, but these things always came as news to Mom.

But this particular evening, Mom wasn't saying a word, and that distracted me so much I asked, "What are you reading about?"

"Nothing," she said, putting down her magazine.

Then five minutes later she said, "Mandy, I'm going to find my mother."

Like, "Mandy, I think I'll get a leather belt for my new slacks."

Mom got up, pulled a package of cookie dough from the freezer, and knocked her knuckles against it. "You think this would thaw pretty quick?"

"Is that what you were reading about, finding parents?"

Mom shoved the dough back. "I guess I don't need the calories. There's a story about how adoption records used to be sealed up, but now they're being opened. More and more people are being reunited with their birth parents."

Poor Mom. I could see the signs—we were going to move again. This time in search of her birth mother.

And she probably expected to find some loving, real-cookie-baking woman delighted to see us. Right. Just the way she'd expected to find sunshine and good jobs and a great life at the end of our other moves.

My mom may have been well into her

forties, but sometimes she didn't have a clue about how the world worked.

"So when do we leave?" I asked. "And where to?"

Hannah's voice startles me, and for an instant I struggle to remember where we are.

She says, "Mandy, let's start back. My feet are getting cold."

But then she stops me. "Mandy, I wish you could see that cow over by the watering trough. Her sides are bulging so far out she must be going to have twins."

"I don't think cows do, at least not very often."

"Do you think there will be any babies soon?"

"Uncle Abe says the first calves will be born in early February."

Without warning, Hannah switches subjects. "Mandy," she says, "you've never told me about your accident. What happened?"

"Why?"

"I don't know." She sounds hurt but goes on. "I guess I've been thinking how strange it is, how I thought my life was all settled. And now my folks are probably getting divorced, and because of that one thing, all of a sudden everything else is different. Wasn't the accident like that, for you?"

I consider what she's said.

"It was and it wasn't," I finally answer. "It made everything different, but . . . there wasn't much in my life really settled before, either."

Although, I remember, I'd had hopes that things might settle down.

I remember how, for the briefest time, Mom and I had thought maybe we were going to stop being just the lonely pair that we were.

It had taken Mom several weeks and a staggering phone bill to get the name of the place that had her adoption records. But, finally, she had an agency's name and address, and it wasn't all that far north of Baltimore, where we were living.

"They said I'd have to come in person with my questions," she said.

We went up together, catching an early morning Amtrak, and by eleven we were watching a woman examine all the identification papers Mom had brought with her.

Finally the woman put them down and opened a folder.

"Actually, Karen," she said, talking to my mom, "this record of your adoption has never been sealed. Your mother left instructions to provide her name, should you ever request it."

And then she wrote several lines on a paper, which she handed, folded, to Mom. "Of course," she added, "you must understand that this address is quite old."

We were in the hall before Mom looked, her fingers trembling just a little bit, and a red spot on each cheek. I read with her, "Margaret G. McKenney," and an address in California.

Mom dithered all the way home about whether she should write or call. Then, when we got home and telephoned Information, she learned there wasn't any listing for McKenney, not at the address Mom had.

"It's a sign," Mom said. "I should write. The post office will forward a letter if she didn't move too long ago."

Mom spent three more afternoons

composing the perfect letter, finally settling on one that began, "Dear Mrs. McKenney, We have never met, but I am the daughter who . . ."

And then she wouldn't mail it until she had good stationery to copy it on to. "I want her to like me," she said.

"Mom, the kind of paper you write on won't make any difference."

"Let's go buy some," she said.

Outside, bits of dust hung in the air and a low afternoon sun glistened golden red behind them. We got into the car and Mom swung into traffic, just as a delivery truck turned a corner going too fast.

When the truck slammed into us, my seat belt kept me from being thrown through the windshield, but my head still smashed into the dashboard.

Mom had just been pulling her seat belt on when the accident happened, and she was hurled through the windshield and crushed against a utility pole.

I become aware that Hannah is waiting for me to answer and I wonder how long

I've been silent. I think back to what her question was.

"There's not much to tell," I say. "A delivery truck hit us. Mom died in the hospital several days later, and you know what happened to me."

I leave it at that. I've never really heard all the next part anyway, except that while I was starting to learn how to live without my sight, a child services worker was busy trying to figure out where to send me when I left rehab. She first tried to track down Margaret McKenney and learned she'd been dead a couple of years. Then she went to the adoption agency and from there backward to my uncles.

Sometimes I imagine the woman calling. I wonder how she asked, "Want to take in a blind teenager?"

But I suppose that's not fair. She must have worked hard to find me my family.

After Hannah goes home, Emma asks, "Want to go to the grocery store?"

When we're driving I say, "Aunt Emma, can I ask you another question?"

"Certainly."

"When you all found out about me . . . When that child services woman asked if you wanted to help . . . Did you and my uncles say yes right away, or did you have to talk it over?"

"We said yes, of course. You're family, Mandy."

"Without even talking it over?"

Aunt Emma laughs.

"I suppose we did spend an evening at the kitchen table. But the discussion started with your uncle Abe saying he'd make sure the stair railings were all safe. There was never any question what we wanted to do."

"Just because I was family?"

In a curious way I want her to say no. To tell me they wanted me for me, and not because they felt they had to take care of a relation.

Which is stupid, because how could they have wanted me for me when we'd never met?

But Aunt Emma must know what I'm thinking. She pats my leg. "Mandy," she says, "we'd want you if you didn't have a single drop of family blood."

And suddenly I feel the most awful longing for my mom, and I feel so sorry for her.

All those moves after all those things, from religion to good health . . . Maybe if she'd somehow known to move here, she'd have found what she really wanted.

I tell Aunt Emma, "I wish you'd taken my mother in."

"But Mandy," says Aunt Emma, "we didn't even know your mother existed. We never knew Gwen had a baby."

It makes me angry. "You could have known," I say. "Why didn't anybody go after Gwen?"

But I'm the one who knows the answer to that question. Abe and Gabriel were too young when Gwen left, and their mother threw Gwen's letter away.

One woman, and her meanness, spoiled Gwen's life and my mother's life.

"She could have put the envelope back together if she'd tried harder," I say.

"Who, Mandy?" asks Aunt Emma.

But I shake my head. It's too complicated.

Night comes. I open my window, pull the curtains around my shoulders, and call to Gwen.

I want to talk to Gwen, alone and signing the adoption papers that would cut her off from the last person she had a blood tie to. I want to thank her for letting me know what happened, tell her that her granddaughter is going to be OK.

A warm breeze wraps me in soft air, a breeze like the Chinook winds that blew the year Mom and I lived in Montana. I can't tell if I am wishing the words or hearing them, but a woman's voice says, "I'm glad, Mandy."

The breeze stirs, slowly lifting the lace curtains from my shoulders. They drift in front of me, hang still on the sill.

chapter 16

Iᴛ's ꜰɪᴠᴇ more days until Christmas and I still haven't figured out gifts for Aunt Emma and my uncles. I want to be able to give them things *I've* chosen, so they'll really be gifts from *me,* but I also want to be sure the gifts are just right. Hannah has asked a couple more times if I want her help shopping, but I've told her no, I have Christmas under control. I wish.

At least I have presents for the girls at school. I take the wrapped boxes with me since it's the last day before vacation. We do our gift exchange at lunchtime.

Charla goes first, handing me a case with three colors of lip gloss. "They're all in your color family, Mandy," she says. "Just remember, the darkest is on the left and the lightest on the right."

I get a wood box with a croaking frog from Blakney, and Rosa has made ornaments for everyone. She tells me mine says, in gold glitter, ROSA AND MANDY, FRIENDS FOREVER.

And they all say they like the writing paper I give them, which has a design worked around their first names. I did it on the computer with Ted's help, which was all right to take because he's an art student and I'm not, and I printed it on parchment-feeling paper that I bought specially.

The only sad thing about our gift exchange is that Hannah is absent.

I'm surprised she didn't call to tell me she wouldn't be in school because it's not like Hannah not to call. And she didn't say a thing yesterday about not feeling well.

"A crummy time to get sick," I tell Ted as we walk to the resource room.

He *uh-huhs*, like he's not exactly agreeing, or he's thinking something else altogether.

The phone rings not long after class

starts, and a moment later Ms. Z. says the principal wants to see me.

"I'll walk Mandy over," Ted offers. "Mandy, you don't know which one the office door is, do you?" The way he asks it, I know he wants to go along.

"No," I say, "I'm not sure."

I have a sick feeling about the reason the principal has asked for me, a premonition, I guess, except . . . Well, anyway, I'm right.

"Mandy," he asks right off, "do you know where Hannah Welsh is?"

"Isn't she home sick?" I ask, hoping mostly.

"No, her father found she was gone this morning, and he's been looking and calling since." The principal's voice is stern. "Mandy, her father believes that if she's run off, she's probably gone to a friend."

"No," I say with certainty. "If Hannah went to a friend, it would be to me. And I haven't seen her."

Even as worried as I am, I'm also surprised at what I've said, at what I've realized. I am Hannah's best friend.

Ted and I go back into the hall.

"Ted," I say, keeping my voice low but

turning so he can see my mouth. "Hannah's pretty upset about her folks getting a divorce."

"I can imagine," he says. "My mother heard Hannah's mom just took off and left yesterday. For good. But that woman is such a . . . Hannah will be better off without her."

"No! That's not true." I say it so loud someone calls, "Keep it down. We're testing in here."

"Sorry," I mumble to whoever it is.

I know that Hannah was upset about her folks separating, but it would never have occurred to her that one of them might want to get away from her, too. I try to think how she'd take it. I remember the talk we had, how she'd imagined ways to run off.

"Ted, we've got to find her before she disappears forever."

"You know where she's gone?"

"I think so."

We take off right after school lets out, after first calling our folks.

Nobody's home at Ted's house or mine,

but we leave messages on the answering machines, so they won't worry.

We drive the highway in silence, except once Ted says, "That woman," and I know he's thinking about Hannah's mother.

I hear the traffic getting heavy as we get close to the city. I can feel Ted's concentration and guess he hasn't done a lot of this kind of driving. "There's a map in the glove compartment," he says.

I unfold it so that it's ready for him to look at when he gets a chance. "Turn it over," he says. "You've got it wrong side up."

"The bus station's got to be downtown," I shout. I don't want him trying to read my lips.

"We're almost there now. I'm pulling into a gas station."

And between the two of us, we get directions from a young-sounding guy who tries his hardest to act like he doesn't find anything unusual about us at all. "You're only a few blocks away," he says.

The traffic has gotten terrible, cars and trucks all around us. Once Ted jams on the brakes so hard they squeal.

There's no place to park near the depot, and I'm terrified we've arrived too late, that Hannah's already found a bus going someplace that sounds good, and that she's taken it.

"Ted, let me out, please."

He does, saying, "I'll come in as soon as I park."

Then I'm on the sidewalk, and horns are telling Ted to move on. I can't hear what he's shouting about where the depot door is.

Someone walks into my cane, knocking it clattering onto the pavement. It's put back into my hand, and a woman is saying, "Do you need help, Miss?"

And because Hannah needs help, I say, "Yes, please. Would you take me inside?"

We go through an entryway of rushing air into a station that's all echoing noise and smell, and the woman's suddenly eager not to get involved. She leaves me alone in the middle of hundreds of sounds and crowds of people.

For a moment I feel helpless, wish I'd waited for Ted. What good did I think I could do by myself? Even if Hannah's here, she can hide in my blindness.

A loudspeaker voice bounces off hard walls. ". . . to Amarillo, Albuquerque, Flagstaff, Phoenix, with connections to points south and west, now boarding in lane four."

Amarillo. *Albuquerque.* Hannah would like even the words. Flagstaff, Phoenix, they'd both sound good, too, and a desert away.

"Northbound passengers holding tickets to . . ."

That's it, I think, the loudspeaker. Maybe I can get them to put on an announcement for Hannah, say, "Will passenger Hannah Welsh please check in at the counter?"

But first I've got to find it myself.

I walk forward until my cane runs into someone's foot. "Please," I say, "would you show me which way the ticket counters are?"

Someone pushes from behind, and whoever I've asked doesn't answer.

I bump into a child. Hear a slap, a woman saying, "Can't you see she's blind?"

The noise is louder to my left, and I think

that perhaps the counters are that way. I turn, run my cane out but not up, and bang my face into cold metal.

The loudspeaker blares again, "Final call for passengers to Albuquerque, Flagstaff, Phoenix." Its twanging threat echoes through the depot.

Is Hannah outside, waiting to board? Maybe already sitting on the bus?

I have to get to the counter, get someone to look for her quickly.

"Please," I say to whoever can hear. "Would someone please . . ."

Kids start laughing, and a girl says, "She shouldn't be alone."

I bump into another person, a woman who says, "The back of the line's over there." Her voice is bored and thinly hostile.

"This is an emergency," I tell her. "Would you . . ."

She doesn't let me finish. "Why do you people think you shouldn't have to wait in line like the rest of us?"

The panic I've been fighting to hold in starts to well up.

"Hannah," I call out, "Hannah?"

The loudspeaker crackles, blares out, "First call for passengers to Oklahoma City, Tulsa, Springfield, St. Louis. Your bus is now ready for boarding in lane four."

Lane four . . . That means the Albuquerque bus has left. Please, please, don't let Hannah be on it.

Whatever is inside me, despair and frustration, anger, raw screaming panic, it boils up and takes over. "HanNAH!" I shout as loudly as I can, loud, pulling every bit of air from my lungs, "HANNAHHHHHHHHH!" loud, and everyone, everything silences around me.

Silences all for one brief stretching-out-to-forever moment, and I think every person in that depot is holding his breath. Then a titter sweeps around me, a relieved whisper that lets people get on with talking and waiting and saying good-bye to each other, a rising wave of sound that lets them pretend I'm not there.

chapter 17

$$\textit{;; ;;}$$
$$\textit{;;}$$

ALL I'VE DONE is make a fool of myself.

Someone grabs my arm and I flinch. Who would grab so hard?

Close by my face a voice demands, "What are you doing here?" A voice so angry, so harsh, I almost don't recognize it as Hannah's. "Why did you come?"

"To get you, Hannah," I say. "Ted and I want to take you home."

"I don't have a home." Hannah's words hit hot against my cheek, a tiny fleck of spittle wets my neck. "I don't need your help. Why don't you mind your own business and leave me alone?"

"Why didn't you?" I'm suddenly as furious as she is. "You didn't have to come over, help the blind girl, just because I shouted."

"What, I should have just left you?" she says. "I couldn't."

"Well, I couldn't either."

Then the ridiculousness of it reaches us both, how we're mad at each other for doing the same thing. It doesn't make things right, but it's enough that we can talk.

When Ted finds us we're sitting together on a bench, and I'm telling Hannah how afraid I was she'd caught that bus to Albuquerque.

"It was full," she says. "But I'm going to take the next one, to there or anyplace else where I won't ever have to see Texas or my so-called family again."

"How are you going to live?" Ted asks, like he's really curious. Like Hannah going off somewhere to live on her own is even an option.

"Look, I'll be all right." Hannah's words are thick and I think her throat must ache with the strain of not crying. She blows her nose. I imagine her sitting up, straightening her spine. "I got a cash advance on my dad's charge card that I'll pay back. Enough to hold me until I find a job."

"Doing what?" Ted asks. "Working in a fast-food place?"

But they've both lost the point. "Hannah," I say, "you do have a home."

"No. I'm not wanted."

I'd like to tell her, "Of course you are," but I realize that if I'm not honest, she won't listen.

So I say, "Hannah, you don't know if your mother wants you or not. Her going . . . It might not have anything to do with you. I mean, she left your whole family."

I think of Gwen's mother, tearing up Gwen's letter and then trying to piece the envelope back together.

"Hannah, she may not even know herself what she wants, or who."

"But she's my *mother*." Hannah makes it both a plea and a question, and I don't have an answer.

So instead I say, "How about your father and brother? You know they want you."

"They'll get along."

Maybe, I think. And maybe not. Maybe her brother needs her as much as Abe needed Gwen. I'm trying to think how to explain that when I realize what it is that I really have to say.

"Hannah, I want you to come back. You're my best friend."

She waits, and I know I must say the rest of it. "And you're the first best friend I've ever had. I need you."

There's this horrible long moment that she doesn't answer. I feel like I'm standing naked in the middle of a million staring strangers, all pointing and saying, "She's never had a friend."

And then Hannah makes everything right. She says, "Best *girl* friend. Remember, Ted's the sensitive type."

We drive away from the city, all three of us jammed in the front seat, me in the middle.

I think, I'm the one who's holding us together.

Ted's whistling "The Eyes of Texas," and I wonder what he hears in his head, and if he knows he is perfectly on key.

Then, when we're almost home and Ted has shifted to Christmas music and is way down in the low notes of "We Three Kings," I get an idea.

"Ted, can we stop by the mall?"

"Never be able to park," he says, but he takes us there anyway, and after driving around for a while, we get a space.

"Let's call your dad, Hannah," I say. "And then . . . I need to buy presents. Especially for Aunt Emma. Will you help?"

Christmas morning I wake to a springlike breeze coming in my window. I go over, lean out, listen to the voices of my uncles calling to each other and to the cattle they're feeding. Gabriel must see me, because he calls up, "Merry Christmas, Mandy."

I pick up my mother's picture, imagine a face more soft than I used to see it, and with the beginnings of peace in her eyes.

I run my finger down the airman's picture. Maybe his grin is for me, too.

And then I'm washed and dressed and downstairs, and Aunt Emma and the uncles are squabbling about whether we do presents or have breakfast first.

"May as well get ready to starve, Abe,"

Uncle Gabriel says. "Emma's no more patient than a kid."

Only it's Uncle Gabriel who has made a small carpet-covered jungle gym that he can't wait for me to open.

"What's it for?" I ask, and he puts a kitten in my arms.

It's a little bigger than my opossum was the last time he scrambled up the porch steps to me. He didn't stay even for a whole bottle that time, and it made me realize he had stopped needing me. That he'd learned how to live on his own.

But this kitten—oh, I can love this kitten even when it's all grown up. I snuggle it close while it explores with tiny paws to find out who I am.

Then my aunt and uncles are telling me to circle the tree and feel all the other presents under it. "All the velvet bows, those are all for you," Aunt Emma says. "Open one."

But I rub my face in the kitten's fur. I make my voice stay steady because this is a dumb time to get weepy. I say, "It's your turn now."

I want them to like their gifts. Want so much that I ache.

Uncle Abe goes first. I've made him a tiny circus of toothpicks tipped with colored flags, planted in a surface of plaster of paris textured with dust. Little plastic people sit on a ring of pebbles, watching pill bugs climb a slide. Ted made the pill bugs for me out of clay, after pointing out they weren't really bugs at all but a land-living crustacean called an isopod. Right.

Emma and Gabriel don't know what to make of the circus, and for a while I'm afraid Abe doesn't, either. Then he says, "If you can get a message through to Gwen, tell her thanks for remembering."

Gabriel whispers, "What's all that about?"

Emma shushes him.

Then Gabriel opens his gift, a combination knife and screwdriver. "See," I tell him. "It's got two sizes each of Phillips and slot, and three blades and . . ."

"And just what I need," he says. "I'm going to keep it right where I can always get at it."

And then Aunt Emma is lifting tissue paper from the sweater I've bought her. "It's for your pleated skirt," I say. "The new one from the mall."

"I'm wearing it," Aunt Emma says. "Mandy, the color match couldn't be more perfect."

"Hannah helped me. I asked her."

And I give Aunt Emma a big hug. Her cheek is wet against mine.

"Don't cry," I say. "Merry Christmas. I love you."

chapter 18

S PRING has come, and I leave my window open to it all the time. Open to the wind that blows almost constantly, that Emma tells me I'll wish for, once summer gets here.

Ask me what has changed and I'll tell you.

I'll say how the figure that cartwheeled from the sky lies still and rests now. I think of him and the others in graves beneath budding trees, under yellow sun and blue sky and red tulips.

I especially imagine a lot of red tulips about my mother's grave because she liked to respect her contrasts.

Aunt Emma and the uncles act younger than they did when I first came here, even though Gabriel says I'm giving him more gray hair every day. "Mandy," he tells me, "you think of stuff to do faster than I can think of rules for keeping you safe doing it."

But his only real rule is that I don't worry Aunt Emma.

The opossum doesn't come back anymore, but thanks to Uncle Abe I'm still in the stepmothering business, taking care of an orphaned calf now. Abe named her for me, Mandy Girl, because she was born on my sixteenth birthday. I give her milk from a huge bottle, and one of these days she's probably going to get tired of my kitten trying to get in on the feeding.

And Abe likes to talk with me about Gwen. He's remembering more and more about being a boy, more than his pill bug circus.

Yes, ask me what has changed and I'll tell you.

I have.

I can't pretend everything is OK. I can't see, and in some ways I'm just now beginning to realize how huge that loss is. Maybe it took getting past being angry to know.

And to realize how much more I have to learn.

I'm going away for eight weeks this summer, to live in a dorm with other blind kids and work in a day care center. My caseworker helped set it up, and Mr. Burkhart wrote me a great letter of recommendation. It has me scared, both the job and how I'll get along in the dorm, but I keep telling myself the Great Om wouldn't send me off to something I can't handle.

Hannah and Ted have both promised to visit.

The town I'll be in is just a couple of miles from where Mrs. Welsh is living now, and I think maybe Hannah might try to see her, too.

And Ted's been saving money so he'll be able to call often. He's got this special phone that puts the volume high enough that he can usually hear what's said.

And some things are better than they ever have been, maybe the more important things.

Uncle Gabriel says every person's life has a time when he lives the fullest, the most aware. The army was like that for him, he says, the time he goes back to and longs for, with all its good and bad.

Aunt Emma says nonsense, and she can think of lots of years when she's been quite fully alive, thank you. No one tells her how her voice softens and yearns when she talks about the few months she and Uncle Gabriel lived in Mexico, when she was expecting the baby that died.

So I wonder. I hope my time is still out in front of me, that it will be more spectacular, bigger, than it is now, but . . . I don't know. Right now I feel more alive than I ever have.

No, that's not exactly it.

Right now the world feels more alive to me than it ever has, a world for me to reach out to and touch.

And I've changed in one more way.

I've made room for Gwen inside me, and for my mom, and maybe even for Gwen's mother. I know how to feel, and love, for us all.

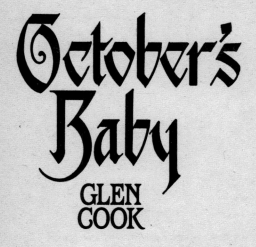

October's Baby

GLEN COOK

BERKLEY BOOKS, NEW YORK

OCTOBER'S BABY

A Berkley Book / published by arrangement with
the author

PRINTING HISTORY
Berkley edition / March 1980
Second printing / January 1984

ISBN: 0-425-06538-3

A BERKLEY BOOK ® TM 757,375
Berkley Books are published by The Berkley Publishing Group,
200 Madison Avenue, New York, New York 10016.
The name "BERKLEY" and the stylized "B" with design
are trademarks belonging to Berkley Publishing Corporation.
PRINTED IN THE UNITED STATES OF AMERICA

CONTENTS

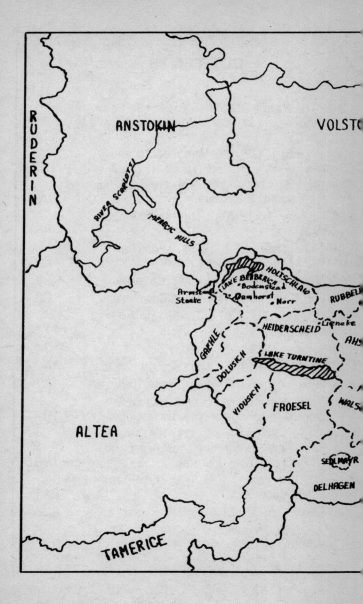

MOUNTAINS OF MYHAND

HIGH GALMICHE

LONCARIC

LOW GALMICHE

SAVERNAKE

oTimpe

Maisak

ERNECKE

BREITENBACH

Berendala

ROHRHASTE

ECHTENACHE

MOERSCHEL

VORGREBERG

FAHRIG

Gudbrandsdal Forest

FORBECK

TRAUTWEIN

UHLMANSIEK

ORTHWEIN

EN RUNG MOUNTAINS

HAMMAD AL NAKIR

KAVELIN
and neighboring
Kingdoms

g. COOK

ONE: Unto Us A Child Is Born

i) He made the darkness his covering around him

Like a whispering ghost the winged man dropped from the moonless winter night, a shadow on the stars whose wings fluttered with a brief sharp *crack* as he broke his fall and settled onto the sill of a high glassless tower window of Castle Krief. His great wings he folded about him like a dark living cloak, with hardly a sigh of motion. His eyes burned cold scarlet as he studied the blackness within the tower. He turned his terrier-like head from side to side, listening. Neither sight nor sound came to him. He did not want to believe it. It meant he must go on. Cautiously, fearfully—human places inspired dread—he dropped to the cold interior floor.

The darkness within, impenetrable even to his nightseeing eyes, was food for his man-fear. What human evil might wait there, wearing a cloak of night? Yet he mustered courage and went on, one weak hand always touching the crystal dagger at his hip, the other caressing his tiny purse. Inaudible terror whimpered in his throat. He was not a courageous creature, would not be in this fell place but for the dread-love he bore his Master.

Guided by whimper-echoes only he could hear, he

found the door he sought. Fear, which had faded as he found all as peaceful as the Master had promised, returned. A warding spell blocked his advance, one that could raise a grand haroo and bring steel-armed humans.

But he was not without resources. His visit was the spearthrust of an operation backed by careful preparation. From his purse he took a crimson jewel, chucked it up the corridor. It clattered. He gasped. The noise seemed thunderous. Came a flash of brilliant red light. The ward-spell twisted away into some plane at right angles to reality. He peeked between the long bony fingers covering his eyes. All right. He went to the door, opened it soundlessly.

A single candle, grown short with time, burned within. Across the room, in a vast four-poster with silken hangings, slept the object of his mission. She was young, fair, delicate, but these traits held no meaning. He was a sexless creature. He suffered no human longings—at least of the carnal sort. He did long for the security of his cavern home, for the companionship of his brothers. To him this creature was an object (of fear, of his quest, of pity), a vessel to be used.

The woman (hardly more than a child was she, just gaining the graceful curves of the woman-to-be) stirred, muttered. The winged man's heart jumped. He knew the power of dreams. Hastily, he dipped into his purse for a skin-wrapped ball of moist cotton. He let her breathe its vapors till she settled into untroubled sleep.

Satisfied, he drew the bedclothes down, eased her nightgarments up. From his pouch he withdrew his final treasure. There were spells on the device, that kept its contents viable, which would guarantee this night's work's success.

He loathed himself for the cold-bloodedness of his deed. Yet he finished, restored the woman and bed to their proper order, and silently fled. He recovered the crimson jewel, ground it to dust so the warding spell would return. Everything had to appear undisturbed. Before he took wing again, he stroked his crystal dagger. He was glad he had not been forced to use it. He detested violence.

ii) He sees with the eyes of an enemy

Nine months and a few days later. October: A fine month for doings dark and strange, with red and gold leaves falling to mask the mind with colorful wonders, with cool piney breezes bringing winter promises from the high Kapenrungs, with swollen orange moons by night, and behind it all breaths and hints of things of fear. The month began still bright with summer's memory, like a not too distant, detached chunk of latter August with feminine, changeable, sandwiched September forgotten. The month gradually gathered speed, rolled downhill until, with a plunge at the end, it dumped all into a black and wicked pit from which the remainder of the year would be but a struggle up a mountain chasing starshine. At its end there was a night consecrated to all that was unholy, a night for unhallowed deeds.

The Krief's city, Vorgreberg, was small, but not unusually so for a capital in the Lesser Kingdoms. Its streets were unclean. The rich hadn't gotten that way squandering income on sweepers, and the poor didn't care. Three quarters was ancient slum, the remainder wealthy residential or given over to the trade houses of merchants handling the silks and spices that came from the east over the Savernake Gap. The residences of the nobles were occupied only when the Thing sat. The rest of the year those grim old skulduggers spent at their castles and estates, whipping more wealth from their serfs. City crime was endemic, taxes were high, people starved to death daily, or any of a hundred diseases got them, corruption in government was ubiquitous, and ethnic groups hated one another to the sullen edge of violence.

So, a city like most, surrounded by a small country populated with normally foibled men, special only because a king held court there, and because it was the western terminus for caravans from the orient. From it, going west, flowed eastern riches; to it came the best goods of the coastal states.

But, on a day at the end of October when evil stirred, it also had:

A holiday morning after rain, and an old man in a ragged greatcloak who needed a bath and shave. He turned from a doorway at the rear of a rich man's home. Bacon tastes still trembled on his tongue. A copper sceat weighed lightly in his pocket. He chuckled softly.

Then his humor evaporated. He stopped, stared down the alley, then fled in the opposite direction. From behind him came the sound of steel rims on brick pavement, rattling loudly in the morning stillness. The tramp paused, scratched his crotch, made a sign against the evil eye, then ran. The breakfast taste had gone sour.

A man with a pushcart eased round a turn, slowly pursued the tramp. He was a tiny fellow, old, with a grizzled, ragged beard. His slouch made him appear utterly weary of forcing his cart over the wet pavement. His cataracted eyes squinted as he studied the backs of houses. Repeatedly, after considering one or another, he shook his head.

Mumbling, he left the alley, set course for the public grounds outside the Krief's palace. The leafless, carefully ranked trees there were skeletal and grim in the morning gloom and damp. The castle seemed besieged by the gray, dreary wood.

The cartman paused. "Royal Palace." He sneered. Castle Krief may have stood six centuries inviolate, may have surrendered only to Ilkazar, but it wasn't invincible. It could be destroyed from within. He thought of the comforts, the riches behind those walls, and the hardness of his own life. He cursed the waiting.

There was work to be done. Miserable work. Castles and kingdoms didn't fall at the snap of a finger.

Round the entire castle he went, observing the sleepy guards, the ancient ivy on the southern wall, the big gates facing east and west, and the half-dozen posterns. Though Kavelin had petty noble feuds as numerous as fleas on a hound, they never touched Vorgreberg itself. Those wars were for the barons, fought in their fiefs among themselves, and from them the Crown was relatively safe, remaining a disinterested referee.

Sometimes, though, one of the nearby kingdoms, coveting the eastern trade, tried to move in. Then the house-divided quickly united.

The morning wore on. People gathered near the palace's western gate. The old man opened his cart, got charcoal burning, soon was selling sausages and hot rolls.

Near noon the great gate opened. The crowd fell into a hush. A company of the King's Own marched forth to blaring trumpets. Express riders thundered out bound for the ends of Kavelin, crying, "The King has a son!"

The crowd broke into cheers. They had waited years for that news.

The small old man smiled at his sausages. The King had a son to insure the continuity of his family's tyranny, and the idiots cheered as if this were a day of salvation. Poor foolish souls. They never learned. Their hopes for a better future never paled. Why expect the child to become a king less cruel than his ancestors?

The old man held a poor opinion of his species. In other times and places he had been heard to say that, all things considered, he would rather be a duck.

The King's Own cleared the gate. The crowd surged forward, eager to seize the festive moment. Commoners seldom passed those portals.

The old man went with the mob, made himself one with their greed. But his greed wasn't for the dainties on tables in the courtyard. His greed was for knowledge. The sort a burglar cherished. He went everywhere allowed, saw everything permitted, listened, paid especial attention to the ivied wall and the Queen's tower. Satisfied, he sampled the King's largesse, drew scowls for damning the cheap wine, then returned to his cart, and to the alleyways.

iii) He returns to the place of his iniquity

Once again the winged man slid down a midnight sky, a momentary shadow riding the beams of an October moon. It was Allernmas Night, nine months after his earlier visit. He banked in a whisper of air, swooped past towers, searched his sluggish memory. He found the right one, glided to the window, disappeared into darkness. A red-eyed shadow in a cloak of wings, he stared across the once festive court, waited. This second visit, he feared, was tempting Fate. Something would go wrong.

A black blob momentarily blocked a gap between crenellations on the battlements. It moved along the wall, then down to the courtyard. The winged man unwound a light line from about his waist. One end he secured to a beam above his head. With that his mission was complete. He was supposed to take wing immediately, but he waited for his friend instead.

Burla, a misshapen, dwarfish creature with a bundle on his back, swarmed toward him with the agility of the ape he resembled. The winged man turned sideways so his friend could pass.

"You go now?" Burla asked.

"No. I watch." He touched his arm lightly, spilled a fangy smile. He was frightened too. Death could pounce at any moment. "I start." He wriggled, muttered, got the bundle off his back.

They followed the hall the winged man had used before. Burla used devices he had been given to overcome protective spells, then overcame the new lock on the Queen's door...

Came a sleepy question. Burla and the winged man exchanged glances. Their fears had been proven well-founded, though the Master had predicted otherwise. Nevertheless, he had armed Burla against this possibility. The dwarf handed the winged man his bundle, took a fragile vial from his purse, opened the door a crack, tossed it through. Came another question, sharper, louder, frightened. Burla took a heavy, damp cloth from his pouch, resumed care of his bundle while the winged man tied it over his twisted mouth and nose.

Still another question from the room. It was followed by a scream when Burla stepped inside. The cry reverberated down the hall. The winged man drew his dagger.

"Hurry!" he said. Excited, confused voices were moving toward him, accompanied by a clash of metal. Soldiers. He grew more frightened, thought about flying now. But he could not abandon his friend. Indeed, he moved so the window exit would be behind him.

His blade began to glow along its edge. The winged man held it high before him, so it stood out of the darkness, illuminating only his ugly face. Humans had their fears too.

Three soldiers came upstairs, saw him, paused. The winged man pulled his blade closer, spread his wings. The dagger illuminated those enough to yield the impression that he had swollen to fill the passageway. One soldier squeaked fearfully, then ran downstairs. The others mumbled oaths.

Burla returned with the child. "We go now." He was out the window and down the rope in seconds. The winged man followed, seizing the rope as he went. He rose against the moon, hoping to draw attention from Burla. The uproar was, like pond ripples, now lapping against the most distant palace walls.

iv) He consorts with creatures of darkness

In the Gudbrandsdal Forest, a Royal Preserve just beyond the boundary of the Siege of Vorgreberg, a dozen miles from Castle Krief, a bent old man stared into a sullen campfire and chuckled. "They've done it! They've done it. It's all downhill from here."

The heavily robed, deeply cowled figure opposite him inclined its head slightly.

The old man, the sausage seller, was wicked—in an oddly clean, impersonal, puckish sort of way—but the other was evil. Malefically, cruelly, blackly evil.

The winged man, Burla, and their friends were unaware of the Master's association with him.

v) Bold in the service of his Lord

Eanred Tarlson, a Wesson captain of the King's Own, was a warrior of international repute. His exploits during the El Murid wars had won renown throughout the bellicose Lesser Kingdoms. A Wesson peasant in an infantry company, Fate had put him near his King when the latter had received a freak, grave wound from a ricocheting arrow. Eanred had donned his Lord's armor and had held off the fanatics for days. His action had won him a friend with a crown.

Had he been Nordmen, he would have been knighted. The best his King could do for a Wesson was grant a commission. The knighthood came years later. He was the first Wesson to achieve chivalric orders since the Resettlement.

Eanred was his King's champion, respected even by the Nordmen. He was well known as an honest, loyal, reasonable man who dealt without treachery, who did not hesitate to press an unpopular opinion upon the King. He stood by his beliefs. Popularly, he was known for his victories in trials-by-combat which had settled disputes with neighboring principalities. The Wesson peasantry believed him a champion of their rights.

Though Eanred had killed for his King, he was neither hard nor cruel. He saw himself only as a soldier, no greater than any other, with no higher ambition than to defend his King. He was of a type gold-rare in the Lesser Kingdoms.

Tarlson, by chance, was in the courtyard when the furor broke. He arrived below the Queen's tower in time to glimpse a winged monster dwindling against the moon, trailing a fine line as if trolling the night for invisible aerial fish. He studied its flight. The thing was bound toward the Gudbrandsdal.

"Gjerdrum!" he thundered at his son and squire, who accompanied him. "A horse!" Within minutes he galloped through the East Gate. He left orders for his company to follow. He might be chasing the wind, he thought, but he *was* taking action. The rest of the palace's denizens were squalling like old ladies caught with their skirts up. Those Nordmen courtiers! Their ancestors may have been tough, but today's crop were dandified cretins.

The Gudbrandsdal wasn't far on a galloping horse. Eanred plunged in afoot after tying his horse where others could find it. He discovered a campfire immediately. Drawing his sword, he stalked the flames. Soon, from shadow, he spied the winged thing talking with an old man bundled in a blanket. He saw no weapon more dangerous than the winged thing's dagger.

That dagger... It seemed to glow faintly. He strode toward the fire, demanded, "Where's the Prince?" His blade slid toward the throat of the old man.

His appearance didn't startle the two, though they shrank away. Neither replied. The winged man drew his blade. Yes, it glowed. Magic! Eanred shifted his sword for defense. This monstrous, reddish creature with the blade of pale fire might be more dangerous than he appeared.

Something moved in the darkness behind Tarlson. A black sleeve reached. He sensed his danger, turned cat-swift while sweeping his blade in a vertical arc. It cut air—then flesh and bone. A hand fell beside the fire, kicking up little sprays of dust, fingers writhing like the legs of a dying spider. A scream of pain and rage echoed through the forest.

But Eanred's stroke came too late. Fingers had brushed his throat. The world grew Arctically cold. He leaned slowly like a tree cut through. All sensation abandoned him. As he fell, he turned, saw first the dark outline of the being that had stunned him, the startled faces of the others, then the severed hand. The waxy, monstrous thing was crawling toward its owner ...Everything went black. But he tumbled into darkness with a silent chuckle. Fate had given him one small victory. He was able to push his blade through the hand and lever it into the fire.

vi) His heart is heavy, but he perseveres

Burla, with the baby quiet in the bundle on his back, reached the Master's campsite as the last embers were dying. False dawn had begun creeping over the Kapenrung Mountains. He cursed the light, moved more warily. Horsemen had been galloping about since he had left the city. All his nighttime skills had been required to evade them.

Troops had been to the campsite, he saw. There had been a struggle. Someone had been injured. The Master's blanket lay abandoned, a signal. He was well but had been forced to flee. Burla's unhappiness was exceeded only by his fear that he wasn't competent to fulfill the task now assigned him.

His work, which should have been completed, had just begun. He glanced toward the dawn. So many miles to bear the baby through an aroused countryside. How could he escape the swords of the tall men?

He had to try.

Days he slept a little, and traveled when it was safe. Nights he hurried through, moving as fast as his short legs would carry him, only occasionally pausing at a Wesson farm to steal food or milk for the child. He expected the poor tiny thing to die any time, but it was preternaturally tough.

The tall men failed to catch him. They knew he was about, knew that he had had something to do with the invasion of the Queen's tower. They did turn the country over and shake out a thousand hidden things. The time came when, high in the mountains, he trudged wearily into the cave where the Master had said to meet if they had to split up.

vii) Their heads nod, and from their mouths issue lies

An hour after the kidnapping, someone finally thought to see if Her Majesty was all right. They didn't think much of their Queen, those Nordmen. She was a foreigner, barely of childbearing age, and so unobtrusive that no one spared her a thought. Queen and nurse were found in deep, unnatural sleep. And there was a baby at the woman's breast.

Once again Castle Krief churned with confusion. What had been seen, briefly, as a probable Wesson attempt to interrupt the succession, was obviously either a great deal less, or more, sinister. After a few hints from the King himself, it was announced that the Prince was sleeping well, that the excitement had been caused by a guard's imagination.

Few believed that. There had been a switch. Parties with special interests sought the physician and midwife who had attended the birth, but neither could be found—till much later. Their corpses were discovered, mutilated against easy recognition, in a slum alley. Royal disclaimers continued to flow.

The King's advisers met repeatedly, discussed the possible purpose of the invasion, the stance to be taken, and how to resolve the affair. Time passed. The mystery deepened. It became obvious that there would be no explanations till someone captured the winged man, the dwarf a guard had seen go monkeying down the ivied wall, or one of the strangers who had been camped in the Gudbrandsdal. The dwarf was working his way east toward the mountains. No trace of the others turned up. The army concentrated on the dwarf. So did those for whom possession of the Crown Prince meant leverage.

The fugitive slipped away. Nothing further came of the strange events. The King made certain the child with his

Queen, at least in pretense, remained his heir. The barons stopped plaguing odd strangers and resumed their squabbles. Wessons returned to their scheming, merchants to their counting houses. Within a year the mystery seemed forgotten, though countless eyes kept tabs on the King's health.

TWO: The Hearth and the Heart

i) Bragi Ragnarson and Elana Michone

Suffering in silence, brushing her coppery hair, Elana Ragnarson endured the grumbling of her husband.

"Bills of lading, bills of sale, accounts payable, accounts receivable, torts and taxes! What kind of life is this? I'm a soldier, not a bloody merchant. I wasn't meant to be a coin counter..."

"You could hire an accountant." The woman knew better than to add that a professional would keep better books. His grumbling was of no moment anyway. It came with spring, the annual disease of a man who had forgotten the hardships of the adventurer's life. A week or so, time enough to remember sword-strokes dangerously close, unshared beds in icy mud, hunger, and the physical grind of forced marches, would settle him down. But he would never completely overcome the habits of a Trolledyngjan boyhood. North of the Kratchnodian Mountains all able males went to war as soon as the ice broke up in the harbors.

"Where has my youth gone?" he complained as he began dressing. "When I was fresh down from Trolledyngja, still in my teens, I was leading troops against El

13

Murid . . . Hire? Did you say hire, woman?" A heavy, hard face encompassed by shaggy blond hair and beard momentarily joined hers in her mirror. She touched his cheek. "Bring in some thief who'll rob me blind with numbers on paper?"

"When me and Mocker and Haroun were stealing the fat off Itaskian merchants, I never dreamed I'd get fat in the arse and pocket myself. Those were the days. I still ain't too old. What's thirty-one? My father's father fought at Ringerike when he was eighty . . ."

"And got himself killed."

"Yeah, well." He rambled on about the deeds of other relatives. But each, as Elana pointed out, had died far from home, and not a one of old age.

"It's Haroun's fault. Where's he been the last three years? If he turned up, we could get a good adventure started."

Elana dropped her brush. Cold-footed mice of fear danced along her spine. This was bad. When he began missing that ruffian bin Yousif the fever had reached a critical pitch. If by whim of fate the man turned up, Bragi could be lured into another insane, byzantine scheme.

"Forget that cutthroat. What's he ever done for you? Just gotten you in trouble since the day you met." She turned. Bragi stood with one leg in a pair of baggy work trousers, the other partially raised from the floor. She had said the wrong thing. Damn Haroun! How had he gotten a hold on a man as bull-headedly independent as Bragi?

She suspected it was because bin Yousif had a cause, a decades-deep vendetta with El Murid which infected his every thought and action. His dedication to vengeance awed a man like Bragi.

Finally, grunting, Ragnarson finished dressing. "Think I'll ride over to Mocker's today. Visit a spell."

She sighed. The worst was past. A day in the forest would take the edge off his wanderlust. Maybe she should stay home next time he went to Itaskia. A night on his own, in Wharf Street South, might be the specific for his disease.

"Papa? Are you ready?" their eldest son, Ragnar, called through the bedroom door.

"Yeah. What you want?"

"There's a man here."

"This early? Tramp, huh, looking for a handout? Tell him there's a soft touch next house north." He chuckled. The next place north was that of his friend Mocker, twenty miles on.

"Bragi!" A look was enough. The last man he had sent north had been a timber buyer with a fat navy contract.

"Yes, dear. Ragnar? Tell him I'll be down in a minute." He kissed his wife, left her in troubled thought.

Adventures. She had enjoyed them herself. But no more. She had traded the mercenary days for a home and children. Only a fool would dump what they had to cross swords with young men and warlocks. Then she smiled. She missed the old days a little, too.

ii) A curious visitor

Ragnarson clumped downstairs into the dining hall and peered into its gloomy corners. It was vast. This place was both home and fortress. It housed nearly a hundred people in troubled times. He shivered. No one had kindled the morning fires. "Ragnar! Where's he at?"

His son popped from the narrow, easily defended hallway to the front door. "Outside. He won't come in."

"Eh? Why?"

The boy shrugged.

"Well, if he won't, he won't." As he strode to the door, Ragnarson snatched an iron-capped club from a weapons rack.

Outside, in the pale misty light of a morning hardly begun, an old, old man waited. He leaned on a staff, stared at the ground thoughtfully. His bearing was not that of a beggar. Ragnarson looked for a horse, saw none.

The ancient had neither pack nor pack animal, either. "Well, what can I do for you?"

A smile flashed across a face that seemed as old as the world. "Listen."

"Eh?" Bragi grew uneasy. There was something about this fellow, a *presence* . . .

"Listen. Hear, and act accordingly. Fear the child with the ways of a woman. Beware the bells of a woman's fingers. All magicks aren't in the hands of sorcerers." Ragnarson started to interrupt, found that he could not. "Covet not the gemless crown. It rides the head precariously. It leads to the place where swords are of no avail." Having said his cryptic piece, the old man turned to the track leading toward the North Road, the highway linking Itaskia and Iwa Skolovda.

Ragnarson frowned. He was not a slow-witted man. But he was unaccustomed to dealing with mystery-mouthed old men in the sluggish hours of the morning. "Who the hell are you?" he thundered.

Faintly, from the woods:

"Old as a mountain,
Lives on a star,
Deep as the ocean flows."

Ragnarson pursued fleas through his beard. A riddle. Well. A madman, that's what. He shrugged it off. There was breakfast to eat and the ride to Mocker's to be made. No time for crazies.

iii) Things she loves and fears

Elana, who had overheard, could not shrug it off. She feared its portent, that Bragi was about to hie off on some hare-brained venture.

From a high window she stared at the land and forest they had conquered together. She remembered. They had come late in the year to a landgrant so remote that they had had to cut a path in. That first winter had been cold and hard. The winds and snows pouring over the

Kratchnodians had seemed bent on revenge for the disasters wrought there the winter previous, in Bragi's last campaign. The blood of children and wolves had christened the new land.

The next year there had been a flareup of the ancient boundary dispute between Prost Kamenets and Itaskia. Bandits, briefly legitimatized by letters of marque from Prost Kamenets, had come over the Silverbind. Many hadn't gone home, but the land had also drunk the blood of its own.

The third had been the halcyon year. Their friends Nepanthe and Mocker had been able to break loose and take a grant of their own.

Things had turned bad again late in the fourth year, when drought east of the Silverbind had driven men from Prost Kamenets into a brigandry their government ignored as long as its thrust lay across the river. Near the rear of the house, the granary stood in charred ruins. A half-mile away the men were rebuilding the sawmill. There were contracts for timber to be delivered to the naval yards at Itaskia. Those had to be met first.

Counting wives and children, there had been twenty-two pioneers. Most were dead now, buried in places of honor beside the greathouse. She and Bragi had been lucky, their only loss a daughter born dead.

Too many graves in the graveyard. Fifty-one in all. Over the years old followers of Bragi's and friends of hers had drifted in, some to stay a day or two out of a journey in search of a war, some to settle and die.

The grain was sprouting, the children were growing, the cattle were getting fat. There was an orchard that might produce in her lifetime. She had a home almost as large and comfortable as the one Bragi had promised her during all those years under arms. And it was all endangered. She knew it in her bones. Something was afoot, something grim.

Her gaze went to the graveyard. Old Tor Jack lay in the corner, beside Randy Will who had gotten his skull crushed pulling Ragnar from between a stallion and a mare in heat. What would they think if Bragi threw it up now?

Jorgen Miklassen, killed by a wild boar. Gudrun Ormsdatter, died in childbirth. Red Lars, brought down by wolves. Jan and Mihr Krushka. Rafnir Shagboots, Walleyed Marjo, Tandy the Gimp.

Blood and tears, blood and tears. Nothing would bring them back. Why so morbidly thoughtful? Break yourself out, woman. Time goes on, work has to be done. What man hath wrought, woman must maintain.

Maxims did nothing to cheer her. She spent the day working hard, seeking an exhaustion that would extinguish her apprehensions.

In the evening, as twilight's pastels were fading into indigo, a huge owl came out of the east, flew thrice round the house widdershins, dipping and dancing with owls from beneath the greathouse eaves. It soon fled toward Mocker's.

"Another omen." She sighed.

iv) Mocker and Nepanthe of Ravenkrak

Mocker's holding lay hip by thigh with Ragnarson's. Both were held under Itaskian Crown Charter. On his own territory each had the power and responsibility of a baron—without the privileges. Though neighbors, both found distance between homes a convenience. They had been friends since the tail-end years of the El Murid wars, but each found the other's extended company insufferable. The disparity in their values kept them constantly on the simmering edge. A day's visit, a night's drinking and remembering when, that was their limit. Neither was known for patience, nor for an open mind.

Ragnarson covered the distance before dinner, pretending that once again he was racing El Murid from Hellin Daimiel to Libiannin.

Mocker wasn't surprised to see him. Little astonished that fat old reprobate.

Ragnarson reined in beside a short, swarthy fellow on his knees in mud. Laugh lines permanently marked his moon-round brown face. "Hai!" he cried. "Great man-bears! Help!" Tenants came running, grabbing weapons. The fat man rose and whirled madly, dark eyes dancing.

A boy the age of Bragi's Ragnar ran from a nearby smokehouse, toy bow ready. "Oh. It's only Uncle Bear."

"Only?" Bragi growled as he dismounted. "Only? Maybe, Ethrian, but mean enough to box the ears of a cub." He seized the boy, threw him squealing into the air.

Wiping her hands on her apron, a woman came from the nearby house. Nepanthe always seemed to be wiping her hands. Mocker left a mountain of woman's work wherever he passed. "Bragi. Just in time for dinner. You came alone? I haven't seen Elana since..." Her smile faded. Since the bandit passage last fall, when Mocker's dependents had holed up in Ragnarson's stronger greathouse.

"Pretty as ever, I see," said Ragnarson. He handed his reins to Ethrian, who scowled, knowing he was being gotten rid of. Nepanthe blushed. She was indeed attractive, but hardly pretty as ever. The forest years had devoured her aristocratic delicacy. Still, she looked younger than thirty-four. "No, couldn't bring the family."

"Business?" She did most of Mocker's talking. Mocker had never mastered the Itaskian tongue. His vanity was such that he avoided speaking whenever he could. Ragnarson was not sure that inability was genuine. It varied according to some formula known only to Mocker himself.

"No. Just riding. Spring fever." Shifting to Necremnen, an eastern language in which Mocker was more at home, he continued, "Strange thing happened this morning. Old man appeared out of nowhere, mumbled some nonsense about girls who act like women. Wouldn't answer a question straight out, only in riddles. Weirdest thing is, I couldn't find a trace of him on the road. You'd think there'd be fresh droppings, coming or going."

Nepanthe frowned. She didn't understand the language. "Are you going to eat?" Pettishly, she brushed long raven hair out of her eyes. A warm breeze had begun blowing from the south.

"Of course. That's why I came." He tried charming her with a smile.

"Same man," Mocker replied, proving he could mangle even a language learned in childhood, "beriddled self. Portly pursuer of pre-dawn pissery, self, rising early to dispose of excess beer drunk night before, found same on doorstep before sunrise."

"Impossible. It was barely sunup when he turned up at my place . . ."

"For him, is possible. Self, having encountered same before, know. Can do anything."

"The Old Man of the Mountain?"

"No."

"Varthlokkur?"

They were at Mocker's door. When Ragnarson said the latter, Nepanthe gave him a hard stare. "You're not mixed up with him again, are you? Mocker . . ."

"Doe's Breast. Diamond Eyes. Light of life of noted sluggard renown for pusillanimity, would same, being contender for title World's Laziest Man, being famous from south beyond edge of farthest map to north in Trolledyngja, from west in Freyland east to Matayanga, for permanent state of cowardice and lassitude . . ."

"Yes, you would. How'd you get known in all those places?"

Mocker continued, in Necremnen, "Was famous Star Rider."

"Why?" Ragnarson asked.

"Why what?"

"Oh, never mind. That's why you weren't surprised to see me?"

The fat man shrugged. "When Star Riders come calling on fat old fool sequestered in boundless forest, am surprised by nothings. Next, Haroun will appear out of south with new world-conquering scheme in hand, madder than ever." This he said sourly, as if he believed it a distinct possibility.

"If you two can quit chicken-clucking for a minute, we can eat," said Nepanthe.

"Sorry, Nepanthe," Ragnarson apologized. "Some things . . ."

She sighed. "As long as it's not another woman."
"No, not that. Just a minor mystery."

v) Another strange visitor

The mystery soon deepened. Ethrian returned from the stables and, after having been scolded for being as slow as small boys will, said, "There's a man coming. A funny man on a little horse. I don't think I like him." Having so declaimed, he set about devouring his dinner.

Mocker rose, went to a front window, came back wearing a puzzled frown. "Marco."

It took Ragnarson a moment to recall anyone by that name. "Visigodred's apprentice?" Visigodred was a wizard, an old acquaintance.

"Same." Mocker looked worried. Ragnarson was disturbed himself.

A clatter and rattle at the front door. "He's here."

"Uhn." Both men looked at Nepanthe. For a moment she stared back, a little pale, then went.

"About goddamn time," came from the other room, then, "Oh, beg your pardon, my dear lovely lady. Husband home? I hope not. Seems a shame to let a beautiful chance meeting go to waste."

"Back here."

Marco, a dwarf with the ego of a giant, came strutting into the kitchen, not a bit abashed about having been overheard. "Timing was right, I see." He pulled up a chair, snagged a huge hunk of bread, smeared it with butter. He ignored inquiring looks till he had gorged himself. "Suppose you're wondering what I'm doing here. Besides stuffing my face. So am I. Well same as always, doing the old man's legwork. Got a message for you."

"Humph!" Mocker snorted. "No time. Am occupied with profound compunctions—computations? Constructions?—philosophic. How to get lentils in earth without straining back of and mud-bespattering self of, portly peasant, self. Am no wise interested in problems and peculations of old busybody who would interfere with ponderations on same." He looked at Nepanthe as if for approval.

Ragnarson was irritated. Did Nepanthe control Mocker that much? Once he had been a wild-eyed heller, game for any insane scheme Haroun concocted. Bragi met Nepanthe's eyes across the table. Why the laughter there? He thought, she knows what I'm thinking.

"What the boss wanted me to tell you was this: 'In a land of many kings trust no hand but your own, nor allow you the right far from sight of the left. Men there change loyalties more often than underwear. Stand wary of all women, and tamper not with the place, and name, and cloak, of Mist.' What the hell that means I don't know. He's not usually that hard to pin down. But he's got a stake in it somehow. I guess his girlfriend is in. Well, got to go. Thank you for a delightful meal, my lady."

"Hold on," Ragnarson growled. "What the hell, hey? What's going on?"

"You got me, Hairy. I just work for the man, I don't read his mind. You want to know more, you check with himself. Only he won't see you. Told me to tell you that. I forgot. He said there's no way he can help you this time. Did all he could by sending me. Now, if you don't mind, I'll be getting along. There's two, three little birds at home might pine away if I don't get back to them soon." Refusing to answer further questions, he returned to his pony. The last they saw of him, he was entering the forest at a brisk trot, a bawdy song trailing behind him.

"You'd think a man like Visigodred could find an apprentice with a little more couth," Ragnarson said. "Well, what do you think?"

"Self, am bamboozled. Befuddled by dearth of sense." Mocker's eyes flicked toward Nepanthe. One chubby brown hand made the deaf-mute's sign for "Be careful."

Ragnarson smiled, glad to see the spark of rebellion.

It did not occur to him that, were Mocker visiting him, he would have seemed as henpecked. Ragnarson was not an empathetic person.

"Heard from informant Andy the Bum," said Mocker, returning to Necremnen. "News of Itaskia. Andy was

pestilential mendicant always beside entrance of Red
Hart, intelligent behind ubiquitous flies and filth.
Sometimes remembers old contributor, self, with missives
relating Wharf Street South street talk."

Mocker was talking as plainly as he could. Must be
important. "Month past, maybe more counting time for
letter to make tortuous way from correspondent to
recipient, Haroun visited Itaskia."

Nepanthe caught the name. "Haroun? Haroun bin
Yousif? Mocker, you stay away from that cutthroat . . ."

Ragnarson wrestled with his temper. "That's not
charitable, Nepanthe. You owe the man."

"I don't want Mocker involved with him. He'd end up
using us in one of his schemes."

"It was one of those that got you together."

"Elana . . ."

"I know what Elana thinks. She has her reasons."
Elana was the first real friend Nepanthe had ever had. In a
sort of pathetic, desperate way, she tried to secure that
friendship by making herself a mirror of Elana. Even
Mocker had less influence than Ragnarson's wife.

His curtness upset Nepanthe. Usually he was gentle
beyond the reasonable. He was secretly afraid of women.

Nepanthe sulked.

"What about him?"

"Was putting finger in nasty place, coming out dirty.
Was talking to scurriliousest of scurrils of Wharf Street
South. Brad Red Hand. Kerth the Dagger. Derran One
Eye. Boroba Thring. Breed known for stab-in-back work.
Very secretive. Went off without visiting friends.
Accident Andy discovered same. Whore friend, also
friend of Kerth, relayed story."

"Curious. Men he's used before. When he wanted
murder done. Think he's up to something?"

"Hai! Always. When was Haroun, master intriguer,
not intriguing? Is question like Trolledyngjan, 'Does bear
defecate in wilderness?'"

"Yeah, the bear shits in the woods. The question is,
does he have plans for us? He can't manage on his own. I
wonder why? He's always so self-sufficient." Faced with a
real possibility of becoming involved, Ragnarson's lust

for adventure perished quickly. "Andy have anything else
to say?"

"Men named vanished, no word to friends or
paramours. Seen crossing Great Bridge. Nervous, in
hurry. Self, expect communication from old sand devil
soon. Why? Haroun is one-man nation, yes, but must
justify villainous activities of self to self. Must have
associates, men of respected morals. Kingship thing.
Must have mandate of, license from, men with values,
with judgments of respect. He respects? You see? Itaskian
knife swingers are tools, not-men, dust beneath feet, of
morals to spit on. Hairy Trolledyngjan and fat old rascal
from east, self, not much better, but honorable in mind of
Haroun. Men of respect, us. Comprehend?"

"Makes sense in a left-handed way. An insight, I think.
I always wondered why he never put the knife work on us.
Yes."

Mocker did a most un-Mockerlike thing. He pushed
his chair back while food remained on the table.
Ragnarson started to follow him to the front of the house.

"Don't get involved with Haroun," said Nepanthe.
"Please?"

He searched her face. She was frightened. "What can I
do? When he decides to do something, he gets irresistible
as a glacier."

"I know." She bit her lip.

"We're not planning anything, really. Haroun would
have to do some tall talking to involve us. We're not as
hungry as we used to be."

"Maybe. Maybe not." She began clearing the table.
"Mocker doesn't complain, but he wasn't made for this."
With a gesture she indicated the landgrant. "He stays, and
tries for my sake, but he'd be happier penniless, sitting in
the rain somewhere, trying to convince old ladies he's a
soothsayer. That way he's like Haroun. Security doesn't
mean anything. The battle of wits is everything."

Ragnarson shrugged. He couldn't tell her what she
wanted to hear. Her assessment matched his own.

"I've made him miserable, Bragi. How long since
you've seen him clown like he used to? How long since he's
gone off on some wild tangent and claimed the world is

round, or a duck-paddled boat on a sea of wine, or any of those crackpot notions he used to take up. Bragi, I'm killing him. I love him, but, Gods help me, I'm smothering him. And I can't help it."

"We are what we are, will be what we must. If he goes back to the old ways, be patient. One thing's sure. You're his goddess. He'll be back. To stay. Things get romanticized when they slide into the past. A dose of reality might be the cure."

"I suppose. Well, go talk. Let me clean up." She obviously wanted to have a good cry.

vi) An owl from Zindahjira

Ragnarson and Mocker were still on the front step when darkness fell. They were deep into a keg of beer. Neither man spoke much. The mood was not one suited to reminiscing. Bragi kept considering Mocker's homestead. The man had worked hard, but everything had been done sloppily. The patience and perfection of the builder who cared was absent. Mocker's home might last his lifetime, but not centuries like Ragnarson's.

Bragi glanced sideways. His friend was haggard, aging. The strain of trying to be something he was not was killing him. And Nepanthe was tearing herself apart too. How bad had their relationship suffered already?

Nepanthe was the more adaptable. She had been a man-terrified twenty-eight-year-old adolescent when first their paths had crossed. She was no introverted romantic now. She reminded Bragi of the earthy, pragmatic, time-beaten peasant women of the treacherous floodplains of the Silverbind. Escape from this life might do her good too.

Mocker had always been a chimera, apparently at home in any milieu. The man within was the rock to which he anchored himself. What was visible was protective coloration. In an environment where he needed only be himself, he must feel terribly vulnerable. The lack of any immediate danger, after a lifetime of adjustment to its continual presence, could push some men to the edge.

Ragnarson was not accustomed to probing facades. It made him uncomfortable. He snorted, downed a pint of warm beer. Hell with it. What was, was. What would be, would be.

A sudden loud, piercing shriek made him choke and spray beer. When he finished wiping tears from his eyes, he saw a huge owl pacing before him.

He had seen that owl before. It served as messenger for Zindahjira the Silent, a much less pleasant sorcerer than the Visigodred who employed Marco.

"Desolation and despair," Mocker groaned. "Felicitations from Pit. Self, think great feathered interlocuter maybe should become owl stew, and tidings bound to leg tinder for starting fire for making same."

"That dwarf would be handy now," said Ragnarson. Both ignored the message.

"So?"

"He talks to owls. In their own language."

"Toadfeathers."

"Shilling?"

"Self, being penurious unto miserhood, indigent unto poverty, should take wager when friend Bear is infamous as bettor only on sure things? Get message."

"Why don't you?"

"Self, being gentleman farmer, confirmed anti-literate, and retired from adventure game, am not interested."

"I ain't neither."

"Then butcher owl."

"I don't think so. Zindahjira would stew us. Without benefit of prior butchery."

"When inevitable is inevitable . . . Charge!" Mocker shouted the last word. The owl jumped, but refused to retreat.

"Give him a beer," said Ragnarson.

"Eh?"

"Be the hospitable thing to do, wouldn't it?" He had drunk too much. In that condition he developed a childish sense of humor. There was an old saw, "Drunk as a hoot owl," about which he had developed a sudden curiosity.

Mocker set his mug before the bird. It drank.

"Well, we'd better see what old Black Face wants." Bragi recovered the message. "Hunh! Can you believe this? It says he'll forgive all debts and transgressions—as if any existed—if we'll just catch him the woman called Mist. That old bastard never gives up. How long has he been laying for Visigodred? 'Tain't right, hurting a man through his woman."

Mocker scowled. "Threats?"

"The usual. Nothing serious. Some hints about something he's afraid to mix in, same as Visigodred."

Mocker snorted. "Pusillanimous skulker in subterranean tombs, troglodytic denizen of darkness, enough! Let poor old fat fool wither in peace." He had begun to grow sad, to feel sorry for himself, A tear trickled from one large, dark eye. He reached up and put a hand on Ragnarson's shoulder. "Mother of self, long time passing, sang beautiful song of butterflies and gossamer. Will sing for you." He began humming, searching for a tune.

Ragnarson frowned. Mocker was an orphan who had known neither father nor mother, only an old vagabond with whom he had traveled till he had been able to escape. Bragi had heard the story a hundred times. But in his cups, Mocker lied more than usual, about more personal things. One had to humor him or risk a fight.

The owl, a critic, screeched hideously, hurled himself into the air, fluttered drunkenly eastward. Mocker sent a weak curse after him.

A little later Nepanthe came out and led them to their beds, two morose gentlemen with scant taste for their futures.

THREE: The Long, Mailed Reach of The Disciple

i) A secret device, a secret admirer

Elana rose wondering if Bragi had reached Mocker's safely. How soon would he be home? The forest was a refuge for Itaskia's fugitives. Several bands roamed the North Road. Some had grievances with Bragi. He took his charter seriously, suppressed banditry with a heavy hand. Some would gladly take revenge.

She went to a clothing chest and took out an ebony casket the size of a loaf of bread. Some meticulous craftsman had spent months carving its intricate exterior. The work was so fine it would have eluded the eye but for the silver inlay. She did not know what the carving represented. Nothing within her experience, just whorls and swirls of black and silver which, if studied overlong, dazed the mind.

Her names, personal and family, were inset in the lid in cursive ivory letters. They were of no alphabet she knew. Mocker had guessed it to be Escalonian, the language of a land so far to the east it was just a rumor.

She didn't know its source, only that, a year ago, the Royal Courier, who carried diplomatic mail between Itaskia and Iwa Skolovda, had brought it up from the

capital. He had gotten it from a friend who rode
diplomatic post to Libiannin, and that man had received
it from a merchant from Vorgreberg in the Lesser
Kingdoms. The parcel had come thither with a caravan
from the east. Included had been an unsigned letter
explaining its purpose. She didn't know the hand.
Nepanthe thought it was her brother Turran's.

Turran had tried Elana's virtue once. She had never
told Bragi.

With a forefinger she traced the ivory letters. The top
popped open. Within, on a pillow of cerulean silk, lay a
huge ruby raindrop. Sometimes the jewel grew milky and
light glowed within the cloudiness.

This happened when one of her family was in danger.
The intensity of light indicated the peril's gravity. She
checked the jewel often, especially when Bragi was away.

There was always a mote at the heart of the teardrop.
Danger could not be eliminated from life. But today the
cloudiness was growing.

"Bragi!" She grabbed clothes. Bandits? She would
have to send someone to Mocker's. But wait. She had best
post a guard all round. There had been no rumors, but
trouble could come over the Silverbind as swiftly as a
spring tornado. Or from Driscol Fens, or the west. Or it
could be the tornado that had entered her thoughts. It was
that time of year, and the jewel did not just indicate
human dangers.

"Ragnar!" she shouted, "come here!" He would be up
and into something. He was always the first one stirring.

"What, Ma?"

"Come here!" She dressed hurriedly.

"What?"

"Run down to the mill and tell Bevold I want him. And
I mean run."

"Ah..."

"Do it!" He vanished. That tone brooked no defiance.

Bevold Lif was a Freylander. He was the Ragnarsons'
foreman. He slept at the mill so he would waste no time
trekking about the pastures. He was a fastidious, fussy
little man, addicted to work. Though he had been one for
years, he wasn't suited to be a soldier. He was a craftsman,

a builder, a doer, and a master at it. What Bragi imagined, Bevold made reality. The tremendous development of the landgrant was as much his doing as Ragnarson's.

Elana didn't like Bevold. He presumed too much. But she acknowledged his usefulness. And appreciated his down-to-earth solidity.

Lif arrived just as she stepped from the house.

"Ma'am?"

"A minute, Bevold. Ragnar, start your chores."

"Aw, Ma, I . . ."

"Go."

He went. She permitted no disobedience. Bragi indulged the children to a fault.

"Bevold, there's trouble coming. Have the men arm themselves. Post the sentries. Send someone to Mocker's. The rest can work, but stay close to the house. Get the women and children here right away."

"Ma'am? You're sure?" Lif had pale thin lips that writhed like worms. "I planned to set the mill wheel this morning and open the flume after dinner."

"I'm sure, Bevold. Get ready. But don't start a panic."

"As you will." His tone implied that no emergency justified abandoning the work schedule. He wheeled his mount, cantered toward the mill.

As she watched him go, Elana listened. The birds were singing. She had heard that they fell silent when a tornado was coming. The cloud cover, just a few ragged galleons sweeping ponderously north, suggested no bad weather. Tornados came with grim black cumulo-nimbus dreadnoughts that flailed about with sweeps of lightning.

She shook her head. Bevold was a good man, and loyal. Why couldn't she like him?

As she turned to the door, she glimpsed Ragnar's shaggy little head above a bush. Eavesdropping! He would get a paddling after he brought the eggs in.

ii) Homecoming of a friend

Elana sequestered herself with her teardrop the rest of the

morning. She held several through-the-door conversations with Bevold, the last of which, after she had ordered field rations for dinner, became heated. She won the argument, but knew he would complain to Bragi about the wasted workday.

The jewel grew milkier by the hour. And the men more lax.

In a choice between explaining or relying on authority, she felt compelled to choose the latter. Was that part of the jewel's magic? Or her own reluctance to tell Bragi about Turran's interest?

By midafternoon the milkiness had consumed the jewel's clarity. The light from within was intense. She checked the sky. Still only a scatter of clouds. She returned the casket to the clothing chest, went downstairs. Bevold clumped round the front yard, checking weapons for the twentieth time, growling.

"Bevold, it's almost time. Get ready."

Disbelief filled his expression, stance, and tone. "Yes, Ma'am."

"They'll come from the south." The glow of her jewel intensified when she turned the pointed end toward Itaskia.

"Send your main party that way. Down by the barrow."

"Really . . ."

What Lif meant to say she never learned. A warning wolf's howl came from the southern woods. Bevold's mouth opened and closed. He turned, mounted, shouted. "Let's go."

"Dahl Haas," Elana snapped at a fifteen-year-old who had insinuated himself into the ranks. "Get off that horse! You want to play soldier, take Ragnar and a bow up in the watchtower."

"But . . ."

"You want me to call your mother?"

"Oh, all right." Gerda Haas was a dragon.

Elana herded Dahl inside, stopped at the weapons rack while he selected a bow. The strongest he could draw was her own.

"Take it," she said. She took a rapier and dagger, weapons that had served her well. She had had a bit of success as an adventuress and hire-sword, herself. She added a light crossbow, returned to the horse left by Dahl.

She overtook the men at a barrow mound near the edge of the forest, not far from the head of a logging road which ran to the North Road.

In military matters Bevold was unimaginative. He and the others milled about, in the open, completely unready for action.

"Bevold!" she snapped, "Can't you take me seriously? What'll you do if fifty men come out of the woods?"

"Uh..."

"Get run over, that's what. Put a half dozen bowmen on the barrow. Where's Uthe Haas? You're in charge. The rest of you get behind the barrow, out of sight."

"Uh..." Bevold was getting red.

"Shut up!" She listened. From afar came the sound of hoofbeats. "Hear that? Let's move. Uthe. You. You. Up. And nobody shoots till I say. We don't know who's coming." She scrambled up the mound after Haas.

Lying in the grass, watching the road, she wondered what prehistoric people had built the barrows. They were scattered all along the Silverbind.

The hoofbeats drew closer. Why wasn't she back at the house? She wasn't young and stupid anymore. She should leave the killing and dying to those who thought it their birthright.

Too late to change her mind now. She rolled onto her back, readied the crossbow. She studied the clouds. She had not looked for castles and dragons in years. Childhood memories came, only to be interrupted when a rider burst from the forest.

She rolled to her stomach and studied him over the crossbow. He was wounded. A broken arrow protruded from his back. He clung weakly to a badly lathered horse. Neither appeared likely to survive the day. Both wore a thick coat of road dust. They had been running hard for a long time. The man's scabbard was empty. He was otherwise unarmed.

She glimpsed his face as he thundered past. "Rolf!" she gasped. "Rolf Preshka!" Then, "Uthe, get ready." While the bowmen thrust arrows in the mound for quick use, she waved at Bevold. A lot of horses were coming. She had no idea who their riders might be, but Preshka's enemies were her own.

Rolf had been her man before Bragi, though Ragnarson didn't know the relationship's depth. She still felt guilty when she remembered how she had hurt him. But his love, rare for the time, and especially for an Iwa Skolovdan, was the unjealous kind. The kind that, when at last she had set her heart, had caused him to help her snare Ragnarson.

Preshka, like Bragi, was a mercenary. After Elana's marriage he had joined Ragnarson as second in command. When Bragi had gotten out, Preshka had joined the party that had beat its way in to the landgrant. But he had been unable to put down roots. Two years later, Bragi's foster brother, Haaken Blackfang, and Reskird Kildragon had come by. Rolf had gone off with them, leaving a wife and child mystified and hurt.

In her own way, Elana cared for Preshka as much as her husband. Though their relationship had remained proper since her marriage, she missed him. He had been around so long that he had become a pillar of her universe.

Now he was home. And someone was trying to kill him.

iii) Sons of the Disciple

A flash-flood of burnoosed horsemen roared from the wood. Elana had a moment to be startled by their appearance so far from Hammad al Nakir, another to wonder at their numbers—there were forty or fifty, then it was time to fight. "Go!" she shrieked.

Her bowmen leapt up, loosed a flight that sent the leaders tumbling over their horses' tails, caused tripping, screams, and confusion behind.

Bevold's group swept round the mound, loosed a flight, abandoned their bows for swords. They crashed the head of the line while confusion yet gripped their foes. In the first minute they looked likely to overwhelm the lot.

"The riders!" bellowed Uthe Haas. "Aim at the riders."

"Don't count your chickens, Uthe," Elana replied from the grass. There was little she could do with her crossbow. "Take what you can get." Haas, smelling a victory still far from certain, wanted the mounts as prizes.

They almost pulled it off. Half the enemy saddles were clear before they recovered.

The wild riders of Hammad al Nakir had never learned to handle the Itaskian arrow-storm. The appearance of Itaskian bow regiments had ordained their defeat during the wars. In a dozen major battles through Libiannin, Hellin Daimiel, Cardine, and the Lesser Kingdoms, countless fanatics had ridden into those cloth-yard swarms, through six hundred yards of death, and few had survived to hurl themselves upon the masking shieldmen.

But the commander here wasn't awed. He seized the ground between Lif's men and the barrow, eliminating the screen Bevold could have provided, then sent everyone unhorsed to get the bows.

"Those are soldiers, not bandits," Elana muttered. "El Murid's men." Royalist refugees from Hammad al Nakir were scattered throughout the western kingdoms, but they were adherents of Haroun's. They would not be after Preshka. Assuming Rolf was still a friend of bin Yousif.

She got her chance to fight. Two quick shots with the crossbow, then the attackers arrived. Her first had deep, dark eyes and a scimitar nose. His eyes widened when he recognized her sex. He hesitated. Her rapier slipped through his guard. She had a moment before she engaged again.

The man had been middle-aged, certainly a survivor of the wars. If these were all veterans, they were El Murid's best. Why such an investment to take one man, nearly a thousand miles from home?

Her next opponent was no gentleman. Neither was he a dainty fencer. He knew the limitations and liabilities of a rapier, tried to use the weight and strength of his saber to smash through. As he forced her back, she met his eyes over crashing blades. He could have been the twin of the man she had killed. The fires of fanaticism burned in his eyes, but, having endured the wars, were dampened. He no longer believed El Murid's salvation could be delivered to the infidel with hammer blows. The Chosen, even in the grace and might of God, had to spread the faith with cunning and finesse. The idolators were too numerous and bellicose.

The man wasn't so much interested in killing her as in forcing her out of position. Without a shield, rapier-armed, and physically less powerful, she was the weak point in the defense box they had formed. Her chance lay in taking advantage of his effort.

She parried a feint, thrust short and low at his groin, backed a step *before* he unleashed the edge-blow meant to force her to do just that. She made no effort to parry. His blade slid past a fraction of an inch from her breast. Being a half-second ahead gave her time to thrust at his groin again before he returned to low guard. She scored.

His blocking stroke smashed into her blade near the hilt, bent it dangerously, forced it from the wound. Her own momentum took her to her knees. She used her impetus to prick the thigh of the attacker on her opponent's left. Then she had to get the rapier up to block her antagonist's weak followup.

Instead of raining blows upon her while she was down, he used his greater strength to force his weapon down while he tried to knee her in the face. Again she let him have his way. With her left hand, beneath their locked blades, she used her dagger, going first for the big vein inside his left thigh, then the ligaments behind his knee. Neither blow was successful, but she hurt him. He backed off to let another man take his place.

The man she had pricked went down. Uthe grabbed the opportunity to force her inside the box. No gentlemanly gesture, she realized. She was becoming more a liability than an asset.

Between and over the heads of the fighters, she tried to see how Bevold was doing.

Not well. He was trying to reach the mound, but his men had become hopelessly disorganized and it seemed unlikely any could push through. Half his saddles were empty anyway. As she watched, Bevold himself succumbed to a blow on the helmet.

/And desert men by ones and twos continued to straggle from the forest. Soon they would send a detachment after Rolf.

She looked homeward to check Preshka's progress. There was no sign of him, but she did see something that buoyed her spirits. Riders in the distance, only specks now, but coming fast, straight through the grainfields.

"Bragi!" she shrieked. "Bragi's coming!"

Uthe and the others took it up as a war chant, vented a moment of wild ferocity on their enemies.

Elana felt something underfoot. She looked down. Her crossbow. She still had quarrels. She snatched it up, cocked and loaded it, looked for a target.

Just then the man on Uthe's left, growing too enthusiastic, broke the shield wall. An enemy took instant advantage. He paid the price of his foolishness. The man to his left fell as well.

That two-man hole, for the seconds it existed, loomed ominous. Elana put a bolt into a man trying to open it wider, clubbed a second with the crossbow, bought time for the gap to close.

A square then, with Elana cramped inside, too crowded to do anything but jab with her dagger.

Why was Bragi taking so long?

Only a minute had passed since she had spotted the riders, but it seemed an age. What good help that arrived too late?

iv) To ride against time

This time there was no lack of motivation in Ragnarson's ride. He didn't have to pretend he was racing El Murid. When Elana's messenger met him on the road, he took only a moment to order the man on to Mocker's for reinforcements. He began galloping.

The horse was fresh but incapable of carrying such a

heavy rider so hard so long. It collapsed a mile north of his northernmost sentry post. There was no flogging the animal on. Carrying only his weapons, he ran. That was difficult. His legs were stiff and his thighs were chafed from two hard days in the saddle.

It never occurred to him that Elana might have sent her message before danger was actually upon her. He expected to be too late to do anything but count the dead. But he ran.

By the time he reached the lookout post he was almost as winded as the abandoned horse. Out of shape, he thought, as he staggered the last hundred yards, lungs afire.

The sentry remained on duty. He ran to meet Ragnarson. "Bragi, what happened?"

"Horse foundered," he gasped. "What's going on, Chotty?"

"Your wife got up excited. Put out sentries. Sent Flay to get you. But nothing happened till a minute ago."

"What?" His guts were about to come up. All this action after last night's beer.

"South call. The wolf."

"Uhn. Any others?" They reached the man's hiding place. He had only one horse.

"No."

"No ideas?"

"No."

He had a vague notion of his own, inferences drawn on yesterday's mysteries. "Got your horn? Get up behind me here. She can carry us to the house."

As they rode, Ragnarson sounded the horn, alternating his personal blast with those for the greathouse. Anyone not already in a fight would meet him there.

He found a few men there ahead of him, saw a half dozen more coming. Good. Now, where was Elana?

Gerda Haas came from the house.

"Where's Elana?"

"Crazy fool you married, Ragnarson. Like I told Uthe when you did, you'll get nothing but trouble from that one."

"Gerda."

"Ah, then, she rode off with Uthe and Bevold and the others. South. Took my Dahl's horse, she did, just like . . ."

"How many?"

"Counting her ladyship and the sentries already down there, nineteen I'd guess."

Then all the help he could hope for was already in sight.

Ragnar came running round Gerda, but the old dragon was quick. She caught his collar before he got out of reach. "You stay inside when you're told."

"Papa?"

"Inside, Ragnar. If he gives you any trouble, whack him. And I'll whack him again when I get back. Where's Dahl?"

"In the tower." She scooped Ragnar up and brushed the tears from his eyes. The boy was unaccustomed to shortness from his father.

"Toke," Ragnarson ordered, "get some horses for me and Chotty. Dahl! Dahl Haas!" He bellowed to the watchtower, "What you see?"

"Eh?"

"Come on, boy. Can you see anything?"

"Lot of dust down by the barrow. Maybe a big fight. Can't tell. Too far."

The barrow lay near the tip of a long finger of cleared land pointing south, with the millstream and lumbering road meandering down it. He had been clearing that direction because the logs could be floated to the mill. It was two miles from the house to the barrow.

"Horsemen?" Bragi called.

"Maybe. Like I said, a lot of dust."

"How long?"

"Only a couple minutes."

"Uhn." Bad. Must be something besides, a gang of bandits. His people could take care of that with a flight of arrows.

Toke came round the house with the horses. The women had started saddling them when he and Chotty had come in sight. "All right, everybody that can use one, get a lance. Gerda, get some shields." He was wearing a mail shirt already—a habit when he traveled—so needed waste no time donning that. "And for god's sake, something to drink."

While he waited he looked around. Elana had done well. All the livestock had been herded into the cellars, the heavy slitted shutters were over the windows, the building had been soaked with water against fire, and no one was outside who had no need to be.

A girl Dahl's age brought him a quart of milk. Ugh. But this was no time for ale or beer. Beer made him sweat, especially across his brow, and he needed no perspiration in his eyes during a fight.

"Lock up after us," he told Gerda as he swung into the saddle and accepted shield, ax, and lance from another of the women. "Helmet? Where's my damned helmet?" He had left it with the foundered horse. "Somebody find me a helmet." To Gerda again, "If we're not back, don't give up. Mocker's on his way."

The girl who had brought him the milk returned with a helmet. Ragnarson groaned. It was gold- and silver-chased with high, spread silver wings at the sides, a noble's dress helmet that he had plundered years ago. But she was right. It was the only thing around that would fit his head. If he weren't so cheap, he'd have a spare. He disappeared into the thing, glared around, daring someone to laugh.

No one did. The situation was too grim.

"Dahl, what's happening?"

"Same as before."

Everyone was mounted, armed, ready. "Let's go."

He wasted no time. He rode straight for the barrow, over sprouting wheat.

v) Sometimes you bite the bear, and sometimes the bear bites you

Even while still a long way away, Ragnarson saw that the situation was grim. There were four or five men on the barrow, afoot, surrounded. As many more were below, on horseback, hard-pressed. Men from both sides, unhorsed, were fighting on the ground. There were more attackers than defenders, and those professionals by their look. He couldn't see Elana. Fear snapped at his heart like the sudden bite of a bear trap.

He was not afraid of the fighting—much; a truly fearless man was a fool and certain to die young—but of losing Elana. They had an odd, open marriage. Outsiders sometimes thought there was no love between them, but their interdependence went beyond love. Without one another, neither would have been a complete person.

He slowed the pace briefly, signaled his lancers into line abreast. Those who couldn't handle a lance stayed back with their bows.

Some cavalry charge, Ragnarson thought. Six lances. In Libiannin Greyfells had commanded fourteen thousand horses and ten thousand bows, plus spearmen and mercenaries.

But every battle was the big one to the men involved. Scope and scale had no meaning when your life was on the line. It came down to you and the man you had to kill before he could kill you.

The foreigners weren't expecting more company. Indeed, a freehold this size should have had fewer men about, but Ragnarson's land wasn't a freehold (in the sense that he had been enfiefed and owed the Crown a military obligation), and many of his hangers-on weren't married.

The attackers noticed his approach only after he was less than a quarter-mile distant. They had hardly begun to sort themselves out when he struck.

Ragnarson presented his lance, swung his shield across his body, gripped his reins in his lance hand. His shield was a round one, in the Trolledyngjan style, and not fit for a horseman. He paid the price almost immediately.

As his lancehead entered the breast of his first opponent, a glancing saber stroke slashed his unshielded left thigh. The sudden pain distracted him. He lost his lance as the man he had slain went over his horse's tail.

Then his mount smashed into two others, momentarily trapping him. He couldn't drag out his sword. He clawed at the Trolledyngjan ax slung across his back while warding off swordstrokes with his shield, began chopping kindling from the nearest unfamiliar target.

A progression of dark faces appeared before him, men his own age with deep-set, dark eyes and heavy aquiline noses, like a parade of bin Yousif's. Desert men. But not Haroun's Royalists. What were they doing this far from Hammad al Nakir?

Three opponents he demolished with his berserk, overpowering attack, then, with a sinking in his stomach, felt his mount going down. Someone had slashed her hamstrings. He had to hurl ax and shield away as he leapt to avoid being pinned beneath. The jump threw him face-first into someone's boot and stirrup. A swordstroke proved the small battle-worth of his fancy helmet. A wing came off. A dent so deep that the metal bruised his scalp left him half-unconscious. On hands and knees, with hooves stamping all around, he lifted his visor to heave the milk he had drunk.

With bile in his mouth, thinking the pukes and a dented helmet were cheaper than a shaved ear, he rose in the melee like a bear beset by hounds, sprang barehanded at the nearest enemy not looking his way. With his forearm across the man's throat, using him as a shield, he struggled out of the thickest press.

While strangling his victim, he looked around. The remaining horsemen were drifting toward the forest. Only a handful from either side were still in their saddles. His own people, on the ground, were having the best of a more numerous foe. They were in their element, being infantrymen by trade. Here and there they were linking up in twos and threes. In a bit they would have a shield wall.

Things weren't going that well atop the mound. He saw Elana now. She, Uthe Haas, and another man were trying to hold off three times their number and managing well enough that their attackers had not noticed their comrades withdrawing.

There was no one to send to the mound. Except himself. And he would be no use charging into that mess. Just fodder for the Reaper. But a bowman could help.

There must be a bow somewhere. His people all used them. He trotted over the litter of dead and wounded, and broken, abandoned, and lost weapons. He found a crossbow of the type El Murid's men preferred, but it was useless without a string. He had never gotten the hang of the things anyway. Then he found a short bow of the desert variety, a weak thing easily used from a horse's back, but that had suffered the ungentle caress of a horse's hoof. Finally, as he was about to snatch up a sword and go screaming up the barrow anyway, he found his hamstrung mare with his bow and arrows still slung behind her saddle.

He went to work.

This was the kind of fighting he preferred. Stand off and let them have it. He was good with a bow. Target plinking, he thought.

His fourth victim went down. Yes, much better than getting up toe to toe and smelling your opponent's rotten breath and sweat and fear. And you didn't have to look them in the eyes when they realized they were going to die.

For Ragnarson that was the worst part. Killing was damned discomfiting when he was nose to nose with the fact that he was ending a human life.

His sixth score broke the siege. The survivors followed their comrades toward the forest. Trotting, Ragnarson lofted a few desultory shafts to keep them moving, at the same time shouted, "Let them go!" to Elana and Uthe. "They've had enough. Let's not get anybody killed after we've won."

Elana sent a look toward the forest, then threw herself at her husband. "Am I glad to see you!"

"What the hell do you think you're doing, woman? Out here without even a helmet. Why the hell aren't you at the house? I've a mind to . . . Damn! I will." He dropped to one knee, bent her across the other, reared back to smack her bottom. Then he noticed his men gathering. Grinning, those who had the strength left.

"Well," he growled, "you know what to do. Pick up the mess." He rose, set a subdued Elana back on her feet. "Woman, you pull something like this again, I'll break your butt and not care who's watching."

Then he hugged her so hard she squealed.

As often happened in a wild mixup, there were fewer

dead than seemed likely in the heat of action. But virtually all his people were wounded. The enemy had taken some of their injured with them. The worst hurt had been left behind. Bevold Lif, still dazed, stumbled up to report four of their people killed. The count on the enemy wasn't final. His men were still making corpses out of casualties.

"Damn!" Elana said suddenly. "How's Rolf?"

"Rolf who?"

"Rolf Preshka. Didn't you see him? They were chasing him. He was bad hurt."

"No. Preshka? What the hell? Where'd he come from? Bevold! Take over here. I'll be back in a little while." To Elana, "Let's catch a couple horses."

Of those there was no shortage. The raiders had left most of theirs behind. The animals, once safe from the fighting, had begun cropping wheat sprouts. They would have to be rounded up or the damage they would do would cut into the plunder-profit from their capture. Good desert horses sold high.

"Which way was he headed?"

"Toward the house."

"He didn't make it."

"You think they caught him?"

"Didn't see any of them on the way down. No telling what happened."

They had ridden a mile when Elana said, "Over there." A riderless horse grazed beside the millstream.

They found Preshka not far away. He was alive, but barely. The arrow had penetrated a lung. It would take a miracle to save him. Or perhaps Nepanthe, if they could get her down from Mocker's. She had studied medicine during her lonely youth, with the wizard Varthlokkur as tutor, and she had the magic of her family.

"Here," Ragnarson said, "we'd better make a litter." He drew his sword and set to work on some saplings left to shade the creek. "Might be good fishing this summer," he observed, spotting a lazy carp. "Maybe we can put some up for winter."

Elana, slitting Preshka's jerkin so she could look at his wound, frowned. "Why not just catch them when you get the taste? The rest will be there when you want them."

"Uhn. You're right." He had two long poles cut, was lopping branches. "Thing like today put me in mind of times when there wasn't no coming back. Talking about fish, what do you think of us putting a dam across the creek up where those high banks are?"

"Why?" She was too worried about Rolf to care.

"Well, like I told Bevold the other day, so we'd have water in a dry spell."

"There was water last summer. The springs kept running."

"Yeah, well." He dragged the poles over. "What I was thinking about was stocking some fish. How the hell are we going to finish this thing?"

"Go catch his horse, stupid!" His poking about was frustrating. "He must've had blankets. And hurry."

He ran off. And she was immediately sorry she had snapped at him. It was obvious his leg was giving him a lot of pain. He had claimed the wound was just a scratch. He didn't like to cause concern.

"I've decided," he said when he returned.

"What? Decided what?"

"I'm going to raise some hell about this. I mean, when we took the grant we said we'd do some fighting. In defense of law and order." He sneered his opinion of the phrase. "But not to fight wars on our own. We kept up our end. I didn't even cry about not getting any help the last time raiders came over from Prost Kamenets, even if the army should've been here. But by damn, having to fight El Murid's regulars in my wheat field, a hundred miles *north* of Itaskia, is too much. I got to go down about the timber contract anyway, and pick up some things, so I'll just go early and burn some ears. If them asses at the War Ministry can't keep this from happening, they're going to tell me why. In fact, I'm going to the Minister himself. He owes me. Maybe he can shake some people awake."

"Now, dear, don't do something you'll be sorry for." His friendship with the War Minister was pretty insubstantial, based as it was on a few secret, illegal favors done the man years ago. Men in such positions were notoriously short of memory.

"I don't care. If a citizen can't be safe at home, then why the hell pay taxes?"

"If you don't, you'll get troops up here quick, all right," she replied. They rigged the litter between their horses, hoisted Preshka in.

"Well, I'm going down. Tomorrow."

FOUR: The Narrowing Way

i) Return of the Disciple

Ragnarson did not leave for Itaskia next morning.

He woke to find the household in an uproar.

All his people had spent the night at the greathouse, vainly awaiting Mocker. He assumed Nepanthe, unwilling to let her husband out of sight, would come along and could be put to doctoring.

He went to see what was the matter.

Luck rode with him in a small, left-handed way. Bevold Lif, despite his bashed head, had risen early to go to the mill. He had started out afoot and had quickly returned. El Murid's men were back, waiting for dawn.

Ragnarson quietly tried to get the animals back into the cellars, the building doused down, and weapons readied. If they had the confidence to return, the raiders had picked up reinforcements.

As false dawn lightened the land, he counted their horses. There were nearly thirty surrounding the house, at a distance demonstrating their respect for the Itaskian bow.

"You think they'll attack?" Bevold asked.

"I wouldn't," Ragnarson replied. "But there's no

figuring those people. They're crazy. That's why they did
so well in the wars. That and being able to field every
grown man. Iwa Skolovda and Prost Kamenets have the
same problem on their Shara borders. Nomads don't have
to stay home to get the crops in. And they don't use much
equipment a man can't make himself, so their cavalry
doesn't need a broad peasant base..."

"That'll reassure everybody," Elana said sarcastically.

Bragi, as he aged, had developed a tendency to lecture.
"Uthe and Dahl are in the tower. Uthe said to tell you they
have a 'shaghûn.'"

"Uhn," he grunted. "That's not good."

"Why not?"

"A shaghûn's a sort of priest-knight. They're a fighting
order like the Guild's Knights Protectors. One with a
group this small is unusual."

"So?"

"They're sorcerers too. Not big-time, but they've got
some magic."

"But I thought El Murid killed all the magicians..."

"Sure!" Ragnarson interrupted, sneering. "All that
didn't get religion. You ever hear of a priest who wouldn't
make a deal with his devil to get what he wanted? El
Murid's no different. He's a politician first, same as all of
them. He just started out with ideals. After reality kicked
his ass a few times, he started compromising. The
shaghûn system worked for the Royalists—Haroun is
supposed to be one, but he didn't get much training before
he had to run—so why not for him?"

Bragi was a cynic who disapproved of any organization
structured for purposes other than warfare. His opinions
of governments were as severe as those regarding
priesthoods.

"What can we do?" Elana asked.

"About what?"

"About this hedge-wizard, you lummox!" Mornings
they both could be bears.

"Oh. I'll have to kill him. Or give up and see what he
wants. How's Rolf?"

"Still in a coma. I don't think he'll come out."

"Grim. Where's Mocker? And where's that shaghûn? If

I'm going to get him, I got to know where." He sent someone to get Uthe from the tower.

Elana started to ask why *he* had to do it. She knew. It was his way. The more dangerous the task, the less likely he was to delegate it.

"Let's go to the study," Bragi said. He had a room of his own off the main hall where, supposedly, he attended to business. It was more a museum filled with mementos, and a library. "I hope he stays alive long enough to tell me why I've got El Murid's horses trampling my wheat."

"I'd like to see him live a little longer than that." She revealed too much emotion. Bragi frowned puzzledly, was about to ask something when Uthe arrived.

The men went to four maps hung on a wall. One was of the west, political; another of the Itaskian Kingdom; a third was of the landgrant with inked notations about resources and special features. The last was of the area around the house, with large blank borders where the forest still stood. It was to this that Bragi and Uthe went. Haas pointed out the location of the shaghûn, then of nearby horsemen. Bragi traced an approach route with one heavy forefinger.

"Did you see his colors?" Ragnarson asked. "Did you recognize them?"

"Yes. No."

"Guess we couldn't tell much anyway. Bound to have been a big turnover. Most of them died before El Murid gave up and went home. Well, I don't know what else I can do. Wish I'd known he was out there when it was still dark."

He grabbed Elana, kissed her swift and hard. "Uthe, if it don't work, you take over. Wait for Mocker. He's bound to come—though how much good he'll be I don't know." He kissed Elana again.

ii) His regiment arrives

The ground was cold. His leg ached. The dew on the grass

had soaked through his trousers and jerkin. A breeze from the south did nothing to make him more comfortable. His hands were chilled, shaking. He hoped they wouldn't ruin his aim. There was little chance he would get a second shot. The shaghûn would have a protective spell ready for instant use.

A hundred yards more, at least, before he dared a shot. And they the hardest since he had slipped out the tunnel from the cellars. There was no cover but a fencerow.

Where was Mocker? he wondered.

The yards slowly passed under his belly. He expected an alarm at any moment, or the cry of the shaghûn ordering an attack.

It was light enough to storm the house. Why were they waiting?

From the end of the fence he would have to trust luck to cross five yards of naked pasture to a ditch.

They would get him there for sure.

A sudden outcry and stirring of horses startled him. He almost let fly before realizing the horses were moving away. He raised his head.

Mocker had come.

And how he had come. The column emerging from the forest, both horse and foot, was the biggest Ragnarson had seen since the flareup with Prost Kamenets. At their head, fat and robed in brown and astride his pathetically bony little donkey, rode Mocker.

They were not Royal troops, though they were disciplined and well-equipped. Their banners were of the Mercenary's Guild. But Ragnarson knew few of their names could be found on Guild rosters. They were Trolledyngjans.

The desert horsemen, after first rushing toward the newcomers, retreated. Even a shaghûn was no advantage against such numbers.

Their flight passed near Ragnarson. The shaghûn, in a burnoose as dark as night, was an easy target.

One shaft, from a bow few men could pull, flew so swift its passage was nearly invisible. It burst through the shaghûn's skull.

For a long minute Bragi watched the riders gallop off.

In an hour they would have disappeared without a trace. They came and went like the sandstorms of their native land, unpredictable and devastating.

"Hai!" Mocker cried as Bragi trotted up. "As always, one believed old fat windy fool, self, arrives in nick, to salvage bacon of friend of huge militant repute but, as customary, leaguered up by nearest congregation quadraplegic. Self, am thinking same should admit same before assembled host..."

"Speaking of which," Ragnarson interrupted, "where'd you turn this crowd up?"

"Conjuration." The fat man grinned. "Self, being mighty sorcerer, wizard of worldwide dread, made passes in night, danced widdershins round yew tree, nude, burned unholy incense, called up demon legion..."

"Never changes, does he? Blows hard as a winter wind."

The speaker was a man even more massive than Ragnarson, mounted on a giant gray. He had the shaggy black hair of a wild man, and behind his beard a mass of dark teeth.

"Haaken! How the hell are you? What you doing here?" Haaken Blackfang was his foster brother.

"Been recruiting. Headed south now." Without alcohol in him Blackfang was as reticent as Mocker was loquacious.

"Thought that was where you were. With Reskird and Rolf. Speaking of Rolf, he turned up yesterday, three quarters dead, with that gang after him."

"Uhn," Blackfang grunted. "Not good. Didn't expect them to get excited this soon. Figured another year."

"What're you talking about?"

"Rolf's job to explain."

"He can't. Might never explain anything. Mocker, did you bring Nepanthe? We need medical help."

Before the fat man could reply, Blackfang interjected, "He didn't. I'll loan you my surgeon."

Ragnarson frowned.

"He's good. Youngster with a case of wanderlust. Now then, where to settle this lot? Looks like your fields have been hurt enough."

"Uhn. East pasture, by the mill. I want my animals near the house till this blows over." He wondered if there would be room, though. Blackfang's baggage continued rolling from the forest, wagon after wagon. This looked like a *volkswanderung*. "What you got here, Haaken, a whole army?"

"Four hundred horse, the same afoot."

"But women and children..."

"Maybe word hasn't filtered down. There's trouble in Trolledyngja. Looks like civil war. The Pretender's grip is slipping. Fair-weather supporters are deserting him. Night raiders haunt the outlands. Lot of people like these, whether they favor him or the Old House, don't want to get involved."

A similar desire, after their family had been decimated in the civil war that had given the Pretender the Trolledyngjan throne, had driven Ragnarson and Blackfang over the Kratchnodians years ago.

"Had a letter from the War Minister a while back," said Ragnarson. "Wanted to know why there hadn't been any raids this spring. He thought something like Ringerike might be shaping up. Now I understand. Everybody stayed home to keep an eye on the neighbors."

"About it. Some decided to try their luck with us."

"What about the Guild? They won't like you showing their colors. And Itaskia won't want Trolledyngjans roving round the countryside."

"All taken care of. Fees paid, passes bought. Every man's a Guild member. At least honorarily. Doing everything by the book. We can't leave any enemies behind us."

"Will you explain?"

"Later, if Rolf can't. Shouldn't we put the doctor to work?"

"Right. Mocker, take him to the house. I'll help Haaken get his mob camped. You travel all night?"

"Had to to get here in time. Thought about sending the horse ahead, but they couldn't've gotten here before dark last night, and I didn't figure anything would happen till morning."

"True. True. You're a welcome sight."

iii) Missive from a friend

Rolf came round briefly while the surgeon, who doubted there was much hope, was removing the arrow. He had ridden too far and hard with the shafthead tearing his insides.

Preshka saw the anxious faces. A weak smile crossed his lips. "Shouldn't have...left," he gasped. "Stupid...Couldn't resist...one more try..."

"Be quiet!" Elana ordered while fidgeting, trying to make him more comfortable.

"Bragi...In kit...Letter...Haroun..." He passed out again.

"Figures," Ragnarson grumbled. "This much going on, couldn't be anyone else. Haaken, you feel like explaining?"

"Read the letter first."

"All right. Damn!" He didn't like this mystery piling on mystery, and nobody leaking any light. "I'll hunt the thing up. Meet me in the study."

The country, Haroun's letter began, *is Kavelin in the Lesser Kingdoms, among the easternmost of these, against the Kapenrung Mountains where they swing southwest out of the Mountains of M'Hand, and therein borders on Hammad al Nakir. In the southwest Kavelin is bounded by Tamerice, in the west by Altea, and in the northwest and west by Anstokin and Volstokin. (I am assembling a portfolio of military maps and will get them to you when I can.) El Murid is an enemy, of course, though there has been no action since the wars, which Kavelin survived virtually unscathed. Altea is traditionally an ally, Anstokin mostly neutral. There are occasional incidents with Tamerice and Volstokin. The most recent war was with Volstokin.*

Governmentally, this is a parliamentary feudality, power balanced between the Crown and barons. In force of arms the latter outweigh the Crown, but internecine intrigues dissipate the advantage. Under the current, mediocre King, the Crown is little more than an arbiter of baronial disputes. Although, unlike Itaskia, Kavelin has no tradition of intrigue for the throne, a struggle for succession is taking shape. There is a Crown Prince, but he is not the King's son. By listening at the proper doors one learns that the genuine prince was kidnapped on the day of his birth and a changeling substituted.

Historically and ethnically Kavelin is even more muddled than the usual Lesser Kingdom. The original inhabitants, the Marena Dimura, are a people related to those of the south coastal kingdoms of Libiannin, Cardine, Hellin, Daimiel, and Dunno Scuttari. They form the lowest class, the pariahs. Only the most lucky (relatively) are so well off as to be slaves, bond-servants, or serfs. The majority run wild in the forests, living in a poverty and squalor that would shame a pig.

When, between 510 and 520 in the Imperial dating, Ilkazar occupied the region, Imperial colonists moved in. Their descendants, the Siluro, today form that class which manages the daily work of government and business. They are educated, officious, self-important, and schemers of the first water, and through their hands flows most of the wealth of the kingdom. A lot, in the form of bribes, sticks.

In the last decade of the Imperial era, about 608, when Ilkazar crossed the Silverbind in the north and Roë in the east, whole villages of Itaskians were transported to Kavelin in what has been called the Resettlement. These people, the Wessons (most came from West Wapentake), still speak a recognizable Itaskian and constitute both the bulk of the population and of the peasant, soldier, and artisan/merchant classes. As with Itaskians, they are stolid, unimaginative, slow to anger, and slower to forgive a wrong. Their leaders still resent the Resettlement and Conquest and scheme to set those right.

The final group are the Nordmen, the ruling, enfiefed class. Their ancestors were proto-Trolledyngjans who came south with Jan Iron Hand for the final assault on Ilkazar. They decided life as nobles in a southern clime

was better than going home to become commoners again
in the icy North Waste. Can you blame them?

Everyone does. It has been centuries since the
Conquest and still all three lower groups plot to topple the
Nordmen. Add to actions forwarding these schemes the
almost constant state of warfare among the barons, and
the problem of the succession (for which several
candidates have begun to vie), and you see we have an
interesting political situation.

Native industries include mining (gold, silver, copper,
iron, emeralds), dairying (Kavelin cheese is famous south
of the Porthune), and a modest fur trade. Economically,
Kavelin's major importance is its position astride the
east-west trade route. The fall of Ilkazar and subsequent
drastic climatic changes in Hammad al Nakir forced the
movement of trade northward. Kavelin became its
benefactor by virtue of controlling the Savernake Gap,
only pass through the Kapenrung Mountains connecting
with the old Imperial road to Gog-Ahlan, which is the
only developed way through the Mountains of M'Hand
south of the Seydar Sea. Mocker is familiar with the
eastern trade; he can explain more fully than I. He was in
both Kavelin and the east before the wars.

Do you see the potentialities? Here is a kingdom, rich,
yet small and relatively weak, beset by enemies, ripe for
internal strife. If the King died today, as many as twenty
armed forces with different loyalties might take the field.
Most would be pretenders, but the Queen would attempt
to defend her regency, and independent Siluro, Wesson,
and even Marena Dimura units, under various chieftains,
might align themselves with men they felt likely to
improve their lot. Moreover, nobody would dare go all
out because of greedy neighbors. Volstokin, especially,
might loan troops and arms to a favorite.

Inject into all this a Haroun bin Yousif, with my
backing. (El Murid, much as he may want to, will not dare
interfere directly in Kavelin's internal affairs. He is not yet
ready to resume the wars, which would be the inevitable
result of his interference with a Western state.) Add a
Bragi Ragnarson with a substantial mercenary force.

There would be battles, shifts of loyalties, a winnowing of pretenders. By proper exploitation we should not only become wealthy men, but find a kingdom in our pockets. In fact, I genuinely believe a kingship to be within your reach.

Ragnarson looked up and leaned back, fingers probing his beard. What Haroun really thought and planned was not in the letter. He didn't explain *why* he offered kingship, or reveal what he himself hoped to gain. But it would have to do with El Murid. Bragi rose and went to the map of the west, looking for Kavelin.

"Ah, yes." He chuckled. The mere location of Kavelin cast light on bin Yousif's plan. It was ideally sited for launching guerrilla incursions into Hammad al Nakir. From the border to El Murid's capital at Al Remish was less than a hundred miles. Swift horsemen could reach the city long before defensive units could be withdrawn from more distant frontiers.

That country, rugged, waterless badlands in which small bands of horsemen would be difficult to find, was suited to Haroun's style. It was the same country in which the last Royalists had held out after El Murid's ascension to power.

Haroun's goal was obvious. He wanted a springboard for a Royalist Restoration. Which explained the presence of El Murid's raiders here. They wanted to spoil the scheme. The western states, long plagued by El Murid and weary of supporting rowdy colonies of Royalist refugees, would, if Haroun could manage it, gleefully support a fiat.

Haroun's letter continued. Bragi read it out of a sense of debt to Rolf, but he had made up his mind. Haroun would not drag him in this time. Yesterday's action, and his wounded leg, were all the adventure he wanted. Haroun could find another catspaw.

Haroun always talked fine and promised the moon, but seldom came near delivering.

The only crown Bragi felt likely to win, if he went to Kavelin, was the kind delivered with a mace.

iv) Knives in passing

Another dawn. Behind them the Trolledyngjan women were striking camp. Bragi, Mocker, Haaken, and Blackfang's staff, were already under way. Uthe Haas, and Dahl, rode with Bragi, ostensibly to help with his business in Itaskia, but, he suspected, more as Elana's watchers. He had not had the strength to argue. His wound and another evening of drinking had washed the vinegar out of him.

"Why don't you just ride along till we meet up with Reskird?" Blackfang asked. "He'll want to swap a few lies, too. Been years since we've all been together."

Reskird Kildragon was in the hills somewhere south of the Silverbind, near Octylya, training bowmen for service in Kavelin. These were prosperous times in Itaskia. Kildragon had been able to recruit few veterans. The youngsters he had assembled were all raw, with the customary, bullheaded Itaskian predilection for using their weapons their own ways. Bragi didn't envy Reskird his job.

"I'll think about it." He wanted to say, "No," but he would hear about that all the way to Itaskia. And if he indulged his emotions and agreed, he would hear about it from Uthe. "Ought to ride ready. Might be ambushed."

The ambush didn't come till after he had wearied of staying alert. The least likely place, he thought, was Itaskia itself. El Murid's men would be too obvious there.

He overlooked the national prosperity that had eased suspicions. He was telling Dahl an exaggerated tale as they, Uthe, Mocker, Haaken, and two others entered Itaskia's North Gate. The city watch had insisted that the main party remain outside, Trolledyngjans and alcohol having a reputation for not mixing.

"It was here that business with the rats started," said Ragnarson. "When Greyfalls tried to take over. I was over there, Mocker was up Wall that way, and Haroun was on that roof over there . . ."

Someone was watching from the same spot Haroun had occupied then, a dark-skinned man who vanished the instant Bragi spotted him. "Watch it," said Ragnarson. "We've got friends here."

"We'll be all right on King's," Haaken replied.

"Damned rules. Laws," Ragnarson growled. "Don't know if I want to see the Minister this bad." He slapped his thigh where, till the gate guards had compelled him to check it, his sword had hung. The only personal weapons allowed were blades shorter than eight inches. "Wasn't this way in the old days."

"There was more killing then, too," Uthe observed.

"Fallacy," Mocker interjected. "Same number cadavers in gutter mornings, now as then. Holes just smaller. Self, if decide man wants murdered, will dispose of same. Can exterminate with hands, ropes, rocks, bludgeons..."

"Maybe," Uthe replied, "but it's inconvenient, not being able just to grab a sword and stick him."

They crossed Wall Street and entered King's, a busy artery sweeping grandly to the heart of the city and kingdom with identical names. Bragi had convinced his companions that they should take rooms near the Royal Palace, where he had business.

In New Haymarket Square in New Town, only a few hundred yards from North Gate, the blow fell.

Two men, dusky and hawk-nosed, exploded from a throng watching a puppet show, hurled themselves at Ragnarson and Mocker with daggers and screams.

The dagger thrust at Ragnarson slid over the mail beneath his sleeve as he threw up an arm, then slashed up his chest and along his jaw. His beard kept the gash from being nasty. He brought his right hand across to strike back. His horse, spooked, reared and neighed wildly, dumping him. As he went down he saw Mocker doing the same, heard the screams and squeals of panicky onlookers. Then his head hit cobblestones.

Mocker had a moment more to react. He threw himself, robes flying, off his donkey. His attacker plunged his dagger into an empty saddle. As the assassin bounced back, Dahl Haas kicked him in the temple.

Mocker came up off the pavement shrieking, "Murder!

Watch! Help! Help!" He plumped his considerable weight atop the man Dahl had kicked, began strangling him. "Murder! Dastardest dastard attacks poor old mendicant in middle of street in middle of day ... What kind city this where even poor traveler is prey for assassin? Help!" Which only spurred bystanders to flee before they themselves were butchered or nabbed as material witnesses.

Several city watchmen turned up with amazing alacrity—as everywhere, they were wont to appear only after the dust settled and there was little danger to themselves—but were unable to get through the dispersing crowd.

Haaken, Uthe, and Blackfang's bodyguards piled onto the man who had attacked Ragnarson. Dahl tried to control the horses while complaining that his foot hurt.

The police finally sorted things out. A half-dozen bolder onlookers, who had hung on for the denouement, supported Blackfang's story. Despite an obvious desire to arrest everyone, the officers settled for two battered would-be assassins and Haaken's promise to file a complaint.

Mocker and Dahl then brought Ragnarson around. "Damn!" Bragi growled. "I'm going to start sleeping in a helmet, way my head's getting smacked anymore." He struggled to his feet, cursing the pain. Dahl and Mocker hoisted him into his saddle. "One thing. I'm going to see the Minister while I'm still hurting. That'll keep me ornery enough to growl him down."

"Or get yourself thrown out," Haaken observed. "But it won't hurt to stop off. I'll get my excuses in ahead of time. Moving that gang of mine is touchy. Can't let them get our passes revoked. The Guild wouldn't help."

"Good thinking. Mocker, you need to take care of anything there?"

The fat man shrugged. "Self, always have business at Ministry of War. Ministry has evil habit. Late payment on contracts. No interest, no penalty. Owes guineas six hundred twelve, four and six, on salt pork supplied for winter maneuvers on Iwa Skolovdan border. But let poor old pig farmer be hour late delivering same. Hai! Sky falling, maybe, self thinks when agent shows up threatening repossession of soul." He laughed. "Can have same. Is already in hock to six devils. Take to Debtor's Court, scoundrelest scoundrels of state collectors! See who wins case." He flashed an obscene gesture at the Royal Palace.

v) Secret master, silent partner

The War Minister was a small man, wizened, who had been ancient when Bragi had met him years earlier. Now, within the plush vastness of his private office, he seemed so small and old as to be inhuman.

"So," said Ragnarson. "The heart of the web. Comfortable. Good to see my taxes well-spent." Times past, because of their nature, their conferences had been held in less opulent surroundings.

"Rank and privilege, as they say." The old man extended his hand.

Ragnarson frowned suspiciously. This was going too smoothly. He hadn't been kept cooling his heels. "You'd think I had an appointment."

"In a sense. Make yourself comfortable. Brandy?"

"Uhn." Ragnarson sank into a chair that threatened to devour him. He was not a poor man, but brandy was beyond his means. "Looks like you got something on your mind too."

"Yes. But your business first. And pardon me for skipping the amenities. Time presses."

Ragnarson sketched recent events.

"Oh, my," said the Minister, shaking his head. "Worse than I thought. Worse. And sure to get worse still. Dear me, dear me. But they wouldn't listen. Told me to forgive and forget, not to hold grudges."

"What're you talking about?"

"Greyfells. They brought him back. Inland Ministry. Wouldn't listen to me. Even moved Customs to his control."

"What? No! I don't believe it." The Duke of Greyfells,
as near an arch-traitor as was boasted by Itaskian history,
back in favor? Astounding.

But Greyfells was a bouncer. During the wars, while
commander of Itaskian expeditionary forces and prime
candidate for supreme commander of the allied armies, he
had been in touch with El Murid, plotting treason. Only
astonishing victories by Haroun's Royalist guerrillas,
with the aid of Trolledyngjan mercenaries and native
auxiliaries, in Libiannin and Hellin Daimiel, had forced
Greyfells to maintain his loyalty.

Later, there had been plots to seize the Itaskian Crown.
Greyfells, once, had been in the succession. Haroun,
Mocker, and Ragnarson had ruined his schemes. One of
the favors done the War Minister. Greyfells had
renounced his place in the succession to evade the
embarrassment of a treason trial.

"Politicians!" Bragi snorted into his snifter. The Duke
kept complicating his life, and Itaskia's, and he was
getting tired of it. How many times would the man reach
for the throne?

"My Lord the Duke has bounced back," said the
Minister. "My people at Interior think he's in touch with
his old accomplice. They've struck a devil's bargain. El
Murid to support Greyfells' next power grab. And
Greyfells to keep Itaskia out of the next war, and refuse
passage to troops from our northern neighbors. You
know what that means. Hellin Daimiel, Cardine, and
Libiannin still haven't recovered. Dunno Scuttari and
the Lesser Kingdoms never were powerful. Sacuescu
couldn't keep a gang of old ladies from plundering the
Auszura Littoral. El Murid would be at the Porthune and
gates of Octylya in a month. There'll be a catastrophe if
Greyfells has his way. And he probably will. He grows
more golden-tongued with the years. The King no longer
hears his critics."

"Then my days are numbered," said Ragnarson. His
dreams were smoke if Greyfells was back. Inland oversaw
the management of Royal Grants even when their original
issuance was under the purvue of War. Greyfells would
find an excuse to revoke his charter.

"True," said the Minister. "He's working on it. The raid demonstrates it. That, which came to my attention only yesterday, was meant to rid Greyfells of a pain in the neck, and El Murid's side of a potential thorn."

"Politics don't interest me," said Ragnarson. "That's a well-known fact. All I ever wanted from politicians was for them to leave me alone."

"But there's your friend, the Royalist, and your talent for warfare. Your friend's a threat to El Murid. That makes you a threat."

"I'm just one man..."

"And not that important from where I sit. But important in some minds. And in the mind is reality. It's no objective thing. You pose a threat if only because they think you do. You aren't the sort who won't fight back."

"No. Where do you stand?"

"I always stand opposite Greyfells. And this time, behind your friend. This isn't to leave this room. The Ministry has been making available certain aid. Funds for which we aren't accountable, and weapons. This may have to stop. But I'll remain behind your friend. His success would delay war, maybe prevent it..."

The Minister's secretary appeared. "Your Lordship, there's a gentleman who insists on seeing this gentleman." His nose wrinkled. Ragnarson glanced down to see if he had forgotten to shake the horse manure off his boots.

Blackfang rolled in. "Bragi, one of my lads says they raided your place again. My people caught them. Got most of them. What you want to do?"

For a long time Ragnarson said nothing. Guards came to drag Blackfang away, but the Minister shooed them off. Finally, Bragi said, "I'll let you know in a minute. Wait outside." After Blackfang and the secretary departed, he asked, "What would happen if Greyfells were assassinated?"

The Minister frowned thoughtfully behind steepled fingers. "They'd want heads. Yours if they connected you. His son would take his place."

"If both were to go?"

"He has four sons. Peas from a pod. Chips from the block. But it'd buy a few months. And get the kingdom turned upside down. How many people at your place? Better think about them."

"I am."

"Something could be arranged . . . If I could get them to safety? . . ."

"You'd have a corpse. I hate to lose the place, but it looks like I'm damned no matter what."

"Keeping it could be fixed. Your grant runs to the river. That puts it in a military zone. I could take it over till this blows away. I'll have to put troops in anyway, if you and your eastern friend leave a forty-mile gap unpatrolled. If I don't, I'll have the north woods thick with bandits from Prost Kamenets, and trade with Iwa Skolovda cut off. But getting you, and your eastern friend, off the hook would take some doing. You might have to stay away for years."

"I think," said Ragnarson, "I'll have to do that anyway. To get help reaching Greyfells." He was on the edge of decision. He knew where to buy the knife, but the price would be playing Haroun's game in Kavelin.

"We'll meet tomorrow, then. Where're you staying?"

"King's Cross, but I may move. We had some trouble in New Haymarket. Greyfells might try to have us arrested."

"Uhm. Charge would only have to stick till something regretable happened in the dungeons. He's foxy. All right. Wansettle Newkirk, ten in the morning. You know it?"

"I can find it."

"Good luck then."

Ragnarson rose, shook the Minister's hand, joined Blackfang. He remained uncommunicative the rest of the day.

FIVE: Their Wickedness Spans the Earth

i) But the evil know no joy

At last. The end of a long and tiring journey. Burla glanced back to see if he had been overtaken at the penultimate moment, sighed, slipped into the cave. His friend Shoptaw, the winged man, greeted him with anxious questions. "Fine, now," Burla replied with a wide, fangy grin. "But tired. Master?"

"Come," the winged man said.

The old man was solicitous and apologetic. "I'm sorry you had to go through this. But Burla, you did me proud. Proud. How's the child?"

Swelling in the Master's praise, Burla replied, "Good, Master. But hungry. Sad."

"Yes, so. You weren't prepared to bring him so far. I feared ..."

Burla laid the baby before the Master. The old man opened its wrappings.

"What's this? A girl?" Thunderheads rumbled across his brow. "Burla ..."

"Master?" Had he done wrong without knowing?

The old man held his temper. Whatever had happened, it had not been Burla's fault. The dwarf didn't have the brains. "But how?..." he asked aloud, wondering how a counterswitch had been made. Then he looked closer. The hereditary mark was there.

The King had lied. To support his shaky throne he had announced the birth of a son when a daughter had been born. The fool! There was no way he could have pulled it off...

Realization. His own schemes had been dealt a savage blow. A wildcat was growling in his embrace. Willy-nilly, he had inherited the Krief's plot. "Oh, damn, damn..."

Two days passed before he trusted his temper enough to confront his shadowy ally. The failure was the easterner's fault. He should have used spells to assure the sex of the child. The old man would have done it himself had he suspected the other's sloppiness.

But no one accused the Demon Prince of incompetence. No sorcerer was more powerful or touchy than Yo Hsi, nor had any had more time to perfect his wickedness. He was an evil spanning unknown centuries. Only one man dared openly challenge the Demon Prince, his co-ruler and arch-enemy in Shinsan, the Dragon Prince, Nu Li Hsi. And, perhaps, the Star Rider, the old man thought, but he was irrelevant to the equation.

The old man, who had taken great pains to remain anonymous, was a noble of Kavelin, the Captal of Savernake, hereditary guardian of the Savernake Gap. His castle, Maisak, in the highest and narrowest part of the pass, had seen countless battles fought beneath its walls. Only once had it been threatened, when El Murid's hordes, by sheer numbers, had almost swamped it. The Wesson, Eanred Tarlson, had prevented that. That near-defeat had led the Captal to reinforce his defenses with sorcery.

A greater sorcery was in the Savernake Gap now. That of Shinsan. The Demon Prince's interlocutors had come to the Captal and found a bitter, ambitious man, Kavelin's only non-Nordmen noble gone sour over the treatment he received in Vorgreberg. The emissaries had tempted him with the Crown of Kavelin in exchange for service to Yo Hsi and eventual passage west for Shinsan's legions. Yo Hsi was ready to settle his ancient struggle with the Dragon Prince. A united Shinsan would move swiftly to fulfill its age-old goal of world dominion.

The Captal, from his lonely aerie, had seen little of the world but that contained in the caravans flowing past Maisak. Since the fall of Ilkazar, the west had been weak and divided. The major powers, Itaskia and El Murid's religious state, were deadly enemies evenly matched. Neither showed much interest in using sorcery for military purposes.

Shinsan hinged its strategies on sorcery. Physical combat was a followup, to occupy, to achieve tactical goals. Rumor whispered dreadful things of the powers pent there, awaiting unity to release them.

The Captal had chosen what he thought would be the winning side. Western sorcery and soldiery had no hope against the Dread Empire.

Yo Hsi had established a transfer link between Maisak and a border castle in his sector of Shinsan. Th old man now used it. He bore the child in his arms.

The place he went was dark and misty. There were hints of evils out of sight, evils more grim than any he had created in the caverns in the cliffs against which Maisak stood.

A squad of soldiers, statue-like in black armor, surrounded his entry point. He could see nothing beyond them. He, and they, might have been the entire universe.

Was Yo Hsi expecting trouble? He had never been greeted this way before. "I want to see the Demon Prince. I'm the Captal of Savernake..."

Not a weapon wavered, not a man moved. Their discipline was frightening.

From the darkness, a darker darkness still, Yo Hsi materialized. Fear cramped the Captal's guts. The man hadn't been the same since losing his hand—though, perhaps, the change had begun earlier, with the failure in the child's sex. Consistency of oversight suggested that Yo Hsi was developing a godlike self-image that underestimated everyone around him.

"What do you want? You've dragged me away from sorceries of the highest and most difficult sort."

His face came visible in the sourceless light. It was

drawn and haggard. The eyes were surrounded by marks of strain. The Captal felt a new touch of fear. Had he made an ally of a man incapable of fulfilling the scheme?

"We've got a problem."

"I don't have time for guessing games, old man."

"Eh?" The Captal controlled himself. He had just learned his status in the easterner's thoughts. "The child. Your Prince changeling. It's a girl."

The Captal had been enthusiastic when Yo Hsi had first proposed the switch. Couldn't miss, what with both Princes their creatures...

The Demon Prince flew into a screaming rage.

It was all the Captal's fault, of course. Or his minions had betrayed him, or...

After several minutes of abuse, the old man could tolerate no more. The Demon Prince had slipped over the borders of reason. The ship of alliance was no longer sound. Time to abandon it and cut his losses.

With a slight bow the Captal interrupted, said, "I see I'll find no comfort in the source of our embarrassment. You may consider our alliance dissolved." He spoke the word that would return him to his own dungeons.

As he flickered away, he grinned. The expression on Yo Hsi's face!

The moment he materialized in Maisak he initiated dissociative spells to close the transfer stream. To pursue the discussion Yo Hsi would have to walk from the hold of his nearest secret ally.

ii) He bears the burden of loyalty

Eanred Tarlson was one man who never ceased worrying the mysterious exchange.

Following his encounter in the Gudbrandsdal there was a long period for which he had no memories. His wife, Handte, said he had lain on the borderland of death for a month. Then, gradually, he had recovered. Six months had passed before he could get around under his own power. Kavelin spent that time under intense pressure from its neighbors.

At home, in the taverns with his men, or maneuvering in the field, Tarlson never stopped puzzling. Something kept ragging the corners of his mind. A clue that only he held. Some memory of having encountered the old man before, long ago. But his bout with death had left his mind unreliable.

"Maybe it's a memory from a previous life," his wife observed one evening, a year after the swap. She was the only one he had told. "I was reading one of Gjerdrum's books. There's a man at the Rebsamen, Godat Kothe, who says the half-memories we get sometimes are from other lives."

Gjerdrum had just finished a year in Hellin Daimiel, courtesy of the Krief. Handte Tarlson, with a thirst for knowledge and little opportunity to indulge it, had instantly begun devouring his books.

Eanred frowned. That reminded him of a problem he had to face soon. The Nordmen were upset that a common Wesson, on state funds, was being sent to a university considered a noble preserve.

It had begun without Tarlson's knowledge, during his unconsciousness. There had been strong opposition, which was stronger now. Gjerdrum had outperformed his classmates. Though Tarlson felt immensely honored, he feared he would have to ask the boy to withdraw.

He felt a quirk of irritation. It startled him. It wasn't like him to feel antagonism over accidents of birth. Still, they couldn't accuse him of ambition. He had never asked honors or titles, only the opportunity to serve.

"Maybe. But I'm sure it's a memory from this life. I'll find the handle someday." After a long pause, "I have to. I'm the only one who saw them all."

"Eanred, tell the King. Don't take everything on yourself."

"Maybe." He considered it.

Weeks passed before he spoke with the Krief. The occasion was his induction into the Order of the Royal Star, the Crown's household knights. The endowment was hereditary and carried a small living.

The Nordmen were bitter. But their opposition remained muted. The ceremony took place in Vorgreberg, where Tarlson was immensely popular.

He could be put in his place when the mad King died.

Afterward, in his private-audience chamber, the Krief asked, "Eanred, how are you? I've heard the pressure's bothering you."

"Fine, Sire. Never better."

"I don't believe it. You showed nerves today."

"Sire?"

"Eanred, you're the only loyal subject I've got. You're invaluable as champion, but worth immeasurably more as a symbol. Why do you think the barons hate you? Your very existence makes their treasons more obvious. They resist honoring you because it makes you more prominent, makes your loyalty a greater example to the lower classes. And that's why I refuse to let you take Gjerdrum out of the Rebsamen."

Tarlson was startled.

The King chuckled. "Thought you had that in mind. In character. Bring me a brandy, will you?"

While Tarlson poured, the Krief continued, "Eanred, I don't have much time left. Three or four years. If I do things that seem strange, don't be surprised. I'm chasing a grand plan. So the scramble for succession won't destroy Kavelin. Thank you. Pour one for yourself." For several minutes he sipped quietly while Tarlson waited.

"Eanred, when I'm gone, will you support the Queen?"

"Need you ask, Sire?"

"No, but I don't envy you the task. My remotest cousins will be after the Crown. You'll have no support."

"Nevertheless..." He remembered his wife's suggestion. "Maybe if we found the true Prince..."

"Ah. You know. I guess everyone does. But it's not that easy. There're facts known only to myself and the Queen. And the kidnappers. Eanred, the Prince was a girl. Fool that I was, I thought we could pretend otherwise..."

Tarlson dropped into a chair. "Sire, I'm a simple man. This's a bit complicated... But there's something I've got to tell you. It may help." He described what he had seen the night of the abduction.

"The Captal," the Krief said when Eanred finished. "I suspected it. The creatures in the tower, you know. But I kept asking myself, what did he have to gain? Now I wonder if he was a willing accomplice, or under duress? I've no ideas about your attacker. He must've been a Power..."

"You haven't investigated?" The puzzle had been answered. The old man *had* been the Captal of Savernake. Eanred had seen him briefly during the wars.

"I had my reasons. For now I have a son, though he'll never be King. Meanwhile, I keep hoping there'll be an acceptable heir..." For a moment his face expressed intense anguish. "The girl's no more my blood than the changeling."

"Sire?"

"Don't know how it was managed. But I didn't father the child. Haven't had the capacity since the wars. No need to be shocked, Eanred. I've managed to live with it. As has the Queen, though she wasn't told till recently...I'd run out of excuses. And it was time she knew. She might find a way to give me an heir before it's too late." He smiled a tight, agonized smile.

"I doubt it, Sire. The Queen..."

"I know. She's young and idealistic...But a man has to live by his forlorn, twisted hopes."

Tarlson shook his head slowly. More than the knighthood, the Krief's confessions were honors that showed the high esteem in which he was held. He wished there was something he could do...

He returned home in a dour, bitter mood, silently cursing Fate, yet with a renewed respect for the man who was his lord and friend. Let the Nordmen call him weakling. The man had a strength they would never understand.

iii) She walks in darkness

Three times emissaries of the Demon Prince came to
Maisak. Each time the Captal sent them home with polite
but firm refusals. Then he heard nothing for a long time.

He considered going to the Krief. But temptation
called. He might stumble into something yet...

News came, whispering on demon wings, of a great
thaumaturgic disaster. It stirred awe and fear among
sorcerers throughout the west.

Yo Hsi *and* the Dragon Prince had been destroyed. In
his hidden fortress deep in the Dragon's Teeth, the
sorcerer Varthlokkur, the murderer of Ilkazar, had
stirred and twitched and lashed out with unsuspected
power.

The Captal, like sorcerers everywhere, retired to his
most secure fastness to cast divinations and lay a wary
inner eye on the Power in the north. The possibilities were
unimaginable. The Empire Destroyer loose again. What
would he do now?

And what of Shinsan? Nu Li Hsi's heir-apparent was a
crippled child, incapable of holding the Dragon Throne.
Yo Hsi's daughter was a postulant of a hermitic order,
uninterested in her father's position and power... Would
Varthlokkur seize Shinsan before the Tervola could select
an Emperor?

Across the west, sorcerers gathered their strength, saw
to their defenses.

And nothing happened. The Power in the Dragon's
Teeth quietly faded away. The Captal's probes sensed
only patient waiting, not ambition, not gathering sorcery.

Nor were there thaumaturgic hostings in Shinsan.
Both successions proceeded smoothly.

He returned to his experiments.

She came at night, under a full moon, three years to the
day after the baby change. In her train were imps and
cockatrices, griffins, and a sky-patrolling dragon. She

rode a milk-white unicorn.

She was the most beautiful woman he had ever seen.
He loved her from the beginning.

Shoptaw roused him from slumber with the news.

"Has the alarm been given?" he asked.

"Yes, Master."

"What's the matter?"

"Great magic. Terrible power. Many strange beasts.
Men without souls."

"You've been to see them?"

"I flew with five..."

"And?" A pang of distress. "Someone was hurt?" He
loved his creations as a man loved his children.

"No. Very frightened, though. Not get close. Great
winged beast, eyes and tongue of fire, large as many
horses..."

"A dragon?"

Shoptaw nodded.

Dragons were incredibly rare, and sorcerers who had
learned dragon mastery rarer still. "They didn't act
hostile?"

"No." But the winged man drew his crystal dagger.

The Captal's gaze wandered its edges and planes. There
was a glow almost indiscernable.

"No inimical intentions," he translated. "Well, let's
have a look at them."

She was a half-mile away when first he spied her, a
glowing point below the circling dragon. He recognized
the unicorn, was awed. Unicorns, he had on high
authority, were extinct.

"Mist," he whispered once she had drawn closer. "Yo
Hsi's daughter."

She stopped before the gate, showed the palms of both
hands. The Captal smiled. He knew the gesture was empty
if she intended evil.

Yet it *was* a gesture. No sense antagonizing her when
she had Shinsan's best at her back. A fight would be
hopeless. He would last barely long enough to send a
message to Vorgreberg.

He delayed the message pending outcome of the
parlay.

She understood his position. She did not ask that he

admit anyone to his fortress. "I've come to discuss a matter of mutual interest." Her bell-like voice turned his spine to water.

"Eh?" Her beauty was totally distracting.

"You had an arrangement with my father. I want to renew it.

He gawked.

She descended from her exotic mount, said something to one of her captains. The soldiers of Shinsan began pitching camp with the same precision shown in everything they did. Among the imps there was an increase in erratic, chaotic behavior.

The Captal found his tongue. "I'd heard you weren't interested in the Demon Throne." He glanced at the unicorn. "But I've heard other tales that, obviously, were unfounded."

She rewarded him with a melting smile. "One must create images to survive a heartbeat from a throne. Had my father believed me interested, he'd've had me killed. The greater the power, the greater the fear of its loss."

"The bargain with your father," the Captal said, after he and the woman had made themselves comfortable inside, "became untenable when he lost touch with reality. He made grave errors and blamed them on others."

"I know. And I apologize. He was a brilliant man once. I think you'd find me a more compatible partner."

Oh, the suggestiveness she put into her words!

"Show me the profit. You have the Demon Throne, but do you have its power? Dare you look beyond your borders? The Dragon Prince, too, had an heir."

"O Shing? I haven't run him to ground yet, but it's only a matter of time.

"Tervola have declared." The Tervola were the sorcerer-generals who commanded Shinsan's armies. Traditionally, they gave no loyalties to anything but Shinsan itself. "Not many yet. Lords Feng and Wu support O Shing. Lord Chin has declared for me. You see that I've captured his token."

"The dragon?"

"Yes."

"Uhm. And the unicorn? I'd thought the beast pure fable."

"They're rare. Rarer than dragons. But there'll always be unicorns while there're virgins—though we're rarer than dragons too."

The Captal stirred nervously. "You're not one of those . . . those whose power depends on . . ."

Her perfect lips formed the tiniest pout. "Sir!" Then she laughed. "Of course not. I'm no fool to hinge my strength on something so easily lost. I'm as human as any woman."

The old man felt a twinge of envy for the man who would first reach Mist's bed.

"What's your offer?" he asked.

"The same as my father's. But I won't cheat you."

He was hooked, but he continued to wriggle. "What're your plans?"

"I mean to test my power. On Shinsan's borders there're a few small kingdoms that have been troublesome. And I'll finish O Shing."

"And then?"

"Then the great eastern powers. Escalon and Matayanga."

"Ah?" She was ambitious indeed, though only to fulfill what Shinsan considered its destiny. And he saw an opportunity to hedge his bets. "I might be interested. But you haven't convinced me. *If* you succeed in Escalon, then I'll commit myself." Escalon commanded sorceries as powerful as those of Shinsan.

Mist wanted to reopen the transfer link. She had a friend in the west, an Itaskian named Visigodred. His residence was far from the focus of events and he was completely apolitical. She would leave control of the link in his hands.

iv) Mistress of the night

She looked seventeen. An enemy might have suggested nineteen. But she was old beyond the suspicions of all but the Tervola. She had been an apparent seventeen when Yo Hsi had engineered Varthlokkur into destroying

Ilkazar. She herself was unsure of her age. She had spent centuries cloistered from the temptations of life and power...

Yo Hsi had never forgotten that he and Nu Li Hsi had usurped their father, Tuan Hua. He had always anticipated his own usurpation by descendants... Males he had had murdered at birth. Mist had been allowed life on her mother's promise that she would spend her existence confined to a nunnery.

Survival had been the obsession of her early existence. She had done everything to assure her father that she had rejected ambition.

She succeeded. And cozened him into placing upon her the sorceries yielding eternal youth.

Those victories won, she turned to sorcerous self-education.

With the centuries never ending there was time to learn cautiously, by nibbles, without being obvious. By the time she was exposed she had become as powerful as any Tervola. The Power was in her blood. Still she showed no ambition beyond the scholarly. Her father chose not to destroy her.

But she had ambitions. And patience. Varthlokkur and the destruction of the Empire had shown her that Yo Hsi contained the seeds of his own destruction. She needed but wait.

Varthlokkur had come to Shinsan as a child, a fugitive full of hatred. The master magicians of Ilkazar, trying to evade a prophecy that from a witch would spring the Empire's doom, had burned his mother. Yo Hsi had undertaken his education, forging a weapon with which to demolish the one power capable of challenging Shinsan. But he had not supervised the boy's education himself. He had left that to the Tervola. They had seen no reason to keep him from meeting Nu Li Hsi as well.

Each Prince had thought to use him against the other. He had shaken their mastery, after crushing Ilkazar, and had hidden in the Dragon's Teeth. When, after centuries, they had striven to regain control, he had trapped them both...

Mist had ascended the Demon Throne without risk or effort. Only a little muddying of the thaumaturgic visions of her father and Nu Li Hsi. Just enough to hasten them to their fates.

The conquest of Escalon appeared easy. She needed but overwhelm the magic of the Monitor and Tear of Mimizan. O Shing was on the run. Her back was clear.

Appearances were deceiving. Escalon controlled more Power than she expected, and O Shing's weakness was the pretense of the broken-winged pheasant.

He struck while she was committed in Escalon, during the height of a battle. Only the greater threat of an Escalonian offensive saved her by forcing him to assume control of the armies.

Mimicking O Shing's game, she struck back while he was involved in a gargantuan operation against the Monitor. She forced another change of command, resumed control of the adventure she had initiated.

In Escalon she captured some western mercenaries. Among them were interesting brothers named Turran and Valther, minor wizards who had been involved in the affair that had led to her father's doom. They seemed to have no particular allegiance to Escalon, and no love for Varthlokkur, whom she would have to face someday. She took them into her growing coterie of foreign followers.

The Tervola issued dire warnings about foreigners. She ignored them.

The younger brother, Valther, caught her fancy. He was a pleasant, witty man, sharp of mind, always ready with a quip or tall tale. And he was impressed by her looks. Most men were terrified of what she was.

It developed so subtly that neither recognized more than a surface involvement. They hawked together in lands far from the war, danced on mountaintops deep in Shinsan, skipped through transfer links to cities and fortresses unknown outside the Dread Empire. She showed him the fains and shrines of her father and grandfather, and let him join the hunt for O Shing.

But there was the war, her war, that had to come before all else, that would mean loss of the Demon Throne if she failed.

The bond developed, deepened. The Tervola saw, understood, and disapproved.

There came a night of rites and celebration before the

final assault on Tatarian. Spirits were high. O Shing seemed broken. Escalon had little power left . . . Over the objections of her generals, she invited Turran and Valther.

Her pavilion, huge and rich, had been erected within sight of Tatarian's defensive magicks, and everything in it had been plundered from Escalon. Mist meant to accept the Monitor's surrender there, in humiliating circumstances. He had caused her untold unhappiness.

"Valther," she said, when he and Turran arrived, "come sit with me."

The man flashed a broad smile. The demon-faced visors of sullen Tervola tracked him like weapons. His brother sent a dark look after him. Valther sat, leaned close, whispered, "My Lady looks radiant tonight. And ravishing. Good news?"

She flushed slightly.

The entertainment began. Musicians sounded their instruments. Escalonian dancing girls came in. Valther clapped to the music, ogled them unabashedly.

The Tervola remained stern. One departed.

Mist watched with angry eyes. She foresaw difficulties, a possible power struggle. She held the Demon Throne only by grace of these dark, grim men hiding behind obscene masks.

Did they think she would be a puppet?

She found her hand in Valther's, begging support.

Another of the Tervola departed.

She had to improve her position. How? Only something swift and savage would impress these cold old men.

The evening progressed lugubriously, fatefully, tension building with each new entertainment. Tervola continually departed.

They were sending a message she refused to heed.

Experimentally, clumsily, she responded to Valther.

More Tervola left. Piqued, she allowed Valther more liberties.

Who were they to approve or disapprove? She was the Demon Princess . . .

She drank a lot.

She forgot the war and her responsibilities, relaxed,

devoted herself to enjoyment.

In Shinsan hedonism was forbidden. From bottom to top in that chill culture each person had a position and purpose to which unswerving duty was obligated.

But she behaved like a romantic teenager, caring about nothing.

Finally, just one grim, pale-faced man remained. Valther's brother. And Turran obviously wished he were elsewhere.

The Escalonian captives, entertainers and servants, also wore expressions of desperation.

"Out!" she screamed. "All of you, out of my sight. You cringing lice!"

As Turran left, he sent his brother a look of mute appeal. But Valther was busy tickling a toe.

Damned Tervola! Let them frown behind their devil masks! She was her own woman.

Never a word was said, but, next morning, she realized everyone knew, from the mighty to the spearmen.

When the Escalonian dawn painted her pavilion with bloody rays, her unicorn was gone.

Before she could be challenged, she unleashed the assault on Tatarian, following a suggestion a helpful Valther had whispered deep in the night.

The city that had held so long collapsed in hours.

The Tervola were impressed.

v) Their heads meet, and they spark wickedness

The defense of Escalon had collapsed. Tatarian lay in ruins. Mist, though still unable to claim victory over O Shing, eyed Matayanga.

It was time the Captal decided.

Mist had come to visit often. His infatuation had grown to the proportions of the great romances. Yet he prided himself on being a hard-nosed realist. He considered facts and acted accordingly, no matter the pain.

But he had a blind spot. The child from Vorgreberg.

They had given her the name Carolan, but the nickname Kiki had attached itself. Shoptaw and Burla, her constant companions, preferred the latter. She was a bright-eyed, golden-haired imp, all giggles and bounce. She was happy, carefree, yet capable of seriousness when discussing her destiny, which the Captal had never hidden.

The old man could not have loved her more. Everyone loved her... And spoiled her. Even Mist.

The winged man brought Kiki. The Captal smiled. He no longer worried about himself, he worried about Kiki. Should he subject a child not yet six to the torments of a play for Kavelin's throne?

"It's about Aunt Mist, isn't it Papa Drake?" she asked, eyes disconcertingly big.

"Yes. The thing in Escalon's done. We've got to decide about Kavelin."

She placed her hands on his.

"We've got to figure what's best for you."

"I thought you wanted..."

"What I want isn't important. I've got Maisak. I've got Shoptaw and Burla. And you." The winged man stirred embarrassedly. The Captal reddened. He had begun to understand the costs of Vorgreberg. "But you... got to do what's best."

"Why don't you talk to Aunt Mist?"

"I know what she wants."

"Talk to her anyway. She's a nice lady." Carolan had her determined face on. "But sometimes she's spooky."

The Captal laughed. "She's that. I'll see if she's got time to visit."

She was there in hours.

The Captal generally greeted her with some small flattery. This time she looked terrible.

"What's happened?" he asked.

She collapsed into a chair. "I was a fool."

"You won, though."

"And came out too weak to go on. Drake, O Shing's pet Tervola, Wu, is a demon. A genius. They almost overthrew me..."

"I'd heard. But you came back."

"Drake, legions are fighting legions. Tervola are fighting Tervola. That's never happened before. And Escalon... The Monitor was stronger than I thought. All I won was a desert. He even got the Tear of Mimizan out before the collapse. And a quarter of Shinsan is as lifeless as Escalon. I'm losing my grip. The Tervola are having second thoughts. They would've abandoned me already, except I managed a coup in the attack on Tatarian."

Once again, it seemed, he had joined a loser.

"So you want the Gap as bride-price for their support?"

She smiled weakly. "I don't blame you. No more than the Tervola. We respect strength and ability. In your place, I'd wonder about me too."

The Captal chuckled nervously. She had read his mind.

"Can I sweeten the partnership?"

So she was weak. Desperately so. "No Escalon. No conquest outright. Hegemony and disarmament. Suzerainty without occupation..."

"A return to Empire?" she asked. "With Shinsan replacing Ilkazar?"

"Any rational man could see we need unity. The problem is questions of local sovereignty."

"And how would you enforce *my* sovereignty?"

The old man shrugged. "I'm not worried about the mules, just about loading the wagon. Agree in principle?"

"All right. We'll manage something. What about Kavelin?"

"The King's sick. He'll go soon. The scramble's about to begin. The barons are forming parties. Breitbarth looks strong. El Murid and Volstokin are interested. Which means Itaskia and Altea and Anstokin... Well, you see the possibilities. I'm sending my winged men to watch my neighbors. I should send them farther afield, to where the real plotting will take place."

"And Carolan?"

"I don't know. I want to protect her."

"So do I. But you'll need support. She's the tool you'll have to use."

"I know. I know. A quandary. That's why I asked you here. She insisted I talk to you."

"Why not ask her what she wants? She's got her feet on

the ground. She's thought about it."

Carolan wanted to be Queen.

So the Captal chose to betray his homeland for the sakes of a six-year-old and a woman who should have been his enemy.

SIX: The Mercenaries

i) A matter of discipline

"Looks just like army," said Mocker, as he and Ragnarson descended the slope of the valley where Blackfang and Kildragon had established their training camp. The River Porthune was near, and beyond it, Kendel, northernmost of the Lesser Kingdoms.

They were a week behind Blackfang. It had taken Bragi that long to conclude his business and convince Uthe that he and Dahl dared return to Elana unaccompanied. He had finally explained the situation fully, trusting Uthe's discretion. Even then Bragi had been forced to compose a long explanatory letter admonishing Elana and Bevold to cooperate with the Minister's agents.

"Uhn." Ragnarson grunted. "A baby one. Or an overgrown street gang." He had been sour for days. First, Mocker had insisted on coming south. Bragi would rather he were in charge at home. Elana was unpredictable. Bevold had no imagination. And the two were sure to feud.

His last hope of evading the Kavelin committment had evaporated when Royalist rowdies, at the gate of Itaskia's citadel, had murdered Duke Greyfells.

The shock waves were still rattling windows and walls. A quiet little war between Haroun's partisans and those of El Murid, in the ghetto, was no cause for excitement. But an assassination...

Half of Itaskia had gone into shock. The other half had gone on a witchhunt.

"Look what Reskird's recruited. Children." Ragnarson indicated a line of young swordsmen being drilled by a grizzled veteran.

"Self," Mocker observed with a chuckle, "remember boy from icy northland, big as a horse, bald-chinned..."

"That was different. My father raised me right."

"Hai!" Mocker cried. "'Raised right,' says he. As reever, arsonist, lier in ambush..."

Bragi was in no mood for banter. He didn't argue. He continued surveying the encampment. The area occupied by Kildragon's trainees pleased him. They had even put up a log stockade behind a good deep ditch.

But the Trolledyngjan camp was a despair. He had seen better among savages. This had come on recently, too. There had been no sloppiness when they had camped at his place.

"The families. We'll have to do something, or there'll be trouble. First time some girl gets caught in the puckerbushes with an Itaskian..."

"Self, am no expert... Hai! Such strange expression. Am, admittedly, expert in most things, being genius equal to girth, but even for genius of such breadth, self, all things not known. But don't tell. Public thinks fat old reprobate infallible, omniscient, near divine in wisdom."

"How about turning your omniscience to the point?"

Mocker did so, but Ragnarson paid little attention.

They entered the Trolledyngjan encampment. Ragnarson's nose rose. Trolledyngjans were notoriously undisciplined and unfastidious, but this much filth meant deep trouble and a lack of leadership.

He heard angry voices. "May get to try your suggestion."

"Uhn," the fat man grunted. He, too, had been surveying the surly faces watching from tents and wagons. "Self, will keep hand to hilt."

The voices proved to be those of Blackfang and a large,

brutish young man, arguing amidst a mass of grumbling Trolledyngjans. With Mocker's donkey in his wake, Bragi forced his mount into the press.

The onlookers moved reluctantly, with hard glares. How could Haaken have let it go this far?

Ragnarson thundered. "What the hell is this, Blackfang? A pigsty?" He studied the man facing his foster brother.

A brute. A young swine. But that was more in mind and manner than appearance. Not too bright, greedy, and a catspaw, Ragnarson guessed.

Blackfang saluted, replied, "A bit of difficulty explaining something, sir. Some folks think we ought to be raiding, not running off to some bird-in-the-bush Lesser Kingdom."

"Eh? What kind of fool are you? You recruit suicides? Settle it. Thrash the lout, get this camp cleaned up, and report to my quarters."

Blackfang's antagonist could contain himself no longer. "Who's this old swineherd muck-mouth, and where's she get off giving orders to men?" Ragnarson wore Itaskian dress. "Are we slaves to every eunuch who rides in? . . ."

Ragnarson's boot found his mouth. He looked up from the ground puzzledly, a finger feeling loosened teeth.

"Ten lashes," Bragi said. "Special consideration so it won't be said I spite the children of old enemies. But I'll hang him next time."

The man was about to spring. Discretion bit him. He frowned questioningly.

"Up, you," Ragnarson ordered. "Which of Bjorn Thorfinson's whelps are you?"

"Eh? Ragnar . . ."

"Ragnar? The gall of the man. But no matter. It's an honorable name. Wear it with honor. There's a saying, 'Like father, like son.' I hope it's not true in your case. Blackfang, somewhere there's a man with a purse full of gold. Someone who was poor when he left the north. Bring him when you report."

He nudged his mount forward. Mocker followed, grinning hugely.

ii) Child with the ways of a woman

Ragnarson had met the Trolledyngjans and Itaskians who were to be his staff. Though Kildragon had nominal control of the latter, a question of loyalties might arise. Most of the Itaskians were raw youths, but their officers and sergeants were obvious veterans, and almost as obviously the Minister's hand-picked men, detached from regular service.

But the Trolledyngjans were the pressing problem. Their leaders were solid, experienced men who knew the lay of things. The young men had never seen a real war. They wanted to plunder the countryside, called wiser heads cowards for demurring. Their exposure to Itaskian military procedures had been sketchy. Wolf-strikes by coast-reevers gave the raiders no true picture of the capacity of the attacked.

"Reskird," said Ragnarson, after a lot of useless talk, "clear your drill ground. Dig a trench down the middle, as wide and deep as you can in two hours. Arm your best men with shields and pikes. Scare up blunt arrows for the rest, and pad the tips. Blackfang will attack you in the Trolledyngjan fashion. We'll give your youngsters some confidence and knock the cockiness out of Haaken's."

Kildragon, a dour man, replied, "Two birds, eh? Show them Itaskian firepower, they'll lose interest in plunder. And we'll build some mutual respect."

"Right." To the Trolledyngjan officers, Ragnarson said, "Push the Itaskians hard. Try to break them. Straight frontal attack, no tricks. See how they stand up..."

A racket approached. Blackfang stalked in, pushing a scared Trolledyngjan. "Here's our gold man," he growled. "Caught him trying to sneak into the hills."

Ragnarson considered the youth, who had been one of Haaken's bodyguards in Itaskia. "Took you long enough, and then you didn't get the right one."

"Eh? He had it when we caught him."

"When did he get it? He was with us in Itaskia. Mocker?" The fat man nodded. "He ever give you any trouble before?"

"No."

"Where'd you get it, Wulf?"

The soldier wouldn't answer.

Blackfang drew back a fist.

"Self," said Mocker, "being accustomed to use of brain instead of fist, would suggest is time for brainwork. Who does boy have for friends? Is friend rabble-rouser? Is friend? . . ."

"Don't have no friends," Blackfang interjected. "Just that girl Astrid he's always sniffing round . . ."

"Ah?" said Mocker. "Girl? Is said, 'Look for woman.' Might same be sister of mouth-man in camp in morning? Saw same with boy on trek to Itaskia."

"Bjorn had a daughter?" Ragnarson asked. Vague recollection of a face. Young. What was it the Star Rider had said? Beware of the girl who acts like a woman? "Get her."

"Never thought about a woman," Blackfang said, leaving.

He soon returned with a howling, kicking adolescent in tow and a group of sullen youths trailing. "Where's her brother?" Ragnarson asked. "I want him here too." Ragnar appeared almost instantly. "Wulf, you and Ragnar stand back, out of the way." To Reskird, "If they move, cut them down. Girl, shut up."

The girl had been alternating threats, pleas, and calls for help.

"Blackfang, watch the door. Kill anybody who sticks his head in."

His officers stirred nervously. He was daring mutiny.

"Sit down, girl," said Ragnarson, offering his chair. "Mocker?"

The fat man grunted, began playing with an Itaskian gold piece taken from Wulf. The girl watched fearfully. Sometimes the coin seemed to vanish, but reappeared in his other hand. Over and over it turned. Droning, Bragi told his officers the tale of how her father, while young, had betrayed his father to the Pretender's followers.

The coin turned over, vanished, appeared. Ragnarson spoke of their mission in Kavelin. He talked till everyone was thoroughly bored.

Then Mocker took over whispering. He reminded the girl that she was weary, weary . . .

She had no chance. At last Mocker was satisfied. "Has been long time," he said, "but is ready. Ask questions gently."

"What's your name?" Ragnarson asked.

"Astrid Bjornesdatter."

"Are you rich, Astrid?"

"Yes."

"Very rich?"

"Yes."

"Have you been rich long?"

"No."

"Did you get rich in Itaskia?"

"Yes."

"A man gave you gold to do something?"

"Yes."

"An old man? A thin man?"

"Yes. Yes."

Ragnarson and Mocker exchanged glances. "Greyfells."

"Sorcery!" Wulf hissed. "It's sorcery . . ." Kildragon's blade touched his throat.

"Did the man want you to cause trouble? To keep your people from going to Kavelin?"

"Yes. Yes."

"Satisfies me," said Ragnarson. "You. Ragnar. Want to ask her anything?" The boy did, and showed unexpected intelligence. He followed Bragi's lead and kept his questions simple. It took but a few to convince him that he had been used.

Wulf refused his opportunity. Ragnarson didn't push. Let him keep his illusions.

"Well, gentlemen," Bragi said, "you see a problem partially resolved. My friend will make the girl forget. But what about the men? This can happen again as long as we've got camp followers. I want them left here."

After the gathering dispersed, Bragi told Kildragon, Blackfang, and the fat man, "Keep an eye on Ragnar and Wulf. I tried to plant a seed. If it takes root, they'll handle our problem with the Trolledyngjans."

iii) News from Kavelin

The sham battle had been on an hour. The Trolledyngjans were getting trounced.

"My point's been made," said Ragnarson to a runner. "The Itaskians look good. Tell Blackfang to withdraw." As the messenger departed, a dust-covered rider approached from the direction of the Porthune. He was a tall, lean man, weathered, grim, who rode spear-straight. A soldier, Ragnarson thought. A man too proud to show weariness.

"Colonel Ragnarson?" the rider asked as he came up.

"Right."

"Eanred Tarlson, Colonel, commanding the Queen's Own Guard, Kavelin. I have a letter from Haroun bin Yousif."

Ragnarson took the letter, sent a runner to prepare quarters. "Queen's Own?"

"The King was dying when I left Vorgreberg."

Ragnarson finished Haroun's brief missive, which urged that he waste no time moving south. "You came alone? With trouble brewing?"

"No. I had a squadron when I left."

"Uhm," Ragnarson grunted. "Well, you're here. Relax. Rest."

"How soon can you move?" Tarlson demanded. "You're desperately needed. The Queen had little but my regiment, and that likely to disappear if someone spreads the rumor that I'm dead."

"The problem of succession, eh? The changeling and the foreign queen."

Tarlson gave him an odd look. "Yes. How soon?"

"Not today. Tomorrow if it's desperate. If I had my

druthers, not for weeks. The men are green, not used to
working together."

"Tomorrow, then," said Tarlson, as if yielding a major
point.

Ragnarson recognized a strong-willed man who might
cause problems unless things were made clear immediately. "Colonel, I'm my own man. These men march to my
drum. I take orders only from my paymaster. Or mistress.
I appreciate the need for haste. You wouldn't have come
otherwise. But I won't be pushed."

Tarlson flashed a brief, weary smile. "Understood. I've
been there. I'd rather you took the extra days and arrived
able to fight, anyway." He glanced at the Trolledyngjan
encampment. "You're bringing families?"

"No. They're staying. Shouldn't you get some rest?
We'll start early."

"Yes, I suppose."

Ragnarson turned to greet Kildragon and Blackfang,
who were arguing as they rode up, Haaken claiming
Reskird had cheated. "Looked good. They might do if we
can get them an easy first fight. Any injuries?"

Headshakes. "Just bruises, mostly egos," said Blackfang.

"Good. We move out tomorrow. Haroun says the
arrow's in the air."

Both men claimed they needed more time.

"You can have all the time you want. On the march.
Haaken, get the families settled in the stockade."

The leading elements moved out at first light. By noon
the rearguard was over the Porthune.

An officer from Kendel's army, as if by magic,
appeared to lead them through back country, by obscure
ways, out of the sight of most eyes, to the Ruderin border,
where they were passed on to a Ruderiner for the march
down the Anstokin border to the River Scarlotti, over
which they would ferry to Altea.

Days went by. Miles and clouds of dust passed.
Ragnarson did not push the pace, but kept moving from
dawn till dusk, with only brief pauses to eat and rest the
animals, for whom the march was punishing. Cavalry
mounts were expensive. He had as yet received no
advance from Kavelin's Queen.

Ten days into the march, in Ruderin, near the northernmost finger of Anstokin, he decided it was time for a rest.

Tarlson protested. "We've got to keep moving! Every minute wasted..." Each day he grew more pessimistic, more dour. Ragnarson had tried to get to know him, but the man's anxieties got in the way. He grew ever more worried as no news came north to meet them.

Ragnarson, while his troops were involved in maintenance and training, asked Tarlson if he would care to go boar hunting. Their guide said a small but vicious wild pig inhabited the region. Tarlson accepted, apparently more to keep occupied than because he was interested. Mocker tagged along, for once deigning to mount a beast other than his donkey.

They had no luck, but Ragnarson was glad just to escape the cares of command. He had always loved the solitude of forests. These, so much like those around his grant, infected him with homesickness. For the most part they rode quietly, though Mocker couldn't stifle himself completely. He mentioned homesickness too.

Toward midafternoon Tarlson loosened up. In the course of conversation, Ragnarson found the opportunity to ask a question that intrigued him.

"Suppose we find the Queen deposed?"

"We restore her."

"Even if the usurper is supported by the Thing?"

Tarlson took a long time answering, as if he hadn't considered the possibility. "My loyalty is to the Throne, not to man or woman. But no one could manage a majority."

"Uhm." Ragnarson remained thoughtful. He hoped Haroun's scheme wouldn't put them on opposite sides. Tarlson was the only Kaveliner with any military reputation, and he clearly had the will to manage armies.

Ragnarson wrestled serious self-doubts. He had never commanded such a large force, nor one so green and ethnically mixed. He feared that, in the crunch, control would slip away.

It was nearly dark before they abandoned the hunt, never having heard a grunt.

On the way back they struck the remnants of a road.

"Probably an Imperial highway," Tarlson mused. "The legions were active here in the last years."

iv) A castle in the darkness

Darkness had fallen. There was a quarter-moon, points up, that reminded Ragnarson of artists' renderings of Trolledyngjan warships. "What warriors," he mused aloud, "go reeving in yonder nightship?"

"The souls of the damned," Tarlson replied. "They pursue the rich lands eternally, their captain's eyes fiery with greed, but the shores of the earth retreat as fast as they approach, no matter how hard they row, or how much sail they put on."

Ragnarson started. This was another side of Eanred. He had begun to fear the man was a small-minded, undereducated boor.

"Varvares Codice," said Mocker, "same being attributed to Shurnas Brankel, legend collector of pre-Imperial Ilkazar. Hai! They send fire arrows."

A half-dozen meteors streaked down the night.

"Ho! What's this?" asked Ragnarson. They had topped a rise. Something huge and dark lay in the vale below.

"Castle," said Mocker.

"Odd," said Tarlson. "The guide didn't mention any strongholds around here."

"Maybe ruin left over from Imperial times," Mocker suggested. There was hardly a place in the west not within a few hours' ride of some Imperial remnant.

They drew close enough to make out generalities. "I don't think so," said Ragnarson. "The Empire built low, blockish walls with regularly spaced square towers for enfilading fire. This's got high walls with rounded towers. And the crenallated battlement didn't become common till the last century."

Tarlson reacted much as Ragnarson had minutes before. Mocker laughed.

The road ran right into the fortress, which made no

sense. There were no lights, no watchfires, no sounds or smells of life.

"Must be a ruin," Ragnarson opined.

Curiosity had always been a weakness of Mocker's. "We see what's what, eh? Hai! Maybe find chest of jewels forgotten by fleeing tenants. Pot of gold buried during siege, waiting to jump into hands of portly investigator. Secret passage with skeletons of discarded paramours of castle lord, rings still on finger bones. Maybe dungeon mausoleum full of ancestors buried with riches ripe for plucking by intrepid grave robbers . . ."

"Ghoul!" Tarlson snapped.

"Pay him no mind," said Ragnarson. "Weird sense of humor. Just wants to poke around."

"We should get back."

He was right, but Ragnarson, too, was intrigued. "Like the old days, eh, Lard Bottom?"

Mocker exploded gleefully, "Hai! Truth told. Getting old, we. Calcification of brainpan setting in. We go, pretending twentieth birthday coming still, and no sense, not care if dawn comes. Immortals, we. Nothing can harm."

That was the way they had been, Ragnarson reflected.

"We explore, hey, Hulk?" Mocker stopped his mount beneath the teeth of a rusty portcullis.

"Go ahead," said Tarlson. "I'm going to get some sleep."

"Right. See you in the morning, then." Ragnarson followed Mocker into a small courtyard.

He got the feeling he had made a mistake. There was something wrong with the place. It seemed to be *waiting* . . . And a little surreal, as if he could turn suddenly and find nothing behind him.

Overactive imagination, he told himself. Came of remembering what they had gotten into in the old days.

Mocker dismounted and entered a door. Ragnarson hurried to catch him.

It was dark as a crypt inside. He pursued Mocker's shuffling footsteps, cursing himself for not having brought a light. He bumped into something large and yielding. Mocker squawked like a kicked hen.

"Do something," Bragi growled, "but don't block the road."

"Self, am listening. And trying not to be trampled by lead-footed stumbler about without sense to bring light. Am wondering about sound heard over stampede rumble of feet of same."

"Let's go back, then. We can come by tomorrow."

Logic had no weight with Mocker. He moved ahead.

So gradually that they did not immediately realize it, light entered their ken. Before they had advanced a hundred feet, they could see dimly, as through heavy fog at false dawn.

"Something's wrong here," said Ragnarson. "I smell sorcery. We'd better get out before we stir something up."

"Pusillanimous dullard," Mocker retorted. "In old days friend Hulk would have led charge."

"In the old days I didn't have any sense. Thought you'd grown up some, too."

Mocker shrugged. He no longer was anxious to go on. "Just to end of passage," he said. "Then we follow example of Tarlson."

The corridor ended in a blank wall. What was the sense of a passage that went nowhere, that had no doors opening off it?

"We'd better go," said Ragnarson. The sourceless light was bright now. He turned. "Huh?" His sword jumped into his hand.

Blocking their withdrawal was a curtain of darkness, as if someone had taken a pane of starless night and stretched it from wall to wall.

Mocker slid round him and probed the darkness with his blade. A deep thrust got results. Laughter like the cackling of a mad god.

"Woe!" Mocker cried. "Such petty end for great mind of age, caught like stupidest mouse in trap..." He charged the darkness, sword preceeding him.

"You idiot!" Ragnarson bellowed. He muttered, "What the hell?" when his companion seemed to slide out of existence as he hit the blackness.

"Might as well." He hit the darkness seconds behind the fat man.

He felt like he was tumbling down the entire well of eternity, rolling aimlessly through a storm of color and sound underlaid by the whispering of wicked things. It went on and on and on and ... Without breaking stride he entered a vast, poorly lighted chamber.

That room, or hall, was an assault on rationality. The air was overpoweringly foul. From all-surrounding, shadowed mists came rustlings, and for a moment he thought he saw a manlike, winged thing with the head of a dog, then a small, apelike dwarf with prodigious fangs. Everything seemed unstable, shifting, except the floor, which was of jet, and a huge black throne carved with exceptionally hideous designs. They reminded him of reliefs he had seen in the temples of Arundeputh and Merthregul at Gundgatchcatil. Yet these were worse, as if carved by hands washed more deeply in evil.

Mocker, sword in hand, prowled round that throne. "What is it?" Ragnarson asked, seldom having seen the fat man so upset.

"Shinsan."

They were trapped fools indeed.

The mists stirred. An old man stepped forth. "Good evening," he said. "I trust you speak Necremnen? Good."

The old man turned to the throne, knelt, touched forehead to floor, muttered something Ragnarson couldn't understand. For an instant new mists gathered there. An incredibly beautiful woman wavered in their depths. She nodded and disappeared. The old man rose and turned.

"My Lady honors me. But to business. You're going where My Lady wishes you wouldn't. Kavelin is already too complex. Go home."

Ragnarson retorted, "Simple as that, eh? Might interfere with your plans, so we should turn back?"

"Yes."

"I can't do that." His fingers, in deaf-mute signs, flashed a message to Mocker. "I've given my word."

"I've tried to be reasonable. My Lady won't tolerate disobedience."

"Terrible. Hate to disappoint her."

Mocker suddenly lunged, sword reaching.

A silvery filament lightninged from the old man's hand, brushed Mocker's cheek. The fat man collapsed. By then Ragnarson was moving in. The thread darted out again. Bragi tangled it on his blade, ripped it from the old man's grasp, continued to bore in. \

The sorcerer sprang straight up and disappeared in the mists overhead. Bragi, mystified, tried a few desultory sword swipes that got no result, then knelt to check Mocker's pulse.

A shimmering, sparkling dust drifted down upon him. When the first scintillating flakelet touched his skin, he tumbled across his friend.

SEVEN: Into Kavelin

i) High sorcery

Ragnarson woke with a headache like that memorializing a week-long drunk. The demoniac whispering of his dream-haunts resolved themselves into the mutterings of Mocker.

Their cell was a classic, even to slimy stone walls. Beyond the rusty-barred door stood the winged thing, dog-teeth bared, a glowing dagger in hand. Other creatures stirred behind it, squat things heavily clothed, with faces like owls. The winged man opened the door.

Six owl-faces pounced on Mocker, bound him before Bragi reacted. Bellowing like a thwarted bull in rut, ignoring the agony in his head, he grabbed two, smashed them together, then used his fists on their faces. A neck went *snap!* He lifted the second overhead, hurled it skull-first against the floor.

A tide of weird creatures washed in. He went down. In moments he was trussed and being carried away. He tried counting turns and steps, but it was hopeless. Not only did his head hurt too much, his captors kept jabbing him in retribution for his attack.

They reached a vast room. It might have been the one

where he and Mocker had been received, with the mists removed. It was huge. Every fixture was black. The monsters dumped him onto a stone table. He heard voices. Forcing his head around, he saw the old man arguing with the woman in the mists. The old man suddenly slumped in defeat.

The mist-woman faded. The man turned, selected a bronze dagger from a collection on a table, faced Ragnarson, raised his arms, began to chant.

Ragnarson noticed a pentagram chalked on the floor. A conjuration! He and Mocker were to be delivered to some Thing from Outside. He struggled against his bonds. The porters ignored him, nervously concentrated on their master.

A darkness animate became pregnant and gave birth to itself in the pentagram. The sorcerer stopped singing. Sighs escaped the creatures around Ragnarson.

Bragi shouted, hoping to disturb the wizard. It did no good. Furious with frustration, because his bonds would not yield, he performed the only act of defiance left him. He spit in the eye of one of the owl-faces.

It jumped as if hornet-stung, staggered, flailed its arms. One crossed the barrier of the pentagram.

It withered swiftly, blackened. The creature screamed in soul-deep terror. The sorcerer tried to pull it out, then to chant the demon down. Too late. The owl-face was lost. The darkness in the pentagram gradually sucked it in.

The remainder of the old man's servants fled, shrieking. Their rush washed against and overturned the table where Bragi lay. He hit the floor hard, groaned, found one hand had been wrenched free. And not five feet away lay the sorcerer's dagger, that he had dropped when he had tried to save his servant. Bragi slithered to the blade, cut his bonds, then did likewise for a Mocker whose eyes were wide with terror.

A finger of blackness began to leak from the pentagram where the owl-face had broken its barrier.

The old man had disappeared again.

Staggering weak, Bragi and Mocker prepared to pursue his example. Mocker's gaze fell on a table where their weapons lay. He moved to get them. His fat man's run would have been amusing in other circumstances. He passed perilously near the pentagram, but the darkness within remained preoccupied with its victim.

It finished with the owl-face as Bragi and Mocker considered how best to escape, began slithering from the pentagram, writhing like a cat getting through a small hole.

"Self," said Mocker, "am of opinion any place elsewhere is better than here."

"Where's here?" Ragnarson asked. "Maybe I could figure where I'm going if I knew where I'm starting."

"Friend Bear doesn't want to know," Mocker replied.

"Bullfeathers. If you know, tell me."

Mocker shrugged. "Are in small quill of Shinsan poked through cloth of universe into Ruderin. Are in two places at same time, Ruderin valley and small frontier castle in Pillars of Ivory on Shinsan border with Sendelin Steppe. Could be long walk home if luck turns bad."

"Turns bad?" Ragnarson snorted. "Can't be worse than it is." The darkness still confined had grown visibly smaller. "I vote we walk while we talk."

The darkness chose that moment to strike. They managed to evade it and flee.

The flight was an eon of fear, of oxygen-starved lungs and already punished muscles refusing to be tortured more but going on all the same. Always close behind was a snakelike black tendril.

Something came hurtling at them. Ragnarson grabbed it, Mocker stabbed it, and together they sacrificed it to the tendril. Only after the darkness began surrounding it did they see that it was another of the old sorcerer's servants.

Chance eventually brought them back to the point where their flight had begun. The demon had evacuated the chamber completely. The uproar it had caused echoed from corridors opening on the room.

Feeling momentarily secure, Ragnarson prowled round the throne. "Hey," he said suddenly. "I think I've found a way out." He had noticed that, from a certain angle, he could vaguely discern a rectangle of darkness that obscured the black pillars and walls behind it. It seemed the same size as the curtain they had plunged into getting here.

"Self, would be grateful for same," said Mocker. "Magic binding two localities together is unraveling."

For some time there had been a gentle trembling in the floor. Ragnarson hadn't paid it any heed, thinking it the demon rumbling around. "What if? . . ."

"If fool-headed venturers don't find exit, then long walk home from Shinsan for same," Mocker replied.

"Here, then. Looks like the way we came in." He ran at the rectangle. The whirling, kaleidoscopic sensations returned. After a stench-filled eternity he stepped into the corridor where they had originally been entrapped. Mocker appeared an instant behind him.

They were still trapped.

"Make yourself comfortable," said Ragnarson, sitting with his back to a wall and his sword across his lap. "I'm not going back through that."

"Self, would prefer dying in west, too," said Mocker. "Though in Ruderin back country of own stupidity? Not even battle to end heroic life with heroic death, lots of witnesses to final bravery? Woe!"

Stone grumbled around them. Dust fell from the ceiling.

"Sounds bad," said Ragnarson.

"Crushed to death. Ignominious end for great mind. Am fool. Friend should have pointed out same, dragged fat idiot to camp kicking and screaming if needful."

"Is the light getting weaker?"

"Verity. Magicks devolving. Portal to Shinsan weakening also."

Indeed it was, getting fluttery around the edges and occasionally showing a swift-running shot of color.

"Maybe we can get out. If the place don't fall down first."

"Maybe so."

The curtain winked out of existence. They found themselves staring into the startled faces of several mercenaries. "Ghosts!" one cried.

"Boo!" said Mocker, then cackled madly. "Out of way. Everybody's out of way before very important head, head of self, gets mashed by falling castle."

Fifteen minutes later they were astride their mounts, atop a hill, watching the castle collapse. Fogs of darkness engulfed its base, darkness untouched by the morning sun. A plume of that blackness, like smoke, rose against the dawn and bent its head eastward. The destruction proceeded in unnatural silence.

"Going home," said Mocker.

"We'll hear from them again," Ragnarson replied.

Tarlson and Blackfang, who had been working round the rim of the valley, arrived. "You're lucky I mentioned the castle to the guide," said Eanred. "He said there wasn't any such place, so I scared up a rescue party."

"I'm grateful," said Ragnarson.

They talked at some length. When Ragnarson mentioned the winged man, Tarlson grew silent and withdrawn.

ii) Passage to Kavelin

The march to the Altean ferry was disconcerting. A regiment of Anstokin infantry paced them along the Ruderin border, making no overt moves but slowing their progress by forcing them to remain battle-ready. Crossing the River Scarlotti while Anstokin's force maneuvered nearby was a laborious business that took two days.

Tarlson grew jumpy as a cat. Still there were no messages from Kavelin, just rumors relayed by Altean officers. Those were not good. Skirmishing had broken out all over the kingdom. The Queen still held Vorgreberg, but the populace were being whipped up by a dozen propagandists. Lord Breitbarth, a cousin of the dead King and the strongest pretender, was assembling a major force at Damhorst, near the Kavelin-Altean border, where Ragnarson was expected to cross. Damhorst lay on the great eastern trade route, which linked Vorgreberg with the Altean capital and the coastal city-kingdoms.

Ragnarson, too, grew concerned at the paucity of news. He had expected to hear from Haroun by now. All he knew was what he had coaxed from the Alteans. One went so far as to loan him a map of the border country, a violation of his orders. Though Kendel, Ruderin, and Altea covertly supported bin Yousif's scheme, openly none could do more than grant passage to mercenaries.

There was a point, Ragnarson saw while studying the map, where the borders of Anstokin, Volstokin, Kavelin and Altea all came together. It was hilly country, almost without roads.

"What I'm thinking about," said Ragnarson, meeting with Blackfang, Kildragon, and Tarlson, "is following the highway to this town, Staake, so it looks like I'm committed to it. Then I'll abandon the wagons, make a night march north, and enter Kavelin through the hills above this Lake Berberich. I'll swing around and take Breitbarth in the flank. Assuming he's surprised. Mocker'll let us know."

Mocker had vanished at the ferry.

Tarlson paced, mumbled, shook his head. "Your men are green. They won't stand up to it."

"Maybe not. Now's a good time to find out. I've never had much use for positional warfare."

"Bin Yousif's influence."

Bragi studied Tarlson thoughtfully. How much did he know? Or suspect?

"Possibly. I've followed his career."

"As you said when we met, it's your command. I'll help any way I can."

"What I want is guides. Scouts. Woodsmen for outrunners."

"That's Marena Dimura country. They're touchy people. They could go either way."

"How do they stand on Breitbarth?"

"They'd like his head. He hunts them like animals."

"Lesser of two evils, then. Ride over and sign them up. Promise them Breitbarth if we catch him."

"A noble? You'd buy those savages with the life of a noble?"

"Just another man to me." He was puzzled by Tarlson's

incredulity. Eanred didn't hold the Nordmen in high esteem. "I'm not one of your Kaveliner chevaliers. War's serious business. I fight to win."

"But you'll unite the Nordmen against you."

"They're unanimous already: the Queen, my employer, has to go. They're all against me anyway." He felt like saying more, but held his tongue. They might be enemies some day.

"All right. I'll go."

Reliable news awaited them at Staake, little of it good. None had come before because Baron Breitbarth had intercepted all the messengers. But one of Tarlson's men finally reached Ragnarson.

Breitbarth had convinced several barons that disposing of Ragnarson was the chief business at hand. He had gathered twenty-two hundred men at Damhorst. Further, his claim to Kavelin's crown had been recognized by Volstokin, which threatened intercession. There were rumors of a pact between Breitbarth and Volstokin's King. And, grimmest news of all, Breitbarth had seized the money meant for Ragnarson's mercenaries.

From Vorgreberg the news was better. The Queen's Own had remained loyal, and the Queen herself had managed to still unrest by going to the people in the streets. But bands of partisans had begun raiding in the country.

And there was a letter from Haroun, that came to him he knew not how. It appeared in his tent while he was out.

It covered the same information, in greater detail, and said more about Volstokin.

Not only had King Vodicka made an agreement with Breitbarth, he had made another with El Murid. After the dust had settled and Breitbarth had been crowned, Volstokin, with aid from El Murid, would occupy Kavelin...

After reflection, Bragi called Blackfang. "Make sure there's plenty of wood for the watchfires. I want them kept burning all night." The Kavelin border was just two miles away, and Damhorst only ten beyond. If his ruse were detected, Breitbarth would soon know. He needed every minute.

Moonrise came early, just after nightfall, but it was little help, being a barely visible slice.

"Has Tarlson shown yet?" he asked. He had Alteans to lead him to the border, but after that he would be on his own. Unless Tarlson turned up.

He didn't. They had to start. It took four hours to reach the border, every minute of which Ragnarson grew more worried. The men performed well enough, moving excitedly but quietly. For them it was still an adventure.

Tarlson met them at the border. "They'll help," he said, sounding surprised. "Didn't have to promise anything. Said our victory would be reward enough."

"Uhm." Bragi thought he sensed the touch of Haroun. What had bin Yousif promised?

"But we've got a problem. Two thousand Volstokiners are camped just north of here, right over their border. Rumor is they'll move to support Breitbarth if he needs it."

Ragnarson wondered if he were entering a trap.

As the night waned, his patrols reached Lake Berberich. Going slowed because of heavy fog. He didn't know whether to curse or praise it. It slowed him, but concealed him.

A Marena Dimura runner, badly winded, came sprinting up the column. Tarlson translated.

"Volstokin's moving. Their vanguard's only a mile behind us..."

iii) Saltimbanco

Could an oddly dressed, short fat man on a donkey, remarkable for his inability to handle any language properly, slide unnoticed through a hundred miles of Altean farmlands, cross a heavily patrolled border, penetrate forty miles of soldier-dense Kavelin, then appear as if by magic on the cavern route from Vorgreberg to the west? Mocker had his doubts. But also his years of experience. He dropped out of sight at the

Scarlotti ferries and reappeared days later at the hamlet of Norr, well behind the Kavelin-Altean border.

Mocker arrived after the men had already gone to the fields. The women were gathering at the well. Even the youngest was a tangle-haired mess, but they were Wessons and clean.

"Hai!" the fat man cried, trying to look pathetic and harmless. "Such visions eyes of poor old wanderer have not seen in age. Hand of Queen of Beauty fell heavily on town." Suspicious eyes turned his way. "Where are menfolk? In land of humble traveler, self, husbands never stray from sprites like these." He tried not to wrinkle his nose as a crone smiled and shifted a babe from breast to wrinkled breast.

"But wait. Must observe proprieties. Must introduce self lest same be suspect for wickedry. Am called Saltimbanco. Am student philosophic of Grand Master Istwan of Senske in Matayanga. Am sent west on quest for knowledge, to seek same at academies in Hellin Daimiel." Children too small to work gathered around him. He did a ventriloquism trick and made the donkey ask for a drink. That frightened some women and disarmed others. Then he asked a meal for himself, for which he offered what he claimed was his last copper, and while he ate told several outrageous lies about the shape of the earth. He then traveled on.

He repeated the performance in every hamlet till he reached Damhorst, thus building himself a small reputation. It was a hurry-up specter of his usual meticulous preparation. He hoped that in the disruption no one would have time to check his back trail.

Damhorst was a large town with a substantial castle atop a tall hill. As happened where armies gathered, leeches were common. One more wouldn't be noticed. A common ground at town's center was crowded by the tents of whores, ale sellers, a tattoo artist, fortune-tellers, amulet sellers, and the like. Saltimbanco would fit like a fish in water.

He arrived early. Few of his colleagues were stirring, but he quickly learned that Bragi was approaching Staake. Mumbling, he spread a rug where he would be out of traffic, yet could watch everything.

"Identical spot." He chuckled. A long time ago, when he really had been coming west, he had paused here to bilk a few Damhorsters. "And same props. Should have thrown away, Nepanthe said. Might need someday, self replied. Hai! Here is husband of same, in business at old stand." Around him he spread a collection of arcana that included bleached apes' skulls and bones from little-known eastern animals, moldy books, and glass vials filled with nasty concoctions. "So many years. Am getting old. But bilking widows hard work even for youngest, virilest man." He chuckled again. He had made his first fortune in Damhorst, by making promises to a lusty young widow named Kersten Heerboth, and had gambled it away in Altea.

He settled against a wall, nodded sleepily. Occasionally, when a rider or lady in a litter passed, he would lift his head to call desultorily, "Hai! Great Lady," or Lord, "before you sits mighty thaumaturge out of mysterious, easternmost east, with secrets of life as unlocked by mightiest of mighty eastern necromancers. Have gold-rare vials of water of fountain of youth, to suppliment beauty of already most beautiful damsels of glorious Damhorst. Have potation guaranteed to banish wrinkles forever. Have cream to end eternally ghost of whiskers on great ladies' lips. Husband getting shiny on top? Have secretest dust, made at midnight full moon by Mata-yangan magicians, heretofore unseen west of Necremnos, guaranteed to restore hair on statue. Just mix same with blood of Escalonian snow snake, only furry snake in world, and will correct same. Snake blood also available here, prepared by adepts of bearded turtle cult deep in darkest heart of Escalon." And so forth.

It was river water, mud, and the like, but there had been a time when he had made a living selling it to ladies on the downhill side of thirty.

Near noon a shadow fell on his lap, into which he stared sleepily. He looked up into one of the nastiest faces he had ever seen. It was scarred, one-eyed, neither clean-shaven nor bearded, and wore a grin with several teeth missing and the rest rotten. Before he could say a word, the man left.

"Derran One-Eye," he muttered. "Hired blade of friend Haroun." He looked around quickly, thought he saw a familiar back vanish round a corner a block distant. Haroun? Here? He was tempted to follow. But Haroun would contact him if necessary.

Later, he decided Derran's appearance was an ill omen he should have heeded. He should have gathered his props and fled, and damn finding out what Breitbarth was up to.

Things soured that afternoon. A lady came by, a lady getting a bit paunchy and looking more than a bit wealthy. She appeared a certain victim. Did he still have the true touch? He accepted the challenge.

"Hai! Great Lady, shadow of Goddess of Love and Beauty on Mundane plane, glow of desire, harken to words of acolyte of greatest mage of east, self. Am in possession of one only packet rarest of rare herbs of Escalon, well-known but impossible of finding amantea, famous to corners of world for efficacy of treatment of teeny, tiny bit less than perfect waistlines..."

"It's him!" the woman shrieked. "And he hasn't changed a word. Harlin, Flotron, seize him."

The armed men who had been walking before and behind her sedan, puzzled, started toward the fat man.

"Woe!" Mocker cried, stumbling to his feet. "Of all ill fortunes," he shouted at the sky, "of all potential evils..." He shook a fist, gathered the skirts of his robe, and ran.

He had been seated in one position too long. Kersten's bravos overhauled him. "Self, should have stayed home," he moaned as they dragged him back. "Should have listened to Nepanthe. Should have stayed pig farmer and mud grubber. But evil gods, maybe wicked sorcerer, lured poor foolish self to fateful appointment..."

"You've been a long time delivering those emeralds," the woman said.

"O Light of Life, Doe Eyes, Dove's Breast, humblest of humble cowards encravens self. In past time, still remembered with great joy as happiest hour of otherwise miserable life, while returning from goldsmith, self was set upon by rogues. Fought like lion, armed with love, breaking bones, maiming, leaving five, six crippled for life. But dagger thrust ended resistance. Still have gruesome scar on fundament, result of same . . ."

"Thrash him, boys, before he breaks my heart by telling me how he couldn't possibly face me after losing all my money."

Harlan and Flotron tried to follow orders, but Mocker never accepted thrashings meekly. He got the best of it, briefly, with tricks that would have embarrassed Derran One-Eye. But he got no chance to escape. Kersten carried more weight than avoirdupois. Damhorsters by the dozen piled on. Soon he found himself being hustled to the castle and its dungeon.

There he learned things he feared he would never pass on to Bragi—because the grimmest news was that Kersten had married Baron Breitbarth.

Hour after hour, day after day, he sat on the straw-covered floor and mumbled to himself about his stupidity. When self-pity grew boring, he wondered how Bragi was doing. Well, he trusted. His companions in durance assured him that their turnkeys wouldn't be so tight-lipped and sour were things going the Baron's way.

iv) First blood

"Haaken! Reskird! Close it up! Don't worry about noise. They know we're here. Move it! They're on our ass. Eanred, ask him what's ahead."

"He came from behind."

"He knows the country, doesn't he?"

Tarlson talked with the scout.

"The lake, he says. A talus beach on the right, narrow, along the lakeside. Hills and some bluffs on the left. Very rugged, bushy country, full of ravines, but not high."

"What about this fog? Is it common? How long will it last?"

Questions and answers, questions and answers. It went so slow. "Haaken. Reskird." He gave orders.

The Trolledyngjan infantry, which had been marching at the rear, began double-timing forward. The Itaskians crowded the edge of the road till they were thoroughly mixed.

"Reskird!" Ragnarson bellowed, "get those horses back. I want contact within the hour." He galloped to the head of the column where Blackfang was replacing the vanguard with heavily armed horsemen. "Hurry it up, damn it. If the Volstokiners knew we were coming, so did Breitbarth. He'll be moving north."

Back down the line he galloped, shouting, "Move it! Move it!" at every officer he saw. Dozens of pale, tense young faces ghosted past in the mist. He saw no smiles now, heard no laughter. It had stopped being an adventure. "Tarlson! Where are you? Stick close. And keep your scout. I want to know when we get to the steepest hillsides." By the time he reached the column's rear, Kildragon and the light horse, with a platoon of bowmen, had faded back.

Soon he had done all he could, and was considering prayer. He had fifteen hundred men sandwiched between two superior, better rested, better trained forces—though as yet he had no idea where Breitbarth was. This was not the easy battle he had wanted for blooding.

Trumpets sounded in the distance. Kildragon had made contact.

On the column's right, only yards away but invisible in the mist, the lake waters lapped gently against the shore.

"Here," Tarlson said at last.

"To your left!" Ragnarson shouted. "Upslope. Move it!"

The soldiers began climbing.

The hills, barely tall enough to be called such, rose above the mist. In the dawnlight Ragnarson arranged his troops in strong clumps on their lakeward faces.

He hoped the mist would not burn off too soon.

Reskird's party soon passed below, invisible, raising a clatter, and moments later were followed by a strong force of cavalry. Ragnarson signaled his officers to hold fire.

The mist had begun to thin by the time the enemy main force moved to where Ragnarson wanted them. He could discern the vague dark shapes of mounted officers hurrying their infantry companies . . . He gave the signal.

Arrows sleeted into the mist. Cries of surprise and pain answered them. Ragnarson counted a minute, during which thousands of arrows fled his bows, then signaled a charge. The Trolledyngjans led, shaking the hills with their warcries.

Ragnarson leaned forward in his saddle, wearily, and awaited results.

The Volstokiners had been in good spirits, confident of victory. The sudden rain of death had stunned them. They could see no enemies. And while trying to form up over the dead and wounded, the Trolledyngjans hit them like an avalanche of wolves.

The fog cleared within the hour. Little but carnage remained. The surviving Volstokiners had run into the water. Some, trying to swim away, had drowned. Ragnarson's archers were using heads for targets. Trolledyngjans on captured horses were splashing about, chopping heads. The water was scarlet.

"Won't you take prisoners?" Tarlson asked. He spoke not a word of praise.

"Not yet. They'd just go home, re-arm, and come back. I hope this'll put Volstokin out of the picture."

A messenger from Blackfang arrived. The commander of the Volstokin vanguard, some four hundred men, stunned, had asked terms after only a brief skirmish.

"All right," said Ragnarson, "they can have their lives and shoes. The enlisted men. Strip them and send them packing."

Below, his men, tired of slaughter, were allowing surrender. "Let's see what we've caught." He wanted to get down there before there were disputes over loot. The Volstokiners had even brought a bevy of carts and wagons full of camp followers.

He dismounted and walked slowly through the carnage. His own casualties were few. In places the Volstokiners were heaped. Luck had ridden with him again. He paused a moment beside Ragnar Bjornson—no older than he had been in his first battle—who grinned through the pain of a wound. "Some folks will do anything to get out of walking," Bragi said, resting a hand on the youth's shoulder. Someone had said the same to him long ago.

It was terribly quiet. It always seemed that way afterward, as if the only sound left in the world was the cawling of the ravens.

A dead man caught his eye. Something odd about him. He paused. Too dark for Volstokin. An aquiline nose. Haroun had been right. El Murid had advisers in Volstokin.

He shook his head sadly. This little backwater kingdom was becoming the focus of a lot of intrigue.

Haaken came in with thirty prisoners and hundreds of heavily laden horses. "Got some odd ones here, Bragi," he said, indicating several dusky men.

"I know. El Murid's. Kill them. One by one. See if the weakest will tell you anything." The remainder he had herded together with officers already captured.

Volstokin had lost nearly fifteen hundred men while Bragi had had sixty-one killed. Had his people been more experienced, he thought, even fewer would have been lost. It had been a perfect ambush.

"What now?" Tarlson asked.

"We bury our dead and divide the spoils."

"And then? There's still Lord Breitbarth."

"We disappear. Got to let the men digest what they've done. Right now they think they're invincible. They've got to realize they haven't faced a disciplined enemy. And we'll need time to let the news spread. May swing some support to the Queen."

"And to Lord Breitbarth. Hangers-back would join him to make sure of you. They've got to keep the Crown up for grabs."

"I know. But I want to avoid action for a few weeks. The men need rest and training. Haaken! See the Marena Dimura get shares." He had noticed the scouts, as ragged and bloody as any of his troops, lurking about the fringes, eyeing plunder uncertainly. One, who was supposed to be a man of importance, seemed enthralled by a brightly painted wagon filled with equally painted but terrified women. "Give the old man the whore wagon."

That proved a providential act. It brought him warning, next day, of a party of Breitbarth's horses ranging far ahead of the Baron. In a brisk skirmish he took two hundred prisoners, killed another hundred, and sent the remainder to their commander in a panic. Tarlson said Breitbarth relied heavily on his knights and was a cautious sort likely to withdraw after the setback.

He did so. And more barons rallied to Damhorst. Breitbarth's force swelled to three thousand.

The westward movement of baronial forces left partisans from the under-classes free to slaughter one another elsewhere. More and more Marena Dimura gravitated toward Ragnarson, who remained in the hill country near the Volstokin border, moving camp every few days. The natives kept him informed of Breitbarth's actions.

Those amounted to patrols in force and a weekly sally north a day's march, followed by a day's bivouac, then a withdrawal into Damhorst.

Ragnarson began to worry about Mocker. He should have heard from the fat man by now.

Eanred left him, declaring it was time to resume his command. The Queen was under little pressure, but rumor had marauders riding to the suburbs of Vorgreberg. That had to stop.

It was now an open secret that Breitbarth held the money intended for Bragi's men, but they, fat on loot and self-confidence, weren't grumbling. Everyone told everyone else that the Colonel would take them down to Damhorst and get it back.

EIGHT: Campaign Against Rebellion

i) In flight

The news the Marena Dimura brought caused Ragnarson
to grow increasingly unsettled. Breitbarth grew stronger
by the day. His numbers reached four thousand, many
heavily armed knights. The Baron's sallies became more
daring. Ragnarson's patrols came under increasing
pressure. He had added four hundred men to his force,
but they were Marena Dimura and Wessons without
training. He used them as guides and raiders.

He began to fear Breitbarth would split his force and
move against Vorgreberg.

During his examination of the country toward
Damhorst he had found the place where he wanted to do
battle. It was on the north side of a dense forest belonging
to Breitbarth himself. It began near the Ebeler a dozen
miles northeast of Damhorst. Roads ran round both
sides, from Damhorst to the town and castle of
Bodenstead, but the western route was the shortest and
likeliest way Breitbarth would come to relieve Bodenstead.

This was gently rolling country. A lightly wooded ridge
ran from Bodenstead northwest a mile to the hamlet of

Ratdke, overlooking plains on either side. From Bodenstead through the forest ran a hunting trail, unsuitable for Breitbarth's knights, along which Ragnarson could flee if the worst happened. North of the western route were thick apple orchards on ground too soft for heavy cavalry. The baron would have to come at him through a narrow place, under his bows.

But even the best-laid plans, and so forth.

To taunt Breitbarth, Ragnarson brought his main force south, moving swift as the news of his coming, laying a trail of destruction from one Nordmen castle to the next. He met surprisingly little resistance. The knights and lesser nobility who remained in their fiefs showed a preference for surrender to siege. The fires of burning castles and towns bearded the horizons as Ragnarson's forces spread out to glean the richest loot.

At first he thought Breitbarth was practicing Fabian tactics, but each prisoner he interviewed, and each report he received, further convinced him that the Baron was paralyzed by indecision.

His train and troops became so burdened with plunder that he made a serious miscalculation. Hitherto he had kept the Ebeler, a deep, sluggish tributary of the Scarlotti, between himself and Breitbarth. But at the insistence of his followers, who wanted to get their loot to safekeeping with the men he had left at Staake, he crossed the river at Armstead, a mile from Altea and just twelve from Damhorst. It took two days to clear the narrow ford. Breitbarth missed a great opportunity.

But the Baron didn't remain quiescent long. When Bragi marched east into the wine-growing country on which the Baron's wealth was based, Breitbarth came out of Damhorst in a fury.

Whether Breitbarth had planned this Ragnarson wasn't sure, but he did know that he had gotten himself into a trap. This was relatively flat country, clear, ideal for Breitbarth's knights. He had nothing with which to face those. Even the fury of his Itaskian bows wouldn't break a concerted charge across an open plain.

He found the eastern Ebeler fords closed and had no time to force them. Breitbarth was close behind, his troops raising dust on all the east-running roads. There was nothing to do but run ahead of him.

Breitbarth gained ground. His forces were unburdened by loot, of which Bragi's men had already re-amassed tons, and his men were fresh. In a few days his patrols were within eyeshot of Ragnarson's rearguard.

He was in the richest wine country now, and the vineyards, with the hedgerows around them, reduced the speed he could make by compelling him to stay on the road.

"Haaken," he said as they rose on their fourth morning of flight and saw dust already rising in the west, "we don't run after today."

"But they've got us three to one..."

"I know. But the more we run, the worse the odds. Find me a place to make a stand. Maybe they'll offer terms." He had grown pessimistic, blamed himself for their straits.

Just before noon Blackfang returned and reported a good place not far ahead, a hillside vineyard where Breitbarth's knights would have rough going. There was a town called Lieneke in the way, but it was undefended and the inhabitants were scattering.

Haaken had chosen well. The hill was the steepest Ragnarson had seen in days, hairy with large grapevines that could conceal his men, and the only clear access for horsemen was the road itself, which climbed in switchbacks and was flanked by tall, thick shrubberies. Moreover, the plain facing the hill was nearly filled by Lieneke, which would make getting troops in formation difficult. Ragnarson raised his banners at the hillcrest.

The position had disadvantages. Though he anchored his flanks on a wood at his right and a ravine on his left, neither could more than slow a determined attack. He worried.

He stationed every man who could handle a bow in the vineyards and behind the hedges. The rest he kept at the crest of the hill, in view from below, including the recruits gathered in Kavelin. He feared those, if committed, would flee under pressure and panic the bowmen. Haaken he gave command of the left, Reskird the right. He retained control of the men on the crest.

Breitbarth appeared before Ragnarson completed his dispositions, but remained on the outskirts of Lieneke. Troops began piling up in the town.

Late in the afternoon a rider came up under a flag of truce, said, "My Lord, Baron Breitbarth wishes terms."

So, Ragnarson thought, the man isn't a complete fool. "I want the surrender of himself and one hundred of his knights, and his oath that no vassal of his will again stand in rebellion against the Queen. Ransoms can be arranged later."

The messenger was taken aback. At last he blurted, "Terms for your surrender."

Ragnarson chuckled. "Oh. I thought he'd come to turn himself in. Well, no point you wasting your trip. Let's hear them."

Bragi was to return all plunder, surrender himself and his officers to the mercy of Breitbarth, and his men were to accept service in Breitbarth's forces for the duration of the unrest in Kavelin.

They weren't the sort of terms usually offered mercenaries. They meant death for Bragi and his officers. No one ransomed mercenaries. He had to fight. But he kept up negotiations till dark, buying time while his men dug trenches and raised ramparts along their flanks. Breitbarth showed no inclination to surround the position. Perhaps he expected a diplomatic victory. More likely, he just did not see.

Night brought drizzling rain. It made the men miserable, but Bragi cheerful. The hill would be treacherous for horsemen.

Dawn came, a bright, clear, hot summer's morning. Breitbarth ordered his forces. Ragnarson did the same.

The Baron sent a final messenger. As the white flag came up the hill, Bragi told Haaken, "I'd better get this going before somebody down there suffers a stroke of smarts." Breitbarth, confident in his numbers and knights, had made no effort to surround him or get on his flanks.

The terms offered were no better. Bragi listened patiently, then replied, "Tell the Baron that if he won't come surrender, I'll come down and make him." The negotiations had given him enough insight into Breitbarth to anticipate that the challenge, from a ragtag hire-sword, would throw him into a rage. These Kaveliners, even his Marena Dimura, were bemused by chivalry and nobility. It was a blind spot he meant to exploit mercilessly.

ii) Second blood

The baronial forces stirred. At the crest of the hill, Bragi and a handful of messengers, behind the ranks of Trolledyngjans and Marena Dimura, waited and observed. Ragnarson directed his brief comments to an Itaskian sergeant named Altenkirk, whose service went back to the wars, and who had spent years in the Lesser Kingdoms advising the native armies.

"Now we see if they learned anything from the wars and Lake Berberich," he said.

"He'll send the knights," Altenkirk promised. "We're only commoners and infantry. We can't beat our betters. It's a chance to blood their swords cheaply." His sarcasm was strong.

Ragnarson chuckled. "We'll see. We'll see. Ah. You're right. Here they come, straight up the road."

With pennons and banners flying, trumpets blaring, and drums beating in Lieneke. The townsfolk turned out as if this were the tournament Breitbarth seemed to think. All night knights and men-at-arms had been swelling the Baron's forces in hopes of a share of glory.

As it began, Ragnarson received a messenger from Vorgreberg. The situation there had become grim because news of his entrapment below the Ebeler had reached the local nobility. Several had marched on the capital, hoping to seize it before Breitbarth. Eanred was playing one against another, but his job had been complicated by a Siluro uprising in Vorgreberg itself. A mob had tried to take Castle Krief by surprise, and had failed. Hundreds had been slaughtered. House to house fighting continued. Would Ragnarson be so kind as to come help?

"Tell him I'll get there when I can." He returned to the matter at hand.

Breitbarth's knights started up the road four abreast, apparently unaware that it narrowed on the hillside. At the first turn they became clogged, and the sky darkened with arrows.

Breitbarth broadened his attack, sending more knights to root out Ragnarson's archers. As they blundered about on the soft earth of the vineyards, becoming entangled in the vines, arrows sleeted down upon them.

Turning to Altenkirk, Ragnarson said, "Send a Trolledyngjan company down each side to finish the unhorsed."

It went on. And on. And on. Attacking in three divisions, Breitbarth's best seldom got close enough to strike a blow.

On the left they began to waver. Ragnarson saw Blackfang appearing and disappearing among the vines as he prepared a counterattack.

"I think," said Altenkirk, after having returned and surveyed the situation, "that you've done it again. They'll break."

"Maybe. I'll help them along. Take charge of the Marena Dimura. Hold them back till it's sure." He led the mounted Trolledyngjans down the far left side of the vineyard, outflanking Blackfang, then wheeled and charged a mass of already panicky knights.

Breitbarth's right collapsed. Pressured by Bragi's horsemen, under a terrible arrowstorm, they fled into their center, which broke in its turn and fell back on Breitbarth's left. In a confusion of tripping horses and raining arrows, the slaughter grew grim.

Resistance collapsed. Hundreds threw down their arms. Hundreds more fled in unknightly panic, with Reskird's arrows pursuing.

Ragnarson hastily solidified his line and wheeled to face Lieneke, where the indecisive Baron retained a strong reserve. Such of the enemy as remained on the hill he left to the Marena Dimura.

In brisk order the Trolledyngjans formed a shield wall. The Itaskians, sure they could bring the world to its knees, fell in behind and began arcing long shots at Breitbarth.

"I could still lose," Ragnarson told himself, staring at the massed Kaveliners. The Baron's reserves were mostly spearmen, but there were enough knights to make him uncomfortable.

He need not have feared. Those knights broke at the first flight. Only Breitbarth's infantry stood fast, and they seemed as dazed as the Baron, who did little to defend himself. The arrowstorm, applied from beyond the range of Breitbarth's arbalesters, broke up the infantry formations.

Ragnarson suffered his heaviest casualties in the final mixup. His Trolledyngjans broke formation to wolf in and catch someone who would bring a good ransom.

His men had perfomed near optimum, yet the battle left him unsatisfied. "Haaken," he said after they had occupied Breitbarth's pavilion, "we didn't win a thing."

"What? It's a great victory. They'll be bragging for years."

"Yes. A great slaughter. A dramatic show. But not decisive. That's the key, Haaken. Decisive. All we've gained is loot and prisoners. There're more Volstokiners —the Marena Dimura say they're levying heavily up there —and more Nordmen. They can lose indefinitely, as long as they win the last battle."

Reskird came in. "What's up?"

"Depressed. Like always, after," Blackfang replied. "What's the score?"

Kildragon dropped onto a couch. "Breitbarth had taste," he said, looking around. "We've counted two thousand bodies and a thousand prisoners already. What I came about was, one of Breitbarth's people said they've got a fat brown man in the dungeon at Damhorst. Could be Mocker. Also, Volstokin himself has marched with five thousand men."

"Going to be a hard winter up there, then," said Blackfang, "pulling so many men off the farms."

"Expect they figure they'll live off the spoils," Kildragon replied. "Bragi, what next?"

Ragnarson shook his preoccupations. "You been thinking about replacing the Itaskian officers with loyal people? Haaken, what about your officers? Will they stick?"

"As long as we're winning."

Kildragon, after consideration, replied, "The same. I don't think they've had specific instructions. Yet."

"Good. I've been thinking some things that won't win us any points with Haroun or the Queen."

"Such as?"

"First, putting everyone on a horse, prisoners too, and roaring off to spring Mocker. After that, I don't know. We'll keep out of Volstokin's way, unless we can nab Vodicka himself. He'll take casualties because his people are green..."

"That's what they thought about us," Reskird reminded.

"Uhm. Maybe. We'll see. Maybe we'll go to work on him if he splits his forces. Meanwhile, we stay out of the way till the pieces fall."

"Tarlson won't like that."

"Too bad. He worries too much. Vorgreberg hasn't been taken since Imperial times."

iii) Speaking for the Queen

Getting Mocker out proved easier said than done. Bragi marched swiftly westward, but the Baroness had sealed her gates the moment news of her husband's defeat had arrived. Ragnarson had no stomach for a siege, what with Volstokin just a few days north of the Ebeler. He tried negotiation.

The Baroness knew about Volstokin too. She tried to hold him till Vodicka arrived.

"Looks like Lard Bottom's going to languish a while," Ragnarson told Kildragon. "I'll pull out tonight. All the loot over the border?"

"Last train left this morning. You know, if we quit now we'd be rich."

"We've got a contract."

"You want to try something tonight?"

"No. She'll expect it. Might've worked when we first showed."

"What about Vodicka?"

"He's headed for Armstead?"

"So I'm told. I'm never sure I can trust the Marena Dimura."

"Take two hundred bowmen. Make him pay to cross. But pull out once they get a bridgehead. I'll head south, wipe out a few barons. Catch up when you can."

"Right. You want I should play cat and mouse?"

"No. You might get caught. I can't afford to lose two hundred bows."

Bragi slipped away in the night, leaving Kildragon to keep the campfires burning. He returned to Lieneke, then turned south and plundered the provinces of Froesel and Delhagen, destroying nearly forty Nordmen castles and fortresses, till he came to Sedlmayr, one of Kavelin's major cities and, like Damhorst, a focal point of Nordmen rebellion. This was mountainous country where goat herding, sheep herding, dairying, cheese making, and wool production were important. The snow-topped mountains reminded him of Trolledyngja.

He besieged Sedlmayr a week, but had no heart for it, so was about to move on again when a deputation of Wesson merchants, deep in the night, spirited themselves into his camp. Their spokesman, one Cham Mundwiller, was a forthright, lean, elderly gentleman whose style reminded Bragi of the Minister.

"We've come to offer you Sedlmayr," Mundwiller said. "On conditions."

"Of course. What?"

"That you minimize the fighting and looting."

"Reasonable, but hard to guarantee. Wine? It's Baron Breitbarth's best." The Baron had taken hard the fact that the Baroness refused to go his ransom. "Master Mundwiller, I'm interested. But I don't understand your motives."

"Having you camped here is bad for business. And production. It's almost shearing time, and we can't get the cheese in to the presses, or out to the caves for aging.

Second, we've no love for Baron Kartye or his brother vultures in Delhagen. Their taxes devour our profits. We're Wessons, sir. That makes us the beasts of burden whose backs support the Nordmen. We hear you're correcting that with a sword."

"Ah. I thought so. And your plans for Sedlmayr's future?"

They were evasive. Slippery as merchants, Ragnarson thought, smiling wryly.

"Might they involve Colonel Phiambolis? Or Tuchol Kiriakos? You'd have a hard time convincing me they're tourists accidentally caught by my siege. Too big a coincidence, them being siege specialists. And Baron Kartye, being Nordmen, would be too proud to hire mercenaries." The presence of Kiriakos and Phiambolis, two of the masterminds behind Hellin Daimiel's years-long stand against El Murid, had been one of his reasons for wishing to move on.

"How did you know?..." one merchant gasped.

"My ears are covered with hair, but they're sharp." The presence of the mercenaries had been reported by a Sir Andvbur Kimberlin of Karadja, a Nordmen loyalist he had recently freed.

Enough former prisoners, and recruits picked up here and there, had stuck for Ragnarson to replace all losses as well as to form a native battalion under Sergeant Altenkirk, who spoke Marena Dimura well. He was now considering splitting that battalion and giving Sir Andvbur command of the Wessons.

"You might even be thinking of declaring Sedlmayr a free city—after I've killed your Nordmen for you."

Expressions said he had struck close. He chuckled.

Mundwiller put a bold face on it. "You're right." To the others, who protested, "He might as well know. He'd act on his suspicions." To Ragnarson, "One gold solidi for each soldier, five for sergeants, twenty for officers, and a hundred for yourself."

"Interesting," said Ragnarson. "A fortune for a night's work. But not that much compared to the loot we've already taken. And there's my contract with the Queen. The more I learn about the woman, the more I want to keep it. Were she not saddled with a nation of opportunists, she might be one of the better rulers Kavelin's had." Quote from Sir Andvbur, an idealistic youth who placed the good of the kingdom first, who believed nobles should be curators and conservators, not divinely appointed exploiters.

But even the Queen's enemies had little evil to say of her. There was nothing personal in the Nordmen rebellion. It was generated by power-lust alone.

Ragnarson's admiration for the woman, in large part, stemmed from the fact that she did not interfere. In other times and places he had suffered snowstorms of directives from employers.

Tarlson was another matter. He sent out blizzards of messages.

"What can we offer?" Mundwiller finally asked.

"Your allegiance to Her Majesty."

They did a lot of foot-shuffling and floor-staring.

"Suppose a direct charter could be arranged, with Sedlmayr and Delhagen as Royal fiefs in keeping of a Council of Aldermen? Direct responsibility to the Crown."

That wasn't what the majority wanted, but Mundwiller saw they would get nothing better. "Can you speak for the Queen?"

"No. Only to her. But if Sedlmayr swears allegiance, supports the throne, and faithfully resists the rebels, I'll press your cause powerfully. She should be amenable, coming from the Auszura Littoral. She'll be familiar with the Bedelian League and what those cities have done to hasten recovery from the wars."

"We'll have to consider what might happen if we announce fealty. An army of two, Phiambolis and Kiriakos, isn't much defense against outraged Nordmen."

"I don't think they'll bother you till they rid themselves of the Queen."

"It's your chances we'll be studying."

"You'll get no better offer. Or opportunity," said Ragnarson.

Once the deputation left, Bragi told Blackfang, "Start packing in the morning. Make it look like we're planning to slip away in the night. I don't want to wait while they play games."

Next night Cham Mundwiller was back, upset, wanting to know why Ragnarson was leaving.

"What's your decision?" Bragi asked.

"For. Reluctantly on some parts. Our more timid souls don't think your luck will hold. Personally, I'm satisfied. It's what I've been arguing for all along."

"Tonight?"

"Everything's ready."

"Then so are we."

"One little matter. Some articles for you to sign. That was the hard part, getting them to accept a position from which they couldn't back down."

Ragnarson chuckled as he examined the parchment. "An exchange, then. My own guarantees." He handed the man a document he had had prepared. "And my word, which's worth more. Unless your fealty becomes suspect."

"As an act of good faith, some information which, I believe, only I outside the Nordmen councils possess."

Ragnarson's eyebrows rose questioningly.

"The Captal of Savernake has been making the rounds of the barons. He slipped out of Sedlmayr just before you arrived."

"So?"

"He claims the true child of the old King is in his custody. You've heard the stories about a changeling? He's trying to find backers for his 'real' heir."

"The Captal," Bragi interjected. "He's old?" He described the sorcerer he and Mocker had encountered in Ruderin.

"You've met?"

"In passing. You've told me more than you realize, friend. I'll return the favor, but don't spread it around. The power behind the Captal is Shinsan."

Mundwiller went pale. "What interest could they have in Kavelin?"

"A passage to the west. A quietly attained bridgehead against the day when they move to attain world dominion. All spur-of-the-moment speculation, of course. Who knows the motives of Shinsan?"

"True. We move at the second hour. I'm to lead you to the postern we hold."

iv) Savernake Gap

Bragi occupied Sedlmayr without disturbing its citizens' sleep, capturing the Nordmen and disarming their troops. Baron Kartye had assumed he would decamp in the night.

Sedlmayr taken, Ragnarson secured Delhagen, then decamped in earnest.

Ragnarson departed with twenty-five hundred men, over half of them Kaveliners. None were men he had given Reskird to dispute the Armstead ford. If forced to fight, he would miss those bows.

Kildragon, he learned, had held the ford so successfully that he had almost turned Vodicka back—till the Baroness Breitbarth had surprised him from behind. He had barely gotten out. Fleeing east, he had encountered Volstokiners who had crossed the river above him. He had abandoned everything but his weapons, swum the Ebeler, and was now hiding in the Bodenstead forest.

Vodicka had shown his gratitude to the Baroness by making her prisoner and sacking Damhorst. That gentleman had abandoned all pretense, was destroying everyone and everything as he advanced toward Vorgreberg.

The barons harrying the capital now eyed him as the greater danger.

In Volstokin itself there was trouble, bands of horsemen cutting, in the guerrilla style, at the roots of royal power. Ragnarson suspected Haroun.

Good. Nothing prevented him from doing what he wanted. He marched eastward, passed within twenty miles of Vorgreberg, struck the caravan route east of the city and, spreading panic among the Nordmen, swept on till he entered Savernake, at the juncture of the Kapenrungs and Mountains of M'Hand, where the Savernake Gap debouched into Kavelin. He considered the Captal the most dire threat to the Queen.

His arrow-straight drive didn't slow till he had entered the Gap itself and had climbed above the timberline. Then he stopped cold. He summoned Blackfang, Altenkirk, Jarl Ahring, subbing for Kildragon, and Sir Andvbur Kimberlin of Karadja, in command of the new Wesson battalion.

The five considered the Gap above. Behind them, men seized the opportunity to rest.

"I don't like it," Ragnarson said. "Too quiet." The pass did seem as still as a desert.

"Almost as if time had stopped," said Blackfang. "You'd expect an eagle or something."

Altenkirk spoke to one of the Marena Dimura. The man examined the road ahead.

Ragnarson, blue eyes frosty, studied the sky. He had scouts out. They were to send up smoke in case of trouble.

"I've been this way before," said Sir Andvbur, "and have heard tell it gets like this when the Captal's expecting a fight."

The Marena Dimura said something to Altenkirk, who translated, "The scouts are still ahead of us."

"Uhm. The Captal knows we're coming. In Trolle-dyngja they defend passes by rolling rocks down on people. Altenkirk, put a company on each face. Have them root out anything bigger than a mouse. It'll be slow, but caution's more important than speed now."

"It's only four or five miles to Maisak," said Sir Andvbur. "Around that bluff that looks like a man's face. It's built against the mountain where the pass narrows. The Imperial engineers used natural caverns for barracks, laying the least possible masonry."

Bragi had gone through the Gap to Necremnos once, a few years after the wars, but his memories were vague. He had been in a hurry to see a woman.

Marena Dimura filtered up the rugged slopes. The troops below perked up, saw to their weapons. The day-after-day, week-after-week grind of the march, without a pause to loot or fight or carouse, had eroded morale. Prospective action lifted that.

"What's that?" asked Ragnarson, indicating a wisp of

blackness over the formation Sir Andvbur had pointed out. "Not smoke?"

"The Captal's sorcery, I'd guess," said the knight.

"Send your people for more firewood. We'll make our own light. Have some men stand by with what we've got. Ahring, bring your best bowmen up to support the Marena Dimura."

Once they had left, Ragnarson told Blackfang, "Maybe it's mother's witch-blood, Haaken. I've got a bad feeling."

"You're sure this's the sorcerer from Ruderin?"

"Reasonably."

"Think I'll have a bad feeling myself." He chuckled. "Here we sit without even Mocker's phony magic, getting ready to storm a vassal of Shinsan."

"That's my worry, Haaken. The Captal's just supposed to be a dabbler. But what's Shinsan put in?"

"Imagine we'll find out."

"Haaken, I don't know what I'd do without you." He laughed weakly. "Don't know what to do with you, either, but that's another problem."

"Don't start your death dance yet."

"Eh?"

"We've been through the campaigns. You're going to tell me how to run things after you've found the spear with your name."

"Damn. Next time I'm using new people." He laughed.

Marena Dimura shouted on the slopes. Something broke cover, ran a few yards toward them, then fled the other way. A bowstring twanged. The creature jumped, screamed, fell. Ragnarson and Blackfang moved up, a dozen bowmen at their backs.

"What is it?" Blackfang asked. The body was the size of that of a six-year-old. It had the head of a squirrel.

"Coronel!"

Bragi glanced up. A Marena Dimura tossed something. He caught it. A child-sized crossbow.

Haaken caught a quiver of bolts, pulled one out, examined its head. "Poisoned."

Ragnarson had the word passed, saw shields start to be carried less sloppily.

"Poor fellow," said Blackfang, turning the corpse with

a foot. "Didn't want to fight. Could've gotten off a shot."

"Maybe the light was too bright." Ragnarson studied the black cloud growing over the bluff with the face of a man.

During the next hour, as the sky darkened, the Marena Dimura flushed two score creatures of almost as many shapes. Several of Ragnarson's people learned the hard way about the poisoned bolts. The little people weren't aggressive, but they got ferocious when cornered.

"Wait'll you see the owl-faced ones," Ragnarson said as they reached the natural obelisk he had marked as their goal for the hour. "Some as big as you, and even uglier."

"Speaking of ugly," Haaken replied with sudden grimness.

They had found the missing scouts.

The men hung on a gallows-like rack, from curved spikes piercing the bases of their skulls. The flesh was gone from their faces, fingers, and toes. Their bellies had been ripped open. Their bowels hung to the ground. Their hearts had been cut out. Painted in blood on a pale boulder were the Itaskian words, "Leave Kavelin."

"That's Shinsan work, sure," Blackfang growled.

"Must be," Sir Andvbur agreed. "The Captal's dramatics were never this grisly."

"Get that writing cleaned up," said Ragnarson. "Then let the men see this. Ought to get them vengeance-mad."

The sight did stir a new, grim determination, especially among the Marena Dimura. Hitherto they had done no more than flush the Captal's timorous creatures. Now they hunted for blood.

Intensity of resistance rose sharply. Bragi moved more archers up to support the Marena Dimura, and Trolledyngjans to shield the bowmen from any sudden charge. He had fires and torches lighted and slowed the advance to an even more cautious pace.

A little later, while they waited for the Trolledyngjans to clear the road of a band of armored owl-faces behind a boulder barricade, he asked Sir Andvbur, "How long before the snows come? Soon?"

"Within the month, this high up."

"Bad. We've got to take Maisak or they'll have all winter to strengthen it."

"True. We couldn't maintain a siege once winter came."

"Not with what we've got. Haaken, get those boulders cleared. We don't want bottlenecks behind us."

Against continually increasing resistance, Ragnarson's men had the best of the casualty ratio.

It became completely dark. The men grew concerned about sorcery. There was little Bragi could do to reassure them.

As they neared the bluff, resistance ceased. Ragnarson ordered a halt.

"I'd trade my share of the plunder for a staff wizard," he muttered. "What do we do now? Even during the wars nobody rooted the Captal out. And then he was using more normal defenses. Why should he fear an attack from this direction?"

"It's the caverns," said Sir Andvbur. "Maisak's built over their easternmost mouths. There're lots of openings here on the west slope. During the wars, once he'd pushed some scouts past, El Murid almost took Maisak by sending men back underground. Most vanished in the maze, but some did reach the fortress."

"He didn't seal them?"

"Those he could find. But what's been sealed can be unsealed."

"Uhm. Altenkirk, pass the word to look for caves. But not to go in."

The next phase of the Captal's defense exploded on leathery wings. Flying things, from man-sized like the one Ragnarson had seen in Ruderin to creatures little bigger than the bats they resembled, suddenly swarmed overhead. Bragi's staff were the focal point, but escaped injury. The winged things' only weapon was a poisoned dart impelled by gravity.

"This can't be his last defense," Ragnarson declared.

"There's an open, flat place the other side of Stone Face," said Sir Andvbur. "Suitable for battle."

"Uhm. Could we see it from up top?" Ragnarson

indicated the highest point of the formation. No one answered. "That's what we'll do. Haaken, take over. Don't go past the bluff. Altenkirk, give me three of your best men. One should speak a language I do. Sir Andvbur, come with me."

v) Woman of the mists

The peak provided a god's eye view of the pass and Maisak. From it Ragnarson saw things he hadn't cared to view. In the open area Sir Andvbur had described, drawn up in line of battle, statue-still among hundreds of illuminating fires, were the most fearsome warriors he had ever seen, each clad in black, chitinous armor.

"Shinsan," he whispered. "Four, five hundred. We'll never cut our way through."

"We've beaten armies three times our number."

"Armed rabbles," said Ragnarson. "The Dread Empire trains its soldiers from childhood. They don't question, they don't disobey, they don't panic. They stand, they fight, they die, and they retreat only when they've got orders. And they're the best soldiers, fighting, you'll find. Or so I'm told by people who're supposed to know. This's my first encounter."

"We could bring bowmen up."

"Right. Having come this far, I can't pull out without trying." He turned to send a Marena Dimura to Blackfang and Ahring. "Sir Andvbur. What do you make of that?" He indicated the far distance, where countless fires burned.

"Looks like the eastern barons have gotten together."

"Uhm. How far?"

"They're still in high pastureland. Near Baxendala. Three days. Two if they hurry. I don't think they will, considering the showing you've made. They'll piddle around till it's too late to back out."

"Think they'll come after us? Or wait there, hoping we get the worst of the Captal?"

Sir Andvbur shrugged. "You never know what a Nordmen will do. What's unreasonable to a logical mind. Tell you what. If you want to go ahead here, I'll take my Wessons down and set an ambush. We won't be much help against Shinsan."

"This requires a staff meeting," said Ragnarson. "Those Shinsaners will wait. Let's slide back down."

To his surprise, he found his officers unanimous. They should try taking Maisak. They found the presence of Shinsan unsettling, but an argument for immediate attack. The advance base must be denied the Dread Empire. The baronial forces they would worry about later.

They were getting a little blasé about the barons, Bragi feared.

He detailed Sir Andvbur, the Wessons, Altenkirk, and half the Marena Dimura to prepare a reception for the barons twelve miles west, in the pines around the tiny lake and marshy meadow where the Ebeler had its headwaters. As always, he chose ground difficult for horsemen.

He prepared meticulously for his engagement with Shinsan, bringing up tons of firewood, having his men erect a series of rock barricades across the floor of the pass, preparing boulders for rolling down on those positions as they were lost, and locating dozens of snipers on the slopes to support the Trolledyngjans, who would do the close fighting. He had several thousand arrows taken to the bluff top. And he sent Marena Dimura to hunt ways to bring small forces against Maisak itself, and to locate every possible cave mouth. He invested a day and a half preparing.

From the bluff it looked as though the enemy hadn't moved, though Bragi knew they rotated for rest. "Well," he muttered, looking down at all that armor, "no point putting it off." Blackfang was awaiting the first onslaught. "Loose!"

Twenty shafts began their drop. In the gloom and shifting light, downhill shooting was tricky. Ragnarson didn't expect much, though his bowmen were his best.

But figures toppled, a few with each flight. Their armor wasn't impervious.

"Gods, are they mute?" one archer muttered. Never a cry echoed up. But Shinsan's soldiers fought and died in utter silence. It disconcerted the most fearless enemies.

The enemy commander had to make a decision. From his Marena Dimura Ragnarson knew a force couldn't be sent up the bluff from the Maisak side. Shinsan would have to withdraw into the fortress, or advance, to break through and secure the bluff from behind. Standing fast meant slow but certain slaughter. The peak was high enough that arrows from bows below were spent on arrival.

Shinsan did three things: sent a company against Ragnarson's walls of stone, withdrew forces that couldn't be brought to bear, and rolled out a pair of heavy, wheeled ballistae with which they fired back.

"Take care!" Ragnarson snapped after a shaft the size of a knight's lance growled a foot over his head. "Duck when you see them trigger. You won't see the shaft coming. You, you, you. Put some fire arrows on them."

He had a sudden premonition, pulled five men back and had them watch for an aerial attack.

"Colonel, they're moving a platoon to the canyon."

"Hurt those you can. Mind the ballistae. You men, look sharp. Now's the time they'll come."

And they did, a swarm of leather-winged hellspawn who, though anticipated, exploded upon them in a sudden shower of poisoned darts. The bigger ones tried to force his archers off the bluff. One man plunged to his death. Then they were gone.

Ragnarson searched the rim for grapnels with depending lines, found two, smiled grimly. He would have tried that himself. Those gone, he threw the enemy casualties after them. He expected Shinsan would send the winged things each time reinforcements went in below, and wasn't disappointed. His men soon slaughtered most of them. He lost two more people. The arrow fire scarcely slackened. He plied a dead man's bow himself.

A messenger came from Blackfang. The first barricade had fallen. The spirits of the men remained good, though they were awed by the prowess and determination of their enemies. They knew they were in a real fight this time.

Ragnarson had had seven barricades erected, manning the first four with a hundred men apiece. The rest of his forces were building an eighth and ninth. To beat him Shinsan would have to seize old walls faster than he could build new ones.

The first four hours of fighting were uneventful, Haaken's Trolledyngjans hacked it out toe to toe with Shinsan while the Itaskians showered the enemy with arrows. Casualties were heavy on both sides, but the ratio favored Ragnarson because of his superior bows. Even fighting from barricades the Trolledyngjans got the worst of the close combat.

When Haaken sent word that the fifth wall was weakening, he began withdrawing from the bluff. Otherwise he would be cut off. It would have been nice to have denied it to the enemy, but he thought the battle would be decided before Shinsan could take advantage of it. He left two Marena Dimura to keep an eye on Maisak.

Before he departed, he examined the western slopes. It should be true night down there. He saw no campfires, but did spot the beacon Sir Andvbur was supposed to light when the barons neared his position. Assuming he beat Shinsan, which wasn't likely, could he handle the barons? His men would be weary and weak.

"Colonel."

He turned.

A new dimension had been given Shinsan's attack. He wondered if it were because of his withdrawal.

From Maisak's gate came the woman he and Mocker had seen in mists in Ruderin. She rode a dark-as-midnight stallion trapped in Shinsan armor. Both moved in intensely bright light. Even at that distance Bragi was awed by the woman's beauty. Such perfection was unnatural.

Beside her, on a white charger, rode a child equally bright, perhaps six, in golden breastplate and greaves, with a small sword in hand and a child-sized crown on his head. This was a simple thing, iron, like a helmet with the top removed.

"Must be the Captal's Pretender," Bragi muttered. A

stream of Kaveliners followed the woman and child. The Captal had, apparently, found support for his royal candidate.

The battle was lost, he thought. Shinsan had softened him up for these men to break and give the child-king an imaginary victory. Time to worry about keeping it from becoming a rout.

Which, unhorsed, would dishearten those troops most? He drew a shaft to his ear, released, put a second in the air while the first yet sped.

He let fly at the two stallions, assuming the sorceress would have shielded herself and her puppet with spells.

The first shaft found the heart of the white, the second the flank of the black. The white screamed and threw the child. The black, like the soldiers of Shinsan, made no sound, but it staggered and slowly went down, hindquarters first. Two more shafts whistled in, one missing, the last turning to smoke in the invisible protection around the woman.

She shrieked, a sound of rage so loud it should never have come from mortal lips. She swung a glittering spear round to point at the peak. Mists of darkness enveloped her.

Ragnarson ran. The bluff behind him exploded. He put on more speed as he heard stone grinding and groaning. The bluff was falling apart, sliding away into the pass. Two hundred yards downslope he glanced back. The peak looked as though some antediluvian monster had taken a bite—and was still nibbling.

"What the hell happened?" Blackfang demanded when he reached the canyon floor.

"Witch got mad at me."

"Cut off her nose to spite her face, then."

"Eh?"

"Must've been three hundred Shinsaners where the mountain fell."

Ragnarson's men were finishing the survivors. Some were about to go haring over the rockfall toward Maisak. "She'll really be mad now. Call them back. We're pulling out."

"Why? We've won."

"Uhn-uh. There's still one hell of a mob over there. Kaveliners. But she's the problem..."

"As you say."

"Now the barons," Ragnarson mumbled, as he settled on a rock, exhausted.

After a while he had men collect enough Shinsan armor and weapons to convince any doubters in Kavelin.

NINE: Family Life

i) Ill wind from Itaskia

Elana didn't worry till Bragi had been gone a week. By the end of the second week she was frantic.

The third raid had left her all raw nerves, and Bevold, who had fallen days behind schedule, had become insufferable.

She spent much of her time watching her teardrop, till Gerda chided her for neglecting Ragnar and Gundar. She realized she was being foolish. Why did the women always have to wait?

One bright spot was Rolf. His chances looked better daily.

Came an afternoon when Ragnar, playing in the watchtower, shouted, "Ma, there's some men coming."

They were near enough to count. Six men. She recognized Uthe's and Dahl's mounts.

Despair seized her. "That bastard. That lying, craven son-of-a-bitch with a brain like sheep shit in shallow water trying to make it to dry land. He's let Haroun talk him into it. I'll kill him. I'll break every bone in his body and kill him!"

"Ma!"

Ragnar had never seen her like this.

"All right." She scooped him up and settled him on her hip. He laughed. "Let's go watch Uthe weasel."

She moved a chair to the porch and, with Ragnar and Gundar squirming in her lap, waited.

One glimpse of Uthe's face was enough. Bragi had gone chasing Haroun's dreams. She was so angry she just glared and waited.

Uthe approached reluctantly, shrugged and showed his palms in a gesture of defeat.

"Goodwife Ragnarson?" one of Haas's companions asked. She nodded.

"Captain Wilhusen, Staff, War Ministry. His Excellency offers his apologies and heartfelt condolences for any inconvenience caused by his calling your husband to active service."

Active service? They couldn't do that. Could they?

"Elana?"

She turned slightly, allowed another face to focus. "Turran! And Valther. What?..."

"We work for the army now. Kind of slid into it sideways."

"And Brock?" Her anger she ignored for the moment.

"Poisoned arrow in Escalon."

"Oh. I'm sorry."

"Don't be. We've been dead for years. Just won't lie down."

"You'll see Nepanthe, won't you? She's been so worried."

"There'll be time to catch up. We'll be seeing a lot of each other."

"I don't understand. But come in. You must be tired and hungry."

"You've done well," said Turran, following her in.

"Bragi's worked hard. Too hard, sometimes. And we've had good people helping. It hasn't been easy."

"No doubt. I know what this country was like."

"Well, make yourselves comfortable. Captain. Valther. You. I didn't catch your name. I'm sorry."

"Sergeant Hunsicker, ma'am, with the Captain, and don't go to no bother on my account."

"No bother. Gerda, we've guests. Hungry guests." A moment later, "Some explanations, please," she demanded, unable to control her anger. "Where's my husband?"

"Captain, may I?" Turran asked. He received a nod.

While he talked, Elana considered the changes four years had wrought. He was handsome as ever, but gray had crept into his raven hair, and he had lost a lot of weight. He was pale, looked weak, and at times shook as if suddenly chilly. When she asked about his health, he replied cryptically that, once again, this time in Escalon, they had chosen the losing side.

A shadow ghosted across Valther's face. He looked older than Turran, who had a decade on him. He had been a lively daredevil four years ago; now he seemed almost retarded. When, with a sort of childlike curiosity, he wandered over to stare into the fireplace, Elana whispered, "What happened to Valther?"

"It comes and goes," Turran replied. "He never talks any more. Escalon was hard for him. But the bad periods get shorter. Sometimes he seems almost ready to speak, then his mind wanders...I haven't given up hope." He went on explaining why Bragi hadn't come home.

She didn't understand why she had to turn her home over to Captain Wilhusen, but it was clear she had little choice.

"Where can we go?" she asked. "We can't stay in the kingdom. We can't go north to Bragi's people. We've all got enemies in Iwa Skolovda, Dvar and Prost Kamenets. And we can't go south if Greyfells' partisans want us."

"Enemies all around us, yes," said Turran. "The Minister has offered to let you use his estate on the Auszura Littoral."

"We can't get there from here."

"We can, but it'll be hard."

"How?"

"One way is through Driscol Fens, over the Silverbind, through Shara, south to the Lesser Kingdoms, then down the River Scarlotti to the coast."

"Which means sneaking past Prost Kamenets, then hoping we can get out of Shara without being murdered or enslaved. I trust the alternative's more palatable."

"You go west through the forests to the Minister's manor at Sieveking, then catch a naval transport going south. It looks easier, but there're problems. First, this vessel's too small to let you take any personal effects. Second, it's lightly armed and has a small crew. It wouldn't stand off a determined pirate. There are still some around in the Red Islands."

"A dilemma with more horns than a nine-headed stag. I'll talk it over with my people. And Nepanthe. Her lot will have to go too, I suppose."

"Of course."

ii) Walk to the coast

With one exception, the people chose to abandon everything to Captain Wilhusen. The exception was Bevold Lif. The Freylander refused to budge. They had survived bandits, wolves, weather, and war, he declared, and he would survive Greyfells' political successors. He was staying. Somebody had to keep the soldiers from stealing the silverware.

They left the grant with little but food and clothing. Preshka was the only adult not walking. He rode a donkey. The forest paths were impassable for wagons and horses.

The way led within forty miles of Itaskia, and for two days they had to travel open farmlands above the capital, hurrying to cross a strait of civilization which ran north to Duchy Greyfells and West Wapentake, a strait that separated two great islands of forest in the midlands. Unfriendly eyes found them there. As they reached the western forest, they spied the dust of many riders.

"You think they'll wait for us on the other side?" Elana asked.

Turran shrugged. "They don't know where we'll come out."

"How much figuring would it take? They know where

the Minister's place is..."

"But we've got the jewel. We can slip past them in the dark."

"You hope. You said you'd tell me about it."

"Later."

"It's later. Talk."

"All right. After I make sure they don't come in after us. Go on a few miles. We'll catch up."

She took the trail-breaker's position, following a path tramped by generations of deer. Valther followed her, hand on sword hilt but eyes faraway, as if he were remembering another retreat. Turran had promised to tell that tale too.

After posting sentries she sat with Rolf, who was pale with discomfort. Valther remained near her, as he always did when Turran was absent.

"How're you feeling?" she asked, laying one hand on Rolf's.

"Miserable." He coughed softly. "Lung's never going to be right."

"Think we'll make it?"

"Don't worry. It's out of our hands. We will or we won't. Depends on how much manpower they want to waste. They're not stupid. Catching us won't change the big picture."

"Tell me about Kavelin. I've never been there."

"I've told what's to tell. Except that it'd be a nice country if someone skimmed off about fifty thousand Nordmen and ambitious commoners. I liked it. Might settle there if Bragi straightens them out."

"You think he can? I mean, sixteen hundred men against a whole country, and maybe El Murid?"

"Sixteen hundred plus Bragi, Mocker, and Haroun."

"Who're only men. Rolf, I'm scared. It's been so long since I was on my own."

"I'm here. I'll always be here... I'm sorry."

"No, don't be. I understand. Ah, here's Turran."

The man came over, squatted by his brother, said, "Well, no worse. I was afraid being chased would hurt... Oh, they've posted watchers, but the rest went south again. Guess they'll wait on the other side. How're you making it, Rolf? Pushing too hard?"

"I'll survive. Iwa Skolovdans are fiesty."

Turran smiled wanly. "Won't lay down and die, that's sure." Once, briefly, he had been master of that city. "Might as well make camp. We could do a few more miles, but we'll be better off for the rest. Especially the children."

Elana snorted. "Not Ragnar. Nor Ethrian. They've put in more miles than any of us. But maybe you'll find time to tell the story you've been promising."

Turran's dark eye went to Valther. "All right. After supper."

"I'll tell Nepanthe."

iii) War in the east

"I suppose the story begins," Turran told an audience of Elana, Nepanthe, Preshka, and Uthe and Dahl Haas, "when Valther talked Brock and me into going to Hellin Daimiel. Jerrad wouldn't go. He went back to the mountains. I guess he's probably hunting and trying to rebuild Ravenkrak. Fool. Anyway, in Hellin Daimiel we were approached by a representative of the Monitor of Escalon. He was recruiting westerners to help in a war.

"We became part of a devil's catch of hedge wizards, assassins, mercenaries, and marginal types that might be useful in a wizard's war.

"It was a long journey east. By the time we reached Tatarian, Escalon's capital, there were a thousand of us.

"We found out that the country was at war with Shinsan. Escalon was strong, but no match for the Dread Empire.

"Escalon was losing. The whole kingdom lay under a siege of night. Demonic, poisonous hordes of hell-things fought for both sides.

"We foreigners were thrown in right away. And we stalled Shinsan for a while. But then they started advancing again.

"The Monitor decided to chance everything on one vast thaumaturgic battle. It defies description. It lasted nine days. When it was over an area as big as Itaskia had

been wasted. Millions died. In Escalon only Tatarian and
the major cities survived. In Shinsan, we don't know. We
hadn't lost, but we hadn't won, and that, in the long run,
meant our defeat.

"It was during that battle that we lost Brock. We got
too involved to look out for ourselves. An arrow got
through and wounded him.

"That it had been loosed a thousand miles away in
Shinsan was no excuse. We'd been provided with ways of
sensing the attack. We just didn't pay attention.

"The wound was minor, but the shaft bore soul-
devouring spells. In the end he begged us to give him a
clean death."

Turran paused for a moment, locked in his memories.

"Afterwards, the Monitor decided Escalon was lost.
He summoned Valther and me. He told us that Shinsan
would turn on Matayanga next. He believed the world's
hope, ultimately, lay in the west because Yo Hsi and Nu Li
Hsi had been destroyed here. What he was trying to do, he
told me, was to buy time. He hoped somebody like
Varthlokkur or the Star Rider would see what was
happening and do something about the west's political
choas.

"That's when he gave me the jewel, Elana. The one I
sent you. You've been using it for a warden, its least
important power.

"The Monitor believed it was one of the Poles of
Power. How he came by it I don't know, and I don't think
it really is a Pole, but one thing's sure. It's important. I
saw him use it. He could move mountains . . . He wanted
me to get it to the Star Rider. But I don't think so. I don't
know why. When this's over, I'm going to try to take it to
Varthlokkur. He knows the Dread Empire. I think he'd
have the best shot at stopping them."

Silence closed in, drawing a tight circle round the
campfire. For several minutes Turran's audience digested
what he had had to say. Then his sister, glancing at a
fitfully dozing Valther, asked, "Why didn't you come
home? You lost Brock, and the war was over . . ."

"It wasn't over. Just lost. There was time to buy. We
thought we could help. After the great wizards' battle
both sides had to rely on ordinary soldiers for a while. It's

generally conceded that I'm a pretty good general. Impetuous and over-optimistic, they tell me, but less so when I'm working for somebody else. I managed to take the battle to Shinsan for several months."

"I'm confused. You've mentioned Nu Li Hsi's heirs, and Yo Hsi's. Who were you fighting?"

"Both. Sometimes one, sometimes the other. They were feuding. Shinsan's army wasn't. It took the orders of whoever gave them. When we first got to Escalon, we fought Yo Hsi's daughter. After the great battle, it was O Shing. I don't know when they made the changeover. The transition couldn't be detected. A few months later we were fighting Mist again."

"I saw the woman... Unbelievable. So much evil in such a beautiful package."

"But what about Valther?" Nepanthe demanded.

"You never did have any patience, did you? Well, it's a complicated story. Try not to interrupt." Nepanthe and Turran had been bickering for years.

"By some snare of the Power he still had, the Monitor caught one of the Tervola. He managed to keep the man alive long enough to find out that Mist herself would take charge of the final assault on Tatarian.

"The Monitor planned one last cast of the dice. Its only objective was Mist's death.

"Valther and I were heart and soul of the plan. And we blew it.

"Our job was to get captured." Turran talked in little gusts, like an indecisive breeze. During his pauses he poked the fire with a stick, threw acorns at tree trunks, used the fingernails on one hand to clean those on the other. He didn't want to relive these memories. "Because we'd been involved in her father's death. The Monitor thought she'd want to question us. If she did, we were supposed to change sides, then kill her when we got the chance.

"It worked too good.

"The woman has a weakness. Vanity. Make it two. Insecurity, too. We played to them. And she started keeping us around like pets. She had a million questions about the west.

"Things started going wrong when Valt started

believing what he was saying..."

Sighs escaped his listeners. They became more attentive. Turran stirred the fire again.

"It was my fault...I should've...In Shinsan they use herbs to increase their grasp of the Power. It stops you from getting older, too. But once you use them, you have to keep on..."

"You?..." Nepanthe interjected.

"In the service of the Dread Empire, one must. After he had betrayed Escalon, Valt tried to make it up by killing Mist. It didn't work.

"I don't know. Maybe her wickedness was polluted by mercy. Maybe an accidental thread of love got woven into her tapestry of evil. Whatever, of all the possible punishments, she chose the simplest. She took away our supply of herbs."

"That's why he's this way?" This time it was Elana who couldn't restrain herself. "How come you recovered?"

"I'm not an expert on the human mind. Yes, I recovered. That was six months ago, in an asylum in Hellin Daimiel. For a while I didn't know if what I remembered was true or just a nightmare. Nobody knew anything about us. The Watch had found us in the street and committed us for our own protection. The scholars who studied us told me Valther is using drug withdrawal as an excuse not to come back and face his guilt."

"If only Mocker were here," Nepanthe mused. Her eyes were sad as she gazed at Valther. "He might be able to reach Valt."

"Time is the cure," Turran told her. "It worked for me. So I keep hoping."

iv) Auszura Littoral

With Elana's jewel guiding them, they slipped through their enemies to Sieveking. But the transport wasn't yet there. When *Dingolfing* did arrive it was in no condition to sail to the Auszura Littoral. The ship had encountered heavy weather shortly after leaving Portsmouth, then had met a Trolledyngjan reever off Cape Blood. Her captain, Miles Norwine, said rigging repairs might take a week. Heavy damage, where the Trolledyngjan had rammed, would have to wait for the yards at Itaskia.

"It seems," said Elana, standing on the quay with Turran and Nepanthe, "that somewhere in the house of the gods, probably in the jakes, there's a little pervert who gets his pleasure making me miserable."

Turran chuckled. "Know what? I'll bet the head man over there's been thinking the same thing." He indicated tents crowning a hill overlooking the estate.

Later, a messenger brought the news that Bragi had crossed the Porthune.

"The renegades," said Turran, "might try their luck when they find out. I'd better get something ready."

That night he and the men laid an ambush at the edge of the estate. Elana, with Dahl Haas under her wing, went to observe.

Sure enough, near midnight, men came sneaking through the brush. Turran sprang his trap. The surprise was complete. In minutes a dozen had been slaughtered and the rest sent whooping up the hillside.

Dahl, half-wild, used his dagger to finish a casualty who came staggering toward Elana, then, realizing what he had done, heaved his supper and began crying. Elana was trying to calm him when his father appeared.

"What happened?" Uthe asked.

Elana explained.

Uthe put his arm around his son. "You did well," he said. "It's always hardest the first time. Lot of men do their conscience-racking first, get themselves killed hesitating."

Dahl nodded, but reassurances did little good. The experience was too intensely personal.

Captain Norwine got his rigging repaired and a patch on his hull. He was willing to risk the trip. Elana put it to a vote. It went in favor.

Dingolfing put out and beat round Cape Blood, sailed south past the Silverbind Estuary, Portsmouth, and the Octylyan Protectorate without mishap. Norwine hugged the coast like a babe his mother. He was prepared to go aground if trouble developed. They weathered a minor storm off the Porthune, spending two nervous days at the pumps and buckets, but came through with no damage other than to landlubbers' stomachs.

"Sail ho!" a lookout cried just north of Sacuescu. Norwine put his helm over and ran for shallow water. Turran and the shipboard Marines prepared for a fight. But the vessel proved to be the *Rifkin,* out of Portsmouth. The fat caravel dipped her merchant's colors to *Dingolfing*'s naval ensign.

Norwine kept everyone at stations once they passed Sacuescu. They were near the Red Isles where, despite regular patrols by the Itaskian Navy, pirates lurked. But their luck held. They made the fishing port of Tineo, midway between Sacuescu and Dunno Scuttari, without incident.

From Tineo it was a twelve-mile walk to the Minister's villa, which occupied a headland with a spectacular view of the sea. The staff expected them. They seemed accustomed to hiding friends of the Minister.

The Auszura Littoral was all Turran had promised, and utterly peaceful. So peaceful that, after a few months, it began to grate. There was nothing to do but wait for rumors from Kavelin, which were unreliable by the time they filtered through to Tineo.

Rolf began wandering, sometimes accompanied by Uthe, to Sacuescu and Dunno Scuttari. Elana didn't weather his absences well. He was her last touchstone, almost her conscience. His absences grew more frequent and extended. She found herself thrown more and more into the company of Nepanthe, Turran, and Valther.

Nepanthe, after Rolf, had been her best friend for years, but her constant company was wearing. Nepanthe was a worrier.

Turran remained a perfect gentleman, ever attentive and willing to entertain. She began to fear what might happen. She tried to stay near Gerda, whose basilisk eye could still the passion of a cat in heat.

Then Rolf and Uthe disappeared. She thought it another of their jaunts till she discovered their weapons missing.

"Gerda, where've they gone?" she demanded. Like certain gods, the woman saw the sparrows fall.

"Where do you think? Kavelin, of course. With help for himself. Who'll be coming home someday, I'll remind you, and be expecting everything as he left it."

Why couldn't Rolf stay put? Was he sublimating his love? Or just searching for the spear with his name?

Autumn leaves were falling on the Littoral. Would it be getting on winter in Kavelin?

The night Rolf left she sat up late with the Tear of Mimizan. Troubled, she used the thing more as a focus for her attention than as a means of checking Bragi's well-being.

The jewel suddenly seized her attention. The light within was strong and growing stronger. Bragi was in trouble.

The light flashed suddenly, so brightly she was momentarily blinded. At the same instant there was a scream from another room.

"The children!" she gasped. She rushed toward the sound. It went on and on. Behind her, the ruby painted her bedroom shades of blood.

The screamer was Valther.

"She's here!" the man kept saying. "She's here. She's loosed her magic..."

"Who?" Nepanthe asked repeatedly.

"Must be Mist," Turran guessed. "Nothing else could've done this."

"But why?"

"Who knows the ways of Shinsan?"

"The jewel," Elana interjected. "Before he screamed, it flashed so bright it almost blinded me."

Nepanthe's eyes met hers. Neither woman voiced her fear.

"She's in Kavelin, then," said Turran. He remained thoughtful while Nepanthe and Elana calmed Valther, who began asking, "What happened?" and "Where am I?"

"It grows too complex," Turran mused aloud. "A three-sided war...Nepanthe, get a couple of horses ready. And weapons. I'll look after Valther."

"But..."

"Looks like we're getting a second chance. Elana, the

Tear is the most valuable thing in the west right now. Guard it well. If Kavelin goes, get it to Varthlokkur."

Things went so fast Elana had no time to protest. Before she exploded in frustration, the brothers had gone. Valther remained puzzled, but seemed determined to rectify his treason.

She and Nepanthe stood on a balcony and watched them ride toward the coast road. Turran hoped to overtake Rolf and Uthe.

A stir in the gardens caught her eye. She said nothing to Nepanthe, merely peered intently till she could make out a small old man nodding to himself. He had spoken to Bragi at the landgrant. Quick as a bolting rabbit, he scooted out a small side gate.

A moment later she gasped. The old man, astride a winged horse, rose toward the moon and sped eastward.

TEN: The Closing Circles

i) From the jaws of despair

Ragnarson collapsed onto a rock. He could scarcely remain awake. The Nordmen gave up their weapons meekly, though puzzledly. They couldn't believe that they had been beaten by lesser men.

For Bragi, too, it seemed a dream. It had taken two man-breaking weeks, but he had slipped out of the destroying vise.

He had fled Maisak certain he would never escape the Gap. Enemies had lain before and behind him, and there had been no way to turn aside.

He had outrun the Captal, almost flying into the arms of the eastern barons, who were pursuing Sir Andvbur Kimberlin, then had *made* a way to the side, out of the inescapable trap of a box canyon. At least, his enemies had thought it inescapable.

While they had taken the measure of one another and he had goaded them into fighting, his men had cut stairs up the canyon wall. Abandoning everything but weapons, they had climbed out one by one. Meanwhile, with a few Trolledyngjans and Itaskians, Ragnarson had harassed the Captal's surviving Shinsaners so they wouldn't get the best of the barons.

The desultory, constricted, unimaginative combat between pretenders had taken four days to resolve itself. The barons had had numbers, the Captal sorcery and men fanatically devoted to his child-pretender.

Ragnarson felt that, this time, he had won a decisive victory. He had won time. The Captal couldn't muster new forces before winter sealed the Gap. The succession might be determined by spring. And the eastern Nordmen had been crushed. For the moment he and Volstokin commanded the only major forces in Kavelin. If he moved swiftly, while winter prevented external interests from aiding favorites, he could fulfill his commission.

And he could return to Elana.

If Haroun would let him. What Haroun's plans were he didn't know.

He had sent his men up the stone stairs, over mountains, and into the Gap behind the barons. The animals and equipment he had abandoned had become bait. They had rushed to the plunder.

Ragnarson's captains, led by Blackfang, had struck savagely. In bitter fighting they had closed the canyon behind the Nordmen. Bragi and a small group had held the stairs against a repeat of his own escape.

There was no water in that canyon. Ragnarson's animals had already devoured the sparse forage. The arrowstorm, once the mouth narrows had been secured, had been impenetrable. The Nordmen had had no choice.

There had been more to it, as there was to all stories: heroism of men pushing themselves beyond believed limits; inspired leadership by Blackfang, Ahring, Altenkirk, and Sir Andvbur; and unsuspected bits of character surfacing.

Ragnarson studied Sir Andvbur. His judgment of the young knight's coolness and competence had proven out during Kimberlin's operation around the headwaters of the Ebeler. Under him, the Wessons had shown well against the barons, particularly during disengagement and withdrawal.

But the first thing he had done, after getting his troops safely into the box canyon, had been to throw a tantrum.

"Both leaders think they can handle us later," he had said.

"You sound bitter."

"I am. Colonel, you haven't lived with their arrogance. Kavelin is the richest country in the Lesser Kingdoms, and that's not just in wealth and resources. There're fortunes in human potential here. But you find Wesson, Siluro, and Marena Dimura geniuses plowing, emptying chamberpots, and eating grubs in the forests. They're not allowed anything else. Meantime, Nordmen morons are pushing Kavelin toward disaster. You think it's historical pressure that has the lower classes rebelling? No. It's because of the blind excesses of my class... Men like Eanred Tarlson could help make this kingdom decent for everybody. But they never get anywhere. Unless, like Tarlson, they obtain Royal favor. It's frustrating. Infuriating."

Ragnarson had made no comment at the time.

He hadn't realized that Sir Andvbur had a Cause. He decided he had best keep an eye on the man.

Blackfang and Ahring took seats beside him. "We should get the hell out before Shinsan tries for a rematch," said Haaken. "But there ain't nobody here who could walk a mile."

"Not much choice, then, is there? Why worry?"

Blackfang shrugged.

"What about the prisoners?" Ahring asked.

"Won't have them long. We're going to Vorgreberg." He glanced up. The sky was nasty again. There had been cold rain off and on since his withdrawal from Maisak. It was getting on time to worry about wintering the army.

Two days later, as he returned to the march, the Marena Dimura brought him a young messenger.

"Wouldn't be related to Eanred Tarlson, would you?" Bragi asked, as he broke Royal seals.

"My father, sir."

"You're Gjerdrum, eh? Your father said you were at university."

"I came home when the trouble started. I knew he'd need help. Especially if anything happened to him."

"Eh?" But he had begun reading.

His orders were to hasten to Vorgreberg and assume the capital's defense. Tarlson had been gravely wounded in a battle with Volstokin. The foreigners were within thirty miles of the city.

"Tell her I'm on my way," he said.

The boy rode off, never having dismounted. Ragnarson wondered if he could get there in time. The rain would complicate river crossings in the lowlands. And Tarlson's injuries might cost the Queen the support he brought her by force of personality. He might lead his men to an enemy city. "Haaken! Ahring! Altenkirk! Sir Andvbur!"

ii) Travels with the enemy

"Woe! Am foolest of fools," Mocker mumbled over and over."

The dungeon days had stretched into weeks, a parade of identical bores. Kirsten had forgotten him due to other pressures. Those he could judge only by his guards. Always sullen and vicious, they became worse whenever the Breitbarth fortunes waned. News arrived only when another subversive was imprisoned.

One day the turnkeys vanished. Every available man had been drafted to resist Volstokin's perfidy.

After crushing resistance, Vodicka visited the dungeons. Mocker tried to appear small in his corner. The Volstokiners were hunting someone. And he had had a premonition.

"This one," he heard.

He looked up. A tall, lean, angular man with a wide scar down one cheek considered him with eyes of cold jade. Vodicka. Beside him was another lean man, shorter, dusky, with high, prominent cheekbones and a huge, hawklike nose. He wore black. His eyes were like those of a snake.

Inwardly, Mocker groaned. A shaghûn.

"Hai!" He bounced up with a broad grin. "Great King arrives in nick to rescue faithful servant from mouldering death in dungeon of perfidious ally. Breitbarth is treacher, great lord. Was plotting treason from beginning..."

They ignored him.

Mocker sputtered, fumed, and told some of his tallest lies. Vodicka's men put him in chains and led him away. No one explained why.

But he could guess. They knew him. He had done El Murid many small embarrassments. There was the time he had sweet-talked/kidnapped the man's daughter. There was the time he had convinced an important general that he could reveal a short-cut through the Kapenrungs, and had led the man into an army-devouring ambush.

Still, daylight seen from chains was sweeter than dungeon darkness. And at least an illusion of a chance to escape existed.

He could have gotten away. Escape tricks were among his talents. But he saw a chance to lurk on the fringe of the enemy's councils.

He got to see a lot of daylight—and moonlight, starlight, and weather—the next few months, while Volstokin's drunken giant of an army lumbered about Kavelin's western provinces. Vodicka wanted his prizes near him always, but never comfortable.

Mocker didn't get along with his fellow prisoners. They were Nordmen, gentlemen who had barely paid their ransoms to Bragi's agents when taken by Vodicka.

Ragnarson had won himself a low, black place in Vodicka's heart. He had already plundered the best from Ahsens, Dolusich, Gaehle, Holtschlaw, and Heiderscheid provinces. Bragi's leavings were not satisfying the levies, who had been called from their homes for a campaign that would last past harvest time.

Vodicka kept escalating his promises to keep his army from evaporating.

Mocker wished he could get out among the troops. The damage he could talk . . . But his guards, now, were men of Hammad al Nakir. They were deaf to words not approved by their shaghûn. His chance to escape had passed him by.

The looting improved in Echtenache and Rubbelke, though there a price in blood had to be paid. In Rubbelke, sixty miles west of Vorgreberg and fifteen north of the caravan route, a thousand Nordmen met Volstokin on the plains before Woerheide.

Vodicka insisted that his prisoners watch. His pride still stung from the difficulty he had had forcing the Armstead ford.

Vodicka was more talented at diplomacy and intrigue than at war, but refused to admit his shortcomings.

Tons of flesh and steel surged together in long, thunderous waves amidst storms of dust and swirling autumn leaves. Swords like lightning flashed in the thunderheads of war; the earth received a rain of blood and broken blades and bodies.

Volstokin's knights began to flee. Enraged, Vodicka prepared to sacrifice his infantry.

Mocker watched with delight and game-fan commentary. The Nordmen had no infantry of their own. Unhorsed, without the protection of footmen, they would be easy prey for Volstokin's more mobile men-at-arms.

The shaghûn asked Vodicka to hold the infantry. He would turn the tide.

Mocker had encountered many wizards. This one was no mountain-mover, but was superior for a survivor of El Murid's early anti-sorcery program. If he were an example of what the Disciple had been developing behind the Sahel, the west was in for some wicked surprises.

He conjured bears from smoke, unnaturally huge monsters misty about the edges but fanged and clawed like creatures bred only to kill. The Nordmen recognized them harmless, but their mounts were impressed beyond control. They broke, many throwing their riders in their panic.

"Now your infantry," said the shaghûn.

"Woe," Mocker mumbled, "am doomed. Am condemned to hopelessest of hopeless plights. Will never see home of self again." His fellow prisoners watched him curiously. They had never understood his presence. He had done nothing to enlighten them. But he had learned from them.

He knew who planned to betray whom, and when and how, and the most secret of their changing alliances. But Mocker suspected their scheming no longer mattered. Vodicka's and Bragi's armies were the real powers in Kavelin now.

Vodicka's leadership remained indecisive. Twenty miles from Vorgreberg he went into camp. He seemed to be waiting for something.

What came was not what he wanted. From his seat outside Vodicka's pavilion, Mocker listened to the King's curses when he discovered that the Queen's Own, though inferior in numbers, were upon him. While the surprise attack developed, Vodicka and the shaghûn argued about why Tarlson was so confident.

Mocker learned why they had been waiting.

They were expecting another Siluro uprising.

But Tarlson should have anticipated that possibility. Had he rounded up the ringleaders?

Mocker supposed that Tarlson, aware of his position, had elected to rely on boldness and speed.

He brought his horsemen in hard and fast, with little armor to slow them. From the beginning it was obvious he was only mounting a raid in force.

Yet it nearly became a victory. Tarlson's men raged through the camp, trailing slaughter and fire. One detachment made off with cattle and horses, another drove for the Royal pavilion.

Mocker saw Tarlson at their head, shouted them on. But Vodicka's house troops and the shaghûn's bodyguards were hardened veterans.

The shaghûn crouched in the pavilion entryway, chanting over colored smokes. If there had ever been a time for a Mocker trick, this was it. He had begun to despair of ever winning free. He wracked his brain. It had to be something that wouldn't get him killed if he failed.

A not-too-kind fate saved him the trouble.

A wild thrust by a dying spearman slipped past Tarlson's shield and found a gap behind his breastplate. The Wesson plunged from his saddle. With the broken spear still protruding, he surged to his feet.

A youth on a big gray, hardly more than a boy, came on like a steel-edged storm, drove the Volstokiners back, dragged Eanred up behind him. Tarlson's troops screened his withdrawal.

In minutes it was over, the raiders come and gone like a bitter breath of winter wind. Mocker wasn't sure who had won. Vodicka's forces had suffered heavily, but the Queen's men might have lost their unifying symbol...

Mocker reassumed his muddy throne. His future didn't seem bright. He would probably die of pneumonia in a few weeks.

"Ignominious end for a great hero of former times," he told his companions. He cast a promising, speculative glance the shaghûn's way.

iii) Reinforcements for Ragnarson

Two hundred men sat horses shagged with winter's approach, forming a column of gray ragged veterans remaining death-still. The chill wind whipped their travel cloaks and pelted them with flurries of dead leaves while promising sleet for the afternoon. There were no young men among them. From beneath battered helmets trailed strands predicting life's winter. Scars on faces and armor whispered of ancient battles won in wars now barely remembered. Not one of that hard-eyed catch of survivors wore a name unknown.

From distant lands they had come in their youth to march with the Free Companies during El Murid's wars, and now they were men without homes or homelands, wanderers damned to eternal travel in search of wars. Before them, a hundred yards away, beyond the Kavelin-Altean border, stood fifty men-at-arms in the livery of Baron Breitbarth. They were Wessons, levies still scratching where their new mail chafed, warriors only by designation.

Rolf Preshka coughed into his hand. Blood flecked the phlegm. Paroxysms racked him till tears came to his eyes.

From his right, Turran asked, "You okay?"

Preshka spat. "I'll be all right."

On Preshka's left, Valther resumed sharpening his sword. Each time they halted, sword and whetstone made soft, deadly music. Valther's eyes sought something beyond the eastern horizon.

Preshka waved a hand overhead.

The column took on metallic life. The mercenaries spread out. Shields and weapons came battle-ready.

The boys beyond the border saw their scars and battered arms, and the dark hollows where the shadows of the wings of death had passed across their eyes. They could cipher the numbers. They shook. But they didn't back down.

"Be a shame to kill them," said Turran.

"Murder," Preshka agreed.

"Where're their officers? Nordmen might be less stubborn."

The *scrape scrape* of Valther's whetstone carried during a lull in the wind. The Kaveliners shuddered.

Rolf turned. Several places to his right were three old Itaskians still carrying the shields of Sir Tury Hawkwind's White Company. "Lother. Nothomb. Wittekind. Put a few shafts yonder. Don't hurt anybody." Qualifications for the White Company had included an ability to split a willow wand at two hundred paces.

The three dismounted. From well-oiled leather cases they drew the bows that were their most valued possessions, weapons from the hand of Mintert Rensing, the acknowledged master of the bowmaker's trade. They grumbled together, picking targets, judging the breeze.

As one three shafts sped invisibly swift, feathered the heads of leopards in the coats of arms on three tall shields.

The Kaveliners understood. Reluctantly, they laid down their arms.

Preshka coughed, sighed, signaled the advance.

East of Damhorst he encountered a band of Kildragon's foragers. They were lean men with a few scrawny chickens. The larders of twice-plundered Nordmen were growing empty; Kildragon wouldn't permit looting the underclasses. Since Armstead Reskird had been fighting a guerrilla campaign from the Bodenstead forest, hanging on even after his enemies had given up trying to hunt him down. He had lost a third of his Itaskians, but had replaced them several times over with Wessons and Marena Dimura. He and Preshka joined forces, continued along the caravan route toward Vorgreberg. Other than Volstokin's army there was no force strong enough to resist them. The Nordmen had collapsed.

Preshka wondered where Bragi was. Somewhere deep in the east at last rumor. After Lake Berberich, Lieneke, and Sedlmayr, he had disappeared.

Rolf moved fast, avoiding conflict. There was little resistance. The faces he saw in the ruined towns and castles had had all the fight washed out. He always explained that he was bringing the Queen's peace. His force grew as angry, defeated, directionless soldiers abandoned the Nordmen for the Queen.

He passed south of Woerheide, heard the peasants mumbling about sorcery. It was chilling. What did this shaghûn have in his bag of tricks?

And where was Haroun? As much as anyone, bin Yousif was responsible for events in Kavelin. His dark ways were needed now. But there was hardly a rumor of the man.

Then came news of Tarlson's action near Vorgreberg, and of the Queen's forces wavering while mobs bloodied the streets of the capital.

And still no news of Bragi beyond a rumored baronial force having pursued him into the Savernake Gap.

When Preshka's scouts first reported contact with Volstokin's foragers, Rolf told Turran, "We can't handle Vodicka by ourselves." He considered his mercenaries. They had come on speculation, on the basis of his reputation. Would they fight?

"We can distract him," Turran said. "Eat up small forces."

Valther sharpened his sword and stared eastward. Hints of mountain peaks could be seen when weather permitted.

"He's been dallying for months," Reskird observed. "Should've driven straight to Vorgreberg."

"Was it his idea?"

"Eh?"

"El Murid's people might've conned him. So he'll be too unpopular to rule once he's done their catspawing. Want to bet there's a Siluro candidate in the wings, waiting till Bragi's been disposed of?"

"Might take some disposing," Kildragon observed. "He's beaten Volstokin before."

"This mob's got a shaghûn. A first-rater, you can bet."

"We haven't reached a decision," Turran interjected.

Preshka glanced his way, frowned. The man still hadn't explained his sudden urge to join this venture.

"They can't know much about us yet," said Kildragon. "So we sneak up on them, hide out—that's hilly country—and give them a swift kick once in a while. Keep them tottering till Vorgreberg gets organized. Way Vodicka's been vacillating, he won't attack with us behind him."

They sneaked, following a corridor of devastation so thorough Volstokin's foragers no longer wandered there. On a gray, icy morning at winter's head, in a drizzle that threatened to become snow, Preshka hurled his force at Vodicka's. He held no one in reserve.

Vodicka's troops were not surprised. Their trouble with Tarlson had taught them to be alert. They reacted well.

Preshka's lung was so bad his fighting capacity was nil. Though he retained overall control, he assigned Kildragon tactical command. Because of his stubborn insistence on joining the assault, Turran, Valther, and Uthe Haas stayed near to guard him.

Cursing the rain because of the damage it might do their weapons, the Itaskian bowmen generated a shower of their own from behind Preshka's veterans. The recruits held the flanks, to prevent encirclement of the thrust toward Vodicka's gaudy pavilion.

A spasm racked Preshka. He thought about Elana, the landgrant, and the heartaches he had suffered there. Was this better?

The Volstokiners fought doggedly, if with little inspiration. But Preshka's force penetrated to the defenses of the Royal pavilion.

If he could capture Vodicka, Rolf thought . . .

"Sorcery!" Turran suddenly growled. He sniffed the wind like a dog. Valther did the same, his head swaying like a cobra's about to strike.

"Hoist me up," Preshka ordered. A moment later, as his feet returned to the bloody mud, "The shaghûn. And Mocker, in chains."

"Mocker?"

"Uthe, can you see?"

"No."

"We've got to get that shaghûn. Otherwise, we're dead. Kildragon! Put your arrows around the tent door." But his words were swept away by the crash. "I think," he told Turran, "that I just brought you here to die. The attack was a mistake."

Colored smokes began boiling up before the pavilion.

iv) Vorgreberg

It was raining hard. Bits of sleet stung Ragnarson's face and hands. The rising waters of the Spehe, that formed the boundary between the Gudsbrandal Forest and the Siege of Vorgreberg, rushed against his mount, threatened to carry them both away. The far bank looked too soggy to climb.

"Where's the damned ford?" he thundered at the Marena Dimura scout there.

The man, though shivering blue, grinned. "Is it, Colonel? Not so good, eh?"

"Not so good, Adamec."

They had been pushing themselves to the limit for a week, a thousand men strung out along remote, twisty ways, trying to come to the capital unannounced.

His mount fought the current bravely, stubbornly, squished up the far bank. As Ragnarson rose in his stirrups to survey the land beyond, the beast slipped, began sliding, reared.

Rather than risk being dragged under and drowned, Bragi threw himself into the flood. He came up sputtering and cursing, seized the lance a passing soldier offered, slithered up the bank behind him. Across his mind flashed images of the main hall of his home, warm and *dry,* then Haroun's eagle's face. He staggered to his feet cursing louder than ever.

"Move it there!" he thundered. "It's open country up

here. You men, get that safety line across. I'll have your balls on a platter if somebody drowns."

He glanced northeast, wondered how Haaken was coming along. Blackfang, with the bulk of the force and the prisoners, was hiking the caravan route, his function for the moment that of diversion.

Bragi's horsemen, exhausted, on staggering mounts, came out of the river by ones and twos, ragged as bandits. Their banners were tattered and limp. The one thing impressive was that they had done the things they had. He wished he could promise them that the hard days would be over when they reached the city. But no, the business in Kavelin was far from done.

The final rush to Vorgreberg reminded Ragnarson more of a retreat than of a dash to action. He waved to startled Wessons peeping from hovel doors, sometimes gave a greeting in the Queen's name. He had the surviving Trolledyngjans with him, as well as the best of the Itaskians and Wessons. Of the Marena Dimura he had brought only a handful of scouts. They would be of no value in street fighting.

A few columns of smoke rose on the horizon, fires still smoldering in the rain. As they drew nearer Vorgreberg, they encountered bands of refugees camped in the muddy fields. From these he learned that the Queen still ruled, but that her situation was precarious. The rumor was circulating that she was considering abdication to avoid further bloodshed.

That would be in character, Ragnarson thought. All he had heard suggested that the woman was too good for the ingrates she had inherited.

And what of Volstokin?

The refugees knew little. Vodicka had been camped west of the Siege, doing nothing, for a long time. He was waiting. For what?

Ragnarson kept pushing. The rain and sleet kept falling. One thing about the weather, he thought. It would keep the mobs small.

He reached the suburbs unannounced, unexpected, and laughed aloud at the panic he inspired at the guardpost. While his Wesson sergeants answered their challenge, he swept on toward the city wall.

At the gate he again surprised soldiers, men hiding from the weather while the gate stood open. Sloppy, he thought, driving through. In a time so tense, why were they not alert?

Morale problems, he imagined. Despair caused by Tarlson's injury. A growing suspicion that it no longer mattered what they did.

That would change.

The alarm gongs didn't sound till he had reached the parklands around Castle Krief. As the panicky carillon ran through the city, he ordered, "Break the banners."

The men bearing the old, tattered standards dropped back. Others removed sheaths from fresh banners representing the peoples forming Ragnarson's command, as well as standards he had captured in his battles. He made sure Sedlmayr's banner was up near his own. The Royal standard he took in his own hand.

The castle's defenders reached the ramparts in time to observe this bit of drama. After a puzzled minute they broke into ragged cheers.

His eyes met hers the instant he entered the vast courtyard. She stood on a tower balcony. She was a tall woman, fairy slim, small-boned, with long golden hair stringing in the downpour. Her eyes were of a blue deeper than a summer sky at zenith. She wore simple, unadorned white that the rain had pasted to her slight curves . . .

He learned a lot about her in that moment, before turning to survey the mud-spattered, weary, ragged cutthroats behind him. What would she think?

He dipped his banner in salute. The others did the same.

His eyes locked with hers again. She acknowledged the salute with a nod and smile that almost made the ride worthwhile. He turned to shout orders to keep traffic moving. When he looked back, she was gone.

The political picture could be judged by the fewness of the servants who helped with the animals. Nowhere did he see a dusky Siluro face. Among the soldiery, Nordmen were scarce. Virtually all were flaxen-haired Wessons.

One, a youth trying to keep his head dry with his

shirttail, came running. "Gods, Colonel, you made good time."

"Ah, Gjerdrum." He smiled weakly. "You said to hurry."

"I only got back last night myself. Come. Father wants to see you."

"Like this?" He had had time to become awed. This was a Royal palace. In the field, at war, a King was just another man to him. In their own dens, though, the mighty made him feel the disreputable brigand he currently appeared to be.

"No formalities around here anymore, sir. The Queen . . . She's a lady who'll understand. If you see what I mean. The war, you know."

"Lead on, then." He left billeting, mess, and stabling to his sergeants and the Queen's.

Tarlson was dying. Propped up in a huge bed, he looked like a man in the final stage of consumption. Like a man who should have died long ago, but who was too stubborn to go. He was too heavily bandaged to move.

She was there too, in her rain-soaked garments, but she stayed in a shadowed corner. Ragnarson nodded, went to Tarlson's side. He tried to avoid dripping and dropping mud on the carpeting.

"I'd heard you'd picked up another scar," he said.

Eanred smiled thinly, replied, "I think this one had my name. Sit. You look exhausted."

Ragnarson shuffled.

From behind him, "Sit down, Colonel. No need preserving furniture for Vodicka's plunderers." She had a melodious voice even when bitter.

"So you finally came," said Tarlson.

"I was summoned."

"Frequently." Tarlson smiled. "But you were right. We couldn't've won defending one city. If I hadn't been rash, you might still be chastising barons."

"I think they've had enough—though I'm out of touch. About the west and south you know. And the east has surrendered."

"Ah? Gjerdrum suggested as much, but wasn't clear."

"He didn't waste any time asking questions."

"He's got a lot to learn. You came swiftly. Alone?"

"With a thousand. The rest are afoot, with prisoners. As I've said before, I believe in movement."

"Yes, per Haroun bin Yousif. I want to talk about him. When the pressure is off. Maybe your arrival will help."

Ragnarson frowned.

"We intercepted messages from Vodicka to the Siluro community. They're supposed to revolt this week. I hope they'll reconsider now."

Ragnarson remembered the laxity of the Queen's troops. "My men won't be much help if it breaks tonight. And yours don't look good for anything."

"What do you suggest?" Tarlson asked.

His wounds had taken the vinegar out of him, Ragnarson thought. "Lock the gates. Use the palace guard to flood the Siluro quarter. Post a curfew. Enforce it. They can't do anything if you grab them as they leave their houses."

"And leave the palace undefended?"

"In my hands, you mean? Yes. Eanred, you've got your suspicions. I'm not sure why. Let's just say our goals are similar."

Tarlson didn't apologize. "Kavelin makes one suspicious. No matter. Be your intentions good or evil, we're in your hands. There's no one else to stop Vodicka."

Ragnarson didn't like it. He was becoming too much a principal in Kavelin's affairs.

"I know my contract," he said stiffly. "I'll try to keep it. But the loyalties of my men lie differently."

"Meaning?"

"They've been in Kavelin for months, fighting, and dying, for a cause not their own. They're full of spirit. They haven't let loose for a long time. What happens when they go for a drink and realize they haven't been paid a farthing? . . ."

"Ah." Tarlson glanced past Ragnarson.

"Sums have been held in the Treasury, Colonel," said the Queen. "Though you should be rich with the booty you've taken."

Ragnarson shrugged.

"And what's happened to your fat friend?" Tarlson

asked. "As I recall, he disappeared at the Scarlotti ferries."

"That's a ghost that's haunted me since. I don't know. I sent him to Damhorst. All I've heard is that he might be in Breitbarth's hands."

"He may be with Vodicka now," said Tarlson. "I saw a chain of prisoners during the attack . . ."

"Was he all right?"

"Not sure it was him. I just caught a glimpse of a fat man hopping around screaming. Then I got spear bit."

"That's him. I wonder what Vodicka's doing with him?"

"What're your plans?"

"Don't have any. I was called to defend Vorgreberg. I didn't extend my imagination beyond getting here."

"There're two considerations. The Siluro. Vodicka. The Siluro we can handle now. If we can send Vodicka packing before spring, we might have an edge on the barons next summer."

"Next summer you'll have real problems."

"Eh?"

"The Captal of Savernake."

"What about him?" Tarlson's face darkened. He stole a glance past Ragnarson.

"He's got his own army and Pretender up there. A child about six. I tried to get him, but . . ." He stopped because of the emotions parading across Tarlson's face.

"But what?"

"His allies. It was pure luck that we got out. Those people . . . The grimmest soldiers in the world."

"There were suspicions . . . The King told me . . . Who? El Murid?"

"Shinsan."

His sibilant whisper fostered a dreadful silence broken only by a gasp from behind him. Tarlson's face became so pale and immobile that Ragnarson feared he had suffered a stroke.

"Shinsan? You're sure?"

"Blackfang's bringing the proof. Armor from their dead. And the child . . . He's training with Mist herself. She was at Maisak."

"The child . . . Did she seem well?" The Queen's voice held such excited interest that Ragnarson half-turned. Then it added up. The child was hers . . . Then, stunningly, the "She" reached his consciousness.

"Shinsan!" Tarlson gasped.

Ragnarson turned back. Despite his condition, Eanred was trying to rise.

He almost made it. Then he collapsed, fighting for breath. Bloody foam rose to his lips.

"Maighen!" the Queen shouted. "Find Doctor Wachtel! Gjerdrum! Come help your father."

As the boy rushed in, Ragnarson went to the Queen. She seemed ready to faint. He helped her retain her feet.

"Eanred, don't die," she begged softly. "Not now. What'll I do without you?"

When aloofness and dignity abandoned her, Ragnarson caught a glimpse of the frightened woman behind the facade. So young, so defenseless.

Ignoring his filth, she clung to him, head over his heart. "Help me!" she begged.

What else could he do?

v) Hour of reprisal

Mocker thought the crash and clash and screaming meant that the Queen's Own had come back for a sudden rematch. He was so sick that he didn't look up. Why bother?

The clangor moved closer. For a long time he did nothing more ambitious than blow his nose on his sleeve. He was sorry immediately. The stench of the corpse five places to his right reached him despite the downpour. The fellow had died four days earlier. No one had bothered to remove him. As the Siluro uprising continued to be delayed, the Volstokiners became increasingly lax, increasingly defeatist. Vodicka and the shaghûn had had bitter arguments about it. Vodicka himself had become dull-witted and unconcerned.

Mocker's stomach turned. The little he had had to eat had been moldy, spoiled. Staggering to his feet, he dragged his nearer chainmates along in his rush to the cathole latrine five paces away.

While he squatted with the skirts of his robe around his waist, a spent arrow plopped into the mud nearby. He reached, slipped, fell, came up cursing. The other prisoners cursed him back. A quarter of their number had died already, and disease soon would have them all—and Vodicka's army as well. Dysentery was endemic. In the chain, now, there were no friends, just animals who growled at one another.

The arrow was Itaskian. No native weapon would have used one so long.

He wanted to shout for joy, but didn't have the energy.

He had long despaired of having this opportunity, yet he had prepared. It had taken slow, careful work. He had wanted no one, especially his favor-seeking companions, to discover what he was doing.

First there had been the chains. Each man's right hand was linked to the left ankle of the man on his right. He had, for days, been grinding away at a link with bits of sandstone. That done to his satisfaction, he had gone on to provide himself with weapons.

When the shaghûn and his gaudy smokes appeared at the pavilion entrance, Mocker broke the weakened link and took the best of his weapons from within his robe.

Making the sling had been more difficult than cutting the chain. Everyone was always toying with the latter . . .

He had three stones, though he expected to get but one shot before being brought down himself. And it had been years . . .

The sling, twisted of fabric strips from his robe, hummed as he wound up. A few apathetic eyes turned his way.

He let fly.

"Woe!" he moaned. He shook his left fist at the sky, got a faceful of rain. He had missed by such a wide margin that the shaghûn hadn't noticed that he was being attacked.

But no one gave Mocker away. No dusky guards came

to pound him back to the mud. The attack was ferocious. Must be some bad fighters out there, he thought.

He turned, glared through the downpour, almost immediately spied Reskird Kildragon. His hopes surged. The best fighters in this end of the world.

His second stone scored. Not with the eye-smashing accuracy he had had as a boy, but close enough to shatter the shaghûn's jaw. The soldier-wizard staggered from his smokes, one hand reaching as if for help. He came toward the prisoners.

Mocker checked the haggard Nordmen. Some were beginning to show interest.

Wobbling on legs weak with sickness, he went to the shaghûn. He swung his length of chain, beat the man to the mud.

Still no interference. But dusky faces were beginning to glance back from the fighting. He used the shaghûn's dagger to finish it quickly.

"Vodicka now," he said, rising with the bloody blade. But through the uproar he heard Kildragon bellowing for his men to close up and withdraw.

And there was no way he could reach them.

"Am doomed," he muttered. "Will roast slow on spit, no skald to sing last brave feat." His hands, deft as those of the pickpocket he had been when Haroun had picked him up early in the wars, ran through the shaghûn's garments, snatched everything loose. He then scooted round the pavilion's rear, hoping to vanish before anyone noticed what had happened.

The Nordmen watched with eyes now jealous and angry. From within the pavilion came Vodicka's querulous voice. He sounded drunk or ill.

Then came shouts as the murder was discovered.

ELEVEN: Closing Tighter

i) Dying

Death just did not belong in the day. It had dawned bright, warm, and almost cloudless. By noon the streets had dried.

"It isn't right," Gjerdrum said, staring out a window near his father's bed. "In stories it always comes during a stormy night, or on a morning heavy with mist."

The Queen sat beside the bed, holding Tarlson's hand. He had been in a coma since the previous afternoon. "My father calls Death the ultimate democrat," she said. Deep shadows lurked beneath her eyes. "Also the indisputable autocrat and the great leveler. She's not impressed by anything or anyone. Nor by what's fitting and proper."

"Mother wouldn't come. She's locked herself in their bedroom . . . Says she won't come out till he comes home. Because he always did. He'd take wounds that'd kill a bear, but he always came home. But she knows he won't make it this time. She's trying to bring him back with her memories."

"Gjerdrum, if there was anything . . . You know I'd . . ."

"I was conceived in that room. When he was just another Wesson footman. The night before the Queen's

167

Own and the guard went to meet El Murid in the Gap. Why didn't he ever move? He took over some of the other rooms, but he never moved..."

"Gjerdrum!"

He turned.

"His eyes. They moved."

Tarlson's eyes opened. He seemed to be grasping for his bearings. Then, in a hoarse whisper, "Gjerdrum, come here."

"Don't push yourself, father."

"There're some things to say. She came, but I couldn't go. Be quiet. Let me hurry. She's waiting. What's Ragnarson doing?"

"Cleaning up the Siluro. He slept a couple hours, then took the regiment and Guard into the quarter. All we've had from him since is prisoners and wagons full of weapons. Doing a house-to-house. They're screaming. But anyone who argues gets arrested. Or killed."

"Gjerdrum, I don't trust that man. I'm not sure why. It may be bin Yousif. There's a connection. They've fought each other, and while their employers got destroyed, they got rich. He knows too much about what's going on. And he may be working for Itaskia. Some of his 'mercenaries' are Itaskian regulars."

He lay quietly for several minutes, regaining strength. "It's a game of empires," he said at last, "and Kavelin's the board.

"Gjerdrum, I made a promise to the King. I've tried to keep it. I pass it to you, if you will ... Though the gods know how you'll manage. Any way you can ... Tell your mother ... I'm sorry ... My duty ... This time she'll have to come to me. Where the west wind blows ... She'll understand ... I'll ... I'll ..."

His eyes slowly closed. For a moment Gjerdrum thought he had fallen asleep. At last, of the Queen, "Is he? ... Did he? ..."

"Yes."

They spent few tears. Waiting for the inevitable had dulled its painful edge.

"Gjerdrum, find Colonel Ragnarson. Tell him to come to my chambers. And inform the Ministers that there'll be a meeting at eight. Don't tell *anyone* what's happened."

"Ma'am." He snapped a weak salute. In duty there was surcease from pain.

ii) Interview

Ragnarson sat stiffly erect as his horse *clop-clopped* through empty streets. He had to keep an iron grip. He was so tired he had begun seeing things.

A Trolledyngjan rode at either hand, ready for trouble. But they didn't expect anything. The populace had been cowed. They appeared only in brief flashes, in cracks between curtains.

Today Vorgreberg, tomorrow the Siege. Next, Vodicka. And Kavelin before spring. Get the kingdom united in time to meet the Captal and Shinsan.

The palace was as deserted as the city. With the Queen's go-ahead, he had sent out every man able to bear arms. They had met little resistance once it was clear they would not tolerate it.

She was pacing when he reached her, pale, wringing her hands. Her eyes were shadowed.

"Eanred died."

She nodded. "Colonel, it's falling apart. My world. I'm not a strong person. I tend to run rather than face things. Eanred was my strength, as he was my husband's. I don't know what to do now. I just want to get away..."

"Why'd you call me?" He had known from the moment their eyes met that she would appreciate strength and directness more than flourishes and formalities. "I'm a sword-for-hire. An outsider. An untrustworthy one, so Eanred thought."

"Eanred trusted no one but the Krief. Sit down. You've been up long enough."

She was a startling woman. No Royal person he had ever encountered would have treated a blankshield as an equal. And no queen or princess would have had him to her private chambers unchaperoned...

"You're smiling. Why?"

"Uh? Thinking of Royalty. Princesses. A long time ago, in Itaskia . . . Well, no matter. An unsavory episode, seen from here."

"Brandy?"

She had startled him again. A Queen serving a commoner . . .

"They're stuffy in Itaskia? Your Royalty?"

"Usually. Why'd you want to see me?"

"I'm not sure. Some questions. And maybe because I need someone to listen." She walked slowly to a window.

Watching her move, Ragnarson's thoughts slipped into channels far from respectful.

"I've called a conference of Ministers. I'll either abdicate and return to my father . . ."

"My Lady!"

". . . or appoint you Marshal and put it all on you." She turned, her gaze locking with his.

He was flabbergasted. "But . . . Marshal? . . . I never commanded more than a battalion before this spring. No. You'd get too much resistance. Better pick a Kaveliner . . ."

"Who could I trust? Who's commanded who hasn't been in touch with the rebels? Eanred. But he's dead. Even my ministers have hedged their bets."

"But . . ."

"And though I hate to speak ill of the dead, Eanred couldn't've handled it. He was at his best as Champion. As a field commander he was mediocre. The King understood this."

She retrieved the decanter, poured more brandy.

"He wasn't strong, the King. Couldn't force his will. But he knew men. He could talk to someone fifteen minutes and tell all about them. He knew who could be trusted and who couldn't, and who would be happiest and do best in which post. I wish he were here."

"You need to trust me, but don't know if you can. Ask your questions."

She moved a chair to face him. "What's your connection with the Itaskian Crown?"

"Appointive landgrave. Non-hereditary sort of half-title with a reserve commission. Army. Brevet-Captain of

Infantry. I get the use of, and title to, formerly non-productive border territory in return for playing sheriff and defending the frontier. For political reasons I'm currently active on the War Ministry rolls. My assignment is to prevent El Murid from gaining control of the Savernake Gap and flanking the Tamerice-Hellin Daimiel Line. I'm also a genuine Guild Colonel, though on the Citadel's bad side. My Itaskian assignment doesn't conflict with my contract to yourself."

"At the moment. Your orders might change. Anything else?"

He shrugged. "What?"

"Men the King trusted he sent on trade missions. With other assignments. He knew Kavelin's importance. Those men have continued reporting. For instance: Tamerice was in touch with the Wessons in Sedlmayr and Delhagen. Altea has considered annexing Dolusich, Vidusich, and Gaehle. Anstokin plans the same for the lower tier of provinces in Volstokin, all the way to the Galmiches—assuming we best Vodicka."

"One King always tries to profit from another's distress. The Sedlmayr matter is settled. Altea, I'm sure, prefers friendship and cooperation to war over wastelands. And Anstokin has a historical claim to most of those provinces."

"I was leading up to the fact that we have people in Itaskia. Our best. When your King stomps, the ground rocks throughout the west."

Ragnarson's immediate reaction was *so what?* Then he asked, "In whose party?"

"Excuse me?"

"You suspect Itaskian intentions. I want to point out that we're split. Each party controls part of the government. The Greyfells party is pro-El Murid. The other, intensely anti-El Murid. I wondered if your spies took that into account."

"Which line do you follow?"

"Greyfells and El Murid have been my enemies since the wars."

"I believe you, Colonel. But there's still Haroun bin Yousif. What does he want?"

"We're as close as men can be. But his mind is like one

of those puzzle boxes where, when you finally get it open, all you've got is another box."

"But you've got an idea?"

"A guess. Based on geography. He's ready to go back to Hammad al Nakir. There's no better base than Kavelin. Al Rhemish is just over the Kapenrungs. If he could seize the holy places, he might manage a restoration. We only see the fanatics outside. Behind the Sahel, El Murid's support is far from unanimous."

"I see. A problem. But one that can be dealt with when the time comes. He won't have calculated Shinsan into his plans." She rose, returned to the window. "The city? Can it be pacified? The Siege?"

"Those are battles already in hand. I'm looking beyond, to Vodicka."

"Good. There's more to be said and asked, but later. I want you to rest now. That's an order. I want you fresh after the council. If I stay on . . ." She came to him, took his hands in hers, turned them palms up, studied them, then looked him in the eye. "I'd be in these hands. Be gentle."

iii) Confrontations

Ragnarson had the feeling that a long time had passed. He lay drifting on the edge of sleep, his conscience telling him he should be up and busy, but instead he continued wondering how much meaning he dared attach to the Queen's final words.

Came a knock. "Enter," he grumbled, rising to a sitting position. A lone candle illuminated his room.

Gjerdrum stuck his head in. "Sorry to wake you, Colonel. We've caught a vagrant. Hard to understand him, but I think he says he knows you."

"Eh? Fat man? Dark?"

"Looks like he used to be fat. But he's sick now. I'd say he's had a rough time for a couple months."

"Where is he? Let me get my pants on. How's the

chances of me getting something new to wear?"

Gjerdrum glanced at the near-rags he was donning. "I'll try to find something."

"The Queen. How'd her council go?"

"Still on."

"Lead away. Where's he at?"

"Dungeon. We thought that'd be safest."

It was Mocker. Mocker in pathetic shape. He snoozed on a straw-strewn floor.

"Open up," he told the turnkey. "Quietly. Don't wake him."

There had to be a trick. He could not welcome Mocker without one. He hunkered down and tickled the fat man's ear. He had grown an ugly, scraggly beard. This Ragnarson tweaked gently. "Wake up, darling," he said in a squeaky falsetto.

Mocker smiled, placed one hand over Ragnarson's. He frowned in consternation—then bounced up ready for a fight.

Bragi roared, rocked back on his heels. "Got you!"

"Hai!" Mocker groaned in a weak imitation of his former self. "Greatest of great spies risks life and limb of very self-important self, endures months of incarceration, debilitation, and torture at behest of friend, weary unto death and on edge of pneumonia, with Volstokiners hordes pursuing, treks thirty miles godforsaken country after redoubtedly—redoubtably?—singlehandedly slaying arch-shaghûn of Volstokin advisers, shaghûn-general direct from councils at Al Rhemish, thereby saving bacon of ingrate associates Preshka and Kildragon, and am welcomed to saved city by dungeon-chucking natives too ignorant to recognize renowned self, there to be set upon by hairy Trolledyngjan of dubious masculinity and questionable morals. Woe! In whole universe is no justice. Very demons of despair pursue self through vale of tears called life..."

Ragnarson got lost in the twists and turns. "Rolf's here? In Kavelin?" If Rolf had joined Reskird, Elana might have too.

"Said same, no? Preshka, Rolf. Iwa Skolovdan. Former Guild Captain. Age thirty-six. Nineteen years service. Began with Lauder's Company..."

"All right. All right. Give me the part about the shaghûn again."

Mocker regained his verve while he detailed his escape.

"Come on," said Ragnarson. "We'll clean you up and have the Royal physician look you over." On the way, Ragnarson bombarded his friend with questions. Each answer pleased him more than the last.

"Gjerdrum," he said, as they neared his room, "scare up the physician. Then have all officers assemble in the officers' mess. Have them bring maps of the area where Vodicka's camped. And I want my Marena Dimura there. Then meet me at the council chamber. How do I get there?"

"But you can't..."

"Watch me. I could care less about being respectful to a gang of lard-assed Nordmen hypocrites. Tell me."

Reluctantly, the youth gave directions.

"Carry out your orders. Wait. What the hell time is it, anyway?"

"Around midnight."

Ragnarson groaned. He had wasted eight hours sleeping.

Two palace guards blocked the council chamber door. "Announce me," he told the senior.

"Sorry, sir. Lord Lindwedel left instructions that they weren't to be disturbed for any reason."

"Eh? Why? What if something happened?"

The soldier shrugged. "I got the idea they were going to have it out with Her Majesty."

"Ah." The old snake had found out about Eanred.

"You'd better get out of the way." His cold determination made the younger guard gulp.

"No, sir," the senior said. "Not till my orders change." His knuckles whitened on the haft of his short ceremonial pike.

Bragi hit him with a left jab. His helmet clanged off the wall. Ragnarson snatched his pike, knocked the second soldier's feet from beneath him, rattled the first's brains again, then hit the door. It was neither locked nor barred. He crashed through.

Just in time.

Seven old Nordmen surrounded the Queen like lean gray wolves a terrified fawn. She had been weeping, was about to sign a document. The triumph on the ministers' faces, before they turned, told Ragnarson he had guessed right. They had bullied her into abdicating.

He took three swift steps, smashed the pike head down on the document. Hurling ministers aside, Bragi seized the document, flung it into a nearby fireplace.

Lindwedel shouted, "Guards!"

"Keep your mouth shut, you old vulture!" Ragnarson growled, drawing his sword. "Or I'll cut you a new one about four inches lower." He backed to the door, locked and barred it.

He wished he had a few Trolledyngjans along. He would have to hurry instead . . .

"You men get over against that wall." He moved to the Queen's side. She appeared uncertain whether to be grateful or angry. He scowled at a minister edging toward the door.

"If I were younger, I'd . . ."

"You'd get your ass killed. Haven't met a Nordmen yet who could butcher a chicken without help. Let's get this settled civilly. We'll let the lady make up her mind on her own."

Their glares promised trouble. There would soon be plots to eliminate the foreigner who defended the foreign Queen.

"Why'd you bust in?" the Queen whispered.

"Friend of mine just arrived," he replied softly. "From Vodicka's camp. Wanted you to know what he said. When I got trouble outside, I figured these old buzzards were up to something."

"What was so important?"

"Vodicka's shaghûn is dead, Vodicka has gone insane, and his army has been decimated by sickness. His men are deserting. My associate Kildragon has placed a force west of them as an anvil against which I can hammer them. I'll begin tightening the noose in the morning."

"You're pushing too hard. Killing yourself. You've got to rest sometime."

"You rest between wars," he muttered. Then, "We can't ease off. There're still too many variables. And Shinsan's vultures are perched on the crags of the Kapenrungs."

"You won't wait for your man Blackfang?"

"No. But he'll be here soon. I don't intend getting in a fight anyway, just to maneuver Vodicka into a bad position."

"The numbers don't look good."

"Numbers aren't important. Still want to run away? To quit when we've got a glimmer of hope?"

"I don't know. I wasn't made for this. Intrigue. War."

"I promise you, if it's within my power, that I won't go till I can leave you with the quietest country in the Lesser Kingdoms. If I have to leave rebels hanging like apples from every tree."

"But you're a mercenary. And have a family and home, I hear."

Did she sound just the least disappointed? "I have no home while the Greyfells party retains any power. The appointment?"

"They'll never agree."

"Bet?" He turned to the Ministers. "Her Majesty wishes your confirmation of my appointment as Marshal of Kavelin."

Some turned red and sputtered. Lord Lindwedel croaked, "Never! No base-born foreigner..."

"Then we'll hang you and appoint some new Ministers."

The door rattled as someone tried it. The Ministers perked up.

Ragnarson could force his will here, he knew, but how would he keep them from reneging?

Haroun's would be the simplest solution. *He* would have them murdered.

"You wouldn't dare!"

Men smashed against the door.

"Try me. The charge is treason. I believe Her Majesty will support it."

Axes began splintering the door.

The Queen touched his arm. "Appearances will decide this. Back into the corner like you're defending me."

She had chosen. He smiled, did as she suggested. She attached herself to his left arm in the classic pose of damsel hanging on protector.

Lord Lindwedel surrendered. "All right, damn it. Have the documents prepared."

Bragi held his pose long enough for Gjerdrum and the Queen's troops to catch a glimpse. Thus it was that, dishonestly, he won their loyalty.

iv) The challenge

There was snow on the ground, a sprinkling scarcely thicker than frost, tainted ruby in the dawnlight. A harsh cold wind stirred skeletal trees. Bragi, astride a shivering horse at wood's edge, glanced up the road that snaked over the hill masking Vodicka's camp. With him were the irrepressible Mocker and a dozen of his own and the Queen's men. Mocker blew into shaking hands and bemoaned the impulse that had brought him into the field.

For a week Ragnarson had maneuvered his forces into position, hoping for a fiat that would spare lives. He would need every man in the spring.

To the north, blocking the route to Volstokin, were Blackfang and Ahring with the Trolledyngjans and Itaskians. Sir Andvbur, for the moment commanding the Queen's Own and palace guard, held the routes eastward. In the south lay Altenkirk with eleven hundred Wessons and Marena Dimura. The woods behind Vodicka were held by Kildragon and Preshka.

Everyone had been in position since the day before. The men had been given a night's rest and plenty to eat . . . This one he wouldn't hurry. It would be his most crucial battle, one that, in its handling more than its winning, could make him as Marshal of Kavelin.

"You'd better get going," he told Mocker.

The fat man kicked his new donkey into a walk. He had volunteered to find Haroun. He would skirt the battle zone and, hopefully, would know the outcome before passing Kildragon's last outpost. He also bore messages to Vodicka's family.

Ragnarson turned to another of his companions. "Bring her out."

Against his advice and over the protests of her supporters, the Queen had insisted on joining him.

In minutes she was at his side, bundled in furs that concealed ill-fitting chain mail. She bubbled.

Ragnarson nodded. "We begin." He urged his mount forward. She kept pace. His party trailed by twos.

Ragnarson's heart hammered. His stomach flipped and knotted. Doubts plagued him. Had he chosen the best course? Sure, it was the way to slay the rumors about him not leading from the front, but... What if Vodicka refused his challenge?

He leaned toward the Queen, said, "If you bring as much excitement and stubbornness to ruling as you do to getting in a fight, you'll..."

Her thigh brushed his. He wasn't sure, but it seemed she'd guided her mount the slightest bit closer to his. He remembered riding thigh by thigh with Elana, with mortal dangers waiting to strike.

"You're a beautiful woman," he croaked, forcing the compliment. Then he ameliorated his boldness with, "You shouldn't risk yourself like this. If we're taken..."

There was red in her face when she looked his way. Had he angered her?

"Marshal," she said, "I'm a woman. Noble by birth, Queen in marriage to a man *long* dead, and leader by circumstance. But a woman."

He thought he understood. And that was more frightening than anything that might be waiting beyond the hill.

They crested that hill. "You're sure the messages went out?" He had asked her to send commands to every Nordmen to post public pledges of fealty or face banishment or death. News of today's events would pursue the messengers, would convince or condemn.

"Yes. Slight exasperation.

He studied the encampment. Vodicka had restructured

it along Imperial lines, throwing up ramparts and cutting trenches. Towers for archers were under construction. It had taken two attacks for Vodicka to learn that he wasn't on bivouac.

"Banners," Ragnarson growled over his shoulder. They had been noticed.

The Krief family ensign broke beside a white parlay flag. Ragnarson advanced till they were just beyond the range of a good Itaskian bow. This would be the point for one of Greyfells' rogues to materialize.

They waited. And waited. The nearest gate finally opened. Horsemen came forth.

"Here," Ragnarson told the Queen, "is where, if I were Haroun, you'd learn the difference in our thinking. He'd make some innocuous signal and our bowmen could cut them down. Haroun goes for the throat."

Vodicka wasn't with the party.

"They look like they've spent a year besieged already," the Queen remarked. She was old enough to remember the bitter sieges in her homeland.

Ragnarson signaled an interpreter. The common speech of Volstokin was akin to Marena Dimura. The upper classes used a different dialect.

The party was a mixed bag including several senior officers of Volstokin's army, a few of El Murid's advisors, Kaveliner turncoats, and a man with a bow who looked Itaskian.

A Kaveliner recognized the Queen, babbled excitedly to his companions.

"Tell them our business is with Vodicka," Ragnarson told his interpreter. The lingua franca of the upper classes was the speech of Hellin Daimiel.

An officer replied, "I speak for King Vodicka. No need for the interpreter." He spoke flawless upper-class Itaskian. "I'm Commander of the Household, Seneschal Sir Farace Scarna of Liolios."

"Guild Colonel Bragi Ragnarson, Marshal of Kavelin, with and speaking for Her Supreme Highness Fiana Melicar Sardyga ip Krief, Queen of Kavelin, daughter and ally of His Highness Dusan Lorimier Sardygo, Lord Protector of Sacuescu, the Bedelian League, and the

Auszura Littoral, and Prince Viceregal to Their Majesties
the Kings of Dunno Scuttari and Octylya." Which didn't
mean much, Sacuescu being powerless, Dunno Scuttari
still recovering from the wars, and Octylya an Itaskian
Protectorate as subject to pressure from the Queen's
enemies as friends.

"What do you want?"

Ragnarson was pleased by Sir Farace's businesslike
manner. A fighting man all his life, Bragi judged.

"I challenge Vodicka to individual combat. And
demand the surrender of himself and his forces. The
former as Champion, the latter as Marshal."

"Champion?"

"Your King has had that much success, Sir Farace,"
the Queen interjected.

Sir Farace said something in his own tongue.
Reluctantly, all but he withdrew a hundred yards.

"Pull back the same distance, Dehner," Bragi ordered.

"The lady too, and it please you."

Ragnarson turned. She was putting her stubborn face
on. "My Lady."

"Must I?"

"I think so."

Once they were alone, scant swordswings apart, Sir
Farace asked, "Man to man? Not as Seneschal and
Marshal?"

"All right."

"Can you beat us?"

"Easily. But I'll starve you out instead. I've talked to
deserters. I know what's going on inside."

"Damned foreigners...Intrigues and magic. And
greed. Destroyed an army and a King." He paused, spat.
"I'd surrender. Save what I could. But I'm not His
Majesty. The weaker he gets, the more he grows sure we
can finish Kavelin if we'll just hold on till we get another
sorcerer from Al Remish." He spat again. "He won't
surrender. He might fight."

"You could sally, come over the hill, and surrender."

"No."

"I didn't think so. How bad is he?"

"Very. Healthy, he'd give you a battle. He fought

Tarlson to a draw once. Years ago. He wears the scar proudly."

"What happens if I kill him? In Volstokin?"

"You wouldn't notice the change. His brother, whom you defeated at Lake Berberich, succeeds. The war goes on."

"How, with Volstokin in ruins and threatened by famine?"

"The rumors are true?"

"I know bin Yousif."

"Why this confrontation?"

"This army's a nuisance. I've got more dangerous enemies to worry about. Suppose I grabbed Vodicka and threw him in a cell somewhere? Kept him in style, but didn't ransom him?"

"A regency. Probably the Queen Mother. His Majesty's brother, Jostrand, isn't that popular."

"And this infamous alliance with El Murid?"

"Dead. Dead as the Emperors in their graves."

"Then imprisonment might best serve both Volstokin and Kavelin."

"Perhaps."

"A gift to show my feeling that there should be peace between us. Anstokin moves with spring. They intend to take the provinces above Lake Berberich, all the way to the Galmiches."

Sir Farace grew pale. He started to say something, nodded. Then, "Of course. We should've anticipated it."

"Our sources are unimpeachable."

"I believe you. I'll talk to His Majesty, but I guarantee nothing. Good fortune."

"The same." He said it to Sir Farace's dwindling back.

v) Personal combat

"Well, what'd he say?" the Queen demanded.

"We might work something out."

"You won't attack?"

"Not if I can help it."

"But..."

"I didn't get this old fighting for fun. Let's get back to the woods. This wind's killing me."

While the others piled brush into a windbreak and got a fire going, and saw to the horses and weapons, Bragi and the Queen sat on a log and stared at Vodicka's encampment. Bragi was looking for weaknesses, she the gods knew what.

"Beckring," Ragnarson said presently. "Find Sir Andvbur. Tell him I need a crossbow, a pony or his runtiest horse, and a Cerny." The Cerny, a breed developed near that small city in Vorhangs, was a gigantic horse meant to bear the most heavily armored knights.

"Now what?" the Queen asked.

"Hedging my bets. That's another way you stay alive in this business."

"I don't understand."

"I just remembered. Haroun isn't the only guy who thinks his way. His whole race... Can you kill a man? If he's trying to kill you?"

"I don't know."

"Better think about it. Better be ready when the time comes." He began fiddling with his boots.

Beckring brought the animals and weapons just as a party left Vodicka's camp. Ragnarson explained as he hurried his people to the meeting point. He rode the Cerny, she the pony. The men crowded close so they could hear.

When the Volstokiners arrived, without Vodicka or Sir Farace, Ragnarson had the Cerny sideways to them with the Queen masked behind him. He presented his shield side.

Sir Farace had been replaced by an idiot, a terrified, drooling victim of some disease that had crippled both brain and body.

Ragnarson had anticipated the action. Vodicka had done the same in other wars. He ignored the man, concentrated on the "advisers."

They were too studiedly disinterested. He locked gazes with a hawk-nosed veteran who wore a mouth-corner scar that drew his lips into a permanent smirk.

Smirk-mouth's eyes flicked, for the scantest instant, to the man who was to provide his diversion...

Ragnarson spurred the Cerny. His right hand, already low, yanked the throwing knife from his boot, snapped it at Scar-mouth's throat. The Queen, no longer masked, discharged the crossbow into the chest of a second rider while all eyes remained on Bragi. His party produced their weapons and surrounded her. Before the startled Volstokiners, unprepared for their allies' treachery, recovered, Bragi had gotten round their flank. There he met a third adviser in a flurry of swordplay, unhorsed him, and faced the Volstokiners as they turned to run.

The mixup was brief. Bragi lost one man. The other party lost five before they surrendered.

Ragnarson dismounted, removed his ax from his wargear, separated Scar-mouth's head from his body. He handed it to the idiot. "Tell Vodicka this's the game I play with treachers. Tell him I say he's a coward, a baseborn whoreson who sends assassins after people he's too craven to face himself."

"We better get out of here," said one of Bragi's men.

"Yeah." He scrambled onto the Cerny.

While they watched Sir Andvbur's men skirmish with Volstokiners who had come out to aid their fellows, Bragi told the Queen, "You look ill. He would've killed you."

"It's not that. I've seen men die... The head..."

"Didn't give me any joy either. But gruesome doings sometimes save lives."

"I know. I understand. But that doesn't make me like it."

His own stomach was in poor shape.

The skirmishing died away. After transferring his gear to a fresh horse, Ragnarson mounted, said, "Time for the next phase." He took a Royal standard from a bearer, spurred downhill.

He went at a trot, carefully studying the ground and distant ramparts. He went to a canter, then, at bowshot, to a gallop. Volstokiners watched in surprise as he spurred past their earthworks, shouting insults at Vodicka. A few desultory arrows reached for him.

One whirred past his nose. He laughed like one of the battle-crazy berserker heroes of his boyhood homeland. His hair and beard whipped with the speed of the horse's passage. He hadn't felt such exhilaration in years.

He stopped beyond bowshot and waited. Then his high spirits got the better of him. He made a second passage, this time planting the Queen's standard on a mound near Vodicka's gate.

"You're mad!" the Queen cried, when he returned for a fresh mount. "Completely insane!" But she was laughing. And there was a new, more promising sparkle in her eyes.

"He's got to come out now. Or admit he's a coward to his whole army."

"He'll come in full knight's regalia," said Sir Andvbur, who had grabbed an opportunity to put himself near the Queen. "You won't be able to handle him..."

His spirits still soared. "Watch me!" Despite the cold, he shed garments till he was down to basic Trolledyngjan war gear. He hung helmet, shield, and sword on his horse, then ran into the woods where a Guard's infantry company lay hidden. He returned with a long pike.

"What you got to do," he explained, "is outgut them. When they *know* you're easy meat, but you stand your ground and grin, they get nervous. And make mistakes."

He realized he was showing off, but what he saw in the Queen's eyes made rational behavior impossible.

He rode to the meeting point, dismounted, planted a fresh standard, walked twenty paces downslope, leaned on the pike.

Trumpets winded. The encampment gate opened. A knight came forth.

This time Ragnarson faced Vodicka. He continued leaning on the pike, motionless. The horseman trotted back and forth, getting the feel of the earth, then rode uphill and stopped a hundred yards away.

As Ragnarson examined that mass of blood and steel, weighing nearly a ton and a half, he began to doubt. The horse was as protected as its rider.

Bragi continued leaning as if bored. He was committed.

Vodicka wasted no time talking. He couched his lance and charged.

The King's horse began to loom castle-huge. Bragi dropped to one knee, set his pike, lifted his shield. Could he hold each solidly enough?

He had made a major miscalculation. Vodicka's lance outreached his pike.

He shifted slightly, was unable to finish before impact.

Vodicka came in with his lancehead aimed at Ragnarson's chest, intending to blast him off the pike and finish him with his sword.

Bragi twisted his shield and pushed, to deflect the lance.

It ripped through his shield, down the underside of his forearm. Its impetus bore him over backward. But his right arm and hand remained oak-firm for the instant needed to bring Vodicka to grief. The pike head met the horse at the juncture of shoulder and breastplate. The screaming beast's momentum levered it into the air.

Ragnarson's sprawl forced Vodicka's lancehead into the earth.

Rearing horse and levering lance separated Vodicka from his saddle. As Ragnarson scrambled away, Volstokin's King landed with a horrendous clangor. Bragi was on him instantly, swordtip at the slot in the man's visor.

"Yield!"

"Kill me," muffled, weak.

Ragnarson glanced toward Vodicka's encampment. No rescue mission yet. He wrestled the helmet free. Yes, he had caught the genuine fish. He punched the King's jaw.

"Ouch!" He kissed his knuckles, with a knife cut the straps and laces holding Vodicka's armor. He finished barely in time to get uphill ahead of a band of would-be rescuers.

"He's in bad shape," Ragnarson told the Queen as he rode up. "Better get him to a doctor. To the palace. Won't be worth a farthing dead. Somebody find me some bandages."

While men dragged Vodicka away, the Queen took Ragnarson's hand. "For a minute I thought..."

"So did I. I'll grow up one of these days." Examining his arm, he found no major veins severed. A surgeon put a field dressing on, told him to avoid exertion for a few days.

"Sir Andvbur," he said, "begin the next phase."

The knight's men began pushing earthworks forward.

TWELVE: Complications and New Directions

i) Recovery and preparation

Volstokin's army fell apart. Man by man, then by companies, Vodicka's soldiers surrendered their weapons, and began the walk home. Within a week the encampment was deserted—except for El Murid's advisers and a few high officers. Ragnarson withdrew to the capital. Blackfang and the Trolledyngjans finished the job.

Pledges of fealty flooded in, especially from the provinces wasted. From Walsoken, Trautwein, Orthwein, and Uhlmansiek the response was spotty. From Loncaric and the Galmiches there was a forbidding silence. From Savernake they expected nothing, and nothing was what they got.

Rumors from the east had winged men soaring the cold winter nights, flitting from castle to castle.

Kavelin had two small industrial regions, the Sieges of Breidenbach and Fahrig. Breidenbach served the mines of the Galmiches, Loncaric, and Savernake. The Royal Mint was located there. To secure this, and as an experiment, Ragnarson sent Sir Andvbur Kimberlin north—across Low Galmiche.

Militarily, Fahrig was more important. It lay at the

heart of iron-rich Forbeck, and received ores from Uhlmansiek and Savernake as well. It was there Kavelin's iron and steel were made, and weapons and armor forged.

Both Sieges were heavily Wesson. The Queen would find support there.

Forbeck and Fahrig became Ragnarson's pet winter project. Securing them would not only insure his weapons supply, it would split the still rebellious provinces into two groups. The southern tier were comparatively weak.

They had gotten numerous declarations of fealty out of Forbeck, mostly from lesser nobles whose fortunes depended on open trade routes. The great landholders favored the Captal's pretender.

While Ragnarson studied, pondered, maneuvered his troops through the Siege of Vorgreberg, made requests and recommendations, and wished he controlled some means of communication as swift as the Captal's, the Queen put in eighteen-hour days trying to rebuild a shattered hierarchy. There were banishments and outlawries, and instruments of social import, each bitterly resisted in council.

Most resisted was confirmation of Ragnarson's bargain with the aldermen of Sedlmayr. On confirmation, Sedlmayr sent Colonels Kiriakos and Phiambolos and six hundred skilled arbalesters to Vorgreberg, and raised levies to pacify Walsoken.

Another edict guaranteed certain rights of free men, especially Wessons.

Even for serfs there was a new right. One son in each family would be permitted to leave the land for service with the Crown. For Kavelin, with its traditional class rigidities, this was a revolutionary device for social mobility.

Though they moaned, the Nordmen yielded little there. The chaos in the west had separated countless serfs from their masters. Many had become robbers and brigands. The device would bring them out of outlawry.

Men began filtering into the Siege.

Responsibilities went with rights. Ragnarson, slyly, injected into the decrees the concept of every man a soldier in defense of his own. Each adult male was ordered to obtain and learn to use a sword.

He was surprised how easily that slipped past the Ministers. Men with swords stood a little taller, stopped being unquestioning instruments of their lords' wills.

Two months passed. Warnecke came into the fold. Vodicka became the dour, grimly silent tenant of a tower shared with a manservant sent him by Sir Farace. The Wessons of Fahrig hinted interest in a charter like Sedlmayr's. Rolf Preshka's health deteriorated till he spent most of his time in bed. Turran and Valther disappeared. But their hands could be seen. The winter in the lowlands was unusually mild. In the high country it was bitter beyond memory. Sir Andvbur occupied Breidenbach. And Bragi spent more and more time in the field, drilling his forces in the southeastern portion of the Siege.

One blustery morning his engineers threw a pontoon across the Spehe to the Gudbrandsdal. He invaded Forbeck.

ii) Ghost hunting.

Mocker huddled between buildings in Timpe, a minor city in Volstokin, cursing the weather and his own ill fortune. He had been in the kingdom two months and had yet to uncover a hint of Haroun's whereabouts. The warmest trail hadn't been hot since autumn. A few guerrillas remained, but the big man had vanished.

A ragged party of soldiers appeared, returning from Kavelin. They exchanged bitter words with people in the streets. Mocker retreated to deeper shadows. No point giving foul tempers a scapegoat.

"Well," said a voice from the darkness, softly, "see what the hounds have flushed."

One hand darting beneath his robes for a dagger, Mocker looked around. He saw no one. "Haroun?"

"Could be."

"Self, have been traipsing over half arse-end of world..."

"So I've heard. What's your problem?"

Mocker tried to explain while hunting. He saw nothing but unnaturally deep shadow.

"So what's Bragi want?" the sourceless voice demanded. "He's doing all right. He could make himself king."

"Hai! Enemies thus far ground in mill of great grinder northern friend like ants in path of anteater. But now anteater comes to narrow in road where lion waits..."

"What're you babbling about? El Murid? He won't attack. He's got trouble at home."

"Woe! Know-it-all son of sand witch, spawn of mating of scorpion with open-mouthed jackass, or maybe camel, plotting like little old lady Fates, mouth always open and eyes always closed..."

"I missed something. And I'm being told to shut up long enough to hear what."

"Hai! Is not stupid after all. O stars of night, witness. Is able to add up twos." Carefully, wasting fewer words than usual, he told what Bragi had encountered in the Savernake Gap.

"I should've expected something. Always there're complications. The gods themselves contend against me." Angrily, "I defy them. The Fates, the gods, the thrones in Shinsan. Though the world be laid in ruin and the legions of Hell march forth from the seas, I'll return."

It was the oath Haroun had sworn while fleeing from Hammad al Nakir long ago.

Of all the Royal House, descendants of the Kings and Emperors of Ilkazar, only Haroun had survived to pursue a restoration. He alone had been nimble, swift, and hard enough to evade the arrows, blades, and poisons of El Murid's assassins, to become, in exile, the guerrilla chieftain known as the King Without a Throne.

Mocker decided it was time an old, nagging question got asked. "Haroun, in case Fates serve up wicked chance with left hands, ending life of old marching companion, what of Cause? Are no successors, hey? Leaders of Royalists, yes. Grim old men in dark places, lying poisoned blades in hand for enemies of Haroun. But no sons of same to pick up swords and go on pursuing elusive crown."

Bin Yousif laughed bitterly. "Perhaps. Perhaps not. I've taken roads walked alone, have secrets unshared. Still, if I'm gone, what do I care?

"Well, I've hoarded a trick or two, like a miser. Guess it's time to spend them."

Mocker, still trying to detect something in the darkness, was startled by a sudden wail from a few feet away. "Haroun?"

The answer was a moan of fear. The darkness faded.

Haroun was gone. Always, in recent years, it had been that way. There was no more closeness, no shared truth between them. Yet Haroun continued presuming on friendships formed in younger days.

The sounds of distress continued. Mocker pushed into the dying darkness.

He found an old beggar barely this side of death. "Demons," the man mumbled. "Possessed by demons."

Mocker shuddered, frowned. Haroun had found him, but he hadn't found Haroun. From somewhere else, anywhere, by sorcery, bin Yousif had spoken through the old man. So. His old friend *had* been studying the dark arts.

With the best of intentions, no doubt. But Haroun's character...

The appearance of several soldiers at the street exit, drawn by the beggar's wails, made Mocker take to his heels.

Very dissatisfactory, he thought, his robes flying. The trip had been a waste. He should abandon everything and return to Nepanthe.

iii) The night visitors

Operating armies in winter, even on Kavelin's small scales, presented almost insuperable problems. Bragi crossed the Spehe with rations for ten days. That he entered the Gudbrandsdal was more to take advantage of game than to come at Forbeck unexpected.

He passed through the forest slowly, pursuing routes previously marked by the Marena Dimura, his men scattering to hunt. Two days passed before he allowed his patrols beyond the forest's eastern verge.

The loyalties of the Forbeck nobility seemed proportional to distance from Vorgreberg. They encountered resistance only beyond Fahrig. The Nordmen there supported the Captal's pretender.

Blackfang's Trolledyngjans, who found the winter mild, whooped from town to castle.

After three weeks, Ragnarson passed command to Blackfang and returned to Vorgreberg.

Little had happened in his absence. An assassin, of the Harish Cult of Hammad al Nakir, had been caught climbing the castle wall. He had committed suicide before he could be questioned. Three ministers had been thrown in the dungeon. Her Majesty had coped.

He saw her briefly before retiring. She was haggard.

Deep in the night a daydream came true, something he had both wanted and feared.

At a touch he suddenly sat upright in darkness. His candle was out. He grabbed for the dagger beside it.

A hand pushed against his chest. A woman's hand. "What?..." he rumbled.

A barely audible "Shh!" He lay back. Fabric rustled as clothing fell. Long, slim nakedness slid in beside him. Arms surrounded him. Small, firm breasts pressed against his chest. Hungry lips found his...

Next morning he was still unsure it hadn't been a dream. There was no evidence save his own satiation. And the Queen seemed unchanged.

Had it been someone else? Her maidservant, Maighen, whose flirting eyes had long made her willingness evident? But Maighen was a plumpish Wesson with breasts like pillows.

Each night the mystery compounded itself, though she came earlier and earlier and stayed longer and longer.

The day Haaken sent word of the surrender of the last rebels in Forbeck, Gjerdrum asked, "What're you doing nights, anyway?"

Ragnarson flashed a guilty look. "A lot of worrying. How do you beat sorcery without sorcery?"

Gjerdrum shrugged.

All questions had their answers. Sometimes they weren't pleasant; sometimes the circumstances of resolution were distressing.

The latter was the case the night Bragi unraveled the mystery of his lover's identity.

The first scream barely penetrated his passion. The second, cut off, grabbed like the hand of a clawed demon.

It had come from the Queen's chambers.

He grabbed his weapons and, naked, charged up the corridor.

The guards before the Queen's door lay in a heap. Blood trickled over the edge of the balcony to the floor below.

Ragnarson hit the door, broke the lock, charged through. He roared into the Royal bedchamber in time to seize a man trying to force himself through a window. He clapped the man's temple, knocked him out.

Ragnarson turned to the Queen's bed. Maighen. And over her now, clenched fist at her mouth, the Queen herself, naked. A dagger protruded from Maighen's throat.

Despite the situation, his eyes roamed a body he had known only by touch. She reddened.

"Get something on," he ordered. He grabbed a blanket, tied it around his waist, returned to Maighen.

There was no hope.

Gjerdrum and three guardsmen entered.

"Get those doors closed," Ragnarson ordered. "Don't let anyone in. Or out. You men. Watch that fellow over there. Gjerdrum, get the city gates closed. No one in or out till I give the word."

It looked, he thought, as if Maighen had been sleeping in the Queen's bed and the assassin had tried to smother her. She had fought free, screamed, and had taken a panicky dagger.

Turning again, he found Gjerdrum still there. "I thought I told you...Wait! Gjerdrum, don't let it out who died. Let them think it was Her Highness. Let's see who tries to profit. But do mention that we've caught the killer."

Gjerdrum frowned, nodded, departed.

"You men," Ragnarson told the guardsmen, "are going to be out of circulation a while. I don't want you talking to anyone. Understand?" Nods. "All right. You, watch the door. No one gets in. No one." Turning to the Queen, softly, "Slip back to my quarters. Stay out of sight."

"What do you mean?"

"You know perfectly well. There's a passage you use, else those two in the corridor would've spread tales. Be a good girl and scoot."

The assassin came round. He was a Wesson barely old enough to sport a beard. An amateur who had panicked, and who was now eager to cooperate.

But he didn't know who had hired him, though he provided a weak description of the interlocuter.

Bragi promised him that, if he helped trap his principal, he would be allowed to go into exile.

The youth knew but one thing for certain. He had been hired by Nordmen.

Ragnarson jumped to a conclusion. "If they know we've got you, they'll try to kill you . . ."

"Bait?"

"Exactly."

"But . . ."

"Your alternative is a date with the headsman."

iv) The worms within

There were four men in the cell with the assassin. Two were genuine prisoners. One was a spy who had been set to watch them. The last was Rolf Preshka.

Rumors of the Queen's murder had run like hares before hounds, threatening to undo all that had been won. Heads leaned together, plotting . . .

Virtually no one would accept the succession of Crown Prince Gaia-Lange, who had been removed to safety with his grandfather in Sacuescu.

Ragnarson expected the assassin's employers to move swiftly. He wasn't disappointed. Just before dawn three men stole to the cell where Rolf and the youth lay. One was the night turnkey. A soldier and a Nordmen accompanied him.

Rolf controlled a cough as a key squeaked in the lock. He didn't think they could be handled. They were healthy, armed, and Bragi wanted them alive.

But Bragi was nearby. Using information he had bullied from the Queen, he had brought the guardsmen from her chambers to the turnkey's office by secret ways. He had watched the soldier and Nordmen come to the turnkey, had seen gold change hands. Now, hearing the distance-muted rattle of keys, he led the guardsmen through a hidden door.

Weapons clashed in the gloom below. Bragi signed two men thither, left the third to hold the dungeon door.

Reaching the cell, he thundered, "Give it up, you."

Preshka and the boy had backed into a corner. The spy and prisoners had been slain.

The Nordmen attacked Rolf ferociously. The turnkey threw up his hands. The soldier, for a second, seemed torn. Then he too dropped his weapon. Bragi hurled him and the turnkey outside.

He, Rolf, and the youth subdued the Nordmen, though the man tried to get himself killed.

"To the stairs," Ragnarson growled. Sounds of fighting came from the turnkey's office. The would-be killers had left a rearguard of their own, beyond the dungeon door.

The guardsmen returned with another soldier. Both captives, Ragnarson noted, were from companies recently recruited.

He dumped the soldiers and turnkey in with the corpses. The Nordmen and assassin, blindfolded and with hands bound, he took up the secret ways to his apartment.

"Ah, Sir Hendren of Sokolic," the Queen said with false sweetness, as Bragi removed his blindfold. "So you wanted me dead. And I thought you a loyal knight." She slapped him viciously. "I never saw so many stab-in-the-back cowards. Kavelin's infested."

The man went pale. He saw his death before him, but still stood tall and silent.

"Yes, I'm alive. But you might not be long. Unless you tell me who had you hire the boy."

Sir Hendren said nothing.

"Then we'll do it the hard way." Bragi shoved the Nordmen into a chair, began binding his legs.

"What?..." the Queen began.

"Castrate him."

"But..."

"If you don't want to stay..."

"I was going to say he's Lord Lindwedel's man."

"You're sure?"

"As stoutly as Eanred was the Krief's."

"Is that true?" he asked Sir Hendren.

The knight glowered.

"Be back in a few minutes." Bragi gave the Queen a dagger. "Use it if you have to."

He went to Lindwedel's apartment. Circumstantially, he found the Queen's allegations confirmed.

Lindwedel, who rose before noon only in the gravest times, was awake, dressed, and in conference.

After amenities, Lindwedel asked, "What can I do for you, Marshal?"

It took some tall lying, worthy of Mocker at his most imaginative, but he convinced the plotters that they should come to his apartment. He hinted that there were secrets he had uncovered during his tenure, and that he wanted to discuss bringing his troops round to their cause.

The Queen, he discovered, had anticipated him. She and the assassin had gone into hiding. Sir Hendren had been gagged, moved against the wall, and covered with a sheet like a piece of useless furniture. "Ah," Bragi said, pleased. The Ministers glanced at him, puzzled. He stood beside the door while they filed in.

The Queen stepped from hiding. Ragnarson chuckled as sudden pallor hit Nordmen faces.

"Greetings, my lords," she said. "We're pleased you could attend us." She made a sign. The assassin crossed to Sir Hendren, removed the sheet.

Lindwedel plunged toward the door. "Got you again," said Bragi.

"Lindy, Lindy," said the Queen. "Why'd you have to have it all?"

Drawing himself up stiffly, trying to maintain his dignity, Lindwedel refused to reply.

Not so some of his co-conspirators. They babbled the tiniest details of the plot.

They were still babbling when they were hauled before a tribunal. They named more and more names, exposing a vast conspiracy.

The conspirators, silent or talkative, next noon, wore puzzled expressions as the headsman's ax fell. They didn't understand.

Ragnarson, for symbolism, had chosen a Wesson who abjured the black hood. The lesson wasn't wasted.

There was a new order. The masks were off and the despised Wessons were the real power supporting the Crown.

He expected the nocturnal visits to cease. And for three nights they did. But on the fourth she returned. She woke him, and this time didn't extinguish the candle.

THIRTEEN: In Their Wickedness They Are Blind, in Their Folly They Persist

i) He watches from darkness

Once again the winged man came to Castle Krief, this time gliding noiselessly through a moonless, overcast night. He deeply feared that the men would be waiting for him, their cold steel ready to free his soul, but the only soldier he saw was asleep at his post on the wall. He drifted into an open window unnoticed.

Heart hammering, crystal dagger half-drawn, he stole through darkened corridors. His mission was more daring and dangerous than either previous. This time he truly tempted the Fates.

Twice he had to use the tiny wand the Master's lady had given him. He need only point it and squeeze and a fine violet line would touch his target. The sentry would fall asleep.

The first time he almost fainted. When he stepped in front of the man, he found the soldier's eyes still open. But unseeing. Shaking and sighing, Shoptaw made his way to his goal.

It was tricky, finding the room where the Krief held his secret audiences. The Master had visited Castle Krief but once, and that the day before Shoptaw's last visit. Their

knowledge of the castle's interior came from men the
Master had recruited to help Kiki claim her inheritance.
None had been intimates of the King. They knew of the
room's existence, but not its location.

So Shoptaw had to trust his own judgment. He was
pleased that the Master had such faith in him, but feared
that faith might be misplaced. He knew he wasn't as
intelligent as the real men . . . As always, he persevered,
for his friend Kiki, for the Master. He found a plain small
room down a narrow passage from an ornate large one. It
felt right.

He searched the room carefully, preternaturally
sensitive fingertips probing for the mechanisms hidden in
the walls. It took three hours to find the hidden doorway.
With a half-prayer that no one would use it soon, he
slipped through.

The passage behind had been designed to his purpose.
It ran round three sides of the chamber, had tiny holes for
hearing and seeing. Long-undisturbed dust lay deep
within, a promising sign. He shed the small pack he had
been able to bring, prepared for a long stay.

He had chosen correctly. But for a long time he learned
nothing that would be of interest to the Master.

Then came the break he had been awaiting. He knew it
the moment the chamber door opened, alerting him, and
he reached a peephole in time to see the lean dark man
follow the King in. He didn't recognize the man. He was
new, a foreigner.

The dark man spoke directly. "Her Majesty will need
supporters without a political stake."

"A point you made in your letter."

"None of your Nordmen fit."

"I have the King's Own and the guard. Their loyalties
are beyond question."

"Perhaps. But we're speaking of a time when you won't
be here to guide those loyalties."

The King, thought Shoptaw, was a tired old man. The
wasting sickness was devouring him. He didn't have long
to live. His face often revealed some internal pain.

"Don't overstep good taste, sir."

"You've had time to investigate. You've been stalling

for it. You know tact isn't my strong point."

"No. Yet the reports were, in the balance, favorable."

The dark man smiled a thin smile that made Shoptaw think of hungry foxes.

"Granted, I need someone. Granted, your proposal sounds good. Still, I wonder. Your specialty's guerrilla warfare. How would Fiana use you? You couldn't prevent the barons from taking Vorgreberg. Then you'd be unemployed ... There is, too, the question of what you hope to gain personally."

"Good. You did your homework. I don't mean to conduct the Queen's defense myself. For that I have in mind a talented gentleman in retirement in Itaskia. He'd conduct the conventional campaign. Most of the arrangements have been made. When we conclude a contract, a regiment will begin gathering."

"Yes, no doubt. You've been ducking in and out of Kavelin for years. Spent a lot of time with the Marena Dimura, I hear. Which leads back to your interest in the matter."

"I could lie to you. I could say it's profit. But you'd know I was lying.

"No matter what you do, no matter how well you prepare, there's going to be a period of adjustment after you pass on. Neither Gaia-Lange nor Fiana is acceptable to your nobility. And you have greedy neighbors. They're watching your health now. They'll complicate and prolong it. Itaskia and El Murid will be watching them, to guard their own interests ...

"My intention is to hit my old enemy while he's distracted."

The Krief chuckled. "Ah. You're devious."

The dark man shrugged. "One sharpens the weapon at hand."

"Indeed. Indeed. Your friend. Do I know him?"

"Unlikely. He's not one of your glory chasers. He's preferred to keep his operations small. But he's as competent as Sir Tury Hawkwind. *And* has a good relationship with such as Count Visigodred and Zindahjira, of whom, I'm sure, you *have* heard."

"Ah? Any man might find such friends useful. His name?"

"Ragnarson, Bragi Ragnarson. Guild Colonel. Though he operates independent of High Crag."

"Not the Ragnarson who was in Altea during the wars?"

"The same. He knocked the point off the spear El Murid ran up the north slope of the Kapenrungs."

"I remember. A lucky victory. It allowed Raithel time to block the thrust. Yes. This might be what I need..."

The winged man had heard enough. For the first time in his vigil he became impatient. He had to fly, to warn the Master.

For he had heard the name Bragi Ragnarson before. Ragnarson was one of the men who had destroyed the father of the Master's lady. He must be terrible indeed.

ii) The wicked persist in their wickedness, and know no joy

"Papa Drake," said Carolan, whispering, "why's Aunt Mist always so sad?"

The old man glanced across his library. Mist stood staring out a westward-facing window, deep in her own thoughts. "She lost something, darling."

"Here? Is that why she's here so much now?"

"You might say. Someone she loved very much...Well..." He dithered, then decided he might as well tell her the whole story.

When he finished, Carolan went over, took Mist's hand. "I'm sorry. Maybe someday..."

Mist frowned, glanced at the Captal, then flashed a bright smile. She hugged the child. "You're priceless."

Through the window, over Mist's shoulder, Carolan saw something hurtling across the sky. "Shoptaw! Papa Drake, Shoptaw's coming. Can I go?..."

"You just wait, young lady. Business first. But you can tell Burla."

As she ran out, Mist said, "He's in an awful hurry. Must be bad news."

Within the half-hour they had heard it all.

"Not to deprecate the man's ability," said Mist, as the Captal began fussing, "but he can be neutralized. I can ask Visigodred not to get involved, and bully Zindahjira into minding his own business. And if we slip the word to El Murid, he'll take care of this Ragnarson for us."

"And if that fails?" The Captal remembered that this Ragnarson had been associated with Varthlokkur. He was more frightened of that man than he had been of Mist's father.

"We'll handle it ourselves. But why worry? Unless the economic picture changes and the politics of High Crag shift, he won't gather much of an army. And if he does, he'll find himself facing my troops, assuming he survives the rebels."

"So many difficulties already..."

"We won't win any victories sitting here."

To the Captal it seemed but moments till their first failure. Nothing they did prevented Ragnarson from leaving Itaskia. Try as he might, he couldn't shake his pessimism.

"I feel Death's hot breath on the back of my neck," he once confided to Burla.

One day Mist announced, "He's in Ruderin. He knows the King's dead. I'll need your help setting a trap."

The Captal, with his creatures, transferred to a small fortress in Shinsan, which, with the help of the Tervola, was projected into Ruderin.

There were complications. Always there were complications.

The whole thing collapsed. And the Captal lost dozens of his oldest friends.

He also suffered a crisis of conscience.

Back in his own library, to Mist, he said, "Don't ever ask me to do anything like that again. If I can't kill more cleanly than that..."

Mist ignored him. She had her own problems. The Tervola were growing cooler and cooler. Her followers still hadn't taken care of O Shing. And Valther... He had disappeared. He had been gone from Hellin Daimiel for months.

But that worry she kept secret. Neither the Tervola nor the Captal would understand...

She spent more and more time at Maisak, delegating more and more authority to her retainers.

iii) The spears of dread pursue them . . .

Months passed. The excitement of the succession reached a feverish pitch. The Captal did some quiet campaigning. At first he was received coolly, even with mockery, but the swift parade of rebel disasters scrubbed the disdainful smiles from Nordmen faces. A few began mustering at Maisak.

"There're so few of them," said Carolan.

"They don't know you yet," the Captal replied. "Besides, a lot of them want to be King too."

"The man that's coming . . . He scares you, doesn't he?" There was no longer any doubt that Ragnarson's swift march was aimed at Maisak. "Is he a bad man?"

"I suppose not. No more than the rest of us. Maybe less. He's on the law's side. We're the bad ones from the Crown's viewpoint."

"Aunt Mist's scared too. She says he's too smart. And knows too many people." Shifting subject suddenly, "What's she like?"

"Who?"

"My mother. The Queen."

The Captal had supposed she knew. Burla and Shoptaw could deny her nothing. But this was the first time she had brought it up.

"I don't know. I've never met her. Never even seen her. You probably know more than I do."

"Nobody knows very much." She shook her head, tossing golden curls, almost lost the small iron diadem she wore, symbolic of Kavelin's Iron Crown, a legend-haunted treasure that never left the Royal vaults in Vorgreberg. "She's shy, I guess. They say nobody sees her much. She must be lonely."

The Captal hadn't thought of that. Hadn't thought of Fiana as a person at all. "Yes. Probably. Makes you wonder why she stays on. Practically no one wants her . . ."

Shoptaw appeared. "Master, hairy men very close. In Baxendala now. Traveling fast. Here soon. Maybe two, three day." Though the Trolledyngjans were in the minority in Ragnarson's forces, they had so impressed the winged man that he thought of all enemies as hairy men.

"How many?"

"Many, many. Twice times us, maybe."

"Not good. Shoptaw, that's not good." He thought of the caves, whose mouths he had for years been trying to locate and seal. Ragnarson had a knack for discovering his enemies' weak points. He would know about the caves.

"Shoptaw, old friend, you know what this means?"

"War here." The winged man shuddered. "We fight. Win again. As always."

Carolan hadn't missed their uncertainty. "You'd better tell Aunt Mist."

"Uhn." The Captal didn't like it, though. She would want to bring in her own people. There were more Shinsaners in Maisak now than he liked, a half-dozen grimly silent veterans who were training his troops and keeping their eyes on him.

iv)...And the thing they fear comes upon them

The first troops came through next day, immediately behind Mist and several masked Tervola. She had said she was bringing six hundred. The stream seemed endless to a man who had often heard what terrible soldiers they were. Yet she was honest. He counted exactly six hundred, most of whom left the fortress immediately. Mist was considerate of his sensibilities.

And before long Ragnarson encountered the Captal's little ambushers.

The Captal followed the reports in quiet sorrow, standing rod-stiff in the darkness atop Maisak's wall. It was murder, pure and simple. The little people couldn't cope with the hairy men. He could console himself only

with the knowledge that none of them had been
conscripted. They had asked for weapons.

There was a fierce, bloodthirsty determination in the
enemy's approach that startled and frightened him. It
didn't seem characteristic of the Ragnarson who had
swept the lowlands. Then he learned what had been done
to Ragnarson's scouts.

He was enraged. His first impulse was to confront Mist
and her generals . . . But no, with their power they would
simply push him aside and take over. He did order his
small friends to cease disputing the pass. In a small way, in
lessened readiness and increased casualties, Shinsan
would pay for its barbarity.

Ragnarson didn't come whooping in as expected, as
past performance suggested he would.

Many of the Captal's friends, and a startling number of
Mist's troops, died before the Tervola felt ready to
commit Carolan's men.

Mist visited his station on the wall, from which he
watched Shinsaners being harassed by bowmen. "We're
ready." She had sensed his new coldness and was curious.
He had already told her he wouldn't discuss it till the
fighting ended.

"You're positive she'll be safe?"

"Drake, Drake, I love her too. I wouldn't let her go if
there was a ghost of a chance she'd get hurt."

"I know. I worry like a grandmother. But I can't help
feeling this man's more dangerous than you think. He
knew what he was up against when he came here. Why'd
he keep coming?"

"I don't know, Drake. Maybe he's *not* as smart as you
think."

"Maybe. If Carolan gets hurt . . ."

Mist wheeled and went below. Soon she and Carolan,
leading Kaveliner recruits, departed Maisak's narrow
gate.

When the swift-sped arrows dropped from the
darkness, he said only, "I knew it. I knew it," and plunged
down steps to ground level.

In moments he was beside Carolan. "Baby, baby, are
you all right?"

Subsequent events seemed anti-climactic. He bickered with Mist, dispiritedly.

"Sometimes, Drake," she once murmured, "I wish I could give it all up."

iv) What does a man profit?

Winter came early, and with a vengeance. The Captal had never seen its like. In normal times it would have been cause for distress. But there were no late caravans to be shepherded through the Gap. Hardly a traveler had crossed all summer.

The Captal welcomed the weather. He would have no trouble with Ragnarson before spring.

Mist damned it. She foresaw them facing a united Kavelin next summer.

The Captal kept his winged creatures watching the lowlands. Ragnarson seemed unable to avoid success—yet each redounded to the Captal's benefit. Ever more Nordmen turned to his standard. Because of his power, he thought. Because he was the one enemy Ragnarson hadn't been able to reduce.

He realized these new allies would abandon him the instant the loyalists collapsed, but that was a problem he could solve in its time. For the present he had to concentrate on old enemies.

Though his couriers brought news consisting entirely of lists of towns and castles and provinces lost, he began to hope. In the free provinces several hitherto uncommitted Nordmen were turning rebel for each turning loyalist.

The edicts flowing from Vorgreberg had changed the root nature of the struggle. The issue, now, was a power struggle between Crown and nobility, one which would preserve or sweep away many ancient prerogatives. And it had become a class war. The underclasses, bought by Crown perfidy, strove to wrest privilege from their betters.

The Captal contacted Baron Thake Berlich in

Loncaric, a recidivist who had been captured by Ragnarson in the Gap and paroled by Fiana. The man's response had been to raise stronger forces for the rematch. He had been one of the Krief's commanders during the wars. He was the logical man to bring Ragnarson to heel. But he was a conservative of a stripe judged bizarre even by his own class.

Through Berlich, using the Baron's interlocutors—whom he kept in careful ignorance of the messages they bore—he reached Sir Andvbur Kimberlin of Karadja, in Breidenbach. Kimberlin had publicly voiced displeasure with the Queen's tepid social reforms. The Captal invited the knight to help him build a new society, hinting that while he controlled Carolan, he wasn't long for this world and was looking for someone who understood, who could carry on after he was gone.

As winter lugubriously progressed toward a spring that was no spring at all in the Gap, the Captal grew less and less pessimistic. The rebel coalition, spanning the extremes of political dissatisfaction and opportunism, waxed strong, reaching into Vorgreberg itself.

That fell apart.

"Stupid, greedy pigs!" the old man grumbled for days. "We had it in our hands. But they had to try cutting us out." Even Carolan stayed out of his way.

He decided there was no choice but to bring in eastern troops, to give the rebels backbone. And, to use a little wizardry.

News of the sudden shift at High Crag (where the ruling junta had for a decade discouraged mercenary involvement in actual warmaking), that had led to an offer of three veteran regiments to the Crown, again pushed the Captal toward despair. It was contagious. Mist became a sad, resigned woman. She returned to Shinsan to prepare a legion for transfer to Maisak when the snows melted.

The Captal, self-involved, overlooked her mood. Burla, Shoptaw, and Carolan understood Mist's unhappiness. The man she had lost, and his brother, had reappeared. In Kavelin. Working the other side again.

v) Glitter of an enemy spear

Three men crouched beneath an ice overhang and, when not cursing the temperature, considered the fortress west of them.

"It'll work," promised the one with a single eye. "They can't sense us."

"The spells. The spells," another grumbled. "If that Shinsaner bitch wasn't in there, I'd believe in them."

"Just think about the gold, Brad," said the third. "More than ... More than you've ever dreamed."

"I believe in that less than Haroun's spells. Maybe this's his way of getting rid of us. We know too much."

"A possibility," Derran admitted. "And I haven't overlooked it."

"If there's trouble, it'll come at payoff time," Kerth said.

"Uhm."

"It's dark enough," said Brad.

"Give it a few more minutes," said Derran. "Let 'em start thinking about bedtime. Some of those things can see like cats." For the hundredth time he patted his purse. Inside, carefully protected, lay a small bundle of plans of Maisak's interior, obtained by bin Yousif from a winged man taken several months earlier.

"You're sure there'll be no sentries?" Brad asked.

Derran concealed his exasperation. "No. Why the hell would they be watching for someone in this?" He gestured at deep snow now invisible in darkness. "Probably someone at the gate, but that's all that's logical." He checked the night, the few lights visible in the fortress. "Hell, you're right, Brad. Let's go."

It took a half-hour to slog the short distance to the castle wall, then just minutes to set a grapnel and climb up. Five minutes later they had finished the two owl-faced creatures at the gate and prepared it for their retreat. If all went right, they would be well on their way before their visit caused an alarm.

Maisak was thick with smells and smokes, but in the outer works, in the winter chill, they encountered no other evidence of occupation.

"Lot of men here," Kerth observed. "Wonder how they keep them fed?"

"Probably with transfers from Shinsan," Derran replied. "That door there, with the brass hinges. That look like the one we want?"

"Fits the description."

"Okay. Brad, you open. Kerth, cover." He went in low and fast so Kerth could throw over him, but the precaution proved unnecessary. The corridor was empty.

"All right," said Derran, "let's see. Commissary down that way. Third room this way."

In that room they found a half-dozen odd little people sleeping. "Look like rabbits," Brad said, after they had been dispatched.

"Place's supposed to be full of weirds," Derran replied. "Kerth, find the panel. We'll clean up." Soon they were climbing a dusty circular stair in complete darkness.

The stair ended in a landing. There was a wall with peepholes. Beyond the wall lay an empty, poorly lighted corridor.

"Brad, you watch." Derran felt for the mechanism that would allow access to the corridor. A small panel scraped aside. They awaited a reaction. Brad hastily assembled a crossbow.

"Go." Derran tapped Kerth's shoulder.

Daggers in hand, the man rushed the one door opening off the corridor. He paused beside it. Closed, he signaled. Derran joined him, pointed to the regular stair. Kerth checked it, signaled it was clear. Derran dropped to his stomach and peered beneath the door with his good eye. From his bundle of plans he took one of the Captal's library, indicated the position of each person in the room.

A final problem. Was the door locked? Barred? Haroun's captive had claimed there were no locked doors in Maisak, only hidden ones.

Derran stood, placed his back to the door, took its handle in his left hand, held his sword vertically in his right. Kerth readied his daggers, nodded.

Explosion. Derran slammed the door open. As his

momentum carried him out of the way, one of Kerth's weapons took wing. Its pommel smacked the Shinsaner woman between the eyes.

Derran didn't pause to appreciate the throw. It was what he had expected. Kerth had spent countless hours practicing.

The woman was the key. If she weren't silenced, all was lost.

In passing he crossed blades with the old man, pushed through his guard, left him clutching his wound in amazement. He grabbed the woman, shoved a hand into her mouth, with his free hand tossed Kerth his dagger. Kerth took it on the fly and turned to two weird creatures who had thrown themselves in front of the little girl...

A wall opened up and men with swords stepped in. Ragnarson's men.

FOURTEEN: The Roads to Baxendala

i) In by the back door

Though April was near, the snow remained deep and moist. The two men fought it gamely, but were compelled to take frequent rests.

"Must be getting old," Turran grumbled, glancing up the long, steep slope yet to be climbed.

Valther said nothing, just made sure moisture hadn't reached his sword. He seldom spoke even now.

"Almost there," Turran said. "That bluff up there ...That's the one that looked like a man's face." The last time they had been in the Gap it had been summer and they had been hurrying to their fates in Escalon. Nothing looked familiar now.

Valther stared uphill, remaining statue-still till a bitter gust reached him. "Better camp," he muttered.

"Uhm." Turran had spotted a likely overhang. It would yield relief from the wind while they hunted a usable cave. Though those were reportedly numerous, they had become harder to find near Maisak.

"Think they've spotted us yet?" Turran asked after they made the overhang.

Valther shrugged. He didn't care. He would feel nothing till they had come face to face with Mist.

"That looks like one," said Turran, indicating a spot of darkness up the north slope. "Let's go."

Valther hoisted his pack and started off.

They had little firewood left. Turran used the minimum to heat their supper, then extinguished the blaze. They would wrap in their blankets and crowd one another for warmth. The mouth of the cave was small and inconveniently located anyway. The smoke didn't want to leave.

During the night Turran shivered so hard that when he rose he had cramps.

Valther didn't notice the chill.

For breakfast they had jerky warmed by their body heats, washed down with snow melted the same way.

Afterward, Valther said, "Time to begin."

"Is she here?" Turran asked.

Valther's eyes glazed. For a moment he stared into distances unseen, then shrugged. "I don't know. The aura's there, but not strong."

Turran was surprised his brother showed that much spirit. He seemed genuinely eager for the coming confrontation.

Turran was not. He saw no way they could best the mistress of Shinsan. Surprise was a tool that could be used against anyone, but how did one surprise a power so perceptive it could detect an enemy's heartbeat a hundred miles away?

But the attempt had to be made. Even in full expectation of death. It was a matter of conscience. They had betrayed those who had trusted them. Just trying would help even the balance.

"Ready?"

Valther nodded.

From his purse Turran took a small jewel the Monitor had given him. He set it on the cave floor. They joined hands, stared into the talisman. Turran chanted in liturgical Escalonian, of which he understood not a word.

In a moment he felt little monkey-tugs at the fringes of his soul. There was a sudden, painless wrench, as of roots pulling away, then his awareness floated free.

The sensing was nothing like that of the body. He did

not "see" objects, yet knew the location and shape and function of everything about him.

Valther hadn't shed his clay. He was too distracted by obsessions that Turran could now trace. Valther lay trapped in a sort of in-between, and would remain there till Turran freed him or pulled him back to the mundane plane.

Just as well, Turran reflected. Valther might have gone haring direct to Maisak, to see Mist, and so have given them away.

There was no sense of time on that level. Turran had to concentrate to make events follow one another in temporal parade. He saw why the Monitor had told him not to use the stone unless he had to. He could get lost on this side, and forget his body, which would perish of neglect.

This was how most ghosts had come into being, the Monitor had told him.

While Turran had had no training in this sorcery, the wizardries of his family had taught him discipline. He began his task.

He floated the slopes between their hiding place and the bluff which masked Maisak. He felt no cold, nor any pressure from the wind.

He discovered he could sense not only the realities obvious to corporeal senses, he could look around, beneath, and within things, and it was with this faculty that he searched for entrances to the caverns honeycombing the mountains. Many came clear. Most had been sealed. Those that had not, he probed deeply. He found the one he was hunting.

Just in time. His attachment to his body was attenuating. His will and concentration were suffering moments of vagary.

As he reentered his body, he learned another danger of the magic.

Feeling returned. All the aches and pains of a hard march, more intense for having gone unfelt for a time. And his senses suddenly seemed severely limited. What a temptation there was to withdraw ...

He reached out and brought his brother back.

Turran's eyes opened. Their hands parted.

Valther had less trouble recovering. "Did you find it?" he asked.

Turran nodded. "I don't want to try that again."

"Bad?"

"Just the coming back."

"Let's go." Valther was ebullient.

Turran rose stiffly, got his gear together. "We'll need the torches. It's long . . ."

Valther shrugged, drew his sword, ran his thumb along its edge. He didn't care about the in-betweens, just the destination.

"What I wouldn't give for a bath," Turran grumbled as he hoisted his pack. "I'll lead."

It was snowing again. That was their fault. The past several months they had used their weather magic to confine winter's worst to the high country.

The cave mouth was a half-mile from their hiding place, naturally but cunningly hidden. He had a hard time locating it. It had to be dug out. It was barely large enough to accept a man's body. He sent Valther in, pushed their packs through, slithered in himself.

"I've got a feeling," he told Valther as they prepared the torches, "that we'd better hurry. My memory's getting hazy."

But speed was impossible. The subterranean journey was long and tortuous and in places they had to dig to enlarge passages for crawling. Once they climbed twenty feet up a vertical face. Another time they had to cross a pit whose Stygian deeps concealed a bottom unguessably far below. At a point where several caverns intersected they found skeletons still arrayed in war gear of Hammad al Nakir. Though they pushed hard, they couldn't make the journey in one day. They paused for sleep, then continued.

They knew they were close when they reached caverns where the walls had been regularized by tools. Those would be passages worked during the wars, when the Captal's fortress had had to have space for thousands of soldiers.

Then they came on a large chamber occupied by Kaveliners who supported the Captal's pretender. Those who were awake were bored. Their conversation orbited round women and a desire to be elsewhere. Nobody challenged the brothers as they passed through.

"That was the worst," Turran said afterward. "Now we take a side tunnel to the Captal's laboratories and get into his private ways."

Valther nodded, caressed the hilt of his sword.

It was strange, Turran thought, that their coming hadn't been sensed or forseen. But, then, their weak plan had been predicated on inattention by the enemy.

In the laboratories, in a dark and misty chamber they recognized as one where transfers were made, they encountered trouble.

It came in the form of an owl-faced creature guarding the transfer pentagrams. He was asleep when they spotted him, but wakened as they tried slipping past. They had to silence him.

"Have to hurry now," Turran said. The thing's disappearance would raise an alarm.

Because they followed secret stairs they reached the Captal's chambers before they encountered second trouble. And this came as a total surprise.

They pushed through a secret panel into a room full of murder. It had been a library or study, but now it resembled a paper-maker's dump. Against one wall an evil-faced, one-eyed man, unarmed, struggled with a woman. He had the heel of one hand jammed firmly into her mouth.

An old man lay unconscious and bleeding on the floor. Now, with a pair of long daggers, a second killer stalked two weird creatures guarding a child. One creature was a frail winged thing defending himself with a blazing crystal dagger, the other an apelike dwarf wielding a short, weighted club.

All eyes turned to the brothers. The failure of hope in the winged man and ape-thing spurred Kerth. One of his blades shattered the crystal dagger while the other turned the dwarf's club. Then the first arced over into the dwarf's throat. He went down with a squeal.

"Burla!" the child screeched, falling on him. "No. Don't die."

Workmanlike, Kerth wheeled and dispatched the winged man.

When Kerth wheeled on the child, Valther said, "No." He said it flatly, without the least apparent emotion. The assassin froze.

Kerth and Derran exchanged glances. Kerth shrugged, stepped away from the girl.

Sudden as lightning, a dagger was in the air, hurtling toward Valther. The man got his sword up in time to deflect it. It had been a gut-throw.

And a feint. The second dagger followed by two yards, bit deep into Valther's right shoulder. Turran jabbed with his own blade, missed the block.

There was a *crack* from Derran's direction. Mist sagged in semi-consciousness. The One-Eye blew on his knuckles.

Turran charged Kerth, who had already armed himself with the Captal's weapon...

The universe turned red.

Mist forced herself up on her hands, stared through an open window. In the starkest terror Turran had ever witnessed, she croaked, "O Shing. He's raised the Gosik of Aubochon!"

None knew the name, but each knew Mist. Their conflict ceased. In moments all crowded the window, staring up at a pillar of red horror.

"The portal!" Mist cried. "He'll try the portal while we're distracted. We've got to destroy it."

Too late. The clack of armor echoed up the same stair Turran and Valther had used.

ii) Approaching storm

March sagged toward April. Spring came to the lowlands. The days of reckoning drew rapidly closer. Ragnarson grew ever more dour and pessimistic. Things were going too well. The censuses were in. Crops had suffered less than anticipated. In areas where there had been little fighting there had been surpluses. Only the Nordmen, it seemed, were suffering.

Volstokin hadn't been as lucky. Ambassadors from the Queen Mother were pleading credit and grain in both Kavelin and Altea.

Favorable weather permitted early plowing. This, to Ragnarson's delight, meant more men for summer service. Hedging against the chance they would be in the field at harvest, the Queen was buying grain futures in Altea, a traditional exporter.

The winter had caused changes at every level. Kavelin had shaken her lice out. As the kingdom settled down and vast properties changed hands, the citizens looked forward to a prosperous future. Because good fortune attended the Queen's supporters, her strength waxed. Feelers drifted in from provinces still in rebellion.

With the exception of Ragnarson and his aides, no one seemed worried about the summer.

Bragi never eased the pressure on the rebels. After Forbeck and Fahrig, he launched expeditions into Orthwein and Uhlmansiek, using the campaigns to temper his growing army. He suffered few setbacks. Each victory made the next easier.

Anticipating fat looting in the Galmiches and Loncaric, squads, companies, and battalions poured into the capital. From the Guild-Masters in their fortress-aerie, High Crag, on the seacoast north of Dunno Scuttari, came congratulations, word that Ragnarson had received nominatory votes for promotion to Guild General, and an offer of three regiments on partial advance against a percentage of booty...

On Royal instructions Ragnarson accepted the mercenary regiments. He dreaded leading so many men. What would happen when they learned the real nature of the enemy?

Tents dotted the roadsides and woods of the Siege. Long wagon trains bearing supplies rumbled toward the city. Dust raised by moving soldiery hung like a vaporous

river over the caravan route. Ragnarson was awed by
their numbers, almost as many as Kavelin had raised
during the El Murid Wars. His original mercenary
command now seemed an amusingly small force. But it
still formed the core of his army.

The more he thought about controlling so many men,
the more nervous he became.

Nights the worries slid away in the magic of the
Queen's arms. No one yet seemed suspicious.

In late March Sir Andvbur went over to the Captal.

What negotiations had passed between the two
Ragnarson never learned, but he suspected Sir Andvbur's
idealism had motivated his treachery.

The knight's coup failed. Having foreseen trouble, and
having gotten the man away from the center of power,
Ragnarson then had surrounded him with trustworthy
staffers. Few men joined Sir Andvbur when, after brief
skirmishing, he fled across Low Galmiche toward
Savernake.

Loncaric and Savernake remained in the grip of
unnatural winter. Ragnarson took the opportunity to
pinch off the depending finger of Low Galmiche and
eliminate the last rebel bastions near the Siege.

When he could find nothing else, he wondered what
had become of Mocker, Haroun, Turran, and Valther.
And worried about Rolf. Though Preshka hadn't been
injured in the dungeon confrontation, the exertion had
excacerbated his lung troubles.

Yet everything went so well that he received the bad
news from Itaskia with relief.

Greyfells partisans had driven the Trolledyngjan
families over the Porthune into Kendel. Kendel's military
ran hand in glove with Itaskia's. A light horse company
had swum the river and slaughtered the raiders. Kendel
had decided to send the families on to Kavelin.

What, Ragnarson sometimes wondered, was Elana
doing? She wasn't the sort to sit and wait.

On the last evening of March, Ragnarson gathered his
commanders to discuss the summer campaign. Meticulously prepared maps were examined. Where to meet the
enemy became the point of contention. Ragnarson

listened, remembering an area he had seen the previous fall.

"Here, at Baxendala," he said suddenly, jabbing a map with a forefinger. "We'll meet them with every man we have. Talk to the Marena Dimura. Learn everything you can."

Before the inevitable arguments began, he strode from the room.

The die had been cast. All time was an arrow hurtling toward the decision at the caravan town of Baxendala.

He went walking the castle's outer wall, to bask in the peace of what would soon be a chill April Fool's morning.

Soon, in the white gown she had worn the morning they had first locked eyes, the Queen joined him. Moonlight like trickles of silver ran through her hair, gayly. But her eyes were sad. Ignoring the sentries, she held his hand.

"This is the last night," she whispered, after a long silence. She stopped, pushed her arm around his waist, stared at the moon over the Kapenrungs. "The last time. You'll leave tomorrow. Win or lose, you won't come back." Her voice quavered.

Ragnarson scanned the black teeth of the enemy mountains. Was it really still winter there? He wanted to tell her he would return, but could not. That would be a blemish on his memory.

She had sensed that he would always go back to Elana. Their relationship, though as intense and fiery as a volcanic eruption, was pure romance. Romance demanded a special breed of shared deception, of reality suspended by mutual consent...

So he said nothing, just pulled her against his side.

"Just one thing I ask," she said, softly, sadly. "In the dark tonight, in bed, say my name. Whisper it to me."

He frowned her way, puzzled.

"You don't realize, do you? In all the time you've been here you've used it only once. When you announced me to Sir Farace. Her Majesty. Her Majesty. Her Highness. The Queen. Sometimes, in the night, Darling. But never Fiana. I'm real... Make me real."

Yes, he thought. Even when she had been no more than

a conception spawned by Tarlson's characterizations, he had felt an attraction that he had pushed off with formalities.

"Gods!" a nearby sentry muttered. "What's that?"

Ragnarson's gaze returned to the mountains.

Beneath the moon, over a notch marking the approximate location of Maisak, stood a pillar of reddish coruscation. It coalesced into a scarlet tower.

The world grew silent, as if momentarily becalmed in the eye of a storm.

The pillar intensified till all the east was aflame. A flower formed at its top. The trunk bifurcated, took on a horrible anthropomorphism. The flower became a head. Where eyes should have been there were two vast Stygian pools. The head was far too large for the malformed body that bore it up. Its horns seemed to scrape the moon as it turned slowly, glaring malevolently into the west.

The thing's brilliance intensified till all the world seemed painted in harsh strokes of red and black. A great dark gulf of a mouth opened in silent, evil laughter. Then the thing faded as it had come, dying into a coruscation that reminded Bragi of the auroras of his childhood homeland.

"Come," he said to the Queen when he could speak again. "You may be right. It may be the last time either of us gives ourself freely."

Deep in the night he spoke her name. And she, shaking as much as he, whispered from beneath him, "Bragi, I love you."

iii) Elana and Nepanthe

On the Auszura Littoral, Elana and Nepanthe, up late after a day of increasing, undirected tension, released sharp cries when the Tear of Mimizan took on a sudden, fiery life that was reflected in crimson on the eastern horizon.

iv) King Shanight

From the Mericic Hills, at Skmon on the Anstokin-Volstokin border, Shanight of Anstokin, restless before the dawn of attack, watched the scarlet rise in the east, a head with its chin on the horizon. After meeting those midnight eyes he returned to his pavilion, called off the war.

v) Mocker

In Rohrhaste, near the site of Vodicka's defeat, Mocker suddenly erupted from an uneasy sleep, saw scarlet beneath the moon. For one of the few times in his life he was stricken dumb. In lieu he loaded his donkey and hurried toward Vorgreberg.

vi) Sir Andvbur Kimberlin of Karadja

Sir Andvbur and two hundred supporters, traveling by night to evade loyalist patrols, paused to watch the demon coalesce over the Gap. Before it faded, half turned back, preferring the Royal mercy. Kimberlin continued, not out of conviction, but for fear of appearing weak before his companions.

vii) The Disciple

In the acres-vast tent-Temple of the Disciple at Al Rhemish, a sleepy fat man moaned, staggered to the Portal of the North. This gross, jeweled El Murid bore no resemblance to the pale, bony, ascetic fanatic whose angry sword had scourged the temples and reddened the sands in earlier decades. Nor was his insanity as limited. The red sorcery stirred a mad rage. He collapsed, thrashing and foaming at the mouth.

viii) Visigodred

At Castle Mendalayas in north Itaskia a tall, lean insomniac paced a vast and incredibly cluttered library. Before a fireplace a pair of leopards also paced. From a ceiling beam a monkey watched and muttered. Between the pacer and leopards, on a luxurious divan, a dwarf and a young beauty cuddled.

The lean old man, sporting a long gray beard, suddenly faced south southeast, his nose thrusting like that of a dog on point. His face became a mask of stone. "Marco!" he snapped. "Wake up. Call the bird."

ix) Zindahjira

In the Mountains of M'Hand, above the shores of the Seydar Sea, lay a cave in which dwelt the being called Zindahjira the Silent. Zindahjira was anything but silent now. The mountains shook with his rage. He did not appreciate being involved in intrigues not his own. But by his own twisted logic he had a responsibility to right matters in the south. When his rage settled, he called for his messenger owls.

x) Varthlokkur

Fangdred was an ancient fortress poised precariously atop Mount El Kabar in the Dragon's Teeth. There, in a windowless room, tiny silver bells tinkled. A black arrow inlaid with silver runes turned southward. In moments a tall young man, frowning, hurried in. His haunted eyes momentarily fixed on arrow and bells.

He was Varthlokkur, the Silent One Who Walks With Grief, sometimes called the Empire Destroyer or the Death of Ilkazar. He was the man who had ended the reign of the Princes Thaumaturge of Shinsan. Those Princes remained like trophies in an impenetrable chamber atop Fangdred's Wind Tower. Kings trembled at the mention of Varthlokkur's name.

He was old, this apparent young man. Centuries old, and burdened heavily with the knowledge of the Power, with his guilt over what he had wrought with the Empire.

He spoke a Word. A quicksilver pool in a shallow, wide basin ground into the top of a table of granite shivered. Iridescences fluttered across its face. A portrait appeared.

Varthlokkur stared at a gargantuan, megacephalic demon whose ravenlike feet clutched the feet of mountains.

This manifestation couldn't be ignored.

He began his preparations.

xi) Haroun bin Yousif

The long, cautious cavalry column was less than thirty miles from Al Rhemish when the northern sky went scarlet. Filtering four thousand Royalists through the Lesser Kingdoms and the Kapenrungs undetected had been a military feat which, meeting success, had astonished even its planner.

The demon head loomed. Haroun gave the order to turn back.

xii) The Star Rider

On the flank of a snow-deep peak high in the Kapenrungs, on a glacier that creaked and groaned day and night, one surprised and angry old man stood between gigantic pillars of legs and stared miles upward at scarlet horror. He spat, cursed, turned to his winged horse. From its back he unlashed the thing known as Windmjirnerhorn, or the Horn of the Star Rider. He caressed it, spoke to it, glanced, nodded. The demon began to fade.

He then sat and pondered what to do about these dangerous ad libs. O Shing was getting out of hand.

xiii) King Vodicka

Half an hour after the night had regained its natural darkness Volstokin's King concluded that he had been used by greater, darker powers to play attention-grabber while Evil slithered in to gnaw at the underbelly of the West.

After writing brief letters to Kavelin's Queen, his mother, and his brother, he threw himself from the parapet of his prison tower.

FIFTEEN: Baxendala

i) The site

Baxendala was a prosperous town of two thousand twenty-five miles west of Maisak. Its prosperity was due to its being the last or first chance for commerical vices for the caravans. The mountain passage was long and trying.

Ragnarson had chosen to fight there because of topography.

The townsite had once marked the western limit of the huge glacier that had cut the pass. The valley, that became the Gap, there narrowed to a two-mile-wide, steep-sided canyon, the floor of which, near the town, was piled with glacial leavings.

Baxendala itself was built against the north flank of a sugarloaf hill half a mile wide, two long, and two hundred feet high, astride a low ridge that ran to the flank of Seidentop, a steep, brush-wooly mountain constricting the north wall of the canyon. The River Ebeler ran around the south side of the loaf where the valley, in a long, lazy curve, had been dug a bit deeper, and, because of barriers a dozen miles farther west, had formed a shallow marsh three-quarters of a mile wide. The marsh lay hard against both the sugarloaf and the steep southern wall of the valley. A narrow strip of brushy, firm ground ran below the southern face. It could be easily held by a small force.

Atop the sugarloaf, commanding a good eastern view, stood a small fortress, Karak Strabger. From it Ragnarson could follow every detail of battle. By anchoring his flanks on Seidentop and Baxendala, along the ridge, he could defend a space little more than half a mile wide. There was no more defensible site to the west, and but one equaling it farther east. And Sir Andvbur, having fought there last autumn, knew that ground better than he.

Ragnarson descended on the town two weeks after the night of the demon. The Strabger family fled so hurriedly they left breakfast half-cooked in the castle kitchen. The rebel forces were training farther east, near the snow line. Three days after Bragi's arrival an attempt was made to dislodge him. Baron Berlich led the rebel knights into another Lieneke. His attack collapsed under a shower of Itaskian arrows. Berlich himself was slain.

The survivors, to Ragnarson's dismay, suffered an attack of rationality. When they selected a new commander they chose the man he believed most dangerous, Sir Andvbur Kimberlin.

Kimberlin opted for Fabian tactics. He took up a defensive position at the site of his previous year's battle. His patrols tried to lure Ragnarson into attack. Bragi ignored them.

Though Kimberlin's force, at eight thousand, was the largest Ragnarson had yet faced, he was more concerned with the sorcery-rich army the Captal would bring out of Maisak.

Bragi waited, skirmished, fortified, scouted, husbanded his resources. He constantly reminded his officers of the need to stand firm here. To, if necessary, endure the heaviest casualties. The enemy would be stopped at Baxendala, or not at all. The west depended on them. There would be no stopping Shinsan if this stand failed.

ii) The waiting

Ragnarson stood on the parapet of Karak Strabger's lone tower and surveyed the power that was, for the moment, his. He had twenty-five thousand Kaveliners, plus the men he had brought south. In the west, on the horizons and beyond, great clouds of dust hung in the spring haze. Surprising allies were hurrying to join him.

One cloud, on the caravan route, marked Shanight of Anstokin with the regiments raised to invade Volstokin. North of him came Jostrand of Volstokin and three thousand puzzled veterans of Lake Berberich and Vodicka's defeat. In Heidershied, rushing in forty-mile marches, was Prince Raithel of Altea, a hard-driving old warrior who had won glory and honor during the wars. Ragnarson hoped Raithel would arrive in time. His ten thousand were the best soldiers in the Lesser Kingdoms.

He had heard there were troops on the move in Tamerice and Ruderin and kingdoms farther away.

This curdling of the Lesser Kingdoms into a one-faced force with chin thrust belligerently eastward had begun the night of the red demon.

The sudden power and responsibility awed Ragnarson. Princes and kings were coming to be commanded by a man who had been but a farmer a year ago...

There were others who awed him more than Shanight, Jostrand, or Raithel.

Beside the sugarloaf, above Baxendala, stood a dozen tents set off by ropes. One housed his old friend Count Visigodred of Mendalayas, another Haroun's dread acquaintance, Zindahjira. The denizens of the others he knew only by repute: Keirle the Ancient; Barco Crecelius of Hellin Daimiel; Stojan Dusan from Prost Kamenets; Gromachi, the Egg of God; The Hermit of Ormrebotn; Boershig Abresch from Songer in Ringerike; Klages Dunivin; Serkes Holdgraver of the Fortress of Frozen Fire; and the Thing With Many Eyes, from the shadowed deeps of the Temple of Jiankoplos in Simballawein.

One tent stood alone, as if the others had crowded away. Before it stood a battered Imperial standard. Within lurked the man whose capital-hopping had started so many armies toward Baxendala, whose name frightened children into good behavior and made grown men glance over their shoulders.

Varthlokkur.

His appearance guaranteed the gravity of the conflict. The high and the mighty, from Simballawein to Iwa Skolovda, would hold all else in abeyance till they knew what was afoot.

Even the Greyfells party, Ragnarson had heard, had joined the truce.

Ragnarson had mixed feelings about Varthlokkur's presence. The man could, without a doubt, be an asset. But what about old grudges? Varthlokkur owed himself and Mocker.

But Mocker, who had most to fear, was in and out of the wizard's tent constantly, when not hiding from soldiers he had bilked with crooked dice.

Ragnarson smiled weakly. Mocker was incorrigible. A middle-aged adolescent.

He spied signal smoke up the Gap. Heliograph operators bustled about him. He returned to the war room he had set up in the castle's great hall.

While awaiting the report, he asked Kildragon, "How's Rolf?" Preshka had insisted on coming east.

"The same. He'll never heal if he won't take time out."

"And the evacuation?" He had been trying to get civilians to leave the area.

"About hit the limit. The rest mean to stay no matter what."

"Guess we've done what we could. Can't force people . . . Colonel Kiriakos?"

He had surveyed the man's work from the parapet. He and Phiambolos were working hard to complicate Shinsan's attack.

Kiriakos was the sort who, finding a pot of gold, would worry about getting a hernia hauling it away. "Too slow. I won't get done if you don't give me more men." His projects were straining the army already. Trenches, traps,

fortifications, cheveaux-de-fris, a pontoon across the
marsh a few miles west, and finding raw materials, were
devouring hundreds of thousands of man-hours each day.
But Kiriakos was a bureaucrat born. There was no project
that couldn't be done bigger and better if only he were
given more money and men . . .

Am I getting old? Ragnarson wondered. What
happened to my penchant for motion? His cavalry
commanders had been asking too. Shinsan's was an army
mainly infantry in orientation, with little missile weap-
onry. But Sir Andvbur was out there . . . All he could say
was that he felt right fighting positionally.

A Sedlmayrese sergeant came from the tower, drew
Bragi aside. "Captain Altenkirk," he whispered, "says he's
taken prisoners. The men called Turran and Valther, and
a woman. The Captain thinks she's the one you saw at
Maisak."

Ragnarson frowned. A windy message for heliograph,
susceptible of error. But justified if true. They had
captured Mist? How?

"Thank you. Send 'Well done.' And keep it quiet." He
retreated to a corner to think. So many possibilities . . . But he would know the truth when Altenkirk came
in.

He would have to take precautions. He headed for the
wizards' compound.

iii) Prisoners

Altenkirk had taken no chances. He brought his prisoners
in gagged, bound, and blindfolded, unable to twitch,
inside the large wicker baskets farmers filled with grain
and hung from their rafters to beat the rats and mice.
Each was litter-borne by prisoners from Kimberlin's army
and surrounded by Marena Dimura ready to destroy
baskets and bearers in an instant. Each litter was piled
with oil-soaked faggots. Horsemen with torches rode
nearby.

In other circumstances Ragnarson would have been

amused. "Think you took enough precautions?" he asked.

"I should've killed them," Altenkirk replied. "It's got to be a trick . . ."

"Maybe. Let's let the witchmen have them."

The baskets were grounded before the sorcerers. Soldiers who could do so absented themselves. Zindahjira, the Egg of God, and the Thing With Many Eyes failed customary standards of what was human.

"What's the smell?" Ragnarson asked Visigodred, near whom he had positioned himself for his nerve's sake.

"The Thing's project. You'll see."

"Uhn." They had to make everything a mystery. He nodded to Altenkirk. "Turran first."

Altenkirk cautiously pried the lid off a basket. Sorcerers tensed like foxes waiting at a rabbit hole.

But Turran had been confined so long that he needed help getting out. Ragnarson went to the man, removed his gag. He beckoned Visigodred.

To Turran, "I'm sorry. Altenkirk's a cautious man."

"Understand."

"Water," Visigodred said, offering a cup. Turran drained it. While Bragi and a soldier supported Turran, Visigodred rubbed his legs. To Altenkirk the wizard said, "Let the others out. They'll cause no trouble."

There was a stir just before Mist came forth. Ragnarson turned. His eyes met the Queen's. So. She had ignored his advice again, had come to join the final battle. With perfect timing, he thought. Her eyes, on Mist, were hard and jealous.

"All I need," he mumbled, "is for Elana to turn up now."

A long draught of wine gave Turran a little life. He asked for a physician, to examine his brother, then admonished, "I thought we were on the same side." And, after a pause, "She's come over."

Hum and buzz. Sorcerers' heads nodded together. Visigodred, who had a relationship with Mist that seemed almost fatherly, fussed round the woman like a hen.

"Did you ever see such a mantrap?" Ragnarson mumbled to Preshka, who, despite continued ill health, had come to investigate the commotion.

"It's obscene. No woman ought to look like that."

Turran gained more life. "They'll be here soon. They started bringing troops through last week."

"Uhn?" Ragnarson's suspicions hadn't died completely. "Let's hear about it."

"We couldn't use the back stairs," he said, after recounting the confrontation in the Captal's library, "so we picked up Brad Red Hand and tried the hallways . . ."

"You joined forces?"

"No choice. O Shing's people would've killed us all. Enemy of my enemy, you know. We picked up Brad and went through the halls to the stairs Derran had used to reach the old man's floor. But it opened in a hall already occupied by O Shing's men. We had to fight through. Valther picked up his wound there. Derran was killed. Kerth, the Captal, and the little girl were captured. Brad tore a muscle in his left arm. We got through, but we couldn't save anybody but ourselves."

"And Mist? She couldn't use a spell or two?"

"Colonel, there were six men in that room. Three were Tervola. You know what that means? We tried. We killed the soldiers. She barely handled the sorcerers. But when it settled out, we couldn't carry the wounded. I was lucky to get Valther out. And the child wouldn't leave the old man. If there was anything that could've been done . . ."

"I wasn't criticizing." He had had to leave people behind too. He knew the spear thrusts of guilt that drove to the heart of one's being.

"We hoped to reach the main gate or the Captal's creatures, but the fight gave O Shing's men time to cut us off. The only escape was the caverns. It may've been my memory or their sorcery, but for a long time we couldn't find a way out. Every passage we took led back to Maisak. Each time we returned something more grim had happened. They tortured Kerth till he told all he knew about Haroun. They enchanted the Captal and girl into being cooperative. They've done the same to the rebel captains. We kept stealing food and trying to find a way out. When they started bringing troops through, I knew I couldn't put off leaving my body anymore. It'd become imperative that I get Mist to you."

"And Brad?"

"They detected the sorcery. Came hunting. His bad shoulder betrayed him. They got him before Mist could drive them off."

"And Mist? Is she a refugee? Does she want help to regain her throne? I won't help her. There's no way I'll do anything to benefit the Dread Empire. I *will* help destroy it. It's like a poisonous snake. Any good it does is incidental to its deadliness."

"I think," Turran said softly, "that's she's run out of ambition. O Shing's successes have crushed her." He nodded her way. She was fussing over Valther. "There's her subliminatory device."

"Ah?"

"I don't know how long it'll last. Long enough for us to benefit, though."

"I can't ask much more." With great reluctance, Ragnarson took his eyes off Mist, studied the assembled sorcerers. Each indicated he believed Turran. Only Varthlokkur expressed reservations, and those weren't related to Mist's turn of coat.

"Power won't affect this battle's outcome," he said. "The divinations are shadowy, but they suggest its result will depend on the courage and stamina of soldiers, not on any efforts of my ilk." He seemed mildly puzzled.

Varthlokkur knew his business. He was probably right. But Ragnarson was puzzled too. He could not see how, with so much thaumaturgic might moving toward collision, massive destruction could be avoided. "See if you can get this straightened out," he told Preshka, then went to welcome the Queen to Baxendala.

iv) The enemy arrives

Sir Andvbur's rebels came down the canyon like leaves driven by an autumn wind, without organization, whipping this way and that, mixing units inseparably. Before and among them fled bands of Ragnarson's horsemen and Marena Dimura. Signal smokes rose rapidly nearer, climbing toward a cloud of darkness driving down from Maisak like the grasping hand of doom. Sir Andvbur's people pelted against Ragnarson's defenses in such disorder that his own men became mildly infected. He had a brisk afternoon's work keeping order.

Night fell without the true enemy appearing. But his campfires, as they sprang into being, were disturbing in their numbers. Ragnarson got little sleep. He stayed up studying a blizzard of conflicting reports.

By morning it had sorted itself out. The Captal and his Kaveliners had moved to Ragnarson's extreme right, beyond the marsh, where Blackfang and Kildragon held the narrows. Sir Andvbur's thousands had taken positions against the flank of Seidentop, facing the mercenary regiments from High Crag. Shinsan held the center, facing Prince Raithel's Altean veterans.

A quarter-mile behind the front line, which was sixteen thousand strong, Ragnarson had drawn up a more numerous but potentially weaker second line. Volstokin he had anchored against Seidentop, in touch with the fortifications and heavy weapons Colonel Phiambolos had installed there. In the center were the Kaveliners, his hand-picked veterans scattered among them as cadre. On the right, their backs against Baxendala, lay Anstokin's army. They maintained close contact with the ramparts and trenches Tuchol Kiriakos had constructed between level ground and Karak Strabger's wall. The main engagement Ragnarson meant to be infantry against infantry, the lines holding while heavy engines on the flanks and bowmen behind the lines decimated the enemy. Only two thousand horsemen, the best, did he allow to retain their animals. These he stationed west of Baxendala, out of view behind the slope running to Seidentop.

Dawn was a creeping thing, a dark tortoise dragging in from the east and never quite seeming to arrive. But gradual visibility came to the valley.

Ragnarson, the Queen, Turran, Mist, Varthlokkur, Colonels Phiambolos and Kiriakos, runners and heliograph men crowded the top of Karak Strabger's lonely tower. When O Shing's camp became visible, Ragnarson's heart fell. He beckoned Mist.

Shinsan was in formation already. Mist peered into the morning haze. A small, sharp intake of breath. "Four legions," she said throatily. "He's brought four legions. The Eighth. On the right. His left. The Third. The Sixth. Oh. And I thought Chin mine body and soul." The remaining legion stood in reserve behind Shinsan's center. "The First. The Imperial Standard. The best of the best."

Her knuckles whitened as she squeezed the stone of the battlements.

"The best," she repeated. "And all four at full strength. He's made a fool of me."

Bragi wasn't disappointed. He hadn't expected good news. But he had hoped O Shing would make a smaller showing. "He's here himself?"

She nodded, pointed. "There. Behind the First. You can see the tower. He wants to watch our destruction from a high place."

Ragnarson turned. "Colonel Phiambolos, relay the word to Altenkirk." The engineer departed for Seidentop, "Varthlokkur? You've seen enough?"

The wizard nodded. "We'll begin. But I doubt we'll do any good." He departed.

"Colonel Kiriakos?"

The Colonel clicked his heels and half bowed. "Gods be with you, sir." He left to assume command of the castle and sugarloaf.

"Turran?"

The man shrugged. "You've done all you could. It's up to the Fates."

"Your Majesty, everything's ready."

She nodded coolly, regally. There was the slightest strain between them because, after her journey from Vorgreberg, he had spent the night in battle preparations.

"Now we wait." He glanced at O Shing's tower, willing it to begin.

Though he concealed it, he didn't think he had a chance. Not against four legions, nearly twenty-five thousand easterners. With so many O Shing might not commit his auxiliaries...

But he did. At some unseen signal Sir Andvbur threw his full weight against the mercenary regiments, all his people fighting afoot.

"That man," said Turran, "needs hanging. He learns too fast."

The mercenaries, though better fighters, were hard-pressed till Phiambolos's engines found the range.

After an hour, Ragnarson asked Turran, "What's he doing? It's obvious that he can't break through."

"Maybe trying to weaken them for the legions. Or draw them out of line."

Ragnarson glanced toward the mountains. The dark cloud from Maisak was fading. "They'll let us have the sun in our eyes." He had hoped they would overlook that.

Mist interjected, "He's buying time to ready a sorcery."

And Turran, "There goes a wagonload of the Thing's poison." In time Visigodred had admitted that the foul stench from the sorcerers' enclave was caused by their distillation of a drink to be served weary troops on the fighting line. There was little if any magic involved, but the liquor would combine the encouraging effects of alcohol with a drug that staved off exhaustion. Little sorceries like that, Ragnarson thought, might be more important than the ground-shakers.

"Marshal," said the Queen, "you have smoke across the marsh."

Bragi turned. It was Haaken's signal. He allowed himself a small grin. "Good. Runner." A man presented himself. "Tell Sir Farace to cross the pontoon."

A key adjunct to his plans, hastily developed during the night, after the enemy's dispositions had become clear, was developing perfectly. Blackfang and Kildragon had laid a trap. The Captal had been lured in.

"The witchery begins," said Mist. Arm spear-straight, she indicated a mote of pinkish light at the foot of O Shing's tower. "The Gosik of Aubochon again." Awe and horror filled her voice. "In the flesh. The man's mad! There's no way to control it . . ."

"Kimberlin's breaking off," said Turran.

Ragnarson had noticed. "This's the critical point," he said, looking down at the still untested Alteans. "Will they hold when they realize what's happening?"

"Back!" Mist snapped. "I need room!"

The pink became scarlet flame; from it rose dense red smoke. In moments, within the smoke, an immense horned head with Stygian eyes formed. This thing was no moonscraping monster such as had loomed over the Kapenrungs, but Bragi guessed it would stand a hundred yards tall. It seemed to grow from the earth itself.

Mist stood with arms outstretched and head thrown back, screaming in a tongue so liquid that Ragnarson wasn't sure she was using words. A strong chill wind began to blow, whipping her hair and garments.

He checked his tame sorcerers.

As the Gosik took on awesome solidity, the twelve hurled their counter-weapons. Bolts of lightning. Spears of light. Balls of fire in weird and changing colors. Stenches that enveloped the tower. A misty thing the size of several elephants that coalesced between the armies and trailed bloody slaughter through immobile legions before attaching its hundred tentacles and dozen beaked mouths to one of the Gosik's legs...

Mist brought her hands together sharply. Down the canyon, echoing from wall to wall, ran a deafening, endless peal of thunder. Over the Gosik a diadem of lights appeared, sparks in rainbowed rings racing angrily. The diadem began to fall.

Ragnarson wasn't sure, but from its enclosing circle, it seemed, a nebulous face as ugly as the Gosik's glared down, swelled till all the interior was a gap through which a hungry mouth prepared to feed.

A touch of shadow crossed the parapet. A few hundred feet up, a lonely eagle patrolled, above Mist's unnatural wind, apparently unconcerned with the human follies below. For an instant Bragi envied the bird its freedom and unconcern. Then...

He released a small, sharp gasp. For an instant the eagle flickered and was an eagle no longer. It became a man and winged horse far higher than he had thought, almost above visual discrimination. He turned to ask Turran's opinion.

Turran had missed it. Everyone had. All attention was on the Gosik.

Every magick in the valley had perished.

The Gosik itself came apart like a crumbling brick building, chunks and dusts falling in a rain that masked O Shing's tower. It bellowed louder than Mist's thunder had done.

Turran groaned, clawed at his chest, staggered. Ragnarson stared, thinking it was his heart.

Mist screamed, a cry of pain and deprivation. She fell to her knees, beat her forehead against parapet stone.

"It's gone," Turran groaned. "The Power. It's gone."

The Queen tried to stop Mist. "Help me!" she snapped at the messengers.

Ragnarson leaned over the parapet. His wizards appeared to have gone insane. Several had collapsed. Most were flopping about like men in the throes of the falling sickness. The Thing sped round and round in a tight circle, chasing its own forked tail. Only Varthlokkur seemed unaffected, though he might have been a statue, so still was he as he stared at the Gosik of Aubochon.

Ragnarson looked up again. The eagle slid toward Maisak, to all appearances a raptor going about its business. He frowned. That old man again. Who was he? What? Not a god, but certainly a Power above any other the world knew.

Ragnarson's companions remained unaware of anything but the sudden vacuum of sorcery. For Turran and Mist it was a loss beyond description, almost a theft of the soul.

v) Opening round

O Shing wasted no time. The legions moved. High on the Thing's brew and Bragi's quickly spread tale that western sorcery had conquered the eastern, the troops waited with renewed confidence.

Shinsan advanced behind a screen of Sir Andvbur's infantry, the rebels more driven than leading the assault. Theirs was the task of neutralizing the traps. Their casualties were heavy. Ragnarson's bowmen had a tremendous stock of arrows, and easy targets.

Before the lines met, Ragnarson's troops sprang one of their surprises. He had had the Alteans armed with javelins, a tactic unseen since Imperial times. Their shower reassured his troops of the foe's mortality.

"Runner!" Ragnarson snapped. He sent orders to ready the second line.

"So much for being Shinsan's ally," Bragi muttered. Several thousand rebels, between his own and Shinsan's lines, were being cut down by friend and foe.

Bragi's first line held better than he had expected. He blessed the Thing.

The Alteans held the Third. The flanking legions, under merciless bombardment from Phiambolos' and Kiriakos' engines, had increasing difficulty maintaining formation.

The enemy commander sent Sir Andvbur to clear Seidentop. Karak Strabger he would not be able to reach unless the Alteans broke. Kimberlin's men got entangled in nasty little battles in brushy ravines and around Phiambolos' fortifications.

Ragnarson had his heliographers send a message.

Altenkirk and a thousand Marena Dimura were hidden on the slopes east of Seidentop. They were to take the rebels and Sixth Legion in the rear. Ragnarson didn't expect them to do more than keep the enemy off balance.

What Ragnarson wanted most was to compel O Shing to commit his reserve. The First Legion, waiting patiently before their emperor's tower, would be the key.

The first line wouldn't compel its commitment. The Altean left had begun to waver. He ordered his archers withdrawn behind the second line. He didn't want them lost in a sudden collapse. He then sent messages reminding his second-line commanders that under no circumstances were they to leave their positions to aid the first line.

The Alteans yielded slowly. The enemy wedged open their junction with the mercenaries. Altenkirk attacked. The fighting round Seidentop grew bloody. The Marena Dimura, high on the Thing's brew, refused to be driven off till they had taken terrible casualties. They, too, did better than Ragnarson had expected. They forced Sir Andvbur to abandon his assault. And they gave better than they got. Kimberlin's troops were unable to pursue them. But in the meantime the Alteans had gotten split off the mercenaries. The commander of the Third Legion was ready to roll up both halves of the line.

Ragnarson expected the reserve legion to drive through the gap, against his second line. But no. O Shing held it.

"They're burning the bridge," Turran said from behind him. The man had recovered, though now he seemed a little insubstantial.

Bragi turned. Yes. Smoke rose from the pontoon. Haaken had either lost or won his part of the battle. There would be no knowing which for a long time yet. He wished he had arranged some signal. But he hadn't wanted any false hopes raised or despair set loose.

The mercenary regiments began to crumble. Crowding Seidentop for its supporting fire, they withdrew. Prince Raithel tried to do the same, but had more difficulty. The fighting washed up the foot of the sugarloaf. Kiriakos couldn't give him much support.

Ragnarson glanced at the sun. Only four hours of light left. If Shinsan took too long, the battle would stretch into a second day. For that he wasn't prepared.

Clearly victorious, the legions disengaged, puzzling Ragnarson. Then he understood. O Shing would send the fresh legion against the center of the second line while the third backed off to the reserve position.

For a time the battlefield was clear. Bragi was awed by the carnage. It would be long remembered. There must have been twenty thousand bodies on the field, about evenly distributed. The majority of the enemy fallen were rebels.

Sickening. Ragnarson loathed the toe-to-toe slugfest. But there was no choice. A war of maneuver meant enemy victory.

O Shing allowed the legions an hour's rest. Ragnarson didn't interfere.

Before, the numbers had been slightly in the enemy's

favor. This time they would be strongly in his. But his men would be greener, more likely to break.

Two and a half hours till sunset. If they held, but Haaken couldn't carry out his mission, could he put anything together for the morrow?

It began anew. The First Legion drove its silent fury against Kaveliners who outnumbered it three to one. The flanking legions held Anstokin and Volstokin while strong elements of each turned on Seidentop and Karak Strabger.

The Thing's false courage continued to work. The Kaveliners stood and continued believing their commander was invincible.

Ragnarson turned away after an hour. Even with the support of the most intense arrow storm Ahring could generate, Shinsan was getting the best of it.

And, redoubt by redoubt, Kiriakos and Phiambolos were being forced to yield their fortifications. By nightfall Karak Strabger would be cut off. Seidentop would be lost. Captured engines would be turned on the castle come morning.

Then he caught moving glitter at the eastern end of the marsh. It was Sir Farace and the horse, come round the marsh through the narrow strip where Haaken and Reskird had pulled a near repeat of Lake Berberich.

At first O Shing was unconcerned, perhaps thinking the column was the Captal's returning. How long would it last?

A while. Long enough for Sir Farace and Blackfang to ford the Ebeler. O Shing and his Tervola were intent on the slaughter before them. Anstokin was being driven into the streets of Baxendala. The Kaveliners were being decimated, though the arrow storm was wreaking its havoc too. Volstokin was desperately trying to retain contact with Phiambolos, who had begun evacuating Seidentop. A hundred pillars of smoke rose from pyres marking abandoned engines. The main battle was lost.

"Turran." Bragi glanced at the sun. "Can we hold till dark? Would they keep on afterwards? Or wait till dawn to finish it?"

"We can hold. But you may have to send the mercenaries and Alteans back in."

"Right." He sent orders to Prince Raithel to stand by.

Peering toward Sir Farace, he saw that Haaken and Reskird had brought their infantry. Blackfang had had good reason for burning the pontoon. If Sir Farace failed, there would be no one to hold the right bank. Trolledyngjans. Proud men. Fools eager, even facing incredible odds, to balance their earlier defeat at Maisak.

The knights formed hurriedly, in two long ranks. O Shing's generals finally awakened, began to form the reserve legion facing them.

Shrieking trumpets carried over the uproar around Karak Strabger; the best knights of four kingdoms trotted toward the best infantry in the world. Haaken, Reskird, and their infantry ran at the stirrups of the second wave.

Had he known there would be no magic, Ragnarson reflected, he would have chosen a knights' battle. It wasn't a form of warfare with which the easterners could easily cope.

The first wave went to a canter, then a full charge, hit before the Third Legion had finished reforming.

What followed was a classic demonstration of why heavy cavalry had become the preferred shock weapon of western armies. The horsemen plowed through the enemy like heavy ships through waves, their lances shattering the front ranks, then their swords and maces smashing down from the height advantage.

Had the Shinsaners been anyone else they would have been routed. But these men stood and silently died. Like automatons they killed horses to bring knights down where their heavier armor would be a disadvantage.

The second wave hit, then the infantry. Without that second wave, Ragnarson reflected, the first might have been lost simply because the enemy didn't have the sense to run. They would have stood, been slaughtered, and have slowly turned the thing around . . .

If the legionnaires would not panic, O Shing would. With trumpets and flags he began screaming for help.

Altenkirk and his Marena Dimura, now completely cut off, launched a suicide attack on Kimberlin, made sure the rebels did nothing to save the eastern emperor.

"We'll survive the day," Ragnarson said, spirits soaring. He drew his sword, gathered his shield. "Time to

counter-attack." The Tervola were trying to disengage
forces to aid their emperor, who was in grave danger.

As he and his staff howled out the castle gate to join
Kiriakos, Ragnarson saw that Sir Farace had shifted his
attack. While the stricken Third Legion ordered itself
around O Shing, Volstokin's seneschal had wheeled his
lines and charged the First from behind.

Ragnarson's immediate reaction was anger. The man
should have gone for checkmate...But he calmed
himself. The knight had seen more clearly than he. O
Shing was only a man. This battle was no individual's
whim, it was a playout of a nation's aspirations. The
Tervola could and would replace O Shing if necessary,
and could win without him. With few exceptions their
loyalties were to ideas, not men.

The sun had reached the peaks of the Kapenrungs. The
slaughter continued shifting in favor of the west. The
Sixth and Eighth tried to close a trap but were too weary
and heavily engaged to act quickly enough. Sir Farace
withdrew before the jaws closed and formed for yet
another charge. Before dark all four legions had suffered
the fury of the western knighthood, the sort of attack
Breitbarth had meant to hurl against Ragnarson at
Lieneke. The assault on Baxendala had been broken.

Shinsan disengaged in good order. Ragnarson sent
riders to Haaken and Reskird, ordering them to recross
the Ebeler before they were trapped. Altenkirk he ordered
off Kimberlin. Sir Farace he had stand off from the
withdrawal. The mercenaries and Alteans, who had had a
respite, he kept in contact. With the remnants of one
mercenary regiment he launched a night assault on the
rebels.

He had judged their temper correctly. Most of the
common soldiers yielded without fighting. Sir Andvbur
accepted the inevitable.

Though it meant straining men already near collapse,
Ragnarson kept the pressure on Shinsan throughout the
night, allowing only his horsemen to rest. All of them,
even those who had fought afoot. With the rebel knights
out he could afford to launch cavalry attacks.

O Shing resumed operations at dawn, withdrawing

toward Maisak with the First Legion in rearguard, masking his main force with trenches dug during the night. The situation left Ragnarson in a quandary. As soon as he sent his horse in pursuit, the First, evidently rested, came out to challenge his exhausted infantry. He didn't want to settle for the single legion the enemy seemed willing to sacrifice. There was no predicting when the Power would return. If it did do so soon, Shinsan could still turn it around.

Both sides had been drained. Nearly ten thousand Shinsaners had fallen. Virtually all the rebels were dead or captured. Haaken had sent word that the Captal and his pretender were in hand. And Ragnarson feared his own losses, not yet determined, would include more than half his force.

His allies from Altea, Anstokin, and Volstokin refused to join the pursuit. The Kaveliners and mercenaries grumbled when he made the suggestion, but had less choice. He compromised. They would advance slowly, maintaining light contact, till O Shing had evacuated Kavelin. His allies undertook the destruction of the Imperial Legion.

vi) Campaign's end

Approaching stealthily, cautiously, unexpectedly, the Royalist forces of Haroun bin Yousif came to a Maisak virtually undefended. In a swift, surprise night attack they carried the gate and swept the defenders into eternity. In the deep dungeons they found the portals through which Shinsan's soldiers had come. Bin Yousif led a force through, surprised and destroyed a small fortress near Liaontung, in the Dread Empire.

Returning, he destroyed the portals, then prepared surprises for O Shing's return. If he returned.

He did, skirmishing with Ragnarson's troops all the way. The would-be emperor, trying to salvage control of the Gap, threw his beaten legions at Maisak's walls.

Soldiers of Shinsan did not question, did not retreat. For three bloody days they attacked and died. Without their masters' magicks they were only men. As many died there as had at Baxendala.

When O Shing broke off, Ragnarson, with Haroun, harried him to the ruins of Gog-Ahlan.

There Turran told Bragi, "There's no percentage in pushing him any more. The Power's returning."

Reluctantly, Ragnarson turned back toward Kavelin.

SIXTEEN: Shadows of Death

i) New directions and vanishing allies

When Bragi went looking for Haroun, his old friend was gone. Side by side they had harried O Shing, moving too swiftly to visit, then the Royalists had evaporated.

When Bragi returned, autumn was settling on Vorgreberg. For the first time in years there was no foreboding lying over the capital. The rebellion was dead. All but a few of its leaders had been caught. But recognition of Gaia-Lange and/or Carolan remained unsettled.

In Ragnarson's absence the Queen had restructured the Thing along lines proposed by the scholars of Hellin Daimiel, adding commons drawn from among Wessons, Marena Dimura, and Siluro. Final judgmental authority had been vested in three consuls, one elected by the commons, another by the nobility. The third was the Queen herself. Before he reached Baxendala returning, Bragi learned that he had a painful decision to make.

Representatives of the commons met him in the Gap and begged him to become publican consul.

He was still worrying it when he reached Vorgreberg. The crowds had turned out. He accepted the accolades glumly. Haaken and Reskird grinned, shouted back, clowned. His soldiers wasted no time getting themselves lost in taverns and willing arms.

Sourly, he entered Castle Krief.

And there she was again, in the same place, wearing the same clothing...

And Elana was with her. Elana, Nepanthe, and Mocker.

Haaken leaned close. "Remember the tale of Soren Olag Bjornson's wife." It was a Trolledyngjan folk story about the vicissitudes of an unfaithful husband.

Bragi started. If Haaken knew, the liaison might be common knowledge.

Maybe a consulship would keep him too busy to get in trouble with either woman.

ii) The new life

Ragnarson accepted the consulship, retained the title Marshal, and received a vote of generalship from High Crag. His most difficult task was integrating his arrogant, overbearing Trolledyngjan refugees into Kaveliner society, and, with the Queen, making compensation to the mercenary regiments. Kavelin's finances were a shambles.

There came a time when final action *had* to be taken in the matters of Sir Andvbur and the Captal of Savernake. To Ragnarson's regret, Kimberlin had to be hanged. The Captal was more cooperative. After a long conversation with the Queen, concerning Carolan, he was allowed pen, parchment, and poison.

The best physician in Hellin Daimiel was brought in to attend Rolf Preshka. But the man neither improved nor worsened. The physician believed it was a matter of mind, not disease.

Time eased Bragi's longing for the Itaskian grant. The War Minister wrote that it would be a long time before he could come back. The Greyfells party had grown no weaker. Meantime, Bevold Lif continued his improvements. Ragnarson began looking forward to playing big fish in his new small pool.

There would be a respite before bin Yousif again maneuvered him into the role of stalking horse.

iii) One pretender

Crown Prince Gaia-Lange was playing in his grandfather's garden when the hawkfaced man appeared. The boy was puzzled, but felt no fear. He wondered how the dark man had gotten past the guards. "Who're you?"

"Like you, my prince, a king without a throne." The lean man knelt, kissed the boy on both cheeks. "I'm sorry. There're things more important than princes." He rose, vanished as silently as he had come. The boy's hands touched where lips had touched. His expression remained puzzled.

Hands and expression were still there when his heart beat its last.

It was another Allernmas evening.

iv) Party kill

Shadow from shadow, a lean dark man momentarily appeared in the room where the wine for the leaders of the Greyfells party, meeting before seizing Itaskia's throne, had been decanted. He dribbled golden droplets into each decanter.

Itaskia's morticians were busy for a week.

v) Autumn's child

Like a black ghost that had come on the wings of the blizzard moaning about Castle Krief, the dark man passed the chambers of the Marshal and his wife, the chambers of the Queen, and entered the door of the Princess' room. Drowsy guards never knew he had passed. The child slept in candlelight, golden hair sprayed over cerulean pillows. One small hand protruded from beneath the covers. Into it he emptied a tiny box. The spider was no larger than a pea.

The dark man pricked her palm with a pin. She made a fist.

Death came gently, silently. She never wakened.

He murmured, "October's baby, autumn's child, child of the Dread Empire. Fare you better in the Shadowland." For an instant, before he snuffed the candle and departed, a deep sadness ghosted across his face. One tear rolled down a dark, leathery cheek, betraying the man inside.